D1409894

THE GENERAL'S
MISTRESS

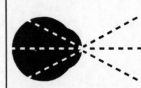

This Large Print Book carries the
Seal of Approval of N.A.V.H.

THE GENERAL'S
MISTRESS

JO GRAHAM

THORNDIKE PRESS
A part of Gale, Cengage Learning

GALE
CENGAGE Learning·

Detroit • New York • San Francisco • New Haven, Conn • Waterville, Maine • London

GALE
CENGAGE Learning®

Copyright © 2012 by Jo Wyrick.
Thorndike Press, a part of Gale, Cengage Learning.

ALL RIGHTS RESERVED
This book is a work of fiction. Names, characters, places, and incidents either are products of the author's imagination or are used fictitiously. Any resemblance to actual events or locales or persons, living or dead, is entirely coincidental.
Thorndike Press® Large Print Romance.
The text of this Large Print edition is unabridged.
Other aspects of the book may vary from the original edition.
Set in 16 pt. Plantin.

LIBRARY OF CONGRESS CATALOGING-IN-PUBLICATION DATA

Graham, Jo, 1968–
    The general's mistress / by Jo Graham.
        pages ; cm. — (Thorndike Press large print romance)
    ISBN-13: 978-1-4104-5473-7 (hardcover)
    ISBN-10: 1-4104-5473-8 (hardcover)
    1. Mistresses—France—Fiction. 2. France—History—18th century—Fiction.
3. Large type books. I. Title.
PS3607.R338G46 2013
813'.6—dc23   2012041289

Published in 2013 by arrangement with Gallery Books, a division of Simon & Schuster, Inc.

Printed in the United States of America
1 2 3 4 5 6 7 17 16 15 14 13

For my mother

Our birth is but a sleep and
a forgetting:
The Soul that rises with us,
our life's Star,
Hath had elsewhere its setting,
And cometh from afar . . .
— William Wordsworth,
"Ode: Intimations of Immortality"

THE CUCKOO'S CHILD

Charles van Aylde was not a nice young gentleman. His fair hair was powdered, swept back from a high, flawless brow. His eyes were blue. Blue eyes were common enough, but his were midnight, the color of sapphires, the color of secrets. His coat was midnight too, his collar reaching to his chin, the shoulders padded wide, the very height of fashion. His cravat was ruched with Valenciennes lace; his hands were long and white. He affected a small quizzing glass, and he wore a diamond on the last finger of his left hand.

I considered him in the mirror, my own reflection, but no longer a girl. In the drawing rooms and spas of the waning eighteenth century, I knew I was prey. Men might play deadly games of war or passion or politics, but the role of a young woman was to be the prize, the lovely and innocent thing for which all others strove for good or ill, to take or defend her virtue and honor as though she were a castle perennially under siege. Such was against my nature. If that was the lot of women, then I would become Charles instead.

I passed through the card parlors where, as Charles, I played conservatively and somehow usually left the table with more than I had brought, though there were no large wins that might call attention to me. Charles did not speak much, and his face was expressionless. In the drawing rooms and at the gaming tables of the baths, in the assembly rooms where young ladies danced the minuet under the careful eyes of their mothers, his manners were polished but not excessive. He was, after all, the scion of an old Dutch family of means, a wealthy man but not a titled one, reveling in the indiscreet pressure of the fingers in the figures of the dance, the brush of his hand against a blushing cheek, the sudden heated look that spoke more of conquest than any kinder passion. And yet, when he left the rooms it was alone.

There were no careful mothers in the inns and taverns that surrounded the baths proper. Instead the taverns were full of soldiers, travelers, tradesmen, and whores. The stakes were higher and the games less genteel. I did not venture here without a sword at my side. It was a dress sword, a pretty thing, but no less sharp.

There were words over cards with a drunk hussar, a recruit hardly more than his own age. Steel rang as the dress sword was drawn sinister, a left-handed fencer in a dirty, crowded room. The hussar's friends stepped between.

"Let's not take this so seriously. There's too much drink all around." An officer barely twenty broke it up. The recruit compounded his difficulties by promptly vomiting on the officer, who swore in Flemish and French both.

I took my winnings and sheathed my blade. The coins we were quarreling over would hardly pay my laundress. With a negligent shrug, I left the disputed coins on the table in the puddle of spilt beer. "Use it to clean up then," I said. I glanced once more at the young officer holding the recruit's arms, raised one eyebrow, and left the tavern, reveling in the sharp spice of danger.

I did watch my back on the way back to the spa, but the only person I met was a whore. "Get you something nice, sir?" she asked, dropping a battered fan from ample cleavage.

I stopped and looked at her appraisingly. "I don't think so just now," I said, cultivating just the right gesture, one finger beneath her chin, tilting her head into the light. "But you are lovely."

I walked back to the spa, to the fine rooms for wealthy people, the suites of travelers with plenty of money to spend taking the waters. Charles van Aylde did not slip in. He strode, the swagger of a blade too young to fear anything. I lit a candle in front of the gilt glass over the sitting room fireplace, the flare illuminating even, handsome features, a mouth too thin and tight for beauty. I closed the heavy velvet drapes and went into the bedchamber on the left.

There, in front of the dresser and washstand, I took off my coat and carefully hung it away. The rooms were silent, though voices still came from the streets. Outside a spring drizzle was beginning. I dipped a cloth and washed the powder from my face with tepid water, looking in the mirror. I opened my shirt, watching one finger trace down from the opened cravat to the top of the contrasting lines of stays, the swell of breasts carefully hidden. "Upon my word," I said, "what are you hiding, Charles?" I smiled at myself in the mirror, and it was not such a nice smile. I opened the top of the stays and rubbed at one pale pink nipple. Charles smiled back in the mirror.

"Lovely, I protest," I whispered. White flesh and white corset, white cravat and shirt opened, man's clothes over woman's body. I ran my hands over my breasts, pulling the nipples free of the top of the corset, drawing and plucking at them, watching them roseate. "You are beautiful," I whispered, but there was no one to answer but myself.

The next afternoon I was taking English tea with my mother in one of the salons, wearing a gown of raspberry-and-white-striped lawn. A lace shawl around my shoulders.

I dropped it. Before I could bend, a hand seized it.

"Allow me," a gentleman said. It was the officer from the tavern. He lifted the delicate lace and handed it to me. "Your servant, Madame."

"Thank you."

He clicked his heels together smartly. "Lieutenant Bleeker, Madame. The honor is mine." He seemed even younger in the light of day.

"Madame Ringeling," I said. "And this is my mother, Madame van Aylde-Versfelt." I indicated my mother. She nodded over her tea.

I saw his eyes widen almost imperceptibly. Yes, he recognized the name. Would he take the bait?

"I believe I am acquainted with your brother, Madame," he said.

"Oh?" I said. Over his shoulder in the great mirrors I could see my reflection. With honey-blond hair, a rose and white complexion, and a pouting mouth stained the color of raspberries, Madame Ringeling resembled her brother, but not so very closely.

"My son is around somewhere," my mother said.

"It was pleasant to make your acquaintance, Lieutenant," I said airily. "Perhaps our paths will cross again." There was a power to it, knowing something he could not possibly guess. It was a polite dismissal, and he made his bows.

My mother took up the lace shawl and began absently shredding it. "Elzelina, I wish you'd be more polite. You're quite too old for competition with your younger brother." At thirty-eight, my mother hardly looked as though her youth was far behind. Her hair was still platinum fair, and her hands were hardly wrinkled at all. "You would never bring me anywhere if Charles

14

didn't insist," she said. "He always thinks of my comfort."

"Mother, it was I who suggested we come to the baths," I said. "Your doctor recommended it, remember?"

"Yes, but I would never have come without Charles," she said. Her beautiful fingers picked at the lace. "I can't imagine traveling without him to protect me. What if we were set upon by highwaymen?"

"In case you hadn't noticed, I'm an adequate shot," I said tightly. "I am quite certain Charles is no better than I."

Mother picked up her teacup. "Oh, I know Leo showed you how to hold a gun, and I'm sure that's all very well, but you can't imagine you're half the man Charles is."

"Mother," I said, getting to my feet, "I assure you that I am entirely the man Charles is." I stalked out of the salon.

I was still fuming when I opened the door to our rooms. Berthe was brushing out my dinner gown. I flung my shoes under the bed and opened the Hungary Water, dabbing it on my temples. My face was bright pink in the mirror.

"Have you quarreled with Madame again?" Berthe asked.

"Charles this and Charles that and all the time Charles," I said. I put down the bottle

15

and ran my hands over my face, breathing in the deep scents of citrus and vetiver. "Charles is dead these ten years."

Berthe came over and stood behind me as I regarded her stout form next to mine in the mirror. "And it's a sad thing, to be sure. But you know your mother would never have come to Bad Bentheim without you playacting at Charles. And her doctor said that staying in Amsterdam was just making her worse."

"Because she thinks there's a curse on the house," I said. I closed my eyes and took a deep breath. "She thinks that her uncle watches her out of mirrors and that there are bloodied monks in the cellar left over from the Spanish and a dead child's ghost moaning around in the attic. Compared to some of the things my mother believes, believing that Charles is alive is fairly sane."

Berthe patted me on the back. "She's not the first mother to lose a child and disbelieve it."

"For ten years?" I asked. "Isn't that carrying it a bit far? Charles would be sixteen if he were alive. He died when I was eight."

We had been in Rome. An elderly cardinal was persuaded that my father was his distant kin, and insisted that we stay in a lovely house

16

he owned in the Eternal City. For all I knew, it was true. My father was a big man, broad-shouldered, and he smelled of tobacco and sweated velvet. He wore his light-brown hair in an unpowdered queue, the strands on the sides coming loose and falling forward over his stubbled cheeks. He shaved before the evening's activities began, so daylight always caught him unshaven, if it caught him at all. My father was the illegitimate son of a Hungarian count, or so he said, but it was his word against that of my mother's kin.

My mother's people, the van Ayldes and the Jonghes, were old merchant families in Amsterdam, men with warehouses and ships and fine multistory houses overlooking the harbor. My mother was an orphan and an heiress who lived with her uncle in an old house full of tiny rooms and teak paneling brought back from the other side of the world. When she was sixteen she climbed out a barred window and ran away with Leopold Versfelt, who might or might not be the illegitimate son of a Hungarian count, and whose income was precisely nothing per annum.

Rome was pestilential. All I could remember was tossing and turning in the bed beside the window, my nurse talking to me in Italian and sponging me off. I knew my parents were sick, and Charles too.

I woke one night from fevered dreams of sacrifices and funeral pyres, shivering and calling out, "My lady, dear lady, don't let him go. The omens are bad, the fire dies in the brazier. Dear lady, do not let him go!"

"Shhhh," my nurse whispered. I saw her face in the firelight, heard her speak to someone behind her: "She is burning up."

"Iras!" I cried. "Come on! Bring the child!"

The priest stepped into the light of the candle. "She's raving," he said, and made the sign of the cross over me. He leaned down. "Dear child, do you understand that I am about to give you Extreme Unction?"

I struggled with the bedclothes. "Iras! Come on! Aurelianus can't hold them forever!"

I felt the priest's cool hand on my brow, heard him speaking the Latin words softly.

It only made me wilder. He could not get the wafer in my mouth.

"Requiescat in pacem," the priest said. The candle flared, illuminating a face like that of a knight on a tomb, then plunging me into darkness.

My nurse sponged me with a cool cloth. "There, sweet child," she said. "There, sweet child."

"The boy, the boy . . ." I whispered.

It seemed to me that her voice broke. "Rest

now, child. Rest now. You can do nothing for him."

"I can't?"

"No," she said, drawing cool water across my lips. "Sleep, little one. Sleep."

"I must get to him," I insisted, curling onto my side. "Sun and moon and the sons of gods. I have failed in every charge and I shall know no peace."

"You've done nothing wrong," she said. "Rest now, little one. There is nothing you must do."

I lay by the window half-open on the Roman night, streets quiet and still. I fell into fevered dreams and woke in the chill hour before dawn. My sheets were damp and twisted, but I was not cold. My hands shook as I sat up, but I did not shiver. In the night, the fever had left me.

"Giulia?" I said.

I heard her voice in the hall talking to someone. It was my father who answered. He sounded shaken, and his voice was thready.

"She's sleeping now," my nurse said. "Her fever's broken, praise to all the saints! But she was that close, I tell you, sir, that close to heaven. And at the worst of it, she was calling for her brother."

My father was weeping. "And he will never

answer," he said, and his voice choked on a sob.

Charles had died, and I lived.

In our second week at the spa, Cousin Louisa arrived. She was my mother's first cousin, raised with her. Like my mother, she was fair, but shorter and plump, with pink cheeks, as lively as my mother was quiet. I was by then incredibly glad to see her.

Louisa embraced me, and then the three of us sat down to the serious business of luncheon and all of the stories about cousins I had hardly sorted out. My mother picked at her food and at last said she was too tired from taking the waters that morning, and that she believed she would retire. I returned to Louisa's rooms instead.

Her maid was still busy unpacking. Louisa traveled with at least ten trunks, all filled with frills and robes and little lawn ruffles. She didn't even wait for us to be seated before she asked, "Well, how is she? The doctor hoped that she would improve."

I shrugged. "She's better than she was in Amsterdam. She knows who I am half the time."

"And Charles?"

"No change," I said. I sat down on Lou-

20

isa's bed. "Surely you don't expect one."

"Not really," Louisa said. "No going out lurking as Charles tonight. You have to stay here and bear your old cousin company!"

I smiled in spite of myself. "Cousin Louisa, it will be a pleasure."

Louisa rang for a collation in her rooms that evening, and we sat beside a comfortable fire that took the chill out of the air, munching on bread and cheese and tiny sausages wrapped in pastry. There was a box of cards on the side table, and I suggested a hand.

Louisa laughed. "You can't play cards with those! Well, I suppose you could, but someone would die!"

Seeing my confusion, she took up the box. "It's an Italian deck for fortune-telling. A friend gave them to me. Parlor tricks, but fun. Will I marry a handsome man? That sort of thing."

"I thought you already did," I said. Her husband, Ernst, was fifty and as wide as he was tall, but he and Louisa seemed to get along.

She laughed again. "Very well, then. Will you find a handsome lover?" She looked at me and raised both plucked eyebrows.

"Now, that's something I'd like to find out," I said. "I'll play."

Louisa lit more candles so we could see better, and I spread the cards out in the light. Round gold coins. Swords interlocked in intricate patterns, printed in blue and green and gold and red. Knights and kings holding the globe in their hands.

"You're supposed to lay out three piles, like this," Louisa said. "You ask a question, and then you shuffle and cut three times. The first one is what, the second one is how, and the third one is why. I can never make them work at all, not even enough to be funny."

I shrugged. They were beautiful. I ran my fingers over them, feeling them warm in my hands, creamy paper flowing like water. Chalices and staves, pages and queens. I pulled one out.

A woman sat enthroned, her blue robe flowing around her feet. Roses surrounded her, and behind her were two pillars with a veil between. She wore a crown surmounted by the horned moon, and her face was serene.

Louisa squinted at it. "So are you going to see about a lover or not?"

I cut the card back into the deck and shuffled, my hands enjoying the familiar feel of the cards. If there was one thing I had learned from my father, it was how to shuffle. "Tell me then," I said to them, "will I find a lover whom I truly love?" The cards flashed, colors bright and gleaming. "Tell me what will happen," I repeated, bending my whole will toward them. "Whom will I find, and how, and why?"

I cut them and laid them out in three, then turned the first one over.

The King of Chalices looked up at me, his red hair garish on the printed paper, a golden cup in his hand. Behind him was the sea, and in his other hand was a sword ornamented with pearls.

"A red-haired man," Louisa said.

"Quick in emotion, in anger or love," I said, peering at the picture carefully, the storm waves tossing behind him. I felt distinctly odd. "That's what the waves mean. Generous and dangerous too."

I flipped the second card over. "Fortune's Wheel," I said. "See, Louisa? How the poor souls bound to the wheel go up to fame and riches and then tumble down to the grave, only to go around again?"

"That doesn't look very nice," Louisa said. "Do you think your fortunes will tumble? Does your husband have any risky financial transactions?"

I shrugged again. "Not that I know of. But with the revolution in France and all, even kings are going to the guillotine. And peasants are coming up." My eyes ran over the wheel. Up, up, up on the wheel of fortune to the dizzying pinnacle, and then suddenly tumbling over. Over and over, up and down, cradle to grave.

"Elzelina?" Louisa touched my shoulder. "Are you all right?"

"Fine," I said. I felt odd, as if the pictures were drawing me into them, unnaturally bright. I smiled at Louisa reassuringly. "I'm fine." I turned the last card over.

An emperor rode in triumph in a chariot, his hair wreathed in victory, his arms extended, holding the reins. One black horse and one white horse drew the chariot, fine, prancing steeds, but they pulled in different directions, the black one stamping at the ground. Only the Emperor's strength kept them yoked together. Behind him the artist had suggested the slave at his shoulder, the one whose task it was to whisper that all glory is fleeting.

"The Chariot," I said. "That's why. The wind through the world. It's starting again. It's already started."

"What are you talking about?" Louisa said.

. . . *A pyre on a beach, the flames rising to the sky, a prince of a people who were no more, his face washed in firelight.*

24

A pyre glittering with gilded ornament and bright with silks beginning to smolder while elephants trumpeted and incense fumed, the smoke rolling over his body beneath its magnificent pall, his eyes weighted with coins, long red hair swept back from a face that was still young.

A red-haired girl turning suddenly, her face lit by flaring torches, illuminating the pale lines of her throat and her old black velvet dress —

Louisa's hand on my wrist. "Elzelina? Are you all right? I think we'd better put the cards away."

I focused on her face. It was real and close, concerned blue eyes, skin a little blotchy along her chin. "Yes," I said. "I think we'd better. I'm sorry. I just felt a little faint for a moment."

I scooped the cards together and put them in the box without looking at them. I should have been frightened, but I wasn't. I wanted to touch them again. I wanted to see. "Would you mind if I kept these for a while, Louisa?"

She shrugged, though she still looked at me a little strangely. "Not at all."

I went back to my room. Mother was asleep in hers. She would never wake, not with her laudanum every night.

I lit one candle and took off my shoes and

25

stockings, garters and all. I unfastened my dress, removed it, and hung it neatly. The stays were next, and then my chemise. In the candlelight, the body in the glass certainly did not belong to Charles. Honey-blond hair fell over my shoulders, not quite covering white breasts, rose-tipped and soft. My thighs were long and muscled, my stomach rounding forward just a little over a mound of Venus covered in gold curls. One hand rose, traced the circle of my navel. I traced it with my finger, round and round. My hand slid lower, entangled in soft hair. I bit my lip.

Abruptly, I turned from the mirror and opened the box, shaking out the cards onto my white bed. Gold and scarlet, garish blues and greens, falling like leaves. Crossed swords entwined with roses. Cups ranged in rows. The golden sun shining over boy and girl twins who stood together hand in hand. A tower fell and the sea lapped about it.

I threw myself on top of them. The soft paper crinkled under my weight. I shook the covers, and the cards fell around me like blossoms.

"Tell me," I whispered, but I did not know what question I was asking.

THE WORLD OF MEN

After two weeks at the spa, I returned home. My husband had secured an appointment in Lille that he thought would advance his career, and of course I traveled with him to take it up.

"Do you mean to send for the children?" I asked.

Jan shrugged. "There is no need. My mother is with them."

"When did your mother arrive?" I asked between gritted teeth. This was the first I'd heard of it.

"A few days after we left." He shrugged and spurred up to the front, ostensibly to talk with our coachman.

I was sure he had arranged her arrival so that he might avoid telling me that she was coming. And once again the children were left behind. Which I supposed was for the best, for what would we do with them if they were there? The travel and the new house would be unpleasant for them, would disrupt Klaas, who hated such things, and really there was no point.

Lille in the fall was lovely. The weather was agreeable and warm, but it was cold enough at night that all the trees turned brilliant colors. It was quite dry, and I could ride every day in the parks, leaving home before sunrise and galloping through the first light of morning before others were about.

The second week in November, we were invited to a dinner party at the house of the French minister, a man named Legros who had somehow managed to keep his footing despite all the changes of government in the last two years.

Since the storming of the Bastille in Paris six years ago, France had gone through one tumult after another, government after government rising and falling. There had been the Committee of Public Safety, Robespierre and other radical leaders of the Revolution, who had put the king and queen to death before their own fall and execution. Now there was a new government in place, less than two months old, the Directory, in which two houses of representatives elected five men to hold executive power. How that would fare we did not know, but it could scarcely be worse than the Committee of Public Safety. Overall, more than thirty thousand people in France had died in the Terror.

Half the world was at war with France since they had done away with monarchy, but in Holland we were France's allies — their only allies except the United States, but that little republic was too weak and too far away to be of any importance. Our new revolutionary government had replaced the autocratic rule of the Prince of Orange and enjoyed wide popular support. Our new leaders were to be elected, and the first written constitution we had ever had was in the works, promising a national assembly that would govern with the consent of the people. My husband hoped to be among its members when it convened in a few months. However, achieving that required a great deal of playing politics, because though he spent freely from my dowry, he was not particularly distinguished as a jurist. In fact, he had not gained any notability at all on his own merits.

For the dinner party I wore a dress that my new dressmaker in Lille had sworn was the latest style from France, a white gown with no panniers or frame at all, with nothing beneath it but a soft corset and a

chemise. While it certainly covered everything my older clothes had, it was so much
lighter that, standing in front of the mirror,
I bobbed and swooped like a little girl. I
could move my legs! I was in no danger of
falling over! The little flat slippers that went
with it were nothing but thin leather drawn
together and embroidered. I could have
climbed trees or ladders in those shoes. I
could run.

My maid put my hair up in the newest
fashion, two gentle knots at the back of my
neck, a tendril on each side escaping and
curled with an iron to cascade over my
shoulder in artful disarrangement à la Lucréce.

I went down and met Jan, who character-
istically had nothing to say except on the
subject of politics.

"I am going to talk with Citizen Legros,"
he said. "Pray be charming and keep others
entertained who might have the same idea."

"I will," I said, "as much as the seating arrangements will allow. If I'm half the table
away from you again, there won't be much
I can do."

And of course, I was. Jan was up at the
top of the table to the left of our hostess,
with Legros opposite. I was two-thirds of
the way down, next to our host's son,

among the younger, gayer people who reigned supreme at that end of the table. Our host's son was much taken with the girl to his left, and spent all of dinner leaning into her plate and giving her pretty compliments in a low voice. The man to my right was a Dutch Reformed minister who did not talk much but applied himself to every course with great enthusiasm. I wondered if my décolletage was incommoding him.

For conversation, this left me the man across and one down, a handsome Franconian officer named Colonel Meynier, who fulfilled his duty admirably. He was dark-haired and moustached, with his left arm prominently in a black sling pinned to his coat.

"And how did you acquire your wound, Colonel?" I asked, helping him to the salt during the game course.

"I am much obliged, Madame," he said. "It was a trifle, and hardly bears repeating. My arm was broken when I was kicked by a horse at Strelnitz. It was not an affair of honor."

"If it were, I am sure you would acquit yourself admirably," I said. He, at least, seemed to appreciate my décolletage.

"I should do so for you, Madame," he

said, laughing. "But I fear I am but a pale shade of gallantry compared to the French officers with whom I have the pleasure of serving." He nodded to the young hussar down the table, who returned the salute in kind. "There are some whose exploits rival the Paladins of Charlemagne."

"Surely you give the gentlemen too much credit," I said. "While I am sure they are gallant indeed, your approbation suggests endeavors of an extraordinary kind, such as are never seen in this late and fallen world."

"Fallen, Madame?" he queried, lifting his glass.

"Say, rather, modern," I amended. "The modern world does not lend itself to poetry. We are no longer allowed to be numinous beings, but rather products of reason. Or so I am told."

"You sound like my friend Ney," Meynier said. "I have a letter from him here, and he tells of his endeavors firsthand."

"You have letters?" interjected the minister to my right. "Why did you not say so before? We are all starved for news."

"Yes," agreed the young lady beside our host's son. "Please, may we prevail upon you to read them aloud?"

"The papers are sporadic in their reporting and boring in the extreme," our host's son said.

Meynier fished a packet out of his coat pocket with some little straining and opened it. "Some of it is quite dull, I assure you."

"Pray go on," the minister said. "If it is from the front, we want to hear it."

Meynier shrugged. "Very well then." He cleared his throat.

" 'Written at Bamberg, this twenty-sixth of August or, as I must style it, 9 Fructidor of the Year III. I can never keep it straight, my dear Meynier. Can anyone?' "

There was a general laugh around the table.

Meynier smiled and resumed. " 'It is, as you know, a pretty town, well situated and not damaged by our latest clashes of arms. A damned good thing, too. It's good to be somewhere peaceful, where there is no stench of blood. Of course, now there is the stench of our latrines —' " He stopped. "Your pardon, Mesdames. I shall skip the part about the latrines.

" '. . . You'll be glad to know that I did manage to purchase a suitable remount. He's a fine bay stallion three years old, with a white blaze and white stockings on his forefeet. I have named him Eleazar ben Yair, after that wily rebel of Josephus's who led the Romans such a chase. He certainly

33

seems clever enough, and like enough to take the arm off any groom who mistreats him. He's large and heavy, but still light on his feet, which is my preference in a horse. And clever enough that if I lack for partners, I shall teach him to play chess.' "

This drew an appreciative laugh from the listeners.

" 'We do not lack provision. Which is one advantage of billeting in unspoiled land. We are purchasing our supplies rather than taking them outright in order that we shall engender respect among the populace, who have no particular love for the Austrians. I am endeavoring to demonstrate that the Devil's Frenchmen have no horns — at least not on their heads —' " Meynier stopped, coloring. "I beg your pardon, Madame. I believe that's the essence of the letter."

Our host's son leaned forward. "A wit, but not a hero," he said. "I do not see this conspicuous gallantry you spoke of."

"You should have seen him at Mainz," Meynier said. "The French and a few allies, such as my humble self, were supposed to take the town. Now, as you may know, Mainz is defended by a star of fortifications, and we were mostly composed of cavalry. Which is not a good situation in the least. I was detailed, with the rest of the allied infantry, to make a skirmish at the outer ring of defenses. My friend Colonel Ney and his cavalry were then to cross into the rear of the defenders while they were occupied with us, and come upon them from the rear. A neat and tidy plan."

"Indeed," the minister said, taking a long gulp of his wine.

Meynier leaned forward. "Only there was a problem. There was a long ditch that ran behind them, fully five feet deep and as wide. A cavalry trap, they call it. Ney's men ran upon it, and their horses refused the jump. I hear a shout, and here's Ney, the only one across, his horse prancing right on the edge of the ditch, yelling for them to come on and jump! So of course the Austrians all wheel about from where I have them engaged, and there he sits all by himself on their side of the ditch. He hadn't room to get his horse up to speed to jump back, with just a dozen feet between him and them on this side. So he looks at me, gives me half a smile, draws his saber and touches his spurs, and wades straight into them. And I give a yell and we all charge in, because now we're in their rear. It was a hot little quarrel, let me tell you! When he finally gets through to us and we to him, he's letting the horse do the steering and he's got his saber in his left hand because he's shot through the right arm. It was bleeding dreadfully by the time we got back to the lines. Broken clean through the upper arm. Then he had lockjaw, and it looked like the arm would have to come off."

"Did it?" I asked.

Meynier looked at my white face, and I suppose he thought he was shocking me. His face softened. "No, Madame. He came through it. He's got an iron constitution to go with that red hair of his."

"How very brave!" the young girl said.

Meynier laughed. "He's that. And there's more than one kind of courage in France these days." He dropped his voice so it was not audible above the conversation at the other end of the table. "Let me tell you about the two priests."

"Priests?" the minister said dryly.

"You know we've standing orders that when we capture certain kinds of personages, they're not to go with the other prisoners. Émigrés, foreigners, aristocrats, and priests are to be detained separately and sent to Paris for questioning."

I took a breath, lifting my chin and trying to shake the ice that had gripped me.

"They go to the Conciergerie, or worse. And then to the guillotine."

"After questioning," I said. My voice sounded perfectly normal.

"Indeed, Madame," he said, and did not meet my eyes. "But it came to the attention of several people last summer that we did not ever seem to capture any such persons. On one occasion, however, we did capture two priests. They were being held with the others, awaiting transport, when somehow they escaped. I went and told my friend Ney about this. He did not seem shocked, and said that it would be a waste of time to look for them, as the area was densely wooded. I saw through his pretense immediately and remonstrated with him for allowing those Agents of Religion and Superstition to escape.

" 'Meynier,' he said, and looked at me sideways, 'if we are the representatives of Liberty, we should remember it.'

"I said nothing to him, Madame, for what should I say? At last I said, 'We have our orders.'

" 'So do I,' he said, 'from a source higher than the Committee of Public Safety.'

" 'You mean God?' I asked him.

"Michel Ney laughed. 'I don't think God is quite on speaking terms with me,' he said. 'I mean my conscience. If we are Liberty, then we must act like it.' He looked at me sideways again. 'Some say I lack intel-ligence. Do you think me a fool, Meynier?'

" 'No,' I said truthfully, 'I think you are something out of the age of chivalry.' "

Those around the table laughed apprecia-tively. I did not. I was struck dumb. It was like looking across a maddened mob, where all is senseless motion, and suddenly meet-ing the eyes of a friend, as though I had suddenly stumbled out of madness into clar-ity.

Michel Ney. My red-haired king from the tarot cards. I knew his name and I knew where he was, some little town in Franconia where he had a new horse and they were digging latrines. I could not think or breathe.

"Michel Ney," I said, trying his name on my tongue. He had red hair. He was a colonel in the French army. "Like a Paladin of Charlemagne."

Meynier nodded. "That is what I said. Are you well, Madame? You have gone white as a sheet. Perhaps all this talk of battles is too much for you?"

"Where is he from?" I asked.

"Saar-Louis. He is a Saarlaender. Ma-dame, you are alarming me. Your face is white and your hands are shaking."

"I'm fine," I said. I moved, and the wineglass tilted, spilling out on the linen. The footmen mopped it up while Meynier apologized.

Jan caught me in the hall, Meynier at my elbow. "For God's sake, Elzelina, I have a lot to do tonight."

"I think I am a little faint," I said. *Michel Ney. Michel Ney.* I knew his name. He was a real person.

"I would be happy to see Madame Ringeling to your door," Meynier offered. "I feel that I have inadvertently caused the lady distress. I should hate to discommode you further."

"That would be very kind," Jan said. "Elzelina, I will see you later." He disappeared into the library, to the political discussion that was beginning.

Meynier helped me into the carriage and climbed in opposite me. The rain was coming down. It made a rhythm on the roof of the carriage that was both lulling and strange. I could not think what was wrong with me.

"I'm sorry I distressed you, Madame," Meynier said. "I should know better than to talk about war in mixed company."

"You did not distress me, Colonel," I said. "I was intrigued by your friend."

"He will be amused to think that he can

cause a lady to faint at a distance," Meynier said. "Usually he needs to be in the same room to cause offense."

"He is not a ladies' man, then?"

Meynier blushed beneath his moustache. "Not really, no. I mean, I'm sure he does well enough, but . . . he is not much given to graces. He is a plain soldier."

"Ah," I said.

We were at my door. Meynier helped me up the step, and I took my leave and went inside. My maid hastened to help me out of my wet clothes, but I dismissed her and sat in the darkness in my chemise. Outside, the rain was pouring over the windowpanes, rolling down into darkness. I did not light a candle. There was some light from the window.

"Michel Ney," I said. "I have no idea why your name hits me like a sounding bell."

I remembered something, and rummaged in my drawer. Wrapped in a silk shawl were Louisa's Italian tarot cards. I opened the box and spread them on the bed. Kings and knights and the Devil, queens and coins and staves.

"Michel Ney," I whispered. The King of Chalices in my hands looked up with printed blue eyes. "I do not know how I know, or even what I know. But I know you."

■ ■ ■ ■

Jan and I returned to Amsterdam for the holidays. Their nurse brought the children from Utrecht, and my mother returned from the spa. It was all very domestic. As long as we could stay at our house, it wasn't terrible; but unfortunately the day before Christmas my mother went into one of her spells again, and I had to set foot in her house.

There were no decorations. My mother did not celebrate holidays, and the house was as dark and cheerless as possible. Night came at barely four in the afternoon.

Berthe met me at the door. "Madame, she's calling out for Charles again."

"I had anticipated that," I said, taking off my cloak and handing it to her. Beneath it I was wearing breeches and a man's frock coat, riding boots, and a cravat. My hair was swept back in a tail instead of pinned up. "I'll go straight in."

"You do make a handsome young man," Berthe said.

I turned on the stairs. "Thank you," I said. "I wish I *were* a man."

"And what would you do, Madame?" Berthe asked.

"I should go to war. And I would be better at it than most men."

Berthe laughed. "Oh, you are something else, Madame!" She dried her brow on her apron.

A little piqued, I went up to my mother's chamber. She was lying in half-darkness as usual, with only one candle lit. "Mother?"

"Charles?" She smiled when she saw me and her hands lifted.

I went and kissed her. "Hello."

"Charles, I have to warn you," she said, clinging to my hands.

I sat down in the chair beside the bed, gently disengaging her. "Mother, I'm fine."

"There is evil in this house. Evil that waits for you."

"Mother, nothing is going to happen to me," I said patiently.

"You aren't taking this seriously," she said, pouting a little. She was still a very pretty and charming woman. "If Elzelina had lived, she would be able to hear them."

I was startled. This was the first time she had ever said that she wished I lived. Even when she knew me and knew who I was.

"It's the women who can hear the voices," she said. "It's the women who are always the Doves in this family. That's how it started. Johan van Aylde killed his own

42

virgin daughter to make a pact with the Devil. Because she was a Dove, and she could see things in the mirror."

A shiver ran down my back, though I did not move. I did not look up at the mirror above her dressing table. "Mother, that's perfectly ridiculous," I said in my best Charles voice.

"I knew something terrible would happen to your father if we came to Amsterdam. And nobody listened to me."

Tears started in my eyes. "Father's death was an accident," I said.

"I warned Leo, but he didn't listen to me!" she said, and rolled over in her bed, her back to me. "You're just like Leo."

I stood up. "Good night, Mother," I said. *I don't know why I even came,* I thought. *It always hurts to no purpose.*

TEMPTATIONS

Spring arrived as it always did, warm and temperate. One of the men associated with the liberal parties was holding an elaborate fête at his country house not far from Brussels. Jan had been unable to wangle an invitation; but as this gentleman, M. van der Sleijden, was a distant relation of mine, a cousin in the third degree, Jan felt that if we simply arrived he would feel that we had some claim upon his hospitality. Not only were the leading men of the liberal party to attend, as well as many of the revolutionaries who had led the rebellion in Brussels a few years past, but also there should be the celebrated French general Pichegru and other military men.

I looked forward to the party and the lively company. I did, however, feel some discomfort with Jan's assumption that we would be welcome because of my tenuous claims of blood with M. van der Sleijden, a man whom I had met perhaps once in my life and could not have picked out of a room full of strangers. Still, Jan was not to be deterred. I smoothed over the awkwardness of our arrival as best I could.

Jan's latest passion was public education, the radical notion that the state should pay for rudimentary schooling for all boys, regardless of their fathers' positions in life. He was attempting to make it his great issue, and we made admirable props. I came in with the children while Jan and the gentlemen were drinking port in the library, knocking politely before I entered. Klaas held my hand, and the nurse followed with Francis in her arms. He was prettily attired in a white dress with blue embroidery around the neck.

"My dear husband," I said, "I hope that you will permit me and your sons to say good night before we retire?" I bobbed a polite curtsy to the gentlemen. The simple white lawn with blue ribbons I wore was becoming and matched the boys' clothes.

"My dear!" Jan rose and led me forward. "Monsieur de Boers, General Moreau, Monsieur van Flecht, allow me to present my wife. Elzelina, these gentlemen are engaged in the great work of assuring liberty for all mankind."

"Charming," said M. van Flecht, bending over my hand. He was the only one wearing a wig, and perspiration showed along the edge of his forehead in the summer warmth.

"What lovely children," M. de Boers said politely. "My felicitations. You have a beautiful family. I can see what inspires you to work so assiduously on behalf of the youth of our fair nation."

"Indeed," agreed M. van Flecht ponderously. "All of our boys should learn to read and write, and to make such mathematical transactions as are necessary for the preservation and enhancement of trade."

I smiled sweetly at him. "And our daughters as well, of course. Don't you agree?"

Jan stepped forward and took my hand from his. "Elzelina, dearest, don't bore the gentlemen with your views on female education." He squeezed my hand rather too tightly. "My wife feels the ardent fires of revolution with the same passion that I do. Only, as is to be expected, it is pure emotion untempered by reason."

"Indeed," said the Frenchman. He looked at me over Jan's shoulder and gave me a sardonic smile. "Is that not the way of women? But in this lies their charm — the ardor of their feelings."

I glanced at him, startled. He was not a

tall man, perhaps Jan's height, and perhaps five years older, soberly dressed, with dark hair tied back with a black ribbon. He had been introduced as a general, but he was not in uniform. His black coat was finely made but far from ostentatious.

"Indeed?" I said coolly. "Do you believe the fair sex incapable of reason, then?"

Moreau made a perfunctory bow over my hand. "Perhaps I find reason unworthy of the fair sex," he said. "After all, are not women made by nature to be the guardians of emotion and mystery? Does it not degrade our Vestals to be reduced to the calculation of coins in a till?"

"The Vestals are eternal virgins," I said. "And I fear that I am rather a matron, a wife and a mother. My service must be pledged rather to the Bona Dea than to Vesta."

Moreau smiled and turned to Jan. "I see your wife is an educated woman. I compliment you. It is through the learning of their mothers that sons gain precocious wisdom."

"Quite," said Jan with a pleasant smile. "Elzelina, perhaps you and the boys should retire. I am sure they are fatigued."

Francis was looking at the gentlemen with interest, one pudgy hand reaching for M. van Flecht's diamond stickpin. I took him

47

somewhat awkwardly from his nurse. "Come then, children. Good night, gentlemen."

"Good night, Madame," M. van Flecht said.

"Until the next time, Madame," Moreau said. As I turned away I felt his eyes on my back, lingering a little too long.

"Good night, Elzelina," Jan said. "Don't wait for me."

As though I expected him. Once I had, but those days were long gone by.

It was early spring in 1789, the spring after I had turned twelve. My father was two years in his grave.

Jan was supposed to be waiting at the bottom of the garden, just where the arbor led off among the trees. For a moment, breathing in the warm spring night, I thought that he was not there, that he had forgotten me. Then a shadow detached itself from the shade of the arbor and beckoned to me. I broke into a run across the grass, the dew splashing my shoes and hem, the heady fragrance of the early roses climbing the trellis almost intoxicating me. Somehow I had stepped out of the ordinary world and into a dream of silence and roses and night.

"Be quiet, Elzelina," he said, a little irritably.

"There is no need to make so much noise. Do you want them to hear us up at the house?"

I stopped in front of him, my cheeks stinging with shame. "I am sorry, Jan. I didn't think."

He stepped back into the shadows of the arbor. "Perhaps you should begin," he said, turning to walk through the tunnel of trellises.

I ran after him, my little bag of belongings bouncing against my back. "Please forgive me! Please don't be angry with me! You know I can't bear it when you're angry with me!" He didn't turn around. "I know I'm stupid and young, but oh, Jan! Please forgive me! It was wrong of me to ruin what should be the happiest night of our lives."

On the other side of the arbor, two horses were tethered beside the stone wall, cropping grass placidly. Jan turned, his handsome face bathed in silvery moonlight. "Of course I forgive you. I'm just concerned that someone will hear us. There are those who would try to prevent us from being together," he said quickly, with a glance back toward the sleeping house. "Now, be quiet." He cupped his hand for me to step in and swing up, as I was still too short to mount alone in skirts without a mounting block.

"I wish I had worn pants," I whispered. "We could go faster."

Jan frowned. "You must get out of that habit,

Elzelina. Riding about in boys' clothes is disgraceful enough in a young girl, but you are about to be a married woman, and you must put aside hoydenish ways."

"Oh yes, Jan. I will," I promised solemnly, petting the mare he held for me, and swinging up with his aid. "I will be very good from now on."

He did not answer, but only mounted his own horse. Together we swung about and trotted off across the fields, under the bright sky. Of course there was a full moon for my elopement. It was part of the scene. There was always a full moon in books. My blue-black cloak belled out behind me, and my long blond hair streamed in the wind. I thought that I must be really lovely tonight for the first time.

Before us the fields stretched out, plowed and planted but not yet greened. I wanted to kick my mare to a gallop, but I knew Jan would tell me to spare the horse. I decided I must start becoming more serious now that I was almost a married woman. I sat up very straight and stiff in the saddle. After a few minutes it was making my tailbone hurt. I supposed I hadn't got the moral backbone for it yet. I allowed myself to relax back into the mare's movements, promising myself I would start sitting up straight tomorrow.

"How far is it?" I asked after a few minutes.

Jan had been glancing back nervously for several minutes.

"It's still a few miles to the border," he replied.

It was three miles to a little village in German Pomerania where we were to be married. It was late when we arrived, with the moon westering behind the trees, and all the buildings locked except the inn. A sleepy stableboy took our horses.

"Jan," I said, touched by the thoughtfulness of it all, "did you tell them we were coming?"

"Of course, my dear," he said, assisting me to dismount. "They are waiting with supper for us."

Inside, the inn was scrubbed as clean as any housewife could want. There was a large, cheery fire, though the night was not cold, and a large woman in a starched apron waiting for us. "Monsieur Ringeling! Mademoiselle Versfelt! What a great honor!" She beamed at us with a beatific expression, a blessing upon young love. "Please sit by the fire! Allow me to bring you something to refresh yourselves while I see to your dinner."

"A bottle of your best burgundy," Jan ordered, allowing her to take his cloak. He was wearing a dark-green velvet coat, dark breeches, black stockings, and a waistcoat worked with silver thread. My heart swelled at the thought of this perfect creature as my husband. When the innkeeper handed him the wine bottle, he uncorked it deftly and poured a full glass of the ruby liquid into a cut-crystal goblet. He presented it to me as though it sanctified our wedding.

"Drink up, Elzelina. It will warm you after the night's chill." He cupped my fingers around it.

Smiling at him, I lifted the goblet to my lips. The wine was full and tasted of fruit and oak barrels, burning a little in my throat. I could feel the blood rising in my cheeks.

Jan nodded approvingly. "I must check on arrangements with the minister. I'll be back in a moment. Just stay by the fire and get warm." He slipped out the door. It was so considerate of him, I thought. So very kind.

I took another big drink of the wine. It tasted so good that I had another. The innkeeper came back in and hung our cloaks near the fire. She looked at me as I kicked off my boots and toasted my toes at the hearth, my blond hair spread across my shoulders. "How old are you, Mademoiselle Versfelt?" she asked.

I giggled. "Sixteen," I said, the lie that Jan and I had agreed on. He said that people wouldn't understand the truth if I said I was twelve, and I was sure he knew best about it. After all, he was twenty-five.

She looked at me as if she didn't believe

me. "Truly?" she said.

"Truly," I agreed solemnly, and giggled again. I took another long drink of the wine. Somehow, I just felt like giggling.

Jan came back and sat down beside me. I giggled. "What are you doing?" Jan said as the innkeeper brought in a tray of roasted meats, bread, and cheese.

"Nothing." I giggled again. *I must have deportment,* I thought. Brides should have deportment.

He lifted the wineglass to my lips, and I drank. It tasted good. He smelled good. Dinner smelled good.

We ate by the fire, drinking the whole bottle of wonderful wine. Wonderful burgundy. "Burgundy must be a wonderful place," I said, trying to sound grown-up and conversational.

Jan stared at me.

"I mean," I said, "it must be nice to travel. I enjoy travel." I giggled.

"I think you should retire," Jan said.

"Oh no!" I said, lunging forward and pouring more wine with unsteady hands. "I'm having a lovely time. Lovely." I simpered, waving an invisible fan in front of my face.

Jan looked nervously back toward the kitchen door. "Elzelina, I think you had best go to bed."

He was so handsome. So concerned. "I

53

don't want to go to bed. I want to talk about Voltaire."

"Not just now, Elzelina," he said, helping me to my feet.

I tripped on something and landed against him, looking up from the middle of his chest. "Hello, Jan," I said.

He took my arm, half-lifting me. "We are going upstairs. It's time you retired." He was nearly dragging me up the stairs, into the nicest room on the second floor. There was a bed and a washstand, a candle by the bed, blue and white curtains drawn tight against the night. He shut the door.

"You smell nice," I said. He was tall. Tall. I wished he would kiss me again like the time he did in the arbor. It was nice. And then he did. The room was spinning around me, and I felt curiously light-headed. I supposed that brides were supposed to faint. I'd never fainted before. I'd never understood why. Brides fainted. I could faint.

The room was spinning and dissolving into a riot of colors and sensations that made no sense. Somewhere there was the softness of the sheet beneath my bare back, the feel of his scratchy face against my chest. I giggled. I could have been floating on a cloud. I was not sure what happened next.

When I awoke, it was morning, and my head

was pounding. Or maybe, I thought, it was the door that was pounding. I covered my head with the pillow to keep out the noise and the brutal light from the window. The door swung open.

"Good God!" I heard a man's voice say. *Oh, I thought drunkenly, I'm not wearing anything but a pillow over my head.* The door slammed shut.

Jan and his father were having a shouting match on the upstairs landing.

"Twelve years old! Jesus Christ! Jan, you're not my son! Jesus Christ! I told you to stay away from her! I ordered you! Jesus Christ!"

"Sir," said Jan dispassionately, "I informed you that I was going to marry Mademoiselle Versfelt."

"You are not!" his father shouted. "That little girl is getting dressed and I am taking her straight back to her mother, where I am going to grovel to her family and hope that you don't face criminal charges. And you are going to be on the next ship to the Dutch East Indies, where you are never going to mess with her again!"

I sat up in bed suddenly, hardly believing that Jan's father could be so cruel. My body was very stiff and sore, a little blood streaking the insides of my thighs.

Jan didn't raise his voice. "No, sir, I am not.

Because if I am, then Mademoiselle Versfelt is ruined. The marriage has already been consummated. If it does not take place, it is she who will be the injured party. No other suitor will ever wed her. She will remain unmarried the rest of her life, cooped up with her madwoman mother."

There was a long silence in the hall, so long that I wondered if they had gone away.

Then I heard his father say, in a low, strangled voice that sounded almost like tears, "Damn you. There's not a drop of human feeling in you, is there? You would do anything for money, regardless of decency."

"That is your opinion, sir," Jan said.

His father's voice was very low. "Tell your fiancée to get dressed. I am taking her back for her mother's blessing and consent. I will not have her speculated about by all good society. You will be married in the First Reformed Church in Amsterdam like respectable people. God help the poor girl, married to you!"

I lay back on the bed, listening to his father's footsteps on the stairs, suddenly frightened to death.

That had been seven years ago, and I was no longer the naïve girl I had been then, blinded by dreams of love. I had given him two sons and brought him a great deal of money. I was a good hostess, a personable wife on the arm of an ambitious man. And of course, I brought my family connections, as awkward as it was to trade upon them, showing up at house parties to which we had not been invited.

As a result, I tried to be as pleasant as possible to our hosts. M. van der Sleijden, my distant cousin, was married to a woman of my mother's age, who immediately bade me call her Aunt Sofie. Their eldest daughter was a lively dark-haired girl of fifteen named Maria.

Maria and I shared many interests, including a love of early-morning horseback rides — Jan was never even up at that time, having stayed up until the wee hours talking politics.

The second day after I arrived, we had a very nice ride, cantering across the fields in the gray morning, the mist rising off every stream and canal, doves calling and crossing the pearly sky. We stopped at the top of a gentle rise and watched the sun come up. Neither of us said anything. It was too beautiful.

Along the line of the canal a man was riding toward us on a black horse, his shadow flung out before him in the morning. I sighed. It was too early for social pleasantry.

"Oh!" Maria said, and I was startled to see her blushing.

I looked at the man again. It was General Moreau. "Do you know Moreau?" I asked Maria.

She bit her lower lip. "I've just met him this week. He's terribly gallant, don't you think? And a bachelor."

"Maria, he's forty if he's a day," I began, but could not finish because Moreau rode up, doffing his hat and making a pretty bow from the saddle.

"My dear ladies," he said.

"Good morning, General," I said.

Maria blushed again. "It's nice to see you again."

"The pleasure is mine," he said. "Surely your fair countenance lends more to the day's beauty than does mine."

I made some sound that might have been a snort.

He raised black eyes to mine, a look of amusement rather than insult there. "Perhaps my countenance does not give Madame Ringeling the same pleasure. The last time we met, she roundly whipped me on the subject of feminine virtue."

I lifted an eyebrow. "I would hardly characterize our brief conversation that way."

Moreau inclined his head. "Believe me, Madame, being whipped by you gave me the greatest pleasure."

"There's no accounting for taste," I said tartly.

Maria was gaping. Her eyes were huge, and she stared at me as though to send me some secret message. "If your presence does not please my cousin, it certainly pleases me. I am by no means ready to return to the house. General, would you accompany me on the rest of my ride? Elzelina was just saying how tired she was."

Moreau inclined his head politely. "Of course, Mademoiselle. I am sure that such an independent woman as Madame Ringeling will have no objection to returning to the house alone."

"Of course," I said sweetly. "I am on my way just now to take breakfast with your mother, Maria. Shall I tell her you will be returning soon?"

"Fine," Maria said. She was looking at Moreau as though he were made of marzipan, a look I distrusted immensely.

At luncheon, Maria would not speak to me. And that evening Jan wanted me at his side constantly to run off anyone who tried to impede his progress at political conversation. I had no chance to talk to Maria until late, when she had already retired. As I came along the corridor, I saw the light under her door and knocked.

"Come in?" she said.

I opened the door. Maria was sitting up in bed, her dark hair braided for the night in two plaits. She was writing in a little journal by the light of a candelabrum beside the bed. "Oh, Elzelina!" she exclaimed.

I shut the door behind me and came and sat on the end of the bed. "Maria," I said, "I feel that I should warn you. You are very young and —"

Maria turned scarlet. "You know nothing about Victor! Nothing! He's one of the finest men ever to walk the earth!"

"I do not doubt it," I said carefully. "And you have told me that he is a bachelor. Indeed, I know nothing to the contrary, and I have enquired of other members of his party this evening. But I think you must be certain that honorable matrimony is his object. He is, after all, more than twice your age —"

"How can you know anything about it?" Maria demanded. "Age is irrelevant when two hearts beat as one."

I folded my hands. "Maria, I am only trying to help. I know from hard experience how men can take advantage of youth and beauty —"

"You're just jealous," Maria said. "You're nineteen and married and nobody looks at you anymore."

Now it was my turn to feel the furious heat rising in my cheeks. "Maria, you are clearly infatuated. And if he returns your feelings and wants to marry you, well and good. But I am warning you that if you slip off alone with him again, I will tell your mother."

Maria threw the journal at me. It caught me at the corner of my left eye, and hurt quite a lot. I resisted the urge to slap her. Instead, I got up and handed it back to her, though my hands were shaking. "I see that you are as stupid as I was. Good night." I slammed the door on my way out and went back downstairs. I had been so very stupid, and certainly no one could have told me so at the time.

The party was ending. A few gentlemen lingered. Jan had General Pichegru in a corner and was wearing his ear out. Our hostess was nowhere to be seen. Nor our host.

Moreau was pouring another glass of Madeira at the sideboard. I walked in directly, my draped skirts whispering over

61

the parquet floors. He looked up, a little startled. "Madame Ringeling? Would you like a glass of this excellent Madeira?"

"I would," I said. "And a word with you in private, General."

His mouth quirked and he made a half bow. "It would be my greatest pleasure. I believe the terrace is unoccupied?"

We stepped out through the French doors. The night was cool and moonlit, but not so chilly that I wished for a wrap. The moon was at first quarter and rising clean above the fields. I took a long drink of the Madeira.

"You had something to say to me?" he asked, waiting in his plain black evening dress.

"I want to know the nature of your feelings for my cousin," I said. "Maria is fifteen, and you have quite turned her head."

"Ah." Moreau cradled his glass in his hands. "You are concerned for your cousin's reputation. An admirable sentiment."

"It would be more admirable if you answered a direct question," I said. "Do you intend to marry her?"

"I wondered why you had enquired after my wife's health with the entire French delegation," he said, "since there is no such lady. I see that this was by way of intel-ligence gathering."

"Are you planning to marry my cousin, or am I going to speak with her father?" I asked. "There are two possible answers, and I will have one or the other."

Moreau looked down at his glass and smiled in amusement. "Touché, Madame. I have no desire to marry at this point in my life. Your cousin is charming, but I have little patience for the state of matrimony. I fear that she has read far too much into some commonplace pleasantries that I produced for the sake of gallantry. And I see that I have no chance at even such innocent pastimes with a Gorgon guarding her."

"Men like to term fierce women such monsters," I said. "But better a Gorgon than a fool, General. Leave my cousin alone, or I will see that her father makes it an affair of honor."

Moreau did not seem upset. "I will comply with your ultimatum, Madame. I seem to have little choice."

I nodded. "That is true. And while Maria will be angry now, it is better than that she should do something she would regret for the rest of her life."

"Does it occur to you that Maria is in every way inferior to you? And that perhaps my ulterior motive in joining you for a ride

63

had nothing to do with the desire to be alone with Maria?"

I looked away and took another drink. "My dear General," I said calmly, "what flattering sentiments! But as you know, I am a married woman and no fool."

"Merely married to one," he said.

I glared at him. Moreau spread his hands. "Madame, do you think I cannot see what a fatuous social climber your husband is? That beneath all his fine talk of democracy and liberty is nothing more than the desire to enhance his own career? His affection for you is a sham, and his principles are the fashion of the day. He is hardly your match in any sense."

"Jan is a gentleman," I said. "I do not think that you . . ."

Moreau took a step closer, his eyes on a level with mine. He was taller than I by a finger's breadth, and in the still night air I caught a faint hint of shaving soap, sandalwood, and oranges. "You cannot tell me that you love him," he said. "You cannot tell me that he satisfies you in any way."

"And you could?" I raised my fan between us, causing him to step back. "You think very well of yourself, General."

"Victor," he said.

"If you think that I will address you

familiarly, you are mistaken," I said. "I am not interested in being your lover. Or anything at all to you."

"Can you tell me honestly that you are a faithful wife?" he asked.

"I do not owe an accounting to you," I said, turning away and taking another sip of my Madeira. Through the French doors I could see Jan still talking with Pichegru. If he looked up, he could see me.

I half-expected Moreau to press, even in full sight of my husband, but he did not. Instead, he carefully balanced his glass beside mine on the railing. "My offer stands," he said. "Should you tire of him, I am willing to provide other options, options perhaps more appealing to a woman of your wit and taste for danger. And obvious sensuality."

I flipped my fan open and looked at him over its bars. "I can't imagine where you would get such vulgar ideas."

Moreau laughed. "As I said, my offer stands. But now . . . good night, Madame." He strolled off across the terrace and through the doors. Jan did not look up.

I stayed out on the terrace until I saw Pichegru take his leave of Jan, and my husband put down his glass and prepared to go up. I followed him and knocked softly at the door of the room he was staying in, adjacent to my own. I entered without waiting for him to answer.

Jan was sitting at a table before the window, already working on some piece of correspondence by the light of several candles. He had removed his frock coat, and his cravat was disarranged. He looked at me and frowned. "Yes, Elzelina?"

I closed the door and came to stand behind him. "Hello, Jan."

"Did you just come up? I hadn't seen you in quite some time."

"Yes," I said. "I was on the terrace talking with General Moreau."

"Good thinking," he said, bending over his letter. "Pichegru has the highest opinion of him. Many consider him a finer general than either Dumouriez or Bonaparte."

"Surely not better than Dumouriez," I said, thinking of the man they called the Liberator of Holland. "I found him rather tiresome." I touched the back of Jan's neck with one finger, running it down to his collar.

"You would. I assume he didn't talk about fashion." Jan waved my hand away. "Elzelina, that tickles."

"No, he tried to seduce me," I said.

"Obviously he failed," Jan said. "Assuming that's what he really meant. The French use so many conversational pleasantries that sometimes it's possible to read in things that aren't really there."

"I'm quite certain he tried to seduce me," I said. I put my hands on Jan's shoulders and began kneading them. "I do know what seduction looks like."

Jan turned around and removed my hands firmly. "Elzelina, I am trying to write a letter. What is it you want?"

"I want you to come fulfill your marital responsibilities," I said, coloring. "If I am going to say no to Moreau, I believe I have a claim on you."

Jan just stared at me. "I can't believe you said that."

"I can't believe you don't even care!"

His voice was perfectly even. "You want me to make some ridiculous display of jealousy over something that may or may not have happened? When even if it did, you handled it both correctly and politely? You have done no more than one might expect of a virtuous wife. And if I can't trust you to talk to a gentleman in public, where would I be?"

Tears were starting unaccountably in my eyes. "Don't you even care if a man has designs on your wife?"

"You handled the matter adequately," Jan said. "There is no reason for any further discussion."

"You could at least be upset!" I snarled.

"Nothing happened! You said so! You expect me to fly off the handle like some quick-tempered Latin —"

"I expect you to act like you love me," I said.

"Elzelina, I expect you to act like an adult," he said. "These girlish fits are unbecoming." He turned back to his letter. "I have some urgent correspondence that must go tomorrow morning. I don't have time for these histrionics. You are acting like your mother."

I felt as though cold water had been thrown in my face. "Fine," I said. "If that's how you feel about it, perhaps I will sleep with Moreau."

"Do you think I care?" he asked dryly. "It might even be helpful, frankly."

"What?"

"Such things happen. I can't imagine that there are any married people of our class without diversions of this sort. As long as you are respectable, do you think I care what you do?"

My tears stopped. I straightened up and turned to look at him. He sat there perfectly calm in his well-tailored coat, his hands at his sides and his hair neatly trimmed, an expression of complete disinterest on his face, as though he were merely getting through some tiresome task before he could get on with politics.

I began to hate him.

He'd been twenty-five when he had married a girl of twelve for her money. And that was all it was. Money. Not even lust. Not even perversion. He couldn't care less if I had a dozen lovers as long as I was a perfect hostess. In fact, he would be happy to pimp me out if it would help his political career, because he did not care about me in the least. My actions mattered less than his valet's or the coachman's. They, at least, had tasks that mattered to him.

"I've told you to be perfectly free. So long as you don't embarrass me."

"I understand," I said. My voice sounded timbreless, even to me.

"Well, then, I'll see you later." He bent over his papers again.

I went back to my room and washed my face and sat down before the dressing-table mirror. Charles was not there. It was my own reflection, white-lipped and pale except for my pink nose. I had loved him, or thought I had, when I was twelve. He had played on that, played me for the fool I had been.

"I am leaving him," I said.

The girl in the mirror had such cool blue eyes.

"I will have more. I deserve more than this. I will have more."

I squeezed my own hands until I was white-knuckled.

"I am leaving him."

THE RUNAWAY BRIDE

Having decided, I was completely, dreadfully calm. The next week Jan was going to The Hague on political business, while I was to remain in Amsterdam. He would be gone for four or five days, so that was the ideal time.

I would leave the children there.

What would I do with them if I had them with me? Klaas hated travel, and he was happy and safe there. Francis hardly knew me. Taking them would bring them nothing but misery and uncertainty. After all, I hardly knew where I was going.

I laid the cards out on my bed that night. Fortune's Wheel was the center card, crossed by the Sword Queen.

"Paris," I said. "Where the low are made high and the high are made low. I am going to Paris." I had never been there. But Paris was Paris, and its name cast a spell.

On the day Jan left for The Hague, I went

to our banker, the man who handled all of the money I had brought to this marriage, and withdrew as much as I could "for shopping" without calling attention to myself. After all, even though the money was my dower, the moment the ring was on my finger everything I owned belonged to Jan. A woman was her husband's, like his horse or his house. I could no more take my own dowry and divorce him than his carriage horses could.

It was safer to travel as a man on a public coach. I reached Utrecht the next day. I took a room at the Hotel du Mail under the name of Charles van Aylde. No one noticed anything or commented. I gave orders I was not to be disturbed, went to my room, and slept the clock around.

In the morning I got up, dressed and pretended to shave, and went down to enjoy a late breakfast in the sun on the terrace. It wasn't much of a terrace, merely a fenced-in area between the dining room doors and the street. There were some low planters full of bulbs that hadn't quite bloomed yet, though I could see they were going to be still more yellow tulips. I crossed my booted feet, ordered café au lait with bread and butter, and sat happily in the early-morning sunshine reading the newspaper and watching the passersby.

If this was what life was like as a man, then I would be a man. To go where I wished and to be my own master was the sweetest taste imaginable.

A Franconian officer was coming up the street, carefully stepping around the puddles and ruts from the mail coach. He glanced at me, glanced away, then stopped and stared. It was Meynier.

I looked coolly back at him, then smiled.

Meynier came over to the fence and looked me up and down, an expression of utter amazement on his face. "Can it be . . . ?"

"It is," I said, "Madame Ringeling. But don't speak so loudly. Come join me for breakfast, if you will."

Meynier stepped over the planter and slid into the seat opposite mine. He leaned over the table. "I hardly recognized you in that. You certainly make a striking young man."

"Thank you," I said. "I thought it safer."

"Safer for what?"

"I have left my husband," I said, "and I am traveling to Paris alone."

Meynier's eyebrows rose to his hairline. "Really? I wondered what a woman like you was doing with a little squirt like him."

"A what?" I chuckled, one hand curving around my coffee.

"A little squirt. A man whose stream is as small as his organ."

I really did laugh out loud at that. I leaned forward conspiratorially. "It is, rather!"

Meynier grinned. "I like you better like this. Is there anything I can do to help you?"

"I need to hire a carriage," I said. "Do you know where I can find a good one?"

He thought for a moment. "Probably. I'll see what I can do, Ma — What should I call you, anyway?"

"Charles van Aylde," I said.

I spent that evening at the hotel, sipping a glass of port in the main room and reading a book. No one bothered me. No one seemed to see through my disguise. I supposed there was something to be said for very long legs. That night I slept quietly in my room.

And I dreamed.

I was climbing a mountain somewhere hot and dry. I heard a mew, and there ahead of me on the path was an orange and white cat. She was waiting, and I followed her.

We came to an overlook, and I caught my breath. The cliff plunged down into desert that stretched as far as the eye could see.

The sky arched blue above, and the sands moved in a thousand shades of light. On the far horizon there was a glitter. I could just make out the faint shapes of towers and gates of brass.

The cat twined around my ankles.

I reached down and touched her. She looked up into my eyes. Hers were sea-green and they knew everything. Her fur was warm under my hand.

I woke.

There was a gray tabby cat on the bed beside me, purring. It was just growing light.

"How did you get in here?" I asked the cat.

A foolish question, since I had left the window cracked. A nimble jumper could get into the second floor from the tree outside. The cat meowed. She turned, and I saw her swollen teats. A nursing mother, or a cat whose litter had been drowned. She butted against my hand.

I petted her absently. Was it the cat that had woken me? I felt a strange urgency, as though someone had whispered in my ear. Something was wrong. I needed to be on the road.

I sat up. I needed to be on the road. It was an irrational feeling, but what good had being rational ever done me? I must go.

I dressed quickly and stowed everything away in my luggage. If Meynier had not found a carriage, I would have to do it myself. There was no time to waste. I had to leave now.

As I came downstairs, I saw Meynier coming in. He grabbed my arm and steered me away from the landlord's wife, who was grinding coffee beans with a hand crank. "Thank God I found you! Listen, you must go immediately. There was a man at the inn down the street by the camp this morning, asking after a golden-haired woman. A runaway wife from Amsterdam. Her mother is mad and her husband is hunting for her before she can do herself harm. The authorities are supposed to help, since the poor woman is a menace and needs to be taken quietly back to Amsterdam and a nice comfortable room."

I clutched his arm. "No."

Meynier nodded. "You're no more mad than I am. But he's going to lock you up. And he's got the law on his side. Is your mother really mad?"

"As a hatter," I said grimly. "And everyone knows it. I imagine society has just been waiting for me to go round the bend."

"There's no chance people won't believe it?"

"None," I said. "I have to get out of here."

Meynier grinned. "Fill your saddlebags, van Aylde! I've got a couple of horses, if you can stick on astride. We'll send your luggage on ahead and whisk you over the border on horseback. Once you're in France, they'll have to apply through official channels to get you."

"They will," I said. "Or they may not wait. Possession is two-thirds of the law. If they take me back by force, will France protest? I have no friends there."

Meynier shook his head. "No, then. Not if you have no friends."

An idea struck me. I stood up straighter, my hand dropping to my side. Could I do it? I could do whatever I needed to do. "Where is General Moreau's headquarters?"

"Menin," Meynier said. "So?"

"We're going to Menin," I said. "Let me grab my saddlebags."

Meynier nodded. "I can go partway with you, at least. I'll find some food for the road while you arrange with the landlord about your luggage."

In less than an hour, we were on the road. Meynier threw me an apple from the saddle, which I caught neatly left-handed. He laughed.

"Madame Ringeling, you have a fine seat!"

Meynier said. "And just what do you pro-
pose to do in Menin? Do you know General
Moreau?"

I looked ahead. The road seemed to meet
the sky, a trick of perspective they taught
nice girls in drawing classes. "Let's see if I
know him well enough."

We reached Menin the next day. Meynier
insisted on coming all the way with me, even
though it would make him a day late returning to his post.

I had no idea what sort of impression I
would make on Moreau wearing men's
clothes, but my own dress from the saddlebags was hopelessly crumpled, and my other
clothes were following in my trunks. I
smoothed my hair down and retied my
queue.

Meynier escorted me as far as the door to
the headquarters, then wandered off to
loiter and watch the groom seeing to the
horses.

One of the young sentries looked me up
and down. I made no attempt to hide my
sex, but rather had opened my shirt at the
throat. My voice was quite steady. "Please
tell General Moreau that Madame Ringeling is here to see him on a matter of some
personal urgency."

"Of course, Madame." He disappeared for a moment, then hastened out. "The general will see you."

I preceded him inside.

Moreau got up from his paper-strewn desk and crossed the room with his hands outstretched. "To what do I owe the pleasure? And you are most charmingly dressed." His eyes raked me up and down, lingering just a moment on the tight legs of the breeches, the buttons on either side at the waist.

I put my head to the side. "Does your offer stand?"

"My offer?" His voice was even, but I saw the flash in his eyes.

"Your offer to teach me better when I left my husband. I have left him."

Moreau laughed. He turned his back and crossed behind his desk. I stood stock-still and immobile.

"I am not laughing at you, Madame," he said. "I am laughing at myself for not anticipating such directness. Of course I should have expected you to be entirely singular in this."

"Does your offer stand?" I asked. "I will be your mistress if you will do one thing for me."

He turned around, and his face was keen.

Victor Moreau was no fool. "What is the thing?"

"My husband wants to return me to Amsterdam. He has sent men to seize me. If you will prevent this and arrange for me to stay in France, I will do what you desire."

"What I desire." He came toward me again. "I must say, I prefer this charming defiance to your slavish submission to that lout. I assume he means to lock you up. I wonder why."

"Because the money is mine," I said. "It's my dower. Jan hasn't a sou that's not mine." He had very dark eyes, and they lingered on my face, on my throat. I did not look away from him. "He has to control me to keep the money. My mother is mad. It's easy to tell people that I am just like her."

"And that he is solicitously caring for an invalid. I see." Moreau reached one hand out and traced the line of my jaw, sensuously and slowly. His fingers pinched down on my earlobe, and I gasped. "Is that the way it is? You do look charming in that ensemble. I wonder how you'd look bent over my desk?"

"I keep my word," I said. I felt a strange excitement rising in me, curling out from between my legs and crawling up my body. "Whatever you desire."

80

"Ah, but what do you desire?" he asked. "Do you even know yet? Playing the coquette for men with no imagination?"

With some difficulty I stepped back. "Do we have a bargain?" I asked. "You will not see me over your desk or anywhere else until I have your word that you will offer me your protection and prevent me being returned to Holland."

He laughed. "You drive a bargain like a burgher, Madame. Very well. You have my word. I will protect you from your husband and guarantee you the protection of France. You are wasted on him, my dear. I think you will like this better."

"Then we have a bargain," I said.

I bade Colonel Meynier farewell with many thanks. He asked me at least ten times if I would be all right left in Menin.

"I will be quite well, I assure you," I said, clasping his hand warmly. "And I will always remember your kindness." I watched him ride away, then returned to Moreau's office. The day was ending and it was growing chilly despite the spring sun.

Moreau looked up as I entered. "Well, Madame?"

"The colonel is gone," I said.

He got up and walked around the desk to

me. The door was closed, but there were two men in the outer office. I did not back up. I would not. I had made this bargain and meant to abide by it.

"You will need a name," he said. "My men know that you are here. If you wish to avoid any unfortunate encounters with your husband's hirelings, then you need a name that is not your own."

I nodded. "St. Elme," I said. "For the fire that illuminates everything and yet is nothing but illusion."

"Very poetic," Moreau said. He stood just a little too close, but he did not touch me. "And perhaps Ida for a first name? It's a common enough name to be believed to be your own, unlike Semiramis or any of the classical names that are all the rage for courtesans these days."

"Why not Lucréce?" I asked, more sharply than I had intended.

"My dear, if rape were what I enjoyed, my profession would give me ample scope for my pleasures." He smiled at me. "You sought me out and offered me this bargain. So there is no need to play the victim with me. Unless that's what you like."

I glanced away. He was still standing too close. Sandalwood and orange, and the scent of his skin after a day of work. Dark hair curling close at the back of his neck, and fine hands.

"Is it?" Victor asked. "The pretense of ravishment? All responsibility for your actions removed? A fairly common fantasy, in my experience, especially among whores who have not admitted it to themselves."

I lifted my hand to slap him, but he caught my wrist. He did not bend it, just held it a trifle too tightly for comfort. He could feel the pulse jumping, my heart beating faster, and I could not hide it.

Victor smiled again, amused and indulgent both. "I don't think so, my dear. I don't particularly like being slapped."

I looked away from his dark eyes. I was too conscious of my body and his, of this heat I was ashamed of and could not control.

He opened his grip and traced the veins in my wrist, circling around my thumb and opening my hand. "You have a fine sensibility, my dear. I saw that immediately. Like a delicate-mouthed mare who has never known anyone but an ironhanded lout. But you have no idea how to play the instrument you own."

"You are mixing metaphors," I said. My heart was racing.

Victor laughed and bent over my hand

with a graceful gesture perfectly suited to the drawing room. "You're clever as well. And of course you know you're beautiful. Everyone must have told you that since you learned to walk."

"Not really," I said.

He raised one eyebrow. "Perhaps that accounts for your poor taste so far. So have you in fact slept with anyone besides your husband?"

"I am not going to answer that," I said. "I don't see that it's any of your business. And you can't make me tell you."

"You will tell me," he said. "Because you have just told me that you want me to make you. That bit of unnecessary defiance was very illuminating." He crossed behind me and did not touch me, just stood close enough behind that I could feel the heat of his body, not quite against mine. "You want to be made to do things so that you don't have to admit that you want them. So that you don't have to accept your own deliciously carnal nature. Why else did you come here?"

"I had nowhere else to go," I said. I waited for him to touch me.

"That's not strictly true, is it, my dear? You could have gone on to Paris in disguise. You could have appealed to Meynier's gallantry. You could have taken a ship to England. In actuality, you had many options."

He did not touch me. When was he going to touch me? He was just standing there at my back, so close that I could feel his breath on my cheek as he leaned forward.

"You could have gone many other places besides here. 'I had no other choice' is an excuse for weak-willed fools. You sought your own ruin. You chased after it gladly."

Now at last I felt his arm go around my waist, felt his lean, muscled form against my back. His hand slid up and cupped my breast, stroking the nipple agonizingly slowly through the cloth of my shirt. I took a ragged breath.

"You want me to take you. You want me to humiliate you utterly, to bring you absolute abasement. And for it all to be my fault. For it to be my perversion, not yours."

Abruptly his fingers snapped my nipple, pinching it painfully. I twisted and let out a moan. He released me. I staggered and almost fell.

"I am not going to do that, my dear," he said. His tone was conversational, but I could see the flush on his cheeks. "Not until you ask me for it. Not until you beg for it."

"That is worse," I said.

"Yes, it is, isn't it?" He smiled at me cheerfully, as though I were a child who had been clever. "You are going to anticipate everything. And you are going to tell me everything."

"No," I said. But I did not move. I wanted him to come close again.

"You are going to describe to me every minute sensation that you feel. You are going to tell me exactly how and where you're becoming aroused. You are going to tell me exactly what filthy thoughts are passing through your mind. And you are going to ask me to do unspeakable things to you, only you are going to speak every word in the crudest possible language. And then, only then, will I do it."

"I do not . . ." I said.

He crossed behind me again, his hip barely brushing mine, but it felt like thunder. He leaned close to my ear. "And when you come, I am going to feel every last shudder, and you are going to tell me exactly what you feel."

"I have never . . . with anyone else . . ." I stammered. I leaned back, and his lips almost brushed my shoulder.

Victor laughed softly. "Only alone?"

I nodded. My breasts were tight, and a wetness was starting between my thighs. My

86

eyes were sparking with tears.

He lifted one stray piece of hair away from my neck. "You see? That wasn't so hard. Your first confession."

I almost sobbed.

He stepped away. "You will dine with me tonight in my quarters. It does not matter what you wear. At eight o'clock. In the meantime, I will have my servant show you to a room where you can be comfortable." Moreau crossed to the desk, picking up papers. "I will see you later."

I nodded. I must pull myself together. I must.

He raised his voice and called for a servant. "Madame St. Elme will be staying. Please put her in the Blue Room and bring her whatever she requires." He nodded at me. "Your servant, Madame."

I followed the man quickly. I was shaking as though I had just faced the most grueling fencing match of my life. *At least I also scored a point,* I thought. As he crossed to the desk, I had seen the bulge in his trousers, uncomfortable if he intended to wait several hours to satiate it. But then, perhaps denial was something he found stimulating.

MOREAU

The Blue Room was a pretty bedchamber at the back of the house Moreau was using for quarters. It was hung with light-blue silk and matching curtains. There was a four-poster with a cream quilt and duvet and blue brocade bolsters, a matching brocade chair, and a bench upholstered in light-blue slipper satin. A wardrobe held the few clothes from my saddlebags. A door gave onto a small, irregularly shaped dressing room with necessary pot, basin, and washing things, all made of plain white china.

It was all perfectly respectable and in good taste. I had half-expected manacles hanging from the ceiling. Or at least silk ropes twined around the posts of the bed.

Had expected or had hoped? That thought rushed to my mind unbidden. Moreau, damn him.

I drew the curtains and lit the candles. The room glowed with a soft light. I opened the wardrobe and shook out my one dress. It was sadly wrinkled. Hopefully the rest of my clothes would be here in the next day or two. The gown was rose pink, with a modest square neckline and a belted waist, the newest English style. It did look nice. I let it air out while I washed up and did my hair. Which did not take two hours.

I heard voices distantly in the house, the sounds of servants, I supposed. I was not locked in. I could have left at any moment. Instead, I prowled around the room, picking up things.

The table held two books and a pamphlet: *The Indelicate Debaucheries of a Crowned Head, Being the Excesses of the Late Marie Antoinette.* I flipped it open, then closed it at once. Then I opened it again. The engraving purported to show the Princess de Lamballe kneeling in front of the queen, her lips on the queen's nether regions, while that lady flung herself backward, caressing her own upturned breast.

"So this is revolution," I said. I doubted seriously that any woman would find that position comfortable, much less pose for an engraver. Nevertheless, it was intriguing. I had certainly never seen anything like it, not even in Italy during my remote childhood. The Dutch said that the French were depraved, and while I found it a bit hard to believe that Marie Antoinette had done anything of the kind, it said something about the audience that a printer found a ready market for things like this. *A different world,* I thought. *Revolution has toppled every barrier.* The idea was rather thrilling.

There was a discreet knock on the door, and I hastened to bury the pamphlet beneath the books on the table. "Come in."

A sober valet stood there. "Madame St. Elme, General Moreau awaits your presence. If you will follow me?"

"Of course," I said.

I followed him down the hall to the door on the other side of the dressing room from mine. It gave into a large room at the front of the house. The nearer part was arranged as a sitting room, while dark-red curtains framed the alcove containing the bed. There was a fire in the hearth and a table drawn up with covered dishes, a large armchair and a backless divan beside it. The floor was covered in a rich red Arabian rug. A bucket of ice held a bottle of champagne.

Moreau came forward to greet me as though we had just met after a long absence. "My dear Madame St. Elme! I am so pleased that you will share my little supper."

The valet withdrew and shut the door.

"Won't you sit and take some wine?" he asked, solicitously helping me to the divan.

"Thank you," I said. I watched him open the champagne deftly and pour some for each of us.

He raised his glass. "To an interesting acquaintance, Madame."

I touched my glass to his.

He looked at me over the table and frowned. "This will not do," he said.

"What?"

"Your attire."

I looked down at my dress. "I'm afraid it's terribly wrinkled. But most of my clothes have not yet arrived."

"It's not a dress for a courtesan," he said, getting up. "Not at all. That is the dress of a young and faithful wife. Which you are not."

I flushed. "Victor . . ."

"Ah, now you call me by my name!" He smiled. "But you are not going to distract me. All my desires, as you recall?"

I nodded mutely.

"Then you will wear what I tell you." He reached down and unhooked only the top hook on my dress, giving it just enough looseness in the bodice. Then he pulled the front straight down beneath my breasts, dress and chemise under it, down to the top

91

of my corset.

I gasped.

He lifted each breast, stretching and pulling it over the top of the corset and crumpled dress, so they stood out pale and white. "Perfect," he said. "Now stand up."

I hesitated.

"Stand up."

I did, feeling my pulse beginning too fast again.

He lifted my skirts, folding them about my waist with my petticoats. Of course I wore nothing beneath my chemise. One hand brushed against my bare hip, but he did not even look. "Sit down," he said.

I sat down on the chaise. The satin was slick beneath my bare bottom. He tucked my dress behind me, leaving me covered only in a narrow strip from chest to hips.

"Now we will eat." He lifted the lid on one of the dishes. "Chicken, Madame?" He resumed his seat.

To sit and eat like that, exposed and half-naked, was humiliating. To be expected to carry on normal conversation was surreal. We talked about books, and about plays that I had read, eating creamy chicken and fresh asparagus in a béarnaise sauce, drinking cold, crisp wine. And all the while, his eyes would go to my breasts, displayed there like sweets in a shop. I had never been so conscious of my body. I had never felt my private parts so keenly as when they rubbed against the upholstery each time I moved. The firelight encircled us, and the warmth from the hearth spread through me.

"Do you like champagne, Madame? I should not have to ask you twice." His sharp tone reminded me that I had fallen into a reverie.

"Yes," I said.

"How much do you like it?"

I shrugged. "Quite a lot."

Victor lifted his glass. "I believe your attention is wandering, my dear. Allow me to recall it to the present." He came around the table and leaned over me. His lips touched my bare shoulder. "Charming, I confess."

I put my glass back on the table with a clatter.

"On your back, Madame," he said.

I hesitated, and he turned me around longways on the divan and pushed me down so that my back was against the arm, my dress up around my waist. "Spread your legs."

I bit my lip and did.

He pressed my knees wider open, all of my most private parts completely exposed.

Looking full in my face, he opened my lips with one hand, smiling at what he felt. "You are soaking wet, my dear. Exposing yourself must agree with you."

I moaned as he fingered my pearl, slid his fingers back and forth provocatively.

"You see," he said, "I do not even need to tie you. I do not need to apply any threat of any kind. Your carnal nature keeps you chained more securely than steel. Nothing whatsoever prevents you from leaving this room. Except that then this would stop." He drew his finger over my pearl again, and I tried not to cry out.

"Is this what you do?" he asked. "Alone in your room at night? When your idiot husband has gone to bed? Is this how you touch yourself?"

I closed my eyes and did not answer.

Victor laughed, a soft, dangerous sound. "You are simply begging to be corrupted. It's very easy. Tell me that you like it."

"Yes," I said, though my breath caught in my throat.

He laughed again, and then I felt his lips brush my breast. I strained upward after them.

I opened my eyes to see him looking down at me. His eyes were dark with passion, but he was still in control. "Not so quickly. Tell me what you want. Don't just thrust your nipples at me."

I felt myself turning red. "No."

"No?" He played with the soft tissues between my legs lazily, separating and stroking each part. "I won't do it unless you tell me."

"I want . . . you to kiss me . . . there. . . ." I said.

"Where?"

"My breast," I gasped.

He smiled. "Very good." He leaned down and took my nipple in his mouth, teasing at it with his tongue, drawing it almost painfully.

I moaned and my back arched involuntarily, my pearl against his hand.

I felt him laugh against my breast. And I felt his hardness against my leg. I was scoring points too. Sooner or later he must take what he wanted. Could I make him? Could I make him lose this infuriating control?

One finger penetrated me, and I almost forgot the thought. My hand clawed at his cravat, at his throat, but he stopped me, taking my wrist with his other hand and shifting his weight to kneel between my knees.

"Not so fast," Victor said. "You will do what I want. And what I want is to hear you beg for release."

I gasped. "I can't. I'll never . . ."

"Never is a very long time. Do you really think you won't if I keep this up? Do you really think that in an hour or however long it takes, you won't come begging like a whore, getting off in full view of me?"

His words were a spur, and I ground against him. I didn't care. I didn't care about anything.

"You're going to come for me, my dear. And you're going to ask for it."

I moaned.

He moved his fingers away. "Ask me for it."

"Victor . . ."

"Ask me for it."

I pumped my hips, trying to get his hand back where it had been. "Please."

"Ask me to let you come." His hand on my wrist was steel.

"Let me come," I whispered. "Victor, please!"

He thrust his hand down, rubbing where I wanted it most. "Say, 'I am a whore. I am a whore and I want you to make me come.' "

"I am a whore and I want you to make me come." The pressure was almost unbearable. I felt suspended, timeless. I was nothing but a knot of craving.

"I am not going to stop until you do," he

said calmly. "You need not worry that you will be unsatisfied. I am going to watch you squirm and writhe with my fingers inside you until you finish."

I screamed and came against his hand. Lights flashed and my head swam, my entire being locked in a convulsion that seemed to come from somewhere deep within. I lay back against the arm of the divan. I could hardly see.

And then he thrust into me, into tissues already overstimulated. My back arched and I almost fell, falling, falling out of the world, sealed together, my body moving against him.

He came hard and lay across me, discipline pushed to the limit. His soft dark hair was against my face, his forehead covered in sweat, our bodies still joined.

I took one breath and then another. And then another.

He stirred, and for a moment his eyes were half-veiled.

"My God," I said.

He smiled, and it was the same mocking poise again. "I doubt if God has anything to do with it." He got up carefully. Despite his best efforts, his clothes were in some disarray.

I tried to sit up. My back hurt from the

uncomfortable position, and my body felt more than sensitive. I moaned involuntarily as my swollen nether lips touched the divan.

Victor looked at me and raised an eyebrow. "That was quite something."

"Yes," I said.

He leaned over me again, parting my legs and touching the tender skin that had just brushed the cloth. I leaned back against his arm.

"Again," he said, and his hand moved on me.

I awoke the next morning in the Blue Room. I stretched luxuriously on the heavy linen sheets. I was stiff and sore, but completely, utterly relaxed. I turned my head. Light came in under the curtains, enough to tell me it was full daylight. The fire was dead and the room was a little chilly, but not cold. Or perhaps it was just that I was naked.

There was a knock. I sat up, pulling the sheet and duvet up over my breasts. "Yes?"

A young chambermaid carrying a bucket of water bobbed a curtsy in the doorway. "Madame, the general thought that you might like a bath."

"Come in," I said. "I would like one very much." The prospect was absolutely delightful. Even more delightful was the idea that he had thought of it, that he had considered my comfort. I looked for my hairpins. I heard the splashing as she poured the water into the tub in the dressing room. "Is the general still here?"

She came out with the empty bucket. "No, Madame. He said that he has a great deal of work to do today. But he told us that we are to do anything you request, and he left a purse with Marcel if you wish to go to the shops today, since your clothes haven't arrived yet."

A nice sensibility, I thought, to leave the purse with the valet for shopping, rather than handing it to me as though it were my price. But I really did want some clothes, at least a clean chemise. My trunks might take three or four days yet. And besides, as he had said, many of my clothes were rather modest.

While the chambermaid finished filling the bath, I looked around the dressing room again. There was plain soap, but no scented soap or oils. For some reason, this pleased me enormously. If women stayed here, it was not often enough to leave their things. Or else Moreau had fastidiously removed them.

"Is there anything else you would like,

Madame?" she asked.

"In three-quarters of an hour, I would like coffee with cream, with bread and butter and jam," I said. "I will take it in here. Also, please brush and hang my dress."

She nodded. "Of course, Madame."

I settled into the warm water gratefully as she left. I did not love him. I wasn't sure if I even liked him. Yet twice this morning he had thought of my comfort and of my feelings. That was a truly novel experience.

He had certainly seemed attuned to my feelings last night, I thought, dreamily splashing myself with water, as though my excitement were the spur to his passion. In my admittedly limited previous experience, men scarcely required that. The mere sight of a breast or a thigh was enough to transport them. My active participation was hardly required. And yet Moreau had gone to vast pains to make me want him.

I didn't know if I liked him, but I certainly desired him. I could admit that to myself.

I had perhaps exaggerated his age to my cousin Maria. He was closer to thirty-five than forty, and if he was not extravagantly handsome, he was certainly good-looking. If he was not tall, he was certainly well made, with the lean body of a man who spent his days in great activity and was abstemious with both wine and food.

Discipline, I thought. *He is about discipline and mastery over himself. That is the key to Moreau. And so perhaps what he craves is its opposite humor, utter abandonment? Is that what completes him?*

I stretched back in the water. Perhaps I would not mind that at all under his cool tutelage.

A New Life

Thus I entered into a period of my life that I liked far better than I had expected. I lived in the house in utter respectability, directing the servants as though I were the lady of the house and doing as I wished. As soon as he learned that I was not a spendthrift, Moreau had no qualms about turning over the running of the household to me, and I was meticulous about keeping his books separate from mine, and his money separate from the money that he gave me. He inspected his own books regularly, and was as thorough and conscientious in that as in everything. My bookkeeping earned a nod of approval, as it never had from Jan.

"I see that you know something of finance, Madame," he said.

"It's common sense," I replied. "And good taste."

"You do have good taste," he said.

While my taste in gowns was somewhat

expensive, it was undeniably good, and if I wore things that previously I would have found too revealing for Madame Ringeling, they were not too revealing for Madame St. Elme.

I cultivated her as I had Charles, considering character and taste. Ida St. Elme did not wear pale pinks and yellows. She wore blue in every shade, from palest dawn to dark sapphire that brought out the color of her eyes. Her new evening gown was of dark blue-purple satin that plunged deeply in the front, with a high-boned corset that made the most of those attributes Moreau appreciated. Her riding clothes were almost navy, a man's coat and buff trousers with a little tricorne with a rakish plume. And her nightclothes . . . Madame St. Elme did not usually wear nightclothes, with the exception of a wrapper of blue and white toile.

There was one very delicate chemise, of the thinnest, lightest lawn with fine lace, the sort of chemise that brides wore. I wore it ripped and torn, one long rent up the side and the lace dangling at the throat, little pink ribbons shredded and trailing. It was the very picture of innocence outraged. When he saw it, Moreau swallowed hard, and a look came over his face that I had waited for.

I wore it pleading at his feet, lavishing him with tears that were half real, begging and sobbing in two languages. And of course he did not fail me.

Afterward, for once we lay quiet together. The candles had burned out. His breathing was even and he had forgotten to send me back to my room. I closed my eyes and was almost asleep when I felt his arm around me.

"My dear," he said quietly. "That was too real."

I licked my swollen lips. "It was," I said. "Too close." There was a long silence. "I was that sort of bride once."

His hand stroked my hair softly and methodically. "So I had guessed. How old were you?"

"Twelve," I said. It was very quiet in the room. Outside, the town and camp were quiet. Far off, a dog barked. "I had a large dowry. Jan talked me into eloping with him, into running away to an inn over the border." Victor's hands were not still, moving softly against my hair. "You can guess what happened then. After that, I had to marry him, even though I no longer wanted to."

"And so you had that costume made up? Not to please me."

"No," I said. I thought about it. For some

reason, thinking was easier around him. If my passion was a spark to his, his thoughts were a spark to mine. "To change the past. To make it as it should have been. If I had married someone . . . different."

His arm tightened around me for a moment, but his voice was still light. "Marriage is a failed institution, my dear. People should stay together only as long as they wish, for whatever reasons they wish."

"That isn't practical," I said, "if women have no place to go, and no way to make their way in the world without men. There is no way not to belong to men."

"You don't belong to me," he said.

"Don't I?"

Victor spread his hand on my naked hip. The rags of the chemise were bunched around my waist. "Do you? You could leave at any time. There are no walls or locks to stop you. You have ample funds and the ability to travel. There is nothing that prevents you from simply walking away. Except, of course, for your desire. There are no chains that are stronger than desire."

"Even desire wanes," I said.

"So it does." His hand slid down my leg and around, into the warm cleft of my buttocks. "And whether yours or mine will cool first, I don't know." He lifted one of the shredded ribbons. "But you will not be the worse for having known me."

He sat up and lifted the torn chemise over my head and pitched it on the floor. "I don't think I care for that game particularly. That is enough of that."

We never played that again.

Three months might have been the limit of my patience with this life, but just short of that time, war intervened. After all, Moreau had more to do than sit in garrison and enjoy his mistress. He was reckoned one of the Republic's best generals, both decisive and brutally swift, and it was a reputation he richly deserved. Keeping the Austrian army on its toes was something at which he excelled.

And so we moved. I did not then understand what he was doing, the continual movement and feints through the summer months, designed to keep the Austrian commanders busy and guessing, without allowing them to draw him into a decisive battle. I thought Moreau's men were splendid. But he knew how outclassed they would be if the Austrians ever brought their numbers to bear. He knew how many more artillery pieces the Austrians had, and how little chance we had of taking any fortified place.

But as long as he had a substantial army in the field, capable of bringing off controlled engagements, there would be no general Austrian advance.

It was a very tricky chess game, and he was the person to play it. It was about nerve and discipline, knowing when to give ground and when to take it, knowing the measure of his officers and of the enemy. I simply enjoyed the freedom of the marches, of riding abroad in my man's clothes, sticking with the column and the baggage train. I liked staying somewhere different each week, the loud, impolite company of the army, the revels and cheap company in each town. I did not mind the rain or the mud.

Sleeping rough was of little consequence to me, or at least I thought it so. There was never a night when Moreau did not have a tent over his head or me to warm him. I rather preferred that, because in the camp he did not send me away when he was done. And if love was quicker and less elaborate than formerly, it was sharper too, seasoned with the scent of danger.

One night at the end of the summer, we had won a fairly substantial skirmish. Some hundred prisoners had been taken, and several hundred of the enemy slain, while our casualties numbered fewer than fifty. Moreau was in high spirits, and so were his men.

As was so often the case after a battle, he could not retire until the wee hours. There was too much to do, reports to be written and dispatched to Paris by courier, captured papers to be examined, supply to be considered. I sat alone in our sleeping tent for many hours. Outside, I could hear a great deal of revelry. I was wearing my riding costume, the buff breeches and blue coat that, in the right light, might look like our uniform. My hair was pulled back, and I wore stout boots.

I waited and I waited and I waited. I thought of simply going to bed, but the noise was too great. There were loud songs and laughter, shouts and swearing and stamping of feet. I should never sleep in this din. It occurred to me that I could go to his day tent, the large one that he used for his headquarters, and find him. Surely he must be nearly done with his paperwork by now. Passing his servant and the sentries at the door, I set out across the camp.

Men were spilling out of pitched tents, going from one gambling game to another, tankards in hand. There was the reek of hard spirits everywhere. In the light of various fires, I could see those who had imbibed too much lying in corners, or sometimes being robbed of their valuables by their fellow soldiers. Drunk men pissed against the sides of the officers' tents or wherever else they chose. I pulled my hat lower over my eyes and walked more quickly.

I was nearly to Moreau's tent when a scream rent the night behind me. I turned. Three men had grabbed a cantinière, a girl scarcely older than I, and were hauling her behind one of the tents. She was flailing and shrieking, trying to ward them off. One of them laughed and grabbed her bodice. I heard the ripping of cloth.

I ran into Moreau's tent, past the startled and bored guards who did not react in time to stop me. He looked up from his papers in astonishment.

I grabbed at his arm. "Victor, you must come. There is a girl being raped not a hundred meters from here."

"The scream I heard?"

"Yes," I said, pulling at him. "A cantinière. Come, Victor."

He looked at me and one eyebrow quirked. "What would you have me do, my dear? Go charging in like a white knight?"

I stared at him.

"If it is a cantinière, then she's used to it.

That's what they do, my dear."

"But . . ."

He took my hand off his arm and held it between his own. "My dear, I told you not to go about the camp at night by yourself, and I am sorry that you had a fright. But these things happen."

"They happen because —"

"They happen because men are men," he said harshly. "You have no idea what you are talking about. These men are volunteers, rabble from streets and farms from one end of France to the other. Some are criminals released when the Republic opened the Bourbon prisons, and others might as well be. They are what I have with which to defend the Republic. I am here to make them a fighting force that can hold, not to make them morally exemplary."

My confusion must have shown on my face.

He took my arm gently. "Now, my dear. Calmly." He looked over the paper-strewn table. "You are frightened. I suppose I can complete this paperwork tomorrow."

Moreau escorted me back to his tent. I did not look in the direction they had taken her. And I did not hear anything over the general uproar.

■ ■ ■ ■

At dawn, the camp was finally silent.

I lay quiet beside him, not sleeping. *I should put it from my mind,* I thought. *What could I have done? What could I be expected to do? These things happen, as I know all too well. What is one more rape, one more prisoner ill-treated, one more complaint from a local?*

Men will be men, and these things happen.

I turned, and Victor curled a little closer to my warm back, affectionate in sleep as he was not when awake.

And what should I expect? Some Paladin of Charlemagne? A white knight wading in with moral fury, an angel of righteousness at his shoulder? This was the age of reason, and he was no more than a man, a general with a nearly impossible task ahead of him, defending the Republic as best he could with the tools he had to hand.

Better to put the entire incident from my mind. I must grow callous if I was to travel with armies. I must grow a thicker skin. I closed my eyes on the tears behind them. This was all there was. I was a fool to imagine anything else.

■ ■ ■ ■

In the morning, I took breakfast with Moreau in his tent. The flaps were spread wide to catch the early breeze, for it was early September, and the days were hot.

He looked up from his coffee. "My dear, I have been thinking that this is not the place for you. It's too rough and too dangerous. I know you were upset last night. There's a reason why army camps are no place for a woman of sensibility." He laid aside his silver knife. "I should send you ahead to Paris. I may not go into winter quarters and be able to return to Paris for several months yet, but there is no reason that I should risk you by keeping you here."

I looked down at my plate, at my buttered bread untouched. "Victor, I do not want . . ." I couldn't continue.

"Do not want what?" he asked softly.

"To end it," I said.

"Because you have nowhere else to go?" The cynical note in his voice stung me and I looked up.

"I could go to Paris alone," I said hotly. "I have the money you have given me. I don't need you."

He stood up smoothly, stepping behind

112

me and gently gathering up my hair. I could not see his face. "I don't want to end it either. That is not what I am proposing." His hands were quiet and methodical, sweeping my hair up into my pins. "I am suggesting that you go ahead to Paris, to a property that I own there. I expect to return in November or December, so if I can trust you in Paris on your own for two or three months . . ."

I rose and turned to face him. "Do you mean it?"

"You know that I do."

I leaned in and kissed him gently on the cheek. He was freshly shaved, of course, and smelled of sandalwood and oranges. "I will miss you," I said. "So very much. You are the best thing that has ever happened to me."

He smiled against my brow. "I shall hope that you continue to believe that."

I left for Paris on a sunny morning in mid-September with quite a cavalcade. There were convalescents on their way to Paris to recover from their wounds, twenty or so transfers who were on their way to other units, and several couriers. I was entrusted to one of these, who was to see me safely to the home of Madame Duferne in the Rue

Saint-Dominique before he took his papers to various people. This lady was the widow of some friend of Moreau's, and acted as housekeeper at this property of his. I hoped she was not young and beautiful.

It was September, and the roads were busy. We had scarcely started when we had to halt to let a column of cavalry pass on their way to join Moreau's camp for the last campaign of the season.

At their head was a magnificent mount, a tall bay stallion with two white socks. His coat was almost blood-colored, and brushed to a high sheen. His rider was similarly red-haired. He wore tight white trousers that displayed his physique accordingly, and the corded muscles in his thighs were plainly visible. His poise was superb. He rode carelessly, yet straight as an equestrian statue, the reins held lightly while he looked about. His shoulders were broad in his tailored coat, which was open in the heat. His face could have been graven in bronze, I thought, for the one moment I saw it, alert and solid, the face of a Roman statue. And then he was past. I admired his posterior as it vanished into the dust of the marching column.

The courier at my side chuckled. "Like a well-turned-out fellow, do you, Madame?"

I had the shame to blush. "I do. I can look, can't I?"

He nodded good-naturedly. "Lots of people look at Colonel Ney."

"Ney?" I squeaked.

The courier nodded. "That's old Red Ney. He's a bastard and a martinet, but a good fellow all the same."

THE WHITE QUEEN

I arrived in Paris on my twentieth birthday, September 28, 1796, and went directly to the house Moreau owned. It was a small townhouse on a quiet and unfashionable street, the kind of house owned by lesser merchants and clerks, professors and junior deputies. Three stories, with no yard at all, it had three bedrooms on the second floor, with a nursery and two tiny servants' rooms on the third floor. The kitchen was in the cellar, and the first floor consisted of a drawing room, a dining room, and a tiny study on the back of the house. The furniture was Louis XVI, in good condition but far from stylish. I wondered how in the world this had come to be Moreau's house. Nothing about it reminded me of him at all.

Madame Duferne explained that the first evening. Not the young, beautiful woman I had feared, she was fifty and cheerful, with a white cap on her unruly dark curls. While the housemaid set dinner on the table, she explained.

"General Moreau has never lived here, Madame. He has a lovely new house in Passy. This is one of the houses he bought up for almost nothing during the Revolution, lock, stock, and barrel."

"Oh?" I said. The beef was well cooked but utterly bland, without a seasoning on it. The cook was obviously no great chef.

"At first, the general made offers to aristos and others who wanted to flee the country. He gave them cash for their homes and furniture, at a greatly reduced price, of course. After all, what good did property do them if they either had to flee and abandon it or go to the guillotine? So he bought a number of properties in nice parts of town for almost nothing. And then some houses, like this one, were seized by the Committee when their owners were executed for treason. The general made offers to the Committee that were accepted. After all, they wanted cash, not houses."

"I see," I said. The table I sat at, the china that held my dinner, had been chosen by some poor woman who had been guillotined. White china with a pattern of roses.

Perhaps the wedding gift of a couple now dead.

"After my husband, Antoine, was killed, I didn't really have anywhere to go. The general rents out houses all over town, but this one didn't bring much in because it's not very fashionable. So the general said I could stay here for absolutely nothing if I would keep house for him and host any of his friends who needed to stay here." She smiled at me across the table. "And I do a very good job, as you can see."

I nodded. "Everything is impeccable, Madame."

I took a drink of my wine. It was decent table wine, sweeter than I liked, but not bad. And I asked the question that I wanted the answer to badly. "Any women, Madame?"

She laughed. "Oh, you want to see if you have rivals! Not many. Once in a while he has had someone stay a day or so, but no one as beautiful as you, and not in some time. Married women, I suspect. Who cannot, of course, be seen at his house in Passy. When they come, I go out, and don't return for hours. But I imagine you have nothing to worry about. You are so very lovely, and he's sent you here from his camp. He must be madly in love with you."

"I doubt that," I said.

Upon retiring, I searched the master bedroom quite closely. The windows were small and hung with thick drapes, and the huge four-poster was very comfortable. The bureau contained several more pamphlets of a "political" nature, as well as a polished wooden box. I opened it and was not surprised to see a pair of soft leather cuffs with silver buckles, a bottle of oil, and an ivory phallus.

I closed the lid, then opened it again and examined it closely. This was more like what I had expected, much more so than this grim decorum. An unlikely love nest, and one where games of passion were hardly to be expected, in a respectable neighborhood where a respectable woman could go in perfect propriety.

No, I had no rivals.

I woke in the night wondering if they had guillotined the children, the ones whose nursery was upstairs with their toys still there, or if the children had been spared to beg in the streets and look up at lighted windows like the ones they had once had.

I closed my eyes and buried my head in my pillow.

The house was absolutely silent.

I had not prayed since I was a child myself, but I found myself whispering words that might have been from my childhood in Italy. "Holy Mary, Mother of God, watch over those children if they live. And if they do not, please take them to your peace."

It was fall in Paris, and the weather was lovely. Unfortunately, I knew no one and had no friends. I had nothing to do. In camp, at least there had always been bustle and excitement. I did not want to stay in the house all day, so each day I hired a carriage and did too much shopping. It was easy to spend time in the shops.

Fashion had changed dramatically in just a few years. All the heavy panniers of my girlhood were gone, exchanged for diaphanous cotton gowns so thin that the shape of the body showed through quite clearly. Some of them were lavishly pleated like those of ancient Egyptian goddesses, worn with little sandals of gilded leather and no stockings at all. To make their feet look beautiful, women had them scrubbed with pumice or sea salt, then rubbed in oil, and had their toenails polished and painted.

By the time Moreau returned to Paris, it was too late in the year to wear those sort of clothes abroad. December had already begun, and the weather had turned rainy and gray.

A message arrived late one night that he had just that moment returned to town, and that he would visit me the following evening. I spent all of the next day in a state of excitement. Would passion have survived a separation of two and a half months? He had been in the thick of war, while I had been reading books and shopping, engaged in perhaps the most useless days of my life.

And the loneliest. When I was brutally honest with myself, listening to what I was beginning to term my Inner Moreau, I could admit that. I had no companions, and Madame Duferne was incredibly boring. I had no responsibilities. I had no occupations, not even bookkeeping. There was, in short, absolutely nothing to do from sunup to sundown except read, shop, and tend my beauty. If this was the life of a grand courtesan, it was dull in the extreme.

So I awaited Moreau's arrival with the breathless anticipation of a harem girl, for whom her lord's summons might be the only event of note in half a year, a lofty fate that might be attained but rarely in a lifetime. For that reason, I chose for our intimate dinner a costume I had had made up, a pair of gauze pantaloons in the sheerest of blue shades, with a bolero jacket of dark-blue velvet embroidered with gold.

Beneath the bolero I wore nothing, and only a frog of gold braid held the bolero closed. I did not expect it to last the night.

Instead of greeting me as I had expected, with harsh words and a command or two, Moreau instead came in quietly, divesting himself of his soaking cloak and hat and putting them before the fire. His face seemed heavily lined in the firelight, and his clothes were black. I lit the candles on the table and went to him.

He did not force me to my knees. Instead, he cupped my chin in his hands and kissed me thoroughly, almost sweetly, sending warmth running throughout my body. I put my arms around him and drew him close. With him in boots and me barefoot, he had a little bit on me in height.

"My dear," he said quietly, his mouth against my ear and my golden hair, "you look lovely."

"And you look tired, Victor," I said. His collar was wet from the rain.

"Well, it was a tiring journey," he said. "But it is over now." One hand ran down my back to the bare skin between the bottom of the bolero and the waistband of the pantaloons. It simply lingered there. "My dear," he said, "I need some time. The transition is too abrupt."

I nodded. I wanted him, but I could wait. And there was something undeniably sweet about being pressed in his embrace like this, as though I were something he valued immeasurably. "Let us have dinner, then. The cook has gone home, but I have kept everything warm in chafing dishes."

The dinner was rather better than the first one I'd had in this house. I had done the sauce with capers myself, rather than leaving it to the cook. We talked about books I had been reading and about the weather, nothing that touched on war or trouble, and I watched him slowly unwind. I poured him a second glass of wine, and a third, and he did not object as he usually did. It was not enough to make him drunk, but it did bring some color and animation back to his face. Afterward I made coffee with water I had kept hot over the fire.

He watched me kneeling on the hearthstone to pour it out, and smiled when I brought the press to the table. "My dear," he said, "I doubt any man in France has ever been waited on so attentively by such a lovely houri."

I had something clever to say, but when I opened my mouth it was not what came out. "I have missed you," I said.

"Did you really? With all the amusements

of Paris at your disposal?"

I shrugged. "I haven't had any amusements. I know nobody, and I have nothing to do."

Moreau took the coffee from me and drank it neat and scalding hot. "We will have to remedy that. I will not be leaving until March. There is ample time to introduce you to congenial society."

"And what is congenial society?" I asked, sitting down and sipping at my own coffee. I put the cheese on the table, but he didn't touch it.

"Politics," he said. "Everything in Paris is about politics. And if you think war is a dangerous game, you have not seen Paris politics. Here, people lose their heads with alarming regularity. This is not your husband's silly games. This is life or death."

"So I had gathered," I said. And I did not mention the house, the constant reminders around me of the losers.

"The Directory is little more than a year old. This tenuous coalition holds together a selection of people who hate each other, but who have three enemies in common. First, none of them want another popular insurrection of the sansculottes, the Paris mob who gave us the Committee of Public Safety and the Terror. Second, none of them want the Austrians to win this war and conquer France. And third, none of them want the Bourbon kings restored. You cannot imagine what life was like then, if this degree of risk seems preferable."

"And what do you want?" I asked, putting my elbows on the table and cupping my coffee in both hands. "To be a Director? To be the Republic's premier general? To be a wealthy man?"

Moreau smiled at me delightedly, as though I had surpassed his expectations. "I already am a wealthy man, my dear. There are army contracts and many other avenues of opportunity."

"And the other two?"

"Why not?" He reached for the cheese knife. "There are no greater talents than mine among the Directors."

I said nothing, for I did not know the Directors or their talents, beyond what I read in the papers.

"And you should have seen some of the members of the Committee of Public Safety. Pigs, my dear."

"They say Barras is capable," I said.

"Paul Barras is all charm and no substance," Moreau said. "He hasn't an idea in his head that wasn't put there by public opinion. He couldn't manage his own household if he didn't have that little Creole that he bought from prison." I raised an eyebrow, and he continued, "It's said that he had a *tendre* for the Creole wife of an aristo. He let her husband go to the guillotine, and then went to her in prison and offered her a choice between his protection and the blade. So Joséphine de Beauharnais agreed, like a sensible woman. And she was a charming hostess. Eventually he grew tired of her and married her off."

"That's terrible," I said quietly.

Moreau shrugged. "If I were you, I should rather pity the women without the interest of a man like Barras. They're dead."

I pushed my chair back from the table. "Is it always like this?"

He got up and crossed the room to stand beside me, to put his arms about my waist, against the bare flesh my bolero did not cover. "My dear, the world is a cruel place. We can either be swallowed up by it or master it. And you are not the sort to be swallowed up. You are a tiger, not some convenient prey."

"And that is what you want," I said. "Some other predator to stalk the drawing rooms with you, glorying in your victories."

"Say, rather, sharing in our triumphs," he said. "I can take you to the very top of

Fortune's Wheel."

"Or together we can plunge into the depths," I said, remembering the card with a shiver.

"Are you the woman I think you are?" Victor asked, tilting my chin up to him. "Are you willing to gamble?"

"Yes," I said.

Three days later, I made my social debut on Victor Moreau's arm. The ball was given by none other than Barras himself, and I was hard-pressed to find something to wear. As many dresses as I had bought, most of them were not quite formal enough. At last I settled on a draped and pleated gown of thinnest muslin, with a chemise of the same beneath it and a corset of the very softest possible material that would not show through. I wore my new sandals, and my hair was pinned atop my head in a style I fancied aped a bust of Agrippina the Younger. My fingernails were likewise cinnabar, and my lips matched them perfectly. I had no appropriate jewelry, so I did without, letting my cleavage be its own ornament. For a wrap, I wore one of the long stoles fashionable that year. It was sapphire blue, and had cost more than many dresses I had had in my old life. I thought I looked quite nice.

So did Victor, when he picked me up in his carriage pulled by a pair of matched grays. I had to ask him if he was sure he wanted me to arrive rumpled, as I had no way of repairing my hair in the carriage if he caused it to fall.

Instead, he reached onto the seat beside him and handed me a velvet-covered box. "I thought you would wear this," he said.

I opened it. Inside was a broad gold collar enameled in red and blue, fitting close to the throat and fastening at the back.

"Victor!" I exclaimed.

He lifted it out of the box and fixed it about my neck. It was very heavy. The gold was not cheap at all.

"Is it a collar or an ornament?" I asked.

He smiled. "That is what everyone will be wondering tonight. Is she or isn't she? Is it fashion or something else? Everyone will be talking about you, my dear." His hand caressed my throat gently, just where the pulse jumped. "But you are not to provide relief to anyone without my permission. Is that understood?"

"I do," I said breathlessly. "May I dance?"

His hand slid down to my breast, caressing my nipple through the thin cloth. "You may dance. You may even press your lips to theirs. But anything further, anywhere else those lovely lips of yours might stray, is beyond the pale. Unless I tell you that you may."

"Or that I must," I said, digging my nails into his coat sleeve.

Victor laughed, low and soft in his throat. His hand caressed the other side. "Or that you must."

The carriage stopped with a jerk. Victor looked out the window with some annoyance and straightened his coat. "We are here," he said.

"General Victor Moreau and Madame St. Elme!" the footman announced. The ballroom was already growing crowded, and many people looked up when we entered. We did make a handsome pair.

Victor wore dark-blue trousers and coat, his lapels thick with gold braid, and a glorious tricolor sash weighted with bullion fringe about his waist. His dark hair shone and his compact form was set off to the best by my white gown, sapphire blue shawl, and golden hair. Beside him, the necklace might have been a beautiful ornament to complement his braid, or it might not have been.

Victor smiled a remarkably genuine smile as a lady approached. She was petite, barely coming to my chin, with a tight-lipped smile and a beautiful figure. Her gown was white, and I saw with some surprise that she was not wearing a chemise under it at all. The shadow of her pubic hair was quite visible.

"My dear lady," Victor said, bending over her hand. "You cannot imagine the pleasure that I take in seeing you again. I had not expected that you would still be playing hostess for Paul."

She smiled, and it was an expression of real warmth. "My dear Moreau, it's a pleasure to have you back in town, rather than rusticating at the front. And of course I am always happy to assist Paul in any way I can. I fear that my husband has already had to return to the field, but he insisted that I should stay in Paris for my safety."

"Well, we must please your husband," Victor said. "And may I present my special friend, a lady recently come to Paris from Holland, Madame St. Elme? My dear, this is Madame Bonaparte."

"Do call me Joséphine," she said, taking my hand. "And tell me if it is true that you are a refugee from some terrible fate! We were all agog when we heard that Victor had been hiding you in Paris for several months and no one had seen you."

"I have not been hiding," I stammered.

130

Half the room seemed to be looking at me. "I have simple tastes and have been living very quietly."

"Ah!" She squeezed my hand and let it go. "I have simple tastes myself, but you would not know it to see this house tonight! Come, let me introduce you to some friends."

I looked at Victor, but he had turned away to talk to two gentlemen in uniform. "I would be honored," I said.

I had no idea who all the people were that I met. It seemed to me that there was an endless series of officers in tricolor sashes and ladies wearing white dresses. All of them said almost identical things. Somehow a glass of champagne appeared in my hand. It was cool and the ballroom was so very warm. I drank it very quickly.

Madame Bonaparte gestured for a footman. She drank her glass with her head down.

"Your husband is with the Army of Italy?" I asked. I wagered he wasn't on the Rhine or I would have heard Moreau speak of him often.

"Yes," she said. "He has command there now. I do not think the Directors want him in Paris." She looked up at me and her eyes were unexpectedly candid. "Successful generals too close to home make them nervous."

"Ah," I said. "Should I take that as a warning?"

"You should," she said. "If you are new to Paris, then you have no idea —" She broke off as a lovely blonde approached us. "Hello, Thérèse! That gown is absolutely beautiful! Where in the world did you get it?"

Her blond hair was rolled on top of her head in a very strange design, and her gown was of thin lavender gauze, clasped with pins in the shape of dragonflies on her shoulders, leaving her shoulders and arms entirely bare. It swept to the floor in glistening folds, and it was perfectly clear that she wore absolutely nothing beneath it. The shifts of shiny material across her uncorseted breasts were fascinating to see.

"Do you like it? I thought I should be the perfect Messalina tonight!" She looked at my hair critically. "And I see you've found us an Agrippina. Unless I mistake the hair."

"Yes," I said.

"I suppose that makes me your rival," she said. "Beware. I like to win."

"Thérèse, for heaven's sake," Joséphine said. "You haven't the slightest interest in Victor Moreau."

"Oh." She put her head to one side. Her

lips were bright red, and her eyes were cool and calculating. "No, I haven't really. I understand he likes whips and chains."

"Bah," said Joséphine. "And where you heard that, I can't imagine."

Thérèse's eyes lingered on my collar. Then she raised her eyes to mine, a little smile playing around her lips. I felt myself blushing. "You can be so naïve, Joséphine. You think every man plays one note, like that little Corsican of yours. We should ask our new friend if what they whisper about Moreau is true. Do you have a first name?"

"Ida," I said. "And please be free with it. But I would not dream of discussing Victor in that way. He is the kindest and most gallant of protectors."

"Of course he is," Joséphine said firmly. "I must go help Paul greet the foreigners before the music starts. Behave yourself, Thérèse."

"I always do," she said.

The music began, but she did not move, only stood at my side. Couples were taking to the floor in the most scandalous dance I had ever seen, dancing nearly in an embrace, with his left arm about her waist.

"The waltz," Thérèse said. "I don't dance." Her beauty was almost too polished. There was something about her that reminded me of Victor. Something of her reserve, something in the way she looked at me knowingly.

"Oh," I said. I looked about for Victor, but he was already on his way to claim me.

Moments later, he led me onto the floor. I did not know the dance, but he led well. He leaned close to my ear and whispered, "I see Thérèse wasted no time."

"What do you mean?" I asked. I was trying not to trip. This dance involved a lot of being propelled backward.

He laughed softly. "You must let her seduce you. But not too quickly. That will take all the fun out of it for her. And it will please her to think she has won something from me."

I felt myself flushing to the roots of my hair. "She is . . . like you?" I asked.

"In some ways," he said. "And in others, not at all. She plays for vanity."

And you play for power, I thought. *Power, and perhaps solace.*

WINTER IN PARIS

I was certainly not bored over the winter. While Victor did not spend every night with me, several times a week we went out somewhere and ended the evening at the house in Rue de Saint-Dominique. Sometimes it was parties and balls. All of the Directors and the leaders of government seemed to feel it was necessary to hold constant entertainments to make up for the austerities of the last few years, so the year's end was filled with a round of one after the other.

We also went to the theater. I had never been before, and I was utterly entranced. I ignored the intrigues among the spectators and the running from one box to another to sit speechless, my fan clasped between my hands, watching the action on the stage. Victor thought this very amusing.

One evening, after we had returned from an evening of Racine, I was trying to remember all the lines I had heard, to capture them. I had a quick memory, and some of the better parts did stick with me. I turned to Moreau as he came in removing his cravat and pointed my fan at him coquettishly.

" 'He had your way of standing, your body, your face. That same noble blush colored his face when to our Crete he traversed the seas to find the daughters of Minos.' " I said the last words walking around him, as though considering the effect of my words on a young Hippolyte.

Victor caught my wrists as I came around. "You would make a lovely Phèdre, my dear. But you do know she copulated with animals, don't you?"

"I think that's Pasiphaë," I said.

He pulled me rather roughly against him, and I gasped. His cravat twisted around my hands, and he dragged them over my head — which had the effect of raising my breasts almost out of the top of my gown. Victor laughed. The color was rising in my face. "You know, it takes almost nothing to arouse you, my dear. Just a few heated words and a bit of humiliation." He lifted my skirts and pulled my dress and chemise over my head in one piece.

I struggled a little with the folds for form's sake.

Victor shook his head. "I don't think so. I don't think I'm going to give you the satisfaction of making you do anything."

I stood there trembling and naked, waiting.

He smiled. "Lie down on the bed and pleasure yourself."

My eyes widened and I didn't move.

"Did you hear me?" he said softly. "I told you to lie down right there and spread your legs. I shall arrange you like a statue."

I lay down. My heart was beating like a drum. Carefully, lightly, he fluffed my hair over my shoulders. "That's better. Now open your legs."

He caressed the inside of my thigh. "That makes a prettier line."

Of course everything was completely exposed, and he made a show of stroking my lips softly. "Now put your hand there. Just as if you were alone."

I did. The jolts of pleasure that went through me were extreme.

"Move your hand just so. I want to watch you." His face was rapt and I could see the passion rising in him, under the leash of control.

I moved my hand, succumbing to the

growing warmth.

"Like that," he said. "Lovely. I think I will have you sculpted like that. As Aphrodite, perhaps. But everyone who sees it will know it's you. Do you want the entire world to see your charms?"

"You wouldn't," I said.

"Are you sure of that?"

His voice was as much the spur as my fingers. I closed my eyes, losing track of everything else. I heard some small movements, but paid them no heed.

"You are lovely that way, my dear. I believe you'd do nearly anything."

"Yes," I whispered. To touch myself this way, to come naked on the bed while clothed he stood watching was . . .

And then there was a cool touch between my legs. The ivory phallus slid inside, oiled and hard. I shrieked and came between his hands and mine.

He laughed.

I sat up unsteadily. It shifted, pressing inside me. He was standing beside the bed. "Don't take it out," he said. "Leave it there."

I could see the strain on his face, and with something like a purr I opened the buttons on his trousers and took him in my mouth, kneeling on my haunches. The phallus inside me slid slick and wet with my movements. It was like being penetrated twice, once there and once in my mouth, where I took him completely.

In the end he had to hold on to the bedpost to keep from falling. He clasped at my hair and called out something I didn't quite understand. I did not let him fall.

Afterward we lay together lazily. Usually he would dress and leave before too late, but that night he showed no inclination to go, lounging next to me wearing his ruffled evening shirt and nothing else. Which was also unusual. Victor usually hated being en déshabillé, and he was never naked if he could help it.

"My dear," he said, "be entirely truthful with me. You hate this house."

"I do," I said. "It is too old and sad. And too far from where you live. It takes you too long to get home at night, and you will not stay with me because you must leave so early. And there is no other suitable room if you wanted to stay in your own bed."

"And you hate it," he said.

"And I hate it," I said. "If I were choosing a place, it would be closer to you and would be both simpler and more elegant. And more modern. Not larger. I don't need more space. Just better arrangement."

"Hmm," he said. "Well, perhaps I can look for something different for you."

I leaned back against his arm. "I will pay the rent out of the money you give me. I'm not asking for more money."

He shrugged. "Which is as well. You know I am no spendthrift. Though" — he brushed the damp hair back from my forehead — "I think it's time I gave an entertainment of my own."

"A ball?" I asked.

"Nothing as grand as that. Perhaps a smaller, more intimate evening with friends."

At the word *intimate,* the hairs on the back of my neck rose. "How intimate?"

Victor smiled down at me. "Are you imagining yourself the main dish, trussed and presented to the company? Nothing that intimate, my dear. Though I imagine you'd like it."

"I would not," I said, though I wondered if I would. It would depend on who was there. I could not help thinking of Thérèse Tallien and her secret smile.

"I was thinking," he said, "of dinner and cards. If you can get your mind out of the gutter, I would like you to plan it. At my house, for the week after next."

I wrenched my mind back out of the gutter with some difficulty. "To do that, I would have to see your house, Victor."

"So you would," he said. "Get dressed and we will go."

"To see your house in the middle of the night?"

He pulled his arm out from under me, dropping my head on the pillows. "Why not? I am going anyway."

"Victor, it's freezing, and I wasn't planning on going anywhere."

"You are a little hothouse flower, aren't you?" Victor said, smiling down at my naked form. "Get dressed. Surely with a warm cloak and boots, you can manage to get across town in a carriage without expiring."

I grumbled, but went to dress. I confess that I was curious. I had never seen his house, though I had been in Paris four months. And in the more than a month he'd been in town, he had never asked me there before.

In the end, I did not see any of it in the dark. A carriage ride through Paris in the moonlight is romantic, regardless of the temperature. Indeed, freezing weather only makes it expedient to huddle more closely together. And then I thought it might warm my hands to put them in his trousers.

So in the end we rushed in rather precipitously. He slammed the door shut in a room of which my only impression was dark and shoved me against the door, his lips on mine urgently while both of us attempted to get winter clothes off without breaking apart.

There was a bed. I ascertained that when I lay back on it at his order while he found the box of English letters in the nightstand. I put my hand over his and drew the sheepskin letter tight over him, bending my head to kiss the indentation at the join of groin and thigh.

Afterward, I heard him removing it and dropping it into the chamber pot beneath the bed.

"I'm glad you remembered," I said sleepily. "It is the wrong time to be without."

"I remembered," he said. "For all that you test my sanity. I want no bastards, my dear."

"Of course not," I said, and settled more closely against him. Surely he would not send me away tonight. It was nearly dawn, and the servants would remark on it if he ordered a guest room made up in the middle of the night. It would not suit his sense of the respectable.

If one could call breakfast at nearly noon respectable, this was. Dressed in an impeccable quilted sapphire-blue wrapper, I breakfasted with him in a small dining room looking out over a formal garden. The walls of the room were white trimmed with gold, and all was modern and airy. Only the lavishly plastered ceiling looped with Louis XV ornament showed the house's age. The carpets were cream-colored and perfectly clean. The furniture was all in the best possible taste.

His own room, where I had spent the previous night, was a model of a gentleman's room, with dark wooden furniture and subdued colors. The bed was not a four-poster, but the elaborate carving of the headboard offered plenty of places to attach ropes, if any were required. Perhaps they weren't, here. Victor was more circumspect than that.

There were no other women here, and probably had never been. There was only one woman's garment in the wardrobe, the quilted wrapper I wore, and it was exactly my size and sapphire blue.

At breakfast, Victor's hair was still a little damp from the bath, and he was shaved and neat, wearing buff trousers and a cream shirt with a buff brocade waistcoat. For him, this constituted great unbending in dress. He helped himself to everything at the table and ate with none of his usual restraint.

I watched him butter a third piece of toast. "Are you quite well, Victor?"

"Absolutely, my dear," he said. "Now, hurry and eat. We have things to do."

"What are we going to do?" I asked.

"I thought you wanted to look at houses," he said. "There is a charming place to rent quite close by."

I shrugged. "That suits me very well."

And indeed it did. It lacked a few days till Candlemas, but the day was sunny and bright, though still cold.

The house Victor wanted me to see was lovely. It was only a few blocks from his own, a beautiful house of weathered red brick, not very large but with a big English garden that swept down to a small stream. I wandered the garden happily, imagining the vistas that would be revealed when the trees greened and the flowers bloomed, pointing out the buds of things to Victor, who seemed bemused.

"Those are tulips there," I said. "I think they are pink or red. I wonder which?"

"How can you possibly tell?" Victor asked, looking down at the pointed leaf spikes that rose two or three inches above the earth in a bare bed.

"The color," I said. "See how dark they are compared to those buds of snowdrop

144

there? The dark pinks and reds show like that. Whites and yellows are pale green. And it is hard to tell with the very pale pinks."

"I had no idea you knew anything about gardening."

I shrugged and took his arm again. "I do have some interests that are not sexual, Victor."

Moreau looked out over the sleeping garden. "I forget that, my dear. And I should not. You are so sensual that it's easy to become entirely beguiled by your face and body."

"You do," I said. "Beguiled, is it?" There was a teasing note in my voice. "Beguile the master himself?"

He raised one eyebrow, but did not smile. "Men are fools, my dear, fools for a pretty face and lovely arms. And when beauty comes with raw, submissive sensuality that would make Ovid blush, it's a terrifying combination. I'd like to think that I am immune to those sorts of charms, but I am not."

I took his arm. "I hardly think I'm a threat to you. It would take an extraordinary woman to beguile you, and I hardly think that I, young and gauche as I am, could do so even if I tried. Which I haven't. I respect you too much to try to use you. After all, is not our friendship based on a certain degree of honesty?"

"Yes," he said, and there was something unreadable in his dark eyes. "How do you like the house?"

"It's beautiful," I said. "I wonder how much the landlord wants for it? It must be quite expensive."

Victor took my gloved hand and turned it up in his own. With his other hand, he dropped a set of keys into my palm. "I am the landlord, my dear. And it is yours."

"Mine?" My incredulous joy must have showed in my face. "This wonderful house?"

"Yours," he said with a smile, closing my fingers over the keys. "Yours to decorate as you wish. I have no doubt you will have many hours of pleasure arranging things in your own nest."

I threw my arms around him and hugged him with delight, quite forgetting his reserve and dignity. "Victor, it's amazing! You have made me so happy!"

"I'm glad that I have," he said, returning my embrace. "You make me very happy too."

I seized his hand and led him under a spreading bare tree. "See? In the summer I can put a table here and hang lanterns from the tree, and we could dine under the stars.

It would be peaceful and beautiful beyond imagining."

"In the summer, I will be in the field, my dear," he said quietly.

During the long months when I'd awaited Victor in the fall, I had written to my mother. It was nothing really, just a quick note posted from Paris, saying that I lived and that I was well. There was no reply, but I had not expected one. I had not given her an address.

Now, settling into my own beautiful house in Passy, I wrote to my cousin Louisa. I knew Louisa's discretion. I had relied on it for years when my mother was ill. I told her that I was in Paris, living with a generous and powerful protector, and that I had no intention of ever returning to Holland or to Jan.

Her response reached me on the day of Moreau's fête. I knew better than to open it but I did anyway.

I expected remonstrances and anger, but instead she told me that my sons were well, and that Francis was safely recovered from a bout of coughing that had kept him ill through Christmas. *Christmas,* I thought. *In places where there is not the Temple of Reason, where the church still exists, there is*

Christmas. We had had none. There'd been balls and pageants galore, theater productions and revels, but no Christmas. Suddenly I longed for snow and happy children, for midnight choirs and all the trimmings I had lacked.

Have always lacked, I said to myself sternly. *It is not as though when you were a child in Italy, anyone took you to church. Or that Carnivale with its masks and licentiousness was not more to your parents' taste than miracles and choirs. And you never saw a drift of snow until you were nine years old and crossed Grand-Saint-Bernard.*

Jan says he will never divorce you. He and his family are adamant on that. He says that you will come crawling home when your money runs out. And that when you do, he will have you confined in the country for the rest of your life, with a strict nurse and a bottle of laudanum for company. He says you are mad. He has filed papers with the government of France to have you extradited to Holland.

That was no more or less than I had expected. But it was the next line that made tears start in my eyes.

He has told the children that you are dead.

AMONG THE MARVELOUS

Moreau's fête was the last week in February. I was a nervous wreck. While of course I had played hostess for Jan for years, I had never planned any sort of social occasion in Paris, and I was keenly aware of how my efforts would reflect on Victor. The wine, the food, the musicians, everything necessary for a simple party took weeks to prepare. In the end, I was beside myself over the flowers. The ones I had wanted were not available, and instead I had gray classical urns, meant to hold flowers outdoors on a terrace, filled with cherry branches forced to bloom early. The effect was both rustic and lovely, and the spare shapes seemed almost opulent in Victor's understated rooms.

The fête went well enough. As I had expected, I did not enjoy myself much. It is far easier to be the guest than the hostess.

I did, however, at last meet Barras. He was of medium height, with brown hair and a handsome face of the sort that every young lawyer aspires to, open and inventive without any trace of cynicism or interest. He took my hand politely and bent over it, saying every conventional thing, making compliment to my clothing and décor. And five minutes later I found it completely impossible to remember a word he had said.

"You are right, Victor," I said when I passed close to him later, "Barras is a cipher."

Victor leaned forward against my arm. "He says everything that everyone wants to hear, and yet says nothing."

I nodded. "But his lady . . ."

Madame Bonaparte had arrived with Barras as usual. She might be married to another, but it seemed in the capital that nothing whatsoever had changed. Whether or not it had changed in the bedchamber was anyone's guess. Personally, I couldn't imagine Barras bothering. But clearly he had loved her once, or at least lusted after her.

She came and joined me greeting arrivals near the door. "Anything interesting?" she asked.

I shook my head and extended my hand to a random officer who had turned up. "Yes, I too am enchanted. No, Joséphine, not a thing."

She waited until the officer had turned away. Her perceptive brown eyes lingered on me. "Something is wrong," she said. "I see it in your eyes."

"It is just a letter I received earlier," I said. "Nothing of consequence." I feared that my voice betrayed me.

It did. She put her hand on my arm. "Do you want to go somewhere quiet and tell me of it?"

I shook my head. "I cannot leave the door. I should have known better than to open the letter before the party."

"My husband sends me upsetting letters often," she said, smiling and nodding to a gentleman who had just come in. "I can't read them when I am to appear anywhere either."

"Does he scold you?" I asked.

"No," she said, her head turning slightly away as she followed the progress of a group with her eyes. "He tells me all of his unrequited passion."

"I think I would prefer those letters," I said.

Thérèse Tallien was coming up the steps on the arm of the banker reputed to be her current lover. Her gown was pure white and her stole was ermine, and a fortune in diamonds dazzled around her neck.

Joséphine leaned forward. "Good Lord, Thérèse! Where in the world did they come from?"

Thérèse gestured to the silent banker, who wore a small smirk. "From my dear friend. They once belonged to Diane de Poitiers, you know."

"Really?"

"Not crown jewels, then," I said rudely.

Thérèse looked at me, and her eyes were like diamonds themselves. "I should never aspire to a crown. It's too easy to lose one's head." She spread her fan carelessly. "Unlike Joséphine, who had some Creole fortune-teller inform her that she was going to be a queen."

Joséphine blushed. "Thérèse, I should never have told you that silly twaddle. You know those things are games and parlor tricks."

"Not always," I said. "I have a deck of cards and they seem to work for me."

Thérèse smiled. "Well, I shall have to get you to tell my fortune someday. And tell me if there is love in it."

"There must be both love and generosity," Joséphine said, graciously gesturing to the banker. "After all, you are the luckiest of women to have found such a friend."

"Indeed," Thérèse said, taking his arm and sweeping into the room.

Joséphine shrugged.

"I thought she was your dear friend," I said.

"She is. But she must always conquer all. It's her way." Joséphine gestured to the footman to close the door. "It's getting cold, and most of the guests are here."

That night after the fête, I spread the cards on the table upstairs in the guest room I used. I put them in three piles, as Louisa had taught me.

Who. Joséphine. The Queen of Chalices sat in her garden surrounded by roses, a woman of sensibility and kindness. Clear enough.

How. The Six of Staves, six rods crossed on a white background. Conflict, war, swift changes.

Why. The Chariot.

I mussed the cards and scattered them as I heard the door open. Victor would laugh at me. "I'm coming, dearest," I said.

There was a low, throaty laugh that was nothing like Victor's. Thérèse stood in the doorway regarding me. "How nice of you to greet me that way!"

I stood up, folding the cards back together.

"So you are playing with your little cards?" Thérèse walked toward me, her fan swinging on its strings. "Do they tell you what waits for you?"

I didn't answer. She lifted the fan. The sticks were heavy ivory. For all her manner, she was several inches shorter than I was. For a moment I thought she was going to strike me across the face with it, but she hesitated. "Victor will object if I mark you," she said.

"So would I," I said. "Moreau has never struck me, and that does not appeal to me in the slightest."

Her eyes narrowed. "How do you know it doesn't if you haven't tried it? Victor may be very good, but I am better."

I took a step back. "I do not plan to be in a position to know," I said.

Instead of being insulted, she smiled. "I see that Victor has taught you saucy protest. Are you entirely his creature?"

"I am his friend," I said. "I do not belong to him."

"Don't you?" Thérèse spread her hands. "You live in his house, wear the clothes he buys, eat his food. You are as much a pet as my little dog. Only prettier and more expensive."

I put my head to the side and looked at

her. "And this is supposed to make me like you? I'm unclear on how insulting me is supposed to make me want to sleep with you."

She laughed, a clear, silvery laugh. "Oh dear! Victor does have more than he bargained for in you, doesn't he? Clearly I'm trying the wrong tack. Does he woo you with sweet words and presents? I imagine he's good at that, hypocrite that he is."

"He is kind to me and treats me with respect," I said. "Whether or not that is hypocrisy, I don't know."

She opened her fan. "Of course it is, my dear. You don't have anything he wants. Victor is a master at flattery and idle banter, among other things. Don't tell me that you take his lavish compliments seriously?"

"I don't," I said, but it hurt. No one had ever told me I was lovely before, nor treated me as though my every wish were important to him.

"He is a man. And underneath it all, they are the same. They're pricks." She raised her fan to her lips, pursed provocatively. "And they all want the same thing. Think about it," she said, and left the room.

I had sat down and was shuffling the cards over and over when Victor came in a few minutes later. "That's the last of them," he said. "Thérèse practically had to be carried out to her carriage. I thought she was planning to stay all night."

"She was," I said, "with me."

Victor came and put his hand on my shoulder. "So that's how it is."

I nodded.

"You seem very downcast for a woman who just had a great social triumph," he said. "Is something troubling you?"

"No," I said.

"Thérèse?"

It was a question I could answer. "She wanted to strike me. Does she do that? For pleasure, I mean?"

"And it does not appeal to you?" I felt him bend over me, his warmth against my back through the thin silk of my dress.

I shook my head.

"Nor to me," he said. "Different tastes. There are women who like that kind of mastery. It's never particularly appealed to me. People who have to enforce their will with whips usually can't control themselves. I have no respect for that kind of weakness."

"And yet you like me to lose control," I said slowly. "To be entirely without pretense or thought."

"That's different," he said. His hand was warm on my shoulder.

"Because I am a woman?" I asked.

"My dear, there is nothing weak about you," he said. "Nothing whatsoever. I am quite aware that a man who tames a tiger has only himself to blame if it bites his hand off."

I turned my head so that my cheek rested against his hand. "Victor, I don't want to hurt you. And I can't imagine that I could. So I don't understand what she wants."

"Who knows? To score off me? To get you into her bedchamber? She is the original Marquise de Merteuil."

"And what am I?" I asked him, and was appalled to find myself almost crying. "Nothing, really. A woman with no future and no past. My husband has filed papers to have me extradited to Holland on the grounds that I am mad!"

"Is that all?" Victor drew me to my feet, his arm about my waist. "My dear, you have nothing to fear from that oaf. I promised you that you would be safe here, and I keep my word. This extradition will come to nothing, documents misplaced somewhere, a lady who cannot be found. After all, who has ever heard of Madame Ringeling?"

I let out a deep breath. I did not like to be afraid, but this frightened me to the core. "You promise?"

"I promise," Victor said gravely. "You have nothing to fear from these papers. I will take care of you."

Moreau left for the front two weeks later. The morning that he was to leave, we breakfasted together at my house, looking out over the garden. It had not quite begun to bloom.

"I wish I were coming with you," I said.

"My dear, it will be far too dangerous. We are not going into garrison, but on the offensive," he said. "And besides, I need you here in Paris."

I nodded. "I understand. And what am I to do about Thérèse? She will be all over me the moment you leave town."

He raised his coffee to his lips and did not look at me. "Sleep with her."

"What?"

"Sleep with her," he said. "If you want her to lose interest, that's the fastest way." Moreau took up his knife and spread his bread with butter. "The more you protest, the harder she will pursue. Simply sleep with her and disappoint her, and she will leave you alone. And you will be free to move in society and politics as you want, one more person on the long list of lovers she has had."

"Does that list include you?" I asked.

"Thérèse and I would not suit," he said.

"And you don't care if I sleep with her?" I was trying very hard to keep my voice light and sophisticated.

"She's a woman, my dear," Victor said, looking surprised. "It hardly counts."

"I see. So you object to another man —"

"I object strenuously," he said. "You are not to go flaunting your beauty to any other men while I am gone, or to have any other lover. I know I shall not hear the faintest word of reproach about your behavior when I return."

"And you will have no other women?" I raised an eyebrow. "That's curious."

"That is entirely different," Victor said. "You can hardly expect a man to go without for eight months."

"Ah, but I am to amuse myself with Thérèse, who is a woman and doesn't count!" I said heatedly. "That's a bit hypo-critical from you, Victor!"

He stood up and walked around the table to me, putting his hands on my shoulders. "My dear, hypothetical Sapphic interludes aside, must we quarrel at the moment of departure?"

"No," I said, and stood up. I would miss him bitterly, hypocrite or no. I would miss his dark eyes and his cynical smile and his hands everywhere. "No, let's not quarrel," I said, so we didn't.

I was right that Moreau had hardly left town before I had an invitation from Thérèse Tallien — not for some intimate tête-à-tête at her house, but to go riding three days later at seven in the morning, with a plan to break our fast at the Dairy at Mont Parnasse, a very rustic retreat.

Bearing in mind what Victor had said about refusing her only encouraging her, I sent word that I would be delighted to join her. I also made certain to look as dowdy as possible on the day, or at least entirely unlike the woman she had seen.

Toward that end, I got out Charles's clothes, entirely neglected since the end of last summer. Instead of a fashionable habit, I wore worn brown trousers, a man's shirt with a coat of dark-blue wool, and a brown hat with no plume at all. Heavy gloves and boots completed the ensemble, and my hair was drawn back in a severe old-fashioned queue.

My surprise was complete when I met her and found that she was dressed much the same.

No one could ever believe that her full-breasted figure was that of a young man, but she wore an old slouch hat over her glorious hair, and her thighs were encased in breeches of soft gray doeskin. Her linen was spotless and her coat was well cut, with soutaches of braid like a hussar's. She laughed when she saw me.

"Ida! I should have guessed that you would be dressed like a veritable Amazon!"

"And you," I said, failing to conceal my surprise.

Thérèse shrugged. "One cannot wear frippery all the time. It's a pleasure, and at the same time a dreadful burden. How free men must be, who can do as they wish!"

"I have often felt the same way," I said.

"Shall we ride, then?"

"Of course," I replied.

She was a surprisingly good rider. As she rode ahead of me at a well-mannered trot, I could not help but admire her fine seat and the way the gentleman's trousers molded closely to the rounded curves of her posterior. I had not seriously thought of it before.

My Inner Moreau objected, reminding me strenuously of the girls Charles had danced with at the spas, of the pleasure of seeing a young girl's rapturous eyes raised to me, of the sweet curve of breasts above the neckline of a gown.

Such things are not done, I thought.

Perhaps here they are, my Inner Moreau replied. *All of these lovely women so free with their affections . . . And it is hardly cheating if your lover told you to. After all, you must have something to console yourself all summer. Why not try it?*

It was in this welter of emotion that we climbed the hill. As we passed a bunch of poor hovels, a gaggle of ragged children ran out. Thérèse halted her horse and smiled down, leaning out of the saddle to give them alms, which they caught in their upturned hands.

Seeing my expression, she removed her hat and smiled ruefully. "The dear children," she said. "I often come this way, and I never forget to bring something for those who are less fortunate. I know that piety and charity are out of fashion, but we are not being women of fashion here, and I must be who I truly am."

"Your feelings do you credit," I said, with Charles's best gallant bow from the saddle.

She smiled and chirruped to her horse.

I rode behind. *Lady,* I thought, *I am not stupid, and I have read* Dangerous Liaisons *too.*

We breakfasted in the Dairy, a former barn

163

that was now an inn. The food was presented on rude trestle tables, and we sat on benches looking out at the perfect spring morning. The butter had been churned that same morning and was sweet as cream, and the bread was warm from the oven. A crock holding the first wildflowers sat on the table. It could not have been more different from my breakfasts with Victor.

Rather than being clever and biting, Thérèse was the model of kindness, telling sweet and complimentary stories about various mutual acquaintances, all calculated to show our friends as generous and wonderful people. Joséphine Bonaparte in particular was the recipient of her good humor.

"She is the kindest, dearest lady," Thérèse said. "And when I consider the crosses she has borne! Her inner strength makes me desire to emulate her in every way. Considering the tragedies in her life makes me regard myself as very fortunate."

"I understand she narrowly escaped the guillotine," I said, stirring cream into my coffee.

"She did," Thérèse said. "At the price of her self-respect."

I did not think it politic to say anything public against Barras, so I said nothing.

"But she saved her two dear children,"

Thérèse said. "And what mother could fail to act as she did?"

"I didn't know that she had children," I said.

"A boy and a girl. I suppose her son is eleven or twelve now, and her daughter is a few years younger." Thérèse dropped her voice and leaned closer over the table. "She saved three other children besides her own from the blade — the little Auguié girls, daughters of a friend of hers. She made Barras release them to her custody. They were eight, six, and four years old when they were thrown into prison to await execution."

I stirred my coffee hard, hoping that no emotion showed. I suspected that it did.

"They are the most darling children," Thérèse said. "She loves them as her own daughters. They are all at school now with Joséphine's girl, Hortense, at Madame Campan's. How that penniless young general pays for them all is a mystery to me!"

How indeed? I wondered.

Thérèse leaned close and whispered confidentially, "You know that all of her friends urged her not to marry him, even her lawyer. A young man with nothing to his name but a cloak and a sword! But Paul Barras wanted it, and what he wants, he gets."

"Why should he want his own mistress to marry a penniless young general?" I asked.

Thérèse smiled at me guilelessly. "To bind him more closely, of course. The Directory would already have fallen into ruins if not for Bonaparte and his artillery. He fired grapeshot into the Paris mob when they tried to storm the assembly."

"Oh," I said, trying not to imagine the consequences of that.

"You are tenderhearted," Thérèse said. When I looked up, her eyes were not calculating, but rather clear and penetrating. "Nothing good can come of that."

"So Victor says. We live in the modern world, and there is no use for tender hearts or human kindness. We are savages in beautiful clothes."

"And you would prefer the world of popes and kings?"

I shook my head. "No," I said. "I can't imagine a world I would like."

"Then it's as well you don't have the ordering of it. What do you really want? Power? Money? Pleasure?"

"I don't know," I said. Certainly all those things were pleasant. I liked having nice things. It was very satisfactory to have the power to order my own life somewhat. But I had no desire to rule, even through Victor.

I had no words for what I truly wanted.

Perhaps Thérèse would have said more, but the innkeeper came to the table to offer us a cut of his beautiful Bavarian ham. I accepted with alacrity, but she refused. "I do not eat meat," she said, "and haven't since my girlhood. I realize that refraining makes very little difference in the world, but I cannot bring myself to eat the flesh of animals who have been raised for slaughter."

"Truly?" I asked.

She nodded. "You may ask my friends if you doubt me. Meat never passes my lips."

I blinked at her.

Thérèse put her hand over mine on the table, a beautiful spontaneous gesture. "Perhaps you have misjudged me just a little, Ida? Allowed Victor's prejudices to cloud your own? He does not love me for certain reasons that are private between us, of which honor forbids me to speak."

"Perhaps I do," I said. "I beg your pardon." Perhaps I had misjudged her somewhat. Her hand under mine was very warm and smooth.

Dangerous Acquaintances

Moreau wrote to me regularly and punctually. Twice weekly he sent me two or three pages. Ever conscious of his dignity, there was nothing in his letters that would have aroused sensation if they were printed in the papers or intercepted by the enemy. They were affectionate, polite, and rather formal.

My dear,
I have taken command of the Army of the Rhine once more, and I have been pleased to see the splendid condition of our men. We are fit and ready to face the enemy at any time.

I trust that you are well. The spring months often lend themselves to chills and colds, and I hope that you have not succumbed to any of the myriad illnesses that seem to circulate at this time. I am sorry that I am not there to see your lovely garden in full bloom. I hope that your flowers will give you much pleasure. I cannot, myself, imagine how all the things you named look, or what their display may be, but it gives me vast pleasure to imagine your excitement and enjoyment of these spring blooms.

I have ordered additional bath linens for my house. Also, I am having new curtains done for the drawing room. I trust that you will oversee the installation of these domestic comforts in my absence. I am sure that your impeccable taste will assure that all these appointments are both appropriate and well crafted. I greatly appreciate your assistance in this matter.

You will no doubt be hearing my name in public circles very shortly, regarding a gentleman of our mutual acquaintance. I recall that you mentioned that you did not think much of him when you met in Holland. I fear that you were right in your assessment of his character, though I would not have believed him guilty of such perfidy had I not seen the evidence with my own eyes. Though in the past I considered him both a gentleman and a friend, I am now forced to revise my thinking. But you have heard of all this, no doubt, through the proper channels.

I shall pass what time is not spent in martial endeavors thinking of you.

Your servant,
Victor Moreau

What in the world? I racked my brains to think of every gentleman I had ever told Moreau that I didn't like. I didn't have long to wonder. The next day the papers blared the truth — General Moreau had captured correspondence between General Pichegru and the Austrians on the twenty-second of April. Moreau had quietly placed the go-betweens under arrest and sent the incriminating papers on to Paris. Pichegru had been arrested for treason.

It was true I had not liked Pichegru when I met him in Holland with Jan. But then, I had also not liked Moreau.

All of that seemed so far away now, so distant, as if it had happened to someone else. Sitting in my lovely garden, branches swaying in sweet breezes, I thought that it had. That had been Madame Ringeling, a mousy little creature who had no knowledge of the world and who yearned for nothing except her husband's affection. I was Madame St. Elme, consort of one of the most powerful men in France.

Of course, there were those who whispered

170

that Moreau had been in the conspiracy with Pichegru and had turned on him when it became clear that the émigrés who claimed they could broker a peace with Austria were lying. That Moreau had thrown Pichegru to the wolves before Pichegru could throw him.

I didn't believe it. Victor carried on many intrigues, and I would not have put betraying a confederate beyond him, but I did not think he would treat with the Austrians. He had no love for the émigrés and the old crown. And I did not think him capable of treason.

Thérèse, of course, believed the opposite.

We often rode together in the mornings before most ladies of fashion were awake. She had given orders to her staff to admit me at any hour, and I often came to her house before she was even up. We would breakfast at some ungodly hour before our morning ride, I in my men's riding clothes, she in her peignoir of white gauze, before our ride.

"Victor is very clever," she said approvingly. "You must know that."

"He is clever," I said, "but he is no traitor. He loves France, and he would do nothing to harm her."

Thérèse handed me the cream for my coffee. "Ida, I know that you wish to give him every benefit of the doubt, but you are naïve in this. I know that you think I have nothing good to say of him, and that he has nothing good to say of me. But in this I think your reason is clouded by your love. You do love him, don't you?"

"Of course I do," I said quickly. Her keen eyes were on me, though she feigned nonchalance. "There is every reason I hold him in great esteem and approbation."

"Esteem and approbation?" Her eyes widened. "That's not a very passionate declaration."

"I don't really want to discuss Victor," I said, looking away. "Of course I find him wildly attractive."

"But do you love him?"

"Yes," I said. I poured more coffee into my half-full cup.

"Forgive me for asking," she said, and her voice was soft. "I suppose I am still upset with Victor for getting us off on the wrong foot. I do want to be your friend."

I looked at her. "What?"

Thérèse toyed with the ribbons on her negligée. "Victor told me that you were a woman who enjoyed games of passion, and that the more violent and abasing they were, the more you preferred them. That you wanted a lover who could rouse in you the strongest and most humiliating instincts, who treated you with the most utter disdain. I took what I thought was his good advice and succeeded in doing no more than offending you. Which I am sure was what he intended. After all, once you had formed such a bad opinion of me, you would never be moved to seek my friendship, much less any more intimate relationship."

I felt the blood rush to my face, and my hands shook. The idea that Victor had casually discussed our encounters with her — with others! — shocked me to the core. I could imagine him dismissing our passions with a shrug and a smile, gossiping with fashionable gentlemen about the most intimate sensations we had enjoyed. About me. Talking about me like his whore. Telling other people what I said, about the games I thought were between us alone.

"Ida, are you well?"

For a moment I had almost forgotten Thérèse. "Fine," I said.

"I hope you don't think that I have repeated his comments," she said. "I wouldn't do that."

"No," I said. "Of course I don't think that."

But others would. All over town. Every

man I met was imagining me as Victor Moreau's collared dog.

Thérèse leaned over and took my hand. "Ida, I'm sorry. I didn't realize you didn't know. Victor talked about you constantly. I suppose he was so taken with you that he didn't realize how it sounded. Men do that when they're in love."

"In love?" I exclaimed, more sharply than I had intended. "Victor does not love me."

"Of course he does," Thérèse said. "I've never seen him make a fool of himself over anyone before. And he makes a perfect idiot of himself over you. Rushing about buying things to please you, dancing attendance on you at the theater, talking about you constantly. I suppose he just got carried away. And no doubt it was jealousy that made him advise me to say things that he knew would anger you. A man can shoot a rival who is a man, but what would he do with me? Call me out?"

"You are not a rival," I said. My chest hurt and I was confused. "I may call you a friend, I hope."

"Of course you may," Thérèse said. "You can always lay your troubles on me."

I don't remember the rest of the day. It was afternoon when I sat down to pen a reply to

Victor, and the quill shook in my hand with both anger and humiliation.

> *Victor,*
> *I cannot imagine what you were thinking to talk to Thérèse Tallien about our intimate relations.*

I tore the paper up and began again.

> *Victor,*
> *If you were here I would throw something at you, but since you are not I shall have to resort to words. I can't believe*

I put my head down on the table, then sat up and started anew.

> *Victor,*
> *I don't know why you did that. I don't know what's true. I don't know if you told her or not. I can't see how she would know if you didn't, but if you did then why? Were you so jealous of someone I had not even spoken with? Why? And why did you tell me to sleep with her? Is this all some depraved game, because if so I don't think I like this part and you told me to tell you when I didn't like it and this is something I don't like because I don't know what's true*

and what isn't and I hate this and I wish you were here so I could kill you. And then you could explain.

Not that you ever do. You never tell me the truth so I know it's true. And I wouldn't know you were lying to me if you were. And I don't know why she said you loved me. You don't say that. You've never said you did. And I can't. I just can't. I mean, I want you and I need you but I don't feel that way and I can't even though I should because why not but I don't. I loved Jan and he was a piece of shit but I did, and I can't love you even though you are the best thing that ever happened to me and I need you so much that sometimes I wake up and I want you so badly that I have to do it and pretend that you're there and you're watching me.

Victor,
I wish you were here because

Dear Victor,
I received your letter today and I am pleased to hear that you are in good health. I have taken care of the domestic details that you recommended to me, including your order with Maille. I will take care of the curtains as well.

I read in the papers of your uncovering

the plot concerning General Pichegru. I am deeply saddened to hear that this gentleman was guilty of such heinous crimes! I had not liked him, but I had not imagined him capable of this kind of perfidy and betrayal.

The garden is lovely. I wish you were here to enjoy it with me. I am out every day walking and finding each new wonderful plant. If you were here, you could enjoy it with me and I would find no greater pleasure than to be with you in this peaceful place.

I have been riding frequently with Madame Tallien, who is kind and has taken a great interest in me. I am of two minds concerning your instructions, and I fear that I am confused by the society in which I move. As you know, I have not your experience in such matters.

Nor your legendary discretion, apparently.

With Warmest Sentiments,
Ida St. Elme

It was the last letter that I mailed.

It took two weeks for a reply. Of course, I received other letters from him in the meantime, dispatched before mine could have reached him.

My dear,
Have I offended you in some way? Your last note was short, and I am mystified by your reference to my discretion, and to my instructions concerning your friendship with Madame Tallien.

I hope that you are not growing too close to this lady, for her character is not irreproachable. May you be guided by me in this and heed my advice to only extend your friendship so far! Remember, I am your protector and more experienced in these matters than you, who are very young and, as you know, an innocent in the sense of the world. I have your best interests at heart always.

Your servant,
Victor Moreau

"Innocent!" I threw his letter down on the table and threw my riding gloves after it.

" 'Remember I am your protector!' Bastard!" I went around the table and picked up his letter for the pleasure of throwing it again. " 'Extend your friendship only so far!' So I should sleep with her, but make sure not to enjoy it? Sleep with her, but only once? You sanctimonious . . ." Words failed me.

■ ■ ■ ■

The next morning I went to Thérèse's house just at dawn and was admitted as usual. I wore my riding costume, gray doeskin trousers and a blue coat with silver buttons, a perfect lace-trimmed cravat.

"Madame is still in her boudoir," I was informed.

"I will go up," I said airily. After all, I usually did. I opened her door and went in.

Thérèse was not only in her boudoir, she was sound asleep in her bed, which was gilt and carved with cherubs. She slept on her side, her long golden hair spread across the pillow behind her, and the sheet draped loosely over her. It was a warm summer morning. She was wearing nothing beneath the sheet. I sat down on the edge of the bed.

Thérèse stretched. "Ida?" she murmured.

The stretch exposed one perfect white breast, the areola of her nipple pink against her pale skin. Her arm extended behind her head, and the lines of her flesh were lovely indeed.

I bent and took her nipple in my mouth. It tasted of warmth and salt.

She squeaked.

I took my hand, still attired in Charles's

dove-gray riding glove, and put it lightly over her mouth. "Don't scream," I said in Charles's best cultured voice. "Women who admit just anyone to their bedchambers are inviting trouble."

Her eyes widened. With my other hand I brushed the sheet back, baring her in all her glory, rounded thighs milky against the sheets.

"Charming, I confess," I said, raking her up and down with my eyes.

She bit down on her lips, her eyes bright.

I bent and kissed her breast again, gathering it in my hand a bit roughly, kneading it and pressing her hard nipple.

Thérèse made a long, low noise in her throat.

"You mustn't scream," I said, "if I take my hand away. You wouldn't want your servants to come rushing in here and see you like this, now, would you?"

She shook her head, and I could see the hungry smile, the faint flutter at her throat.

"Be silent," I said, "or you will be sorry." I opened her legs with my gloved hand. Her hair was brown, giving the lie to her golden tresses above. The seam of my suede glove brushed against the inside of her thigh, and her hips lifted off the bed. I took my hand from her mouth and pressed it against her

180

stomach, right above the mountain of Venus, pressing down with the heel of my hand against the womb inside. Of course she rocked her hips upward, parting them slightly, a deep exhalation coming from her.

I laughed low in my throat. Her lips were pink and full, growing distended with blood. I ran my gloved hand along them.

Her back arched.

"Not a sound," I said. "Not a sound from you. Or I will make you very, very sorry."

Thérèse bit down on her lip.

"Charming," I said. My gloved hand toyed with her pearl. It was quite large and I felt it swelling under my attention. My other hand still pressed down, catching her in the unbearable place between.

It was hard to keep my voice conversational. I could feel the inseam of my trousers very sharply of a sudden, rubbing in a sensitive spot. Charles had more self-discipline than Ida, however. "Turn over," I said.

She made a small whimpering noise.

"Turn over," I said more insistently. "Do you think you can flaunt your charms as you do and not pay the price? On your hands and knees."

She turned stiffly, for I did not remove my fingers from that intimate place. Her ass was rounded and pale, and as she sank onto her knees I could see every part. I ran my hand down her back to the top of the cleft, and she arched her back, moaning. I had counted on this. With my forefingers still on her pearl, I thrust my gloved thumb inside her.

She moaned.

I took my other hand and slapped her hard across the bottom. "Did I not tell you to be quiet?"

She whimpered, and I took that as an invitation. My hand came down upon her again hard, twice, three times. Each time she moved. Each time my thumb thrust into her propelled by her own motion, the seam of my glove caressing her pearl.

I struck her again. I could see the red marks of my hand on her white skin.

Her whole body lifted and she gave a vast shudder. I felt her spasm around my thumb, the embrace of that intimate part giving against me. And then she collapsed into the bedsheets.

My body was throbbing. I could not let go. I could see my gray gloves damp from her body.

Thérèse rolled over, and her eyes were like a cat's. "Ummm, I had no idea," she purred, "that taunting such a handsome young gentleman was so dangerous."

"It is, hussy," I said. "I hope that I have taught you a proper lesson." My voice was shaking.

"You have," she said. "But perhaps you can make it more clear by requiring me to pleasure you."

I undid my trousers as though I were a man, unbuttoning the sides and pulling them down to expose enough. I knelt over her face. "Do it, then," I said. "You have a tongue, bitch."

Thérèse laughed.

Games of Passion

Over the next seven or eight weeks, I saw quite a lot of Thérèse, but we didn't honestly talk very much. Two or three times a week I would come by her house early in the morning and awaken her while the room was still cool and light. It was not a surprise after that first time, but she never failed to respond as though it were — the careless woman of fashion who had provoked a man she should not have, who had played with fire one time too many. She never seemed to tire of Charles's dandy manners and lethal smile. Then we would breakfast and sometimes go for a ride, though in the heat of August we gave up on the riding. She would go about her extensive toilette, and I would go home before it was too hot.

Of course I was now invited to all her dinners and entertainments, but I saw little of her there — the hostess cannot spend a great deal of time with any guest. I spent my evenings in repartee and cards, winning money off gentlemen who thought a lady must be a dunce and whom décolletage robbed of their wits. I did not play for much money. The pleasure was in winning hand after hand off young men who should know better.

Gossip spreads fast. The third week in September I was at a party, playing cards and listening with half an ear to things around me, when I caught Moreau's name in passing. Two gentlemen at a nearby table were talking about him. I glanced about unobtrusively. One was a civilian, the other in uniform, though I did not recognize him.

". . . will be dismissed any day now. I've seen the orders myself."

The civilian shrugged. "Moreau took Stuttgart and then gave it back, what do you expect?"

"Moreau retreated because Archduke Charles was breathing down his neck. What was he supposed to do? Take Stuttgart with him?" the officer countered.

"He's mediocre and he can't bring off a decisive battle. It's time he stepped down and someone more aggressive had the command. Someone who will carry the battle to the Austrians, not just run round and round over the same territory for years on end."

The civilian got up from the card table. "I'm for the necessary. Back in a bit."

I watched him go. Moreau would be dismissed. . . .

I did not even have time to write him. The next day I had a note from Victor that was both brief and to the point.

My dear,
I am arriving in Paris within a day or two. Please make certain that my house is in order and that my staff is prepared for my arrival.

Victor

I went to his house immediately and began ordering his staff around. They were, naturally, thrown into utter confusion by his return a full two months early. The floors were unpolished, the covers had to be removed from the furniture in the public rooms downstairs, and all the decoration needed dusting. The silver was in want of polishing and the windows on the second floor needed washing. Before it was finished, Victor arrived.

I heard his carriage pulling up at the door just at dusk, and I ran down the stairs and out to greet him, my hair still tied under a scarf that I had worn to keep the dirt off while the footmen were cleaning the hall chandelier.

Victor got out and looked at me quizzically. "My dear, what are you doing here?"

"Cleaning your house," I said. He looked very tired and he was rumpled from the road.

"Yourself?"

"Of course not," I said. "But I came to make certain that it was done well and in a timely fashion. I did not want you to come home to a cold house."

"I doubt it would be cold," he said. It was, in fact, a very warm day at the end of September, and felt more like August.

"Figuratively," I said. "But I did not know you would be here tonight or I would have ordered the cook to prepare. Would you prefer to go out?"

Victor shook his head and walked up the steps to me. The sun had just set and the sky had turned a deep and exotic blue. "And face society tonight? I suppose it will be no better another day. All Paris knows that I have been relieved of my command by now, I suppose."

I took his arm. "And no doubt they are incensed by such unfairness! You have done the unlikely on the Rhine, and it is no credit to anyone to expect you to do the impossible! I am wild with fury at this slight to you, Victor! To imagine that there is anyone who could possibly do better . . ."

"I am glad you think so, my dear. But you are no expert on military matters, as you well know. And the mob loves to blame someone. Today I am the goat. Tomorrow it will be another. What goes up comes down."

I leaned against his shoulder there on the street. "Victor, come with me. Your house is in disorder, and there is no supper. Let us go somewhere and dine, and then you can return to the comfort of my house for the evening and give your servants time to finish."

"If it would not trouble you, perhaps we could just dine at your house."

I nodded. "As warm as it is, a cold collation in the garden might be the most pleasant thing."

An hour later, the stars were appearing. We ate under the trees in my garden, moths flying at and bouncing off the paper lanterns in the tree above. There was cool white wine and pâté de campagne, olives and watercress and a little salad, cheese and bread and lovely fresh pears and a delicious crème de marrons. The night was quiet. The sounds of insects were louder than those of distant streets. The stars came out bright in a flawless sky.

It was idyllic enough to relax anyone but Victor. He picked at his food and said little. His shoulders were tense, and even a second glass of wine did not seem to change him. I chattered on about this and that. I did not bring up Thérèse. Whatever he had said or not, my raw anger at him had long since evaporated. Whether he had confided in Thérèse or had tried to discourage her, he had acted out of jealousy, I felt sure. And that I could not blame him for.

At last he put his empty glass on the table and looked at me. "And what was it about Thérèse? Did you sleep with her?"

"I did," I said lightly. "Any number of times. It was very amusing."

"Was it?" His voice was dry.

"She prefers me in men's clothes," I said. "Which is interesting, to be sure. But I do not trust her."

"That is wise," Victor said. He poured himself a third glass. "I don't trust her either. And I mistrust her with you even more."

"I can handle Thérèse," I said. "In fact, I've been handling her with a firm hand, so to speak."

Victor raised an eyebrow. "And do you

find that to your taste?"

I shrugged, coloring a little. "I enjoyed it. But nothing more. How were your women over the summer?"

He laughed. "I enjoyed it. Nothing more." Victor reached across the table and took my hand. "You are exquisite. And I have always been afraid that you would notice it."

"And yet you have given me into the very society that you know presents temptation to me," I said. "Victor, I don't understand. You could have sent me to a country house to live in quiet, or at least not given me the means to meet potential rivals."

"And I could chain you as well," he said. "But it would not serve my purpose. If I kept you solely because you could not leave, what would that say? If you answered to my hand only because there were no others who would have you, how should I take pleasure in that? I do not need to chain you. If passion is not chain enough, there is none that would do." He turned my hand so that mine rested on his, and he caressed my palm, sliding his fingers between my own. The mere touch of a hand should not feel so carnal, as though he had caressed flesh much more tender than this.

I caught my breath. "I will leave off with Thérèse," I said. "I do not need the complications."

"As you like, my dear." He lifted my hand like a gallant and touched it to his lips.

He rolled off me abruptly with an oath. Throbbing with frustrated pleasure, for a moment all I felt was huge, encompassing anger.

His breathing was very harsh. "I can't," he said, and lay on his side facing away from me.

I was shaking with interrupted passion, catching at my breath in the tight black lace corset that was all I wore, my legs spread and tensed. A brief desire to slap him ran through me, but I did nothing, just lay there until it subsided. I didn't move. The faint night breeze played over my private parts.

Victor was in shadow. I could see only the stiff set of his shoulders in his white shirt.

After a long moment, he got up. I heard him dropping the useless letter in the chamber pot and rummaging for his trousers and shoes while I lay like a broken doll. The door closed softly behind him.

I slid one finger down and finished what was begun, coming almost silently in little gasps, the corset tight around me. I turned over and clutched the pillow, face against cool cloth through the inevitable descent.

Minutes passed. The curtains swayed in the breeze. The sweat dried on my skin.

After a while I sat up stiffly and unhooked the corset. One of the stays had dug into my left breast, and there was a painful bruise starting. I got out of bed and found my wrapper, a new summer one of thin white lawn with no embroidery or ribbons at all, meant for use, not for show. I put it on and opened the door. The curtains were open facing the back of the house. I saw a movement and went to the window.

Victor was out in the garden. There was no mistaking his shape or the gleam of his shirt.

I went downstairs and followed him out. The dew was damp on the grass, dragging at the hem of my robe. The breeze felt wonderful, fresh and cool and just beginning to speak of autumn. Dawn was hours away.

I came up beside him. He must have heard me, but he did not turn.

I put one hand on his shoulder, laid my face against the back of his neck silently.

He took and released a deep breath.

"It's very peaceful here," I said.

"It is." He reached back and put an arm around my waist, and I stood next to him, my arm around him, looking up at the stars glittering through the full green leaves, just at their largest. One night soon the temperature would drop. October was almost here. The leaves would change. This was the high tide, but already the summer was over, pulling away like a drag far out to sea.

"Do you love me, my dear?" he asked.

I put my head on his shoulder, so tall that even sideways my brow was against his chin, the faint unfamiliar feel of stubble against my skin. "I love you, Victor," I said, and knew as I said it that it was a lie.

I felt his arm tighten about me. When he spoke, it was with the old mocking tone again, falsely light. "I am sorry to have disappointed you, my dear."

I shrugged. "These things happen. It doesn't matter."

"No?"

"No," I said firmly. "You're tired after a long journey. You don't usually come straight to me, you know." The wind tugged at my hair, and the branches murmured. "You will have another command, as soon as they realize that whoever relieved you is not a miracle worker either. No one can defeat the Austrians decisively."

"Bonaparte can," he said. "In Italy. And they expect a second Bonaparte. Suddenly competence and service are not enough.

They want a poor-man's Alexander."

"Whatever he is, there is only one of him," I said. "And they will need you. You will see. Now that you're here in Paris, you can convince the Directors personally that they need to give you a command again next spring. It's not as though anyone is going to be fighting decisive battles over the winter."

"No, it's not likely."

I ran my finger along his jaw affectionately. "And I can help you. You'll need to entertain a lot. And you'll be glad of the goodwill I've found this summer. I think that instead of hiding in your house as if you have something to be ashamed of, you should give a celebration. You should have a ball to mark your return to Paris. You are not hiding! You are the Republic's finest general, and you know it!"

Victor laughed. "What a Machiavellian little thing you are! I see you've made the most of your time in Paris."

"You sent me to school with Thérèse. Did you expect me to learn nothing?"

"Nothing except?" He raised an eyebrow, and he was smiling.

"Nothing except how to dominate a woman and make her beg for pleasure? My dear Victor, I learned that from you."

"Touché, Madame," he said, laughing.

I put my arms around his neck. "Dear Victor," I said. "I did miss you. Even with Thérèse for company." I kissed him, warm and sweet, then drew him down beside me on the grass. "All summer I've wanted you here to lie outside with me looking up at the stars."

"The grass is wet," he said. "And I don't have a letter with me."

"Lie on the grass," I said, pushing him playfully. "And you don't need anything. We're not going to do anything except lie here looking at the stars."

"Getting wet," he said.

"For goodness' sake, Victor," I said. "You would think you'd never seen grass before!"

"I've seen stars before," he grumbled.

"Not with me," I said, and settled onto his shoulder.

"No," he said quietly. "Not with you."

TEMPERANCE

Midwinter came and the year turned. While it was all still the Year VI by the revolutionary calendar, it was hard for me not to think of 1798 starting with the snows of winter. It was a difficult one. The cold came hard, and soon the gutters and their filthy contents froze over, and some mornings the trees were festooned with ice. In the country, peasants were starving. In the city, there was bread, but for some little else.

We gave parties. On the way back to my house from one of them, my coachman shot a beggar who tried to rob us.

All through the winter, Victor grew more and more testy, driving both of us to extremes. While he had always been cynical and mocked his rivals, now there was a bitter edge to his jokes in company that I thought uneasily was less than funny. Oh yes, it was wicked and amusing! But it also seemed mean-spirited. I didn't think it showed Victor in a particularly good light.

I should have been entirely happy. After all, I had everything, even Victor's apparent devotion. I had money and a beautiful house, fashionable clothes, entertainments and the best society. I might even have influence if I wished. Many a mistress did.

Influence to do what? some part of me whispered. To cause men to give me diamonds in order to have Moreau's ear? To cause women to wear one mode or another, to all dress in lilac or eschew the color completely? What was the point of all that? There must be something more to all of it. Was I born for this? I did not think so in my heart, but what other answer could there be beyond the one I had tried before and found lacking, being a good wife to a man I hated? In my dreams, there were other choices. I stood behind a queen while she heard cases in court, queen and goddess alike in her pleated white linen, crook and flail in her hands. In my dreams, I defended a city hopelessly besieged, Greek fire spattering with eerie light against the stonework I sheltered behind with helmet and shield. I dreamed of smooth green oceans beneath the prow of a sailing ship, of distant mountains beneath the moon, of faces I had never seen, yet that I dreamed with love. But those were fancies. They were not part of life, of the world as it was.

We had a February thaw. The branches began to bud, and there were a few days that were unseasonably warm. The appointments for the spring were not all posted, but if the decisions were not made they would be soon.

We had planned an afternoon reception for one of the Decades, the tenth day of rest that replaced Sunday in the new calendar. Unexpectedly, the day was warm and the sun was bright. The huge pots of forced fuchsia tulips that I had placed all over the downstairs of Victor's house were lovely in alabaster urns, and the buffet table was simply gorgeous. Silver gleamed on cloths of magenta and aqua silk embroidered with gold thread on the tables, and purple and aqua fringed shawls were thrown over Victor's very neutral furniture. The chandeliers had been hung with fuchsia and aqua beads. Candles glowed everywhere.

My dress was aqua silk gauze, fashioned almost like a classical chiton, with brooches on my shoulders in the shape of flowers. A gold chain belt caught the dress just below my breasts, and between them a long gold chain held a single lacquered white rose.

As the party began, I stood with Victor at

the door. We had invited more than a hundred people — all the government types, all the Directors, a good smattering of finance, and a bunch of officers Victor had served with, to underline his experience and his good reputation. I couldn't stay at the door forever. To begin with, it was clear that the buffet line was backing up, and the footmen weren't retrieving used glasses fast enough.

I found the nearest one, who was standing like a rock against the wall. "Go round and pick up all the glassware," I said. "I shouldn't have to tell you not to leave dirty dishes sitting about."

Another footman was circulating with a tray full of champagne. He was mobbed in an instant, and the glasses were gone while some guests were still empty-handed. We needed two footmen doing that.

I nipped back in the kitchen. "More champagne," I said. "We need two men with trays. Gustave, put down those canapés and take the champagne around. Drinks first, then food. Marcel, straighten your cravat." The first footman came in with a tray of dirty glasses. "Get these rinsed out and back out with champagne. Hurry."

I went back to the party, which was in full swing. Victor was talking to Barras and Joséphine Bonaparte across the room. The buffet table had been thoroughly raided and the crowd around it had dwindled. Nothing looked too terribly depleted.

He was standing by the buffet.

I had only seen him once, but I knew him at a glance. He wore white trousers and waistcoat with the dark-blue coat of the Army of the Republic. A general's tricolor sash was around his waist, and the knotting of it did not disguise the hilt of the saber at his side. It wasn't a dress sword. It was a heavy cavalry saber in a battered scabbard, and he wore boots instead of dress shoes. *A poor man's compromise,* I thought. His hair was red and still pulled back in an old-fashioned tail, but he had giant muttonchop sideburns that almost seemed to meet under his chin. He held a plate in one hand and was looking at the pâtés with great suspicion.

He looked up as I approached. His eyes were as blue as I knew they would be.

"Wondering which is which?" I asked.

He looked down at me with his head to the side. I was a tall woman, but the top of my head only came to his chin. "Yes," he said.

"That one is duck with chestnuts," I said, pointing, "and that one is pork with truffles."

"I'll try the duck, then," he said, picking up the serving knife.

I handed him the basket of bread with a smile. "You will like that, General Ney."

He took a few slices. "I'm at a loss," he said. "Do I know you?" His eyes were very keen, light blue, like clear water.

"No," I said. "Madame St. Elme. We've never met."

There was an awkward moment as he tried to figure out how to bend over my hand while holding a plate and a pâté knife. I took the pâté knife and put it back on the table. He bowed quite correctly. "I am enchanted," he said. "You must be our hostess. But how in the world do you know me?"

"I saw you a number of years ago," I said. "And I am acquainted with a friend of yours, Colonel Meynier."

"Ah." He straightened up, looking at me again. "You wouldn't be Meynier's runaway bride, would you?"

"Colonel Meynier was the soul of gallantry," I said. "He promised me he would not talk of it."

"He didn't," Ney said. "At least, not your name or anything. But he said . . ." For a moment he looked embarrassed. "He said you were the most beautiful woman in the

201

world, with eyes like the sea and the face of an angel."

I stared at him. The conventional pleasantries deserted me. "I don't look like an angel," I said. "I am too hard."

Ney smiled, a wonderful, gentle smile that could have lit the room and banished February forever. "How do you know?" he asked. "Have you ever seen an angel?"

I hardly knew how to take it, and so I stood there stupidly, the appropriate compliments dead on my lips. "General . . ."

"Yes?"

I lifted a plate of trout terrine. "Do you like fish?"

He looked at the plate. "Yes," he said.

"It's very good. It has herbs of various sorts. Parsley, maybe. Or dill. I don't know. I didn't make it. I mean, I don't usually cook. The cook does that. But it's very good." I was babbling and wasn't sure how to stop.

"Good," he said. He took the plate out of my hand and looked at it in bafflement. "I like fish very much. Trout is good." I could see him visibly casting about. "I used to fish for trout when I was a boy."

"Did you enjoy it?" I asked.

"Very much," he said. "My brother and I fished. For trout. And other fish."

"I'm glad," I said. "I'm sure fishing is very pleasant."

"It is," he said.

He was smiling as if he could not stop looking at me, those warm blue eyes on my face as though I were some dream that had stepped suddenly to life. "Madame . . ."

"Yes?"

He lifted a tray of tarts. "What are these?"

"Onion tarts," I said. "With port marmalade." Now there was a plate of tarts in the air between us too.

"Are they good?"

"Yes," I said.

"I've never had them before."

"There's a first time for everything," I said. That was a lead line I knew what to do with. "Sometimes you don't know if you'll like something until you try it."

His eyes widened. *Not a gambler,* I thought. *Everything he thinks he shows on his face, transparent as glass.*

"Madame?" One of the footmen was trying to get my attention. "We have a slight difficulty in the kitchen." The man almost had to grab my arm.

"I'm sorry," I said. "There seems to be some crisis I must attend to."

Ney bowed slightly. "Of course. Your servant, Madame."

"I will —" I started to say.

"Please, Madame!" the footman said.

"In a moment," I excused myself to Ney.

The kitchen was on fire. Someone had started a grease fire, and one of the footmen in a fit of helpfulness had thrown a dish tray full of dirty water on it, which of course had only spread the flames and broken all the champagne glasses that were being washed.

The cook had then smothered the fire with flour, covering almost every surface in the kitchen at the same time. It looked like something very large and white had exploded. The glassware was gone, and the raw chickens that were being roasted were now covered in flour. It took me nearly an hour to sort everything out, then clean up and get the flour off my dress. When I went back to the party, Ney was nowhere to be seen. The guests were beginning to go, and the party was winding down.

I went and stood by Victor at the door as we said farewell. "Is Ney gone?" I asked him.

Victor nodded. "He left a few minutes ago. Did you make his acquaintance?"

I took his arm. "Yes," I said. He had not waited. But then, why should he?

"What did you find to talk about?" Victor reached for the hand of an officer who was leaving, and they exchanged farewells and pleasantries.

"Fishing," I said. My heart was sinking. Which was ridiculous.

Victor snorted. "That's about his speed. He's a good officer, but he has the imagination of a side of beef."

"Oh," I said. Eyes like the sea and the face of an angel. The most beautiful woman in the world. Surely I was used to compliments by now, even ones delivered with less than the usual panache. It wasn't what he'd said. It was the way he had looked at me. And I had talked about food. Because I was an idiot.

"Are you feeling well, my dear?" Victor asked.

I nodded. "Just a bit tired," I said.

Victor did not get a command. For three days he paced around both our houses, alternating between silence and ranting. "The Directors are imbeciles," he said.

"Yes, Victor, I know."

"It's all about flash these days. They have no stomach for the kind of hard work we had to do a few years ago."

"Yes, Victor," I said. I refrained from saying that a few years earlier they'd beheaded generals who displeased them, rather than simply not assigning them any troops.

Victor paced all the way down to the long windows that overlooked my flowering garden. "Since that puffed-up Bonaparte signed the Treaty of Campo Formio with the Austrians, there isn't anything to do this year. Half the army is in reserve in barracks."

"Surely peace is a good thing," I said, coming to the window. Ney was in camp at Lille. He had command of several cavalry divisions. I had seen all the posting lists that friends had sent Victor.

"Bah." Victor scowled out at the gardens. "The Austrians aren't serious. We'll be at war again soon. And the English aren't about to abandon the war with us, not when their navy has ours going and coming."

I shrugged. "Perhaps a breather is good for us. Time to reform and time to train and replace. You always tell me how important it is."

Victor leaned his forehead against the glass and said nothing.

"If it's true that the peace won't last, then you know that when war comes they will need more experienced generals. You simply need to make sure the Directors remember you." I put my hand on his shoulder. "You can be patient, Victor. You're clever and you never give up. And in the meantime, so many people will have a chance to heal. Think of all the thousands of children who are glad to have their fathers home!"

Victor smirked. "You are turning into a sentimentalist, my dear. How very sweet."

I looked at him. "Victor, I wish —" I broke off.

"What, my dear?"

"I wish you were someone who cared."

He turned and looked at me, his brow furrowed. "I do care, my dear. I care about you, and about my friends."

"But not about people." I put my hands against the glass, pressing against the rain-streaked panes. "You don't really care if thousands of children are orphaned, or if people starve, or whatever happens. It just doesn't matter to you. I can't explain. I'm not saying this right."

"I am a pragmatist, my dear. I don't believe in God and piety and charity. It was entirely corrupt, if you remember, a scam for priests to live well while doing nothing."

"Is this all there is, then?" I looked out at the rain soaking my gorgeous tulips. "Nothing matters and there is no reason for anything?"

He put his hands on my shoulders gently. "My dear, you are softhearted. If it will make you feel better to involve yourself with some respectable charity, then by all means do it. The Fund for the Orphans of the Army of the Republic is well thought of. You may make a donation of any size you see fit. Or even engage yourself in the production of their receptions or endless bazaars. There is no reason you can't, if it will make you happy."

"It's not about my happiness," I said. It was hard even to find words for the thing I sought. I leaned back against his shoulder. "Surely there is more to the world than my happiness."

Victor slid his arm around my waist. "There's mine," he said.

That night I dreamed. In my dream, I climbed from my bed and walked through Paris, through misted streets like the ones I knew waking.

The only thing that was different was that it was too fast. I had only to think, and I could hear the river running, see the lights shining from the windows of the Tuileries. It was early spring and the night was warm, with a mist rising off the Seine. I was alone.

"Why am I here?" I asked.

Nothing happened. A soft breeze pressed against my face.

"Why can't I remember?" I whispered.

I walked along the quays. Ahead of me Pont Neuf stretched, cool and reflected in the water. I walked out onto the bridge.

A man stood at the railing, looking downstream. For a moment I thought it was my father — the same brown queue, the same breadth of shoulder. Then I realized that he wore the uniform of the Army of the Republic, a sash around his waist. I would have thought it was some friend of Victor's if not for the odd shadow behind him, like folded wings.

"Why don't I remember?" I asked.

"You can," he said, and turned. He was young and tired, with a homely, ordinary face. "You can remember anytime you want to."

I went over and leaned my elbows on the rail beside him. "Why?"

"Because you asked for the Gift of Memory. And I promised I would never take it from you again." He leaned companionably beside me. "It's good to see you."

"You came with him, didn't you?" I asked.

"With Michel, you mean? My namesake?"

I nodded. "I know him, don't I?"

"What do you think?" He looked at me

209

from under long lashes, pretty as a girl's.

"I'm afraid to," I said. "If I do, I will never be safe again."

"Probably not," he said cheerfully. "He does get into a lot of trouble."

I looked out over the quiet water. "This river isn't the Seine, is it?"

This time he grinned. "No."

INDISCRETIONS

Victor rattled around snarling at everything until I suggested that he should join Barras as his guide in a tour of our encampments on the Rhine. As was his habit, Victor wrote me almost immediately.

My dear,
I have reached Strasbourg in company of M. Barras, and our reception in this city has been exceptional. M. Barras is well known to them, and is esteemed as greatly by them as by me.

I am well, though the condition of the roads was somewhat worse than I had expected due to the torrential rains that plagued us. Because of this, I shall require my older pair of boots to be sent to me, as I do not wish to spoil the best ones.

I have received correspondence from my builder regarding the renovations to the kitchen that you and I discussed. I am un-

able to concentrate on these domestic matters at this time, so if you could contact him and relate to him all the particulars, my gratitude should be extreme. Also, I have ordered new table linens. Pray see what has become of them.

I am your servant,
Victor Moreau

I sighed deeply and put the letter in my reticule. I would deal with Victor's builder after lunch. I was meeting Lisette and her theater friends in a café in the Palais-Royal.

The day was gorgeous. The sun was bright, and the weather warm. I took off my shawl and draped it over the back of my chair. Lisette and I were the only women. There was Jean Delacroix, the lead who played Gaius Gracchus, and two more young men, one of whom was wickedly funny. All through lunch he told anecdotes about notable persons who came to the theater, both the Populaire and the Théâtre de la République, which was much more respectable.

"Ah," said Delacroix, "but we are more entertaining!"

"We have Talma," the young man countered, "the very prince of the theater that he is. If only he didn't mingle in politics so much! It makes the rest of the company nervous."

"It's just that he likes to be looked at," Lisette said. "He's as kind as the day is long."

"He likes to be looked at, all right," Delacroix said. "He's posing for Lemot the sculptor now, nude as the day he was born, for a life-size marble, wearing nothing but a pair of manacles!"

"I'm sure that will be decorative," I said dryly. "And pray tell me what the subject is? A Dying Gaul, perhaps?"

Delacroix grinned. "Thettalos Enchained," he said.

I felt a shiver despite the warmth of the day. "Ah," I said. "I haven't had the pleasure of meeting Monsieur Talma yet."

"You spend too much time in military circles," Lisette said. "We can introduce you."

"It must be very boring," the young man remarked. "All those staid soldiers!"

"Not really," I said.

Delacroix poured everyone more wine. "Some of them are as good as players themselves. There was this fellow at Mannheim who took the town without a shot on sheer theatrics."

Lisette laughed. "And how do you do that?"

"Well, he had some inferior number of men or something like that. But the fellow spoke German perfectly well, since he's an Alsatian. So he dressed up in peasant clothes and went in by himself on market day to reconnoiter. Big redheaded fellow, must have looked like he belonged."

"Ney," I said, catching my breath.

Delacroix nodded. "That was his name. Do you know him?"

"I've met him once," I said. "What did he do?"

Delacroix leaned back, obviously relishing his position as storyteller. "He wandered around looking at all the defenses and decided that he could never take the town by force. While he was chatting with people in the market, he saw a young woman with a lot of packages. She was heavily pregnant, and he gave her a hand with her purchases to a cart that was going back outside the walls. He asked her if she wasn't nervous being outside the walls so close to her time."

I could just imagine. His friendly manner and perfect German — who would suspect a thing?

"She said that, no, the commander of the garrison had been very kind and told her that if she needed the midwife, they would be happy to let her in at any time. So this fellow Ney took himself off, acting like some yokel, and made his way back to his men. They found him a dress and an apron and kerchief, and that night good and late he dressed up with a big straw pillow under the dress like a bump!"

I clenched my hand around the wineglass. It was damp from the condensation on the outside, the white wine still cool from the cellar.

"So he had fifty of his picked men wait, and then he staggers up to the gate moaning, with the big bump on the front end and a kerchief over his head. 'Oh, help! Oh, help me! I need the midwife! My time is come!' and carrying on in German in falsetto. They opened the gate, and as soon as they did his men rushed the guards. They took the city of Mannheim without a shot fired, with nothing more than a few bruises all round. He said the best way to win battles was not to fight them."

The company laughed. "How very clever," Lisette said.

"I love him," I said.

Delacroix looked at me. "What?"

"I love him," I said. My hand was perfectly steady on the wineglass and so was my voice. "Lisette, have you ever met someone and just known them? Irrationally, absolutely?"

"I thought you'd just met him," Lisette said.

"I did," I said. "I've only met him once. But I know him. I know him as if it's been a thousand years. I should have said . . . I don't know what I should have said, but I shouldn't have talked about trout."

"Trout?" Lisette said confusedly. "Why would you talk about trout?"

"I don't know," I said. "He was so overwhelming in person. I should have been witty and clever and amazing and unforgettable, and instead I talked about food and fishing."

"Do you know anything about fishing?" Lisette asked.

"No!" I put my head in my hands. "I don't even know why we were talking about fishing. And then the kitchen caught fire."

"And he put it out with his bare hands?"

"No." I rubbed my forehead. "I went to tend to it, and when I came back he was gone. But it had been nearly an hour, even though I'd told him I would be back in a minute, so I suppose he thought I was trying to get rid of him."

"Is he that good-looking?" Delacroix asked.

"He's not good-looking at all," I said. "He has red hair and the most horrible sideburns that wrap around under his chin like he's got some strange animal attached, and he's built like the side of a barn, and his face is ordinary and you can see that his hairline is receding and he's going to be bald, and he doesn't even have a pair of dress shoes."

"Then why . . ." Delacroix began perplexedly.

"I don't know!" I said. "I don't. It's just that he's him. I can't explain. I know him. I've been looking for him since the day I was born."

Lisette and Delacroix exchanged a look. "What about Moreau?" Lisette asked.

I took a quick gulp of my wine. "I can't leave Victor. And he's been wonderful to me in every way. I can't wait until he goes out of town and go dashing off to Lille. It's not fair."

"And he pays the bills," Delacroix said cynically.

Lisette shot him a quick glance.

"He does," I said, "but he's having such a terrible time right now. I can't do that."

"And you don't know if Ney would want you," Lisette said practically. "It's better if you do nothing. Infatuations fade, or they turn into something real. But either way, it takes time."

"You are right, of course," I said.

That night I sat down to answer Victor's letter.

My dear,
I am sorry the weather was terrible for your trip! I hope you took the precaution of wearing your greatcoat and a scarf. I know you are susceptible to colds.

I am sending your boots as you requested, along with several pairs of new stockings. I have taken care of the table linens. The ones you ordered looked terrible when they arrived — the stitching was crude and the quality was not acceptable. I have ordered new linens, and I am sure they will meet your exacting specifications. They are not in the least gaudy, but they do have colored borders for summer dining.

I have not yet talked to the builder about the kitchen. He is on another job and his wife keeps telling me that he will call upon me, but it hasn't happened yet. I shall have to make a pest of myself.

With greatest esteem,
Ida St. Elme

I poured sand on the letter and shook it off carefully, then put it to the side to dry completely.

I could write to him, I thought. *I could write and at least apologize for leaving him so precipitously. I could say the witty things I had meant to say. Or at least say something.*

I picked up another sheet of paper and began to write.

My dear General,
I hardly know how to begin this. I obey my heart without searching for vain excuses. I do not know the art of disguising my feelings. Besides, there is something in the depths of my soul that tells me that if what I am doing wounds the conventions of mundane people, it may still please someone of your character.

I have only spoken with you once, and yet your image is graven on my heart.

Since I first heard your name, I have been one with you in my thoughts. I tremble at all of your perils, rejoice at all of your triumphs, and applaud every recounting of your beautiful deeds.

My life is wonderful. I know that there are women who envy me. But I would joyfully renounce it all to be your companion in danger.

Respect and intimacy unite me with General Moreau. Does it carry the risk of making myself contemptible in your eyes to confess to you in a letter like this? But I don't know how to fight the irresistible demands of my heart!

I have no other reason for telling you of the feelings that trouble my sleep except that you should know that I exist. That there is somewhere a woman to whom your glory is no less dear than it is to you yourself.

I will remember you until the end of the world.

Love,
Ida St. Elme

I blotted the letter quickly, and put both of them in their envelopes. Tomorrow they would set off in different dispatch bags, part of my life and part of my soul.

TEN OF SWORDS

Victor returned to Paris far sooner than I had expected, with not even a note ahead to tell me of his arrival. I was reading in my drawing room late one afternoon. I didn't even hear his carriage on the drive, didn't realize he was there until he opened the door.

"Victor!" I got up to greet him, but he backed away from my embrace.

His face was a study in cold fury. He withdrew a folded paper from his pocket. "Madame," he said, "what is the meaning of this?"

"The meaning of what?" I asked, confused.

"So I assume your lover has not yet warned you of your mistake." His jaw was clinched.

"What?"

"Don't play innocent with me, Madame!" he shouted. "Grant me the respect my intel-ligence deserves." He unfolded the paper and held it at arm's length. " 'My life is wonderful. I know that there are women who envy me. But I would joyfully renounce it all to be your companion in danger.' "

"Oh, my God," I said, grabbing the edge of the table behind me.

Victor stalked toward me. "I want you out of this house, Madame. Now."

"How did you get that?" I said.

"You sent it to me, my dear," Victor snapped. "And I assume that you sent your lover the letter you meant for me. No doubt a much less passionate missive."

"Victor, I can explain —"

"I imagine you can," he said, stopping before me. "I imagine I would hear some very pretty lie. I imagine you are quite used to telling me lies, moneygrubbing little whore that you are."

I reeled as though he had hit me. "Victor, I haven't slept with Ney. I've never even spoken with him in private."

"Ney!" Victor threw the letter on the table. He stood with his back to me but his shoulders were shaking with fury. "I should have thought you had better taste, my dear. He's as thick as a slab of Alsatian beef, but I suppose he's well hung. I wouldn't have thought he had the discretion to go meeting you behind my back."

"I've never met with him behind your back," I said. "I told you, Victor. I've never even spoken to him in private." My eyes were smarting, and I stilled my shaking hands.

" 'But I don't know how to fight the irresistible demands of my heart,' " Victor quoted. "Very passionate for a man you've never even talked to. You shall have to do better than that, my dear." He turned and looked at me, loathing in every line of his face. "I am done with you. You are a treacherous little snake, like all of your kind."

I grabbed his arm. "Victor, you must believe me! I have never lied to you about this."

He slapped me across the face. It wasn't very hard, but it was the first time he had ever struck me, even in play. "Lying cunt! Do you think I'm stupid? Do you think I am so entranced by your beauty that I will be your dog? A laughingstock while you give it to that stupid yokel? While you give him what I am paying for?"

I burst into tears, more from shock than pain. "Victor, please —"

He seized me by the shoulders. "Out! Out of my house, bitch!" He hauled me bodily toward the door.

"Victor, please listen to me. . . ." I was crying and grabbing at him.

The astonished footman stuck his head in.

"Your mistress is a lying whore," Victor said. "This is my house, and she is leaving now. You are not to allow her to set foot in here again for any reason whatsoever. Nor are you to bring her anything or obey her in any way." He shoved me at the door.

I fell, grabbing at his boots. "Victor, please, darling, listen." I pressed my face against his leg.

He shook me off as though I were something slimy. "This is not a game. I am done with you, Madame."

"Victor, I should not have written that letter, but I have never slept with him! I've never even —"

He shoved me and I fell outside, onto my side against the brick steps. "I am done with you. Done!" He slammed the door.

"Victor!" I screamed. I got to my knees and began pounding on the door. "Victor, you ass! Come back here and listen to me!" I pounded and pounded and pounded. "Victor, please! I wasn't unfaithful! I wasn't!"

I sank down on the step, shaking with every breath. My hands hurt. I looked down and saw with an odd sense of detachment that my knuckles were bloody. There were streaks of blood on my front door. And still it didn't open.

I stood up. "I hate you!" I screamed. No curtain moved, no window cracked. "I hate you, Victor Moreau! I wish I'd slept with every man in the French army! I wish I'd let every private in your command bugger me! Do you hear me, Victor?"

There was no reply.

"You're a miserable, pathetic excuse for a man!" I yelled, tears running down my face, but it was fury that possessed me now. "You impotent aesthete!"

The door did not open. Nothing happened.

Night was falling. The stars were beginning to appear.

"If you think I'm going to sit here and beg for you, you're mistaken!" I screamed. "Open the door now, or forget about it!" I picked myself up and dusted off my skirts. Deliberately I walked out the gate and down the street.

Several blocks away, I hailed a hired carriage.

"Where to, Madame?" the driver asked.

And I realized that I did not have my reticule, or any money, or anything except the afternoon dress I stood up in. "Madame Tallien's house," I said, giving him the address. Thérèse would be good for the cab fare.

And she was. Thérèse was dressing to go out for dinner, but she stopped all her preparations when she saw me. "Darling! What happened to you?"

"Victor and I had a terrible fight," I said. "Thérèse, I'm so upset. I can't bear to talk about it."

Thérèse put her arm around me. "My poor dear! How awful! Did he do that to your poor hands?"

I sniffled. My hands did look terrible. "No," I said. "I hit the door when I couldn't get my hands on Victor."

Thérèse laughed. "That's probably good luck for Victor. What were you fighting about?"

"It's so stupid, Thérèse." I felt the tears beginning again, spurred by her kindness. "He thinks I have a secret lover. I don't. I've never been unfaithful to him. I kept telling him that, but he wouldn't believe me."

"Men can be awfully jealous," Thérèse said.

I took her hand. "Thérèse, can I stay here

tonight? So that Victor has time to cool off?"

"Of course," Thérèse said warmly. "You're always welcome. I'm afraid I have to go out. Constant will be waiting for me right now, pacing up and down at the restaurant, or else I would stay with you."

"I don't want to spoil your plans," I said. "Thérèse, if I can just make use of one of your guest rooms . . ."

"Anything you need," Thérèse said. "I'll have my maid draw you a bath, and you can just relax and let Victor cool his heels! It's all the game of love, Ida."

I managed a smile for her, though I didn't feel it. "Thank you."

Thérèse went out, and I took a long bath. At first I lay there enumerating Victor's sins. God, he was so stupid! *And so was I,* I thought. *How could I have misaddressed the letters? That must have been what happened.*

I rubbed my face with my wet hands. And what had Ney thought when he got the letter for Moreau? I tried to remember what the letter had said. Nothing important, just routine household things, I thought.

My eyes felt swollen with crying. I got out of the bath and put on one of Thérèse's night-robes. It was short on me and ended halfway between my knees and my ankles, but it was clean and fresh. I went and lay down on the soft bed in her guest room. Tomorrow I would go talk to Victor and make him see reason. Tomorrow.

I had not expected to fall asleep, but I did.

In the morning, I breakfasted before Thérèse was awake. I felt much better for some sleep, and my dress had been brushed out. Her footman fetched me a hired carriage and I had it take me to my house.

In the carriage I composed myself. Victor would be reasonable. He was a very reasonable person. I should admit my fault in writing the letter and promise never to do it again.

As we turned into my street, I caught my breath. On the curb was a huge mound of goods. I leapt from the carriage. All my clothes, my books, my letters and papers, my shoes, everything was heaped in a huge pile for the garbage.

I stood there dumbstruck, wanting to simply scream.

In the gutter were all my tulips, each one pulled up by the roots, a pile of wilting greenery. I sank down beside them, crying. Each beautiful flower was torn out, bulb and all, simply because I had loved it.

The footman came out, carefully not looking at me. He threw a box of my toiletries on the pile. A bottle of perfume rolled off and broke on the sidewalk, spilling over my underclothing, my crumpled houri costume, my sandals.

I stood up and shrieked at him, "Marcel! What —"

He flinched, but went back to the house for another load.

"You bastard," I swore through my tears, gathering up my white lawn wrapper, the book I had been reading yesterday, my shredded tulips, and clutching them to my bosom. "I hate you till my dying day."

The footman came back. It was my bath oil and cosmetics that he tossed on the sidewalk.

I ran after him, planting myself in front of him, the trailing edges of my nightclothes in my arms. "Marcel, stop this now. Stop it, I say!"

"Please, Madame," he whispered, not meeting my eyes.

I dodged and stayed in front of him. "Marcel, why are you doing this? I was never unkind to you."

"He pays me, Madame," the footman whispered. "The general pays me. He says it all belongs to him."

"I'm going to give him a thing or two about that," I snapped, trying to push around him toward the house.

"The general's not here, Madame," Marcel pleaded. "He left hours ago."

"After he destroyed my flowers," I said.

Marcel could hardly look at me. "Please, Madame. I can't afford to lose my position. I have a family. He said he would dismiss anyone who disobeyed him. And I've never seen a man in such a temper before. I can't imagine calling any woman the things he called you."

"Marcel, please let me in."

"I can't, Madame!" His voice was frightened. "I can't afford for him to let me go! I have four children, Madame!"

I stepped back. There was no more pain. It was just a dullness.

"I understand," I said. "Of course you can't risk your livelihood. The general will get what he wants."

Marcel looked down at the ground, his broader accent betraying his distress. "Madame, you was always decent to me. He told me to pile your things on the curb. But he don't care what happens then. If you was to take some things away with you, how'd he know the difference from if some scrounger took them?"

I nodded. "Thank you. Thank you so very much. . . ."

I started bundling things together, all the ruins of my life. Bottles and one gilded sandal. The pins from my blue reception dress. The black corset I had worn when he got home last year. A new fan I hadn't used yet with the sticks broken. I tied things up in my skirts. Books. Notes. My riding pants. Charles's cravat, the letters from my cousin Louisa.

I know I looked like a madwoman. I made the carriage stay and I piled things inside.

"Hope you've got money for this, Madame," the driver said.

My reticule was on the bottom of the pile, the velvet ruined by the damp. But there was money in it. Not as much as I had hoped, but enough for the carriage.

And I had a bank account. Not for the first time, I was glad of the Revolution. Women could open their own bank accounts that were their own property. Victor couldn't touch my money in the bank.

The money he had paid me.

I ground my teeth. Paid me to be his whore. And despite all his protestations, that's what it was. He was throwing me out like an overpriced whore.

I couldn't get it all. And it would serve him right if our play clothes rotted on the sidewalk.

"Madame Tallien's house again," I told the driver.

If Victor didn't like that, it wasn't his problem anymore.

By the time I got back to Thérèse's house, the sun was high and I was hot and sweaty. I got down from the carriage with my arms full of glass bottles and ran up the walk. Thérèse was just coming down the front stairs in a morning dress.

"Can I borrow a footman to help me get things in?" I asked her.

Thérèse did not smile. Instead, her brow puckered.

"What?"

"Victor is furious," she said. "And I can't risk it politically. It would be better if you stayed somewhere else."

I stopped dead in my tracks. My heart was suddenly pounding. "What?"

"Ida, you can't stay here," she said. "It just won't work."

"Won't work? I thought you were my friend!" I said. "Now you're throwing me out when I have no place to go?"

She frowned. "It's just not a good idea. Victor is a hard man to have for an enemy."

"But you were my friend." I just stood there dumbly.

Thérèse almost shrugged. "Victor is the one with the power, Ida. Without him, you're nobody. Don't you understand that?"

"I see," I said. My jaw clinched, but I would never cry in front of her again. "It's been nice knowing you, then." I stalked back to the carriage.

"No hard feelings," Thérèse said. "You understand. It's politics."

"Yes," I said, and slammed the door.

Thérèse shrugged and went inside.

The driver leaned back. "Where to?"

I gave him Lisette's address.

I had never been to Lisette's house before. She had never wanted to meet me there, despite the fact I knew she didn't live with a man. When I saw it, I understood why. It was a fourth-floor walk-up in a run-down building near Porte de Clichy, a neighborhood full of workingmen and Jews.

I went up and knocked while the carriage waited. It took a long time for her to answer the door.

"Hmm?" she said. Her hair was mussed and she was wearing a robe in the early afternoon. "Ida?"

"Can I come in?" I asked, my voice breaking a little.

Lisette took a longer look at me and her

eyes opened wide. "Ida? What happened to you?"

"Moreau threw me out," I said bitterly. "Literally. With the clothes on my back. And then threw my things after me. They're downstairs in a hired carriage, and, Lisette, I swear I wouldn't have come here and I would never have presumed, but I don't have anywhere to go and Thérèse . . ."

I started crying again as she put her arms around me. "Oh, Ida! Of course it's all right! Come in. Or hold on a minute — I'll dress and help you bring your things up. Things like this happen!"

I returned her hug. She was little and round, unwashed and smelling of last night's perfume and last night's sex. "I can't even start to thank you. . . ."

Lisette patted me on the back. "There's plenty of room. I used to have a roommate, but she moved out with her man. Are you flat or do you have a little put by?"

"I have some money in the bank," I said. "I can split costs with you. I promise I wouldn't take advantage of you that way." There were two bedrooms and a sitting room between, with a fireplace in the sitting room. In the winter, the bedrooms must be freezing. Her furniture was newish, but obviously inexpensive. The gilt was gold paint.

Lisette bustled around helping me bring in my things and hang my clothes. Some of them were ruined, but most were salvage-able. "One option is to go on the stage. That's what most women do. There are some bit-part trials at the Théâtre de la Ré-publique next week. But they aren't going to pay much."

"I still have some money," I said. "I can make it stretch. Not a lot, but for a little while."

Lisette looked me up and down. "You might do for one of the Greek extras. And you don't have to have experience for that." She met my eyes. "And I always have a friend of a friend. There are always plenty of people willing to pay for an introduction to a woman with your looks."

"For an introduction?" I said cynically.

"That's what you call it," she said. "After that, you work out your own terms. But you don't mind kink. There's a lot of demand for girls like that."

I nodded. "If I need to. But I'll try the stage first. I'm sure I can get parts, once I get a chance."

Lisette smiled gently. "That's what every-one says."

AUDITIONS

I wrote to Victor two days later.

Dear Victor,
You have been very unjust to me. You know perfectly well from the letter you received by accident that I have never slept with Ney, nor indeed kissed him or been alone with him or exchanged any tender words. You can see perfectly well that I have never been unfaithful to you with him.

Your reaction is completely out of proportion to my supposed crime.

Yes, I should not have written to him. And I will humbly apologize to you for that. But for you to act as though I have been unfaithful is beyond reason.

Ida

He did not reply.

■ ■ ■ ■

I went for the trials at the Théâtre de la République the next week. There were nearly a hundred young women there for six parts — six lovely Greek slaves who were supposed to fill out the background and go about pretending to serve at the couches in the symposium scene.

I did my recitation from *Phèdre,* the seduction of Hippolyte. Three other girls did the same piece. I sat in the hot theater watching them. The youngest must have been about fourteen, the oldest well over forty. They wore everything from schoolgirl frocks to pseudo-Greek drapery. There were blondes and brunettes, one stunning redhead with a thick Breton accent and skin like cream, a dark girl with gypsy looks, and one girl who was actually African with tightly curling black hair, who spoke her lines (Ismene, from *Antigone*) with the very best Parisian accent. She must have been brought here as some aristocratic woman's pretty slave years ago. The Revolution had freed her but given her no livelihood.

She came and sat in the row ahead of me when she was done. I leaned forward and whispered to her, "You were very good."

She looked back and smiled at me. "Thank you. I didn't hear you. I'm sure you were good too."

I shrugged. "I'm Ida."

"Dorée," she said. We might have whispered more, but the manager turned and shushed us. Not wanting to make a bad impression, we were very quiet.

In the end, she was chosen. So was the redheaded Breton, and four other girls. I wasn't. By that point in the day, I had not expected to be. I was a very ordinary blonde, with a very ordinary dress and a very ordinary recitation.

I wrote to Victor again.

Dear Victor,
I am sorry for my fault. I should not have written to Ney. It was foolishness, the kind of childish infatuation that I should have resisted. Please forgive me.
We were very happy together, weren't we?

Ida

He did not reply.

I did trials at the Théâtre Populaire the next week. Summer had come, and the theater was stifling during the day. I had learned a new piece, a comic one this time in anticipation of the Molière they planned to produce. I knew I hadn't gotten it when I left the stage. I was stiff and my comic delivery was poor. In short, I wasn't funny. And it seemed that the more I tried to be funny, the more I was only frenetic and desperate.

I went back and threw myself on my bed. The windows were all open; if Lisette's apartment would be freezing in the winter, at least there was a breeze in the summer. Lisette came in wearing her wrapper.

"Another late night?" I asked.

Lisette nodded and sat down tailor-style on the foot of the bed. "A private party. I take it the audition didn't go well."

"No," I said, rolling over and staring at the ceiling. "Lisette, I don't think I'm meant for comedy."

Lisette shrugged. "You're only auditioning for roles at the good theaters, not the burlesque in the Palais-Royal or the traveling troupes. Of course it's hard. And you don't have a patron. Or any experience."

"I'm pretty." I kicked my shoes off. "But Paris is full of girls who are pretty."

"I'm doing a private party next week and we need one more girl," Lisette said. "If you're interested. I can tell my friend."

I raised an eyebrow. "What kind of private party?"

Lisette shook her head, smiling. "Not that kind of party. It's really an acting job. An occult ritual."

"What?" I sat up.

"You know how there used to be laws against the occult and witchcraft, yes? Church laws? You could be burned at the stake for being a witch."

"Are there really any such things?" I asked. "I mean, there are fortune-tellers and things like that, but who believes in witchcraft? I suppose some people out in the country somewhere. . . ."

Lisette's face was serious. "What about the Masons?"

I laughed. "My father was a Mason. He joined when he was a soldier, and he was a Mason the entire time we lived in Italy. And I can absolutely guarantee you that there was nothing whatsoever occult about what he was doing. He was an atheist and a rationalist."

"Not all men of substance are," Lisette said. "There were rumors for years about witchcraft at court."

"And there were rumors that Marie Antoinette had orgies with footmen and the Princess de Lamballe," I said, remembering

Moreau's pamphlets. "But that's just dirt. I'm sure people said she paid witches to ensure drought and famine too."

Lisette didn't laugh it off. She regarded me very steadily. "I can tell you for a fact that there are powerful men in France who take the occult very seriously. There are secret lodges all over the place."

"If they're secret, why do they want to hire an actress?"

Lisette looked exasperated. "The legitimate lodges don't! But there are plenty of men who want to get into that kind of thing who can't get invited by the great. My friend knows this man who runs a scam. It's not really a lodge. It's a couple of his friends who invite some marks to pay 'initiation fees' to join a lodge, and they pay to go to rituals for a few months before they're told that they have progressed too far and need to go by themselves on a quest, and that if they're worthy they'll be contacted by the Secret Masters. And of course they never are. But in the meantime, he hires actresses to round out the group." Lisette shrugged. "Men are willing to pay a lot more for atmosphere that includes beautiful girls in classical robes."

"So what's the part? And what does it pay?"

"He's looking for a Spirit of the Dawn. You're supposed to light some incense and walk around with it and say a bunch of lines. I'm the Spirit of Evening. I get to asperge everyone with a sprig of rosemary and some holy water."

"So is there the Goddess of Reason?" I asked. Everyone had heard about Robespierre's plan a few years before to create elaborate festivals to celebrate the Goddess of Reason rather than the festivals of the Church.

"No," Lisette said. "There are four Elemental Maidens, and then Clemence, who does the scrying. She tells them all they're going to be wealthy and have beautiful women pursuing them. Sometimes she says they're going to be glorious in war or have an affair of the heart with a woman who is far above them, that kind of thing."

"All right. Tell your friend I'll do it."

I had a page of lines to learn. There was a long, tedious speech in badly written alexandrines about rosy-fingered dawn and how I was Aurora, the dawn maiden, who spreads her saffron robe over the skies. I also had a saffron robe. It was a muslin chemise dyed yellow, but it actually would look quite nice in limited light. Lisette assured me that these things were always as dark and atmospheric as possible. I wore my sandals with it, glad that I had saved them from the ruin of my life.

On midsummer's night, we took a hired carriage to a house near Saint-Germain-des-Prés. We were early. It was barely nine o'clock.

Charles Lebrun was a well-dressed young man of medium height, the very picture of a junior clerk or a deputy something-or-other. The house was a neat townhouse on a quiet street. The carriages arriving could have been for a respectable party. He greeted Lisette with a kiss on the cheek.

"Hello, lovely lady! I see you brought your friend! Don't worry, I'll pay up afterward."

"Before," Lisette said, still smiling.

He shrugged and grinned at me. "Mademoiselle Bellespoir drives a hard bargain. Before, then." He counted out our money. "Now, Madame, do you know your lines?"

I gave them for him.

He nodded absently. "Good, good. Nice and easy. No need to shout. There's only ten of us. Me and four guests, you maidens, and Clemence. It's not the entire Théâtre de la République. And what is your name, by the way?"

"Charmiane," I said, and had no idea why

I'd said it. Lisette shot me a quick look, but said nothing. It's a bad idea to keep your real name, but to be protective of a name that was already an alias seemed excessive.

"Charmiane, lovely." He was distracted by the sound of another carriage. "Oh, damn. Is that Monsieur Villiers? How can he be so early? Now I have to go take care of him. You two go on up — and for God's sake, don't talk loudly!"

Lisette took my hand as Lebrun hurried out to greet the first guest. "Come on, then. You can see the room." We went upstairs to the second floor.

The room in question was clearly intended to be the dining room, but the furniture had all been removed. There were heavy scarlet drapes at the window, and the walls were painted very nicely with imitations of classical frescoes. The doorways were also hung with heavy scarlet curtains, and an identical sconce had been hung on each wall, lit with tall beeswax tapers like the ones churches used in Italy. There were four small tables, one beneath each sconce. Mine had a heavy brass censer. It looked old. I guessed it had originally belonged to one of the churches in Paris before the Revolution. Inside was a cake of charcoal.

"You light the charcoal," Lisette explained,

"and then you open this box and drop some of it on the charcoal." She held out a pretty little china box.

I opened it. A rich scent rushed out. There were chips of amber-colored resin, some almost the color of honey, some dark brown. "Frankincense and myrrh," I said, bending my head and breathing deeply. The scent was warm and intoxicating, the scent of churches in Italy when I was a child. "I can do that."

Lisette nodded. "Then you just walk around the room that way once, and come back and put it down. The tabletop is tile, so you won't scorch it with the censer, see?"

Two more women had arrived. I assumed they were the other two Elemental Maidens, for Lisette greeted them. I said hello and then pleaded that I wanted to go over my lines. I stood quietly, my head bent over the paper. In the middle of the room there was a low table draped in black, one white candle and a blackened mirror. I kept looking away from it, but then looking back.

In a few minutes Lebrun came dashing upstairs. He closed the door carefully, then spoke quickly. "Clemence isn't coming. She's drunk. Anybody want to be our Sibyl tonight? You'll have to wing it."

"I will," I said, and was startled to hear

myself speak.

Lebrun turned quickly, smiling. "Ah, good! Let me take you aside, then. Give that paper to Lisette." He led me over by the window. "At first, don't say a lot," he said. "Just mumble and drop in some nice classical references if you can. Then when we get to the body of it, I'll try to keep it short. Villiers is going to want to know about his investments. Tell him in vague terms that he'll prosper, but don't get off on any particular stocks. Too easy for him to check. Noirtier will ask about the army. Just prophesy victory after long struggle. That's easy. Again, no specifics. You're not a damned almanac."

I laughed.

"Anything else, they're lucky in love and will meet a fascinating woman. You can go on about dark or fair, but don't give them anything about a particular person. Got it?"

I nodded.

"Good girl." Lebrun patted my arm. "And you can ham it up a bit. Moan. Roll your eyes. Don't make it look easy!"

"I'll do it," I said.

Lebrun stepped away. "All right, places, ladies! I'm going down to get our guests."

Adele stood by the censer. I didn't know what else to do, so I went and knelt by the little table. I didn't touch the mirror. In the darkened room, the faint shadows of people moving reflected oddly off the silvered glass. I looked down at my hands instead. *Breathe,* I thought. My heart was beating very fast.

We are all Doves, my mother had said. *We see things in mirrors. Elzelina would have been able to hear. . . .*

The gentlemen came in. I did not look at them. I knelt quietly and did not raise my head.

Adele said the lines that had been mine. The incense filled the room. Frankincense and myrrh. The scent of time. My eyes closed, and I heard the lines around me as from far away.

". . . for I am the Spirit of Fire, the breath of life. I am the summer sun, the golden orb of heaven. . . ."

In my mind's eye, the sun glanced through stained-glass windows. An angel with a sword of fire glowed bright, a red cloak billowing behind him, a white tabard over his silver armor, red device on white. The window split apart in unbearable brilliance before his glory.

". . . for I am the Spirit of Water, the depths of the ocean." I knew it was Lisette's voice, but it seemed very far away and strange. "I am the movement of mists, the rains of heaven. . . ."

Water beneath a leaping keel, the sound of the endless depths. Blue silence, and an octopus moving among submerged stones.

". . . the dark places of the Earth, cold stones and lost caves . . ."

Sunrise, and a cold morning, a standing stone twice my height at my elbow, watching the sun rising out of the cold North Sea. Far overhead the faint honking of geese, great flocks of them, the children of the sun, the children of this endless day when there would be hardly any night, just the sun dipping low for an hour or two. Out across the windswept straits a ship was coming, her prow curved upwards like a swan or a dragon, a ship to bring a prince home.

"Oh, great Sibyl!" Lebrun said at my elbow. "Will you not speak to us? Will you not look into the depths of time and tell us what you see? Speak! We entreat you!"

I remembered what I was supposed to be doing and opened my eyes. The blackened mirror reflected the vague shape of my face.

"Speak," Lebrun said dramatically to a man out of my line of sight. "Ask your question, my friend!"

"Shall my investments in the banking house of Ouvrard prosper?" he asked.

I moaned. "Ah, ah, ah!"

"Please tell me," he said, and I could hear the note of excitement in his voice.

"Jupiter rules a man of power," I said, trying to be both suitably poetic and obscure. "Power and prosperity are yours. Bright Jupiter ascends the heavens, and gold flows into the laps of the worthy."

There were some small delighted sounds.

"Let Monsieur Noirtier have his turn," Lebrun said. I assumed he was, directing traffic around the Sibyl. I did not move my eyes from the mirror. The candle flame's reflection wavered.

A different voice: "How shall fare Bonaparte's expedition in Egypt?"

This time I did not have to seek for the words. They were there as if they always had been. "He who would conquer Egypt must prepare to be conquered by it." The arching sky looked back at me in the mirror, clear as faience, blue as dreams. My voice ran on, my will somewhere behind it. "There is a ship with an eagle spread upon its sail, great oars moving in unison. Caesar has come in relentless pursuit of his enemy, to conquer and to be conquered. The Black Land does not give up her secrets easily, for we are older than time. We were old when he last came here, golden warrior, son of the gods."

There was a swift intake of breath behind me. Noirtier knelt down. "Can you tell me more?"

The light blurred, streaked like fire on water. "There will be fire on the deep, and Orient's loss will blind the eagle," I said. "It is not the sea that answers to his hand, but the deep-buried mysteries of the land. He has come to Alexandria now as once he came to Siwa, seeking truths that only the Black Land can show him, and there he must find his destiny, in the place where he chose it once before, when he turned away from the rest that was offered. It is easy to descend to the underworld, but returning is the difficulty."

Lebrun put his hand on my shoulder. "Monsieur, you must not tire her. This is very hard." Lebrun guided him gently away. "We are tiring our Sibyl," he said. "Gentlemen, see how she sways!"

I swayed for good measure. "I cannot . . ." I whispered.

"Rest yourself," Lebrun said. He covered the mirror ostentatiously with a piece of silk. I sat still and almost frozen. About me I heard their voices, the Maidens again with their last lines, the gentlemen getting up as it ended. I did not move.

At last Lebrun put his hand on my shoulder again. I lifted my head. He was grinning.

"Charmiane, you are a natural!" he exclaimed. "That was well done!" He helped me to my feet. "And here's a little bonus for you! All that blathering about Bonaparte in Egypt was perfect. You could read into it anything you like. A regular Nostradamus!"

"Thank you," I said. I felt a little unsteady on my feet. "Do you think I might have a glass of wine?"

He fetched me one, and when we left, Lisette and I went out to eat on my bonus at a little café not far away. I thought we deserved it. It was very merry and pleasant, and I felt all the strangeness going, replaced instead by a dawning sense of triumph. Here was something I could do well.

DEBUTS

I wrote to Victor again the next week.

> *Victor,*
> *Since you persist in this silence, this is the last note you will have from me. I am perfectly capable of supporting myself, and will soon be doing so on the stage.*
>
> *Ida*

This received a prompt reply. I tore it open and read it by the window in Lisette's apartment, a cup of coffee in my hand.

> *My dear Madame,*
> *Knowing your imprudent and impulsive nature, I am hardly surprised by your decision to take up acting. However, I beg you to reconsider. Despite the life you have led for the past several years, you are not entirely devoid of reputation in the eyes of the world, and are a woman of some*

consequence and distinguished anteced-
ents.

    *However, if you go on the stage you will
tarnish that reputation irretrievably by ally-
ing yourself with the lowest types of men
and women. Actresses lack your breeding,
birth, and taste, and are engaged in the
lowest forms of commerce. I beg you to
reconsider this hasty decision and consider better alternatives. It is from my abid-
ing respect for you that I speak.*

                      Victor Moreau

For a moment, I could scarcely see straight.

But I would not act precipitously, no. I would wait two days and then answer it. Because my answer would be the same.

My dear General,
*It is unbecoming for the champion of
liberty and social equality to suggest that I
am superior to my sisters because of my
breeding and birth. However, I expected
no less than this hypocrisy from you, who
of course are such a paragon of virtue and
traditional values.*

    *As for my hasty decision, my decision is
based upon necessity that you have forced
upon me. If you had not acted as you did,
for as little reason, I should not find what*

you term "the lowest forms of commerce"
necessary to my survival.

You are not the man I hoped you were.
And for that reason, we have nothing more
to say to one another.

Ida St. Elme

There was no reply. I did not expect one.

The next session with Lebrun was not nearly as spectacular, probably because the questions did not give me as much scope for poetry. "Shall my wife have a son or a daughter?" was particularly problematic. The gentleman in question was soon to become a father for the first time, and the answer must be either one or the other. I prevaricated and said that I could not tell.

Which, it turned out, was the right answer. Lebrun informed me the next week, grinning broadly the entire time, that the gentleman's wife had delivered safely and without incident healthy twin babies, a girl and a boy. It had made my reputation. He wished to engage me weekly as his medium.

This was a good thing, for my bank account was dwindling, I had no stage role, and I was not yet ready to start taking on private parties of a more intimate nature.

Following Lisette's advice, I had started

going to the auditions for the small companies as well as the big, respectable theaters. I was talking with Delacroix after one more endless and fruitless audition at the Théâtre de la République in early fall. He had dropped in to watch and was lounging in the last row of seats, his feet up on the back of the seat in front. I came back and sat with him after it was my turn. I hadn't done well and I knew it.

Delacroix sneezed delicately into a handkerchief. "Look, dear girl, you're never going to get a part this way. Most of the bit parts go to girls who are students of the theater. Sometimes when there's not someone it will go outside, but that's rare. And quite frankly, you're too old. They usually start in their early teens. How old are you, anyway? When's your birthday?"

"Not quite twenty," I said, shaving nearly two years off my age. I gave him Charles's birth date, December 28, 1778.

He shrugged. "You're too old. If you want to get to the top, you have to start at twelve or thirteen. You really need to just face it. Acting is an art. There's a lot more to learn than just being beautiful."

"I know," I said. I wasn't angry with him for telling me the truth. I looked down toward the stage. There was no one reciting right now, and a portly man was talking with the director. I recognized him. I had seen him at dozens of parties last year. I gestured toward him with my chin. "Isn't that Monsieur Chaptal, the Minister of Home Affairs? I wonder what he's doing here."

Delacroix nodded. "Home Affairs oversees the theater censors. Chaptal comes around now and then to look busy. And to look at the girls, of course. He doesn't know anything about theaters and he never bothers us much."

"Good," I said. "Because there's more than one way to get a part." I stood up, brushing the wrinkles from my dress.

"Ida, don't —" Delacroix began, but I was already walking down toward the front.

"Good afternoon, Monsieur Chaptal," I began, smiling and inserting myself next to him. "I thought that I recognized you! I would know you anywhere!"

He glanced at me, and his eyes widened. "Madame St. Elme! Good heavens! I had no idea you were here! I used to see you all the time, but it's been months now!"

I shrugged prettily. "Well, you know I always used to come with Moreau, but since I don't see him anymore, I have no opportunity to see you either."

"Not with Moreau? How can that be?"

I smiled up at him. "Gentlemen's fancies are capricious, my dear sir. We fragile barks are merely buffeted by their charms, and then left to wallow in the cruel waves."

"Can it be that you are without a protector?" Chaptal's face was florid with scarce-concealed delight.

"Unfortunately, it's so," I said. "So I am trying to earn my bread in the theater. But I haven't been able to even gain the opportunity to make my debut."

Chaptal looked at the director, his eyes wide. "Can it be? There is not even so much as a bit part for Madame St. Elme? A woman of her grace and wit?"

The director pursed his lips. "We have many qualified young ladies auditioning, and some must be disappointed."

"Well, of course some must be," Chaptal said. "But surely not her. I mean, what's to stop her?"

The director said nothing. Or perhaps he hadn't time to. "My dear Madame," Chaptal continued, "have you had luncheon yet?"

"I'm afraid not," I said. "I have been waiting all morning to audition, and had just finished when you arrived. I was hesitant to speak with you at first and presume upon old acquaintance, when the exigencies of life have so lowered my expectations."

"You must join me for lunch," he said. "La Belle Armoire? The shade of the gardens is exquisite."

I looked down at my dress in mock dismay. "Monsieur Chaptal, do you think I am quite dressed for such an elegant establishment? I am afraid that I have nothing new this season, and I hesitate to embarrass you in public."

His face clouded for a moment, but the storm was not for me. "You mean to tell me that Moreau didn't provide for you? That he put you off without so much as a purse?"

I glanced down modestly, as though I hesitated to reveal the truth. "I can speak no ill of Moreau," I said.

Chaptal took my arm. "We will go have lunch," he said gallantly. "And you look perfect."

We lunched elegantly on turtle soup with foie gras, then moved on to a variety of other treats, sitting in the shade of the big trees at La Belle Armoire. Chaptal gossiped about people I knew very slightly while I nodded and smiled and made myself very agreeable. We were all the way to the lemon ices before he got to the point. He leaned forward, a look of concern on his face. "I hesitate to pry . . ."

"Yes?" I smiled sadly at him. "Monsieur Chaptal, you are so kind. I could not consider your friendly advice to be prying."

"Is it really true that Moreau put you off with nothing?"

"With nothing except the clothes on my back," I said. "You may ask him if you don't believe me." To my surprise, I did not have to pretend to the choked sound in my voice. "I had nowhere to go. I was fortunate that one of the actresses from the Théâtre Populaire took me in. She has been more than generous to me. She is like a sister."

His kindly face clouded. "Damn. Excuse me, Madame." He cleared his throat. "That's not how a gentleman behaves. Especially not to a companion of many years who has been the ornament of his home. I'd thought better of Moreau."

I said nothing. If it was repeated to Victor's detriment, it was no more than the truth.

Tentatively, he put his hand over mine on the table. "I've always thought you were a fine-looking woman and a perfect hostess."

His hands were white and manicured, but he was no fool if he had not only held on to his head but managed a political appointment, even one as little distinguished as Minister of Home Affairs. There was nothing attractive about him except his admiration. Admiration is always flattering.

"I have always held you in the highest esteem as well, Monsieur Chaptal," I said. I smiled at him warmly. "You know, I do not even know your given name. But I am sure you know mine, and I would not mind if you used it. I consider us intimate enough for that."

"Jacques," he said. "Or you could call me Bobo, as my friends do. I hope you will consider dining with me on Friday. I would say tonight, but I have an engagement. You understand. . . . But the opportunity . . . I am not sure you will be alone long. So many gallant young soldiers . . ."

I lifted my wineglass in salute to him. "There are some things that improve with time. Wine is not the only one. Age brings character and deeper flavor."

Chaptal actually blushed. "Will you do me the honor of dinner?"

"I would be honored," I said. "And your fond regard is recommendation enough. I never had the opportunity to get to know you when I was with Moreau. It would not have been proper to spend much time with someone whom he so clearly would suspect of being a rival. I would not like to be the inadvertent cause of your being forced into an affair of honor."

Chaptal smiled happily. "I should not have liked a duel with Moreau. Fine soldier. But I'm no slack hand with a pistol, either. Challenged party chooses the weapon, you know."

"I am sure you are a fine shot," I said. "But what then should happen to France were you to wound her general thus, as I am sure you would?"

"It's better this way," he said, taking my hand and bringing it to his lips. "Oh, and I'll just have a little word with Monsieur David at the theater about your audition. I'm sure something can be arranged for you."

When I told Lisette about it, she sniffed. "You can do that. But everyone will hate you. They always do, when a girl has screwed her way in rather than getting in on merit."

I shrugged. "So they will hate me. I need the money."

"Chaptal's fickle," Lisette said. "He changes girls every few months. Oh, nothing bad is ever said. He doesn't beat his women or do anything strange. But his attention wanders to whatever is new and interesting. Look how fast he was on to you! He does that all the time."

"I know," I said. "He never brought the same girl twice to a party. But as long as he gets me a part, I'm satisfied if he gets bored next month."

"One part. And then you're never cast again if they hate you," Lisette said. "You were doing better with the medium act."

"It doesn't pay enough to live on. And given the choice between Chaptal and walking the arcades of the Palais-Royal, I'll take Chaptal."

We had dinner at his townhouse on Friday, and then retired upstairs. Compared to Moreau, his tastes were bread-and-butter. Youth and beauty were spurs enough to his passion and he needed no embellishments. For all that he seemed older, he was scarcely more than Victor's age. The Directory was filled with young men, and forty was not old. I told him that he was a stallion, a bull, a fine specimen of manhood indeed. He did not notice that I was not much moved.

Afterward, as his carriage delivered me home, I looked out the window at the crowds still streaming into the Palais-Royal, to the coffee shops and dubious amusements. This felt like the first time I had sold myself. Yes, of course that was what it had been with Victor, but it had not felt that way. He was as conscious of my dignity as of his own. He had not, until the very end, made me feel as though I were his property rather than his lover.

I had not felt repulsed by Chaptal, merely bored. If I had found it disgusting, perhaps I would know that I had some womanly feeling, some decency left. Instead, I had merely wondered, even at the height of the act, how much longer he intended to go on and how much longer I should need to keep up theatrical sighs and moans.

I had never wondered that with Victor. All the sighs and moans had been real.

Perhaps, I thought, *most men are like this. Perhaps I will never be moved again. But at least I know that I have the stomach for it. I can do this. I don't really mind. I do not come home like the ruined women onstage, weeping and lamenting, but simply a bit tired and dissatisfied.*

The next day I had a note from M. David, the Director at the Théâtre de la République. I was cast in an afternoon matinee, a review of famous moral stories from antiquity, told in eight scenes. It would open in seven weeks, and I should be in the third scene, cast as Dido, Queen of Carthage.

DIDO'S REVENGE

"Oh, tell me not that it is fate! Oh, tell me not that you must fly!" I lamented. "Gracious Juno, make this pyre my marriage bed!"

The director cleared his throat loudly. "Try to sound like you're talking to Aeneas, not to the third row. And look at him, not up at the flies."

"I thought I was talking to Juno," I said.

"Juno is not up in the flies either," the director snapped. "You are giving the audience a view of your chin. Get your head down and turn your face to three-quarters like you're talking to Aeneas."

It was a very poor rehearsal, and I said so to Lisette afterward.

"A poor dress rehearsal means a good performance," she said. "Supposedly."

"Thank you," I said. "It's not nerves. It's just that things keep going wrong. People keep stepping on my lines, and I've been late twice because I was told the wrong rehearsal time."

Lisette shook her head. "I told you people would hate you if you got the part because of Chaptal. Is he coming to the opening tomorrow?"

I nodded. "He's bought the best box. And he's having a party for me afterward at Les Palmiers."

Lisette raised an eyebrow. "Very nice. He must be very taken with you."

"I think so," I said. "He wants to see me at least twice a week. And he's told me to order a dress for the party and charge it to him."

The dress was perfectly lovely. It was white silk brocade with a faint jacquard pattern, white on white. It was cut low in the bosom, showing my breasts lifted by the stiff half-corset, and full in the skirts, falling in gorgeous draping folds. A pair of white brocade mules went with it.

Of course, this was not my stage costume. That could not have been worse suited to my complexion or looks. It was a long-sleeved garment of scarlet satin, with long trailing sleeves slashed with gold cord. It was not fitted closely, and the bodice was padded an absurd amount and trimmed with more gold cord. Perhaps it would have looked good on a dark-eyed, dark-haired woman with a vivid complexion. It made me look entirely washed-out, and the gold cord made my hair look dingy in comparison. The cut would have flattered a shorter woman, and given her the height and substance she needed. It merely made me look freakishly large and as broad-shouldered as a dragoon.

Lisette came by to help me dress. I saw her biting her lip.

"What's the matter?" I said, looking in the mirror. I looked like a ghost with dirty hair.

Lisette picked up the rouge pot and began sweeping it over my cheekbones. "You need some color," she said. "You shouldn't be wearing scarlet. Platinum blondes with pale complexions can, but not a honey blonde with a pink complexion."

"I look like a clown," I said.

"I'm doing the best I can," Lisette snapped. "It's supposed to be heavy for the stage, heavier than you'd wear anywhere else." She bent low to my ear. "What did I tell you about people hating you?"

I nodded miserably. "I know. The costume is terrible. But what can I do about it?"

"Nothing. You'll just have to act."

"You're right," I said. "After all, it's not my fault the costume is gaudy. I'll just have to do well anyway."

"That's the spirit," Lisette said. "Just do your best. Anyhow, Chaptal will still be here, no matter how you do."

There was a knock on the door. One of the rigger boys stuck his head in. "Madame St. Elme? Somebody left these for you." He held out a bouquet of white roses tied with white and silver ribbons.

I took them from him. They were almost scentless, and this late in the fall must have been grown in a greenhouse or a sheltered place. There were a dozen of them full-blown, not budding. "How beautiful!" I held them up.

"Who are they from?" Lisette asked.

There was no card with them. I asked the boy, "Who was the gentleman who left these?"

He shrugged. "I didn't see him. Someone came round to the stage door and said they'd been left at the box office."

"And lost the card, I suppose," said Lisette, looking for a vase. "They're lovely. I suppose they came from Monsieur Chaptal."

"They must have," I said. "White roses are my favorite."

There was another knock on the door. "Ten minutes!"

I looked around. "Where are my shoes?" They had been sitting right beneath my costume in this dressing room shared with six other women. They were gone.

"Someone must have picked them up," Lisette said. "Don't get down on the floor in your costume! Let me look under there!" She started crawling around under the tables and chairs.

I hunted frantically through the piles of clothes left lying around. None of the other women helped. They just kept putting their makeup on.

"Two minutes!"

I looked at Lisette and she looked at me. "No shoes," I said. They were very high-heeled gold shoes with pointed toes.

"Shit," Lisette said succinctly. We both knew what had happened.

I went on barefooted. Which made my costume much too long. This was a good thing, since you couldn't see my feet at all. Barefooted was marginally better than wearing my very modern and entirely inappropriate white shoes.

The footlights along the bottom of the stage had been kindled, oil lamps in glass globes that were supposed to shield the lights and keep our skirts from catching fire. Above, the lights hanging from the pin rail were bright. And the house was full.

I looked across the stage, and it seemed very far. The young girl who was playing my sister Anna came up behind me. "Ready?"

I nodded. Across the endless expanse of stage, M. Lamorial waited in his chiton and gilded sandals, a gold wig over his dark curls. I walked on, Anna pacing after.

"Where is beautiful Aeneas?" I asked. "He has said that he would meet me, and yet I wait in vain."

"Here he comes," Anna said.

Lamorial stepped onstage and bowed. "Gracious queen," he said. "Your loveliness eclipses the sun. And yet I must wrong you, gentle soul, generous benefactor."

"What? Oh how!" I exclaimed, trying to walk forward in my too-long skirts. I reached up with my left hand instead of my right, realizing too late that I was gesturing with the wrong arm and blocking my own face. I switched precipitously.

"Father Jupiter has decreed that I must leave your shores, gentle queen," Lamorial declaimed. "For it is a high fate that leads me to the shores of Latium, where in pleasant climes I must found a city worthy of my Dardanian forefathers and the gods of sacred Troy. There it is prophesied that I shall prove the foundation of a mighty race."

"Oh! Oh!" I exclaimed. "My wounded heart! Is there naught that I can say to turn you from this fate? Not my riches, not my love?"

Lamorial took my hand. "Were it only riches or love, I should tarry in Parthenopean glades forthwith. No, it is fate that leads me on, fate and the winds that Father Jupiter encourages to move our fragile ships." He was getting into the scene, and he dropped on one knee before me, looking up at me out of blue eyes. "I pray you, lady, do not despair. I know that you grieve, and that your heart cannot be healed. I fear that I shall see you no more under the sun."

"No," I said, taking my hand from his and looking off into the bright lights. They made my eyes water, and suddenly I felt a wave of strangeness breaking over me, as though I watched this farce from outside. "You shall not see me again beneath the sun. Perhaps in that fair land between the rivers, where luckless mortals dwell forever in starlight, you will see me in the meads of lilies and know that it was your cruelty that drove me there. Perhaps you will regret your folly then. Perhaps in those empty places between the River Styx and the River Lethe, memory at last will fail me and I will be spared the recollection of your face."

I should have eaten, I thought. *Oh, God, I am actually going to faint. Oh, God, for the first time in my life, now is not a good time to faint.* I reached forward and seized Aeneas by the shoulder. "Oh, Dardanian Prince! Oh, beloved son of Venus! Do not wound me thus!"

Lamorial looked shocked that I had grabbed him and staggered off balance on one knee. It didn't help that he was a small, slight man, and in my giant robe with my height, and him down on one knee, I towered over him. I heard a faint titter of laughter run through the audience. "Gracious queen, I must," he said.

Anna took my arm. "Oh, dear sister!"

Aeneas struggled to his feet, shaking off my grip. "I must go. The bounding waves call me, the winds of Aeolus even now fill my sails."

"No!" I shrieked. Three more lines. I felt the world swimming around me.

He backed a step or two away, raising his arm in farewell. "I must go. My heart is breaking! How can I be parted from your bounteous generosity?"

Bounteous brought forth another titter of laughter. I felt the blood rising to my already scarlet-painted face. "I shall die! Oh,

271

tell me not that it is fate! Oh, tell me not that you must fly! Gracious Juno, make this pyre my marriage bed!"

"Farewell!" he said. "My heart too is broken!" and bounded offstage as I collapsed into Anna's arms. Unfortunately, I tripped on my overlong skirts, and would have flattened her with my full weight if the curtain hadn't come swinging down as she staggered beneath me.

I ran off the stage and back to the dressing room. No one else was there. The other women were all in the next scene that was starting. I looked in the mirror. My eyes were bright with unshed tears and my face was a carnival mask, a parody of beauty.

There was a soft knock. It was Delacroix. I looked at him and shrugged.

He came over and patted my shoulder.

"Was it bad?" I asked.

"Darling," he said, "you were horrible."

I burst out laughing. It was terribly inappropriate. But what else was there to do?

I was still laughing when M. David, the director, came back. "I'm glad you find it so funny, Madame," he said. "However, I do not. The Dido and Aeneas scene will not appear in the next performance, or in any future performance. We are not a comedy troupe, Madame. We are the Théâtre de la

République!" He swept out and slammed the door.

Delacroix shrugged. "Well, that's that."

"Go out so I can change," I said. "Chaptal will be waiting, and there is a table at Les Palmiers. I hope you'll join us."

"Of course," he said, and bent and kissed my brow. "I wouldn't miss your best performance of the evening." He closed the door carefully behind him.

I cleaned off my makeup. Lisette had been right. It did no good if they hated me. But I still had Chaptal, and now I must make myself bright and agreeable for him, even if half of Paris was laughing at me. Or perhaps with me. Perhaps I could pass it off as deliberate comedy.

By the time the show ended and Chaptal came around to the stage door, I was wearing my white dress and was fit for company. I carried the bunch of white roses, and I had tucked one into my hair.

If Chaptal had seen anything amiss in the performance, he did not say so. Instead, he greeted me with a huge mixed bouquet and embraced me enthusiastically. "My dear lady! A masterful performance! Amazing! You nearly brought me to tears!"

"Of mirth," Delacroix said in a low voice behind me.

I ignored him and embraced Chaptal. "Bobo, I can't tell you how much that means to me! And to find the lovely flowers from you in my dressing room was simply wonderful!"

"Flowers?" Chaptal looked surprised. He looked at the big mixed bouquet he had been carrying. "Those are the flowers I sent you, dear lady. I didn't send any around to your dressing room."

"Oh." I shrugged. "There was no card and I thought they were from you. Never mind." I kissed his cheek. "I love this beautiful bouquet. Thank you so much!"

He put my wrap around my shoulders and we went out into the rainy street. His carriage was waiting.

I stopped. I glanced back. The street was busy with theater-goers hailing hired carriages or stepping into their own. Others were leaving on foot, or milling about talking with friends and acquaintances in the gathering dusk. I could have sworn that someone was watching me. There was no one, but still I felt odd, as though someone were waiting just out of sight.

"Ida?" Chaptal said, still holding out his hand to help me into the carriage.

"I was distracted for a moment. I thought I saw someone I knew."

■ ■ ■ ■

Chaptal and I lasted through the end of the old year, which I understood was something of a feat with him. True to form, he broke it off handsomely, over dinner in a public place where I could not scream or cry. He gave me a purse and a not terribly expensive topaz ring and thanked me for a lovely time.

I made appropriate noises of dismay, but in truth I wasn't disappointed. My bank account was much improved by the relationship, and I was running out of dramatic sighs for the bedroom. Nothing seemed to excite him like novelty, and after a few months my body was starting to be too familiar.

So I wiped my eyes bravely, told him that I should miss him, and went home to lie on the sofa and eat food carried out from a tavern with Lisette.

I still had a weekly appointment with M. Lebrun to scry for his clients. Most of the questions were quite dull and repetitive. Finances, marriages, affairs, and business ventures of various sorts were the usual questions, and most of those could be managed with stock answers. As the weeks passed, I found it easier and easier to give them without being distracted as I had been the first time, to imagine enough but not too much.

One evening very early in the spring, there was a young man who struck me more than the usual ones. He had his right arm in a black silk sling, and he had come with two friends who were very cheerful. I thought they had all had a few drinks before they arrived, though they calmed down well once the ritual started. I saw from the way they stood and their respectful silences that they had done something of the kind before. I could always tell the people who had some legitimate lodge in their background from the way they moved inside the space delineated by the censer.

I saw, when I lifted my eyes for a moment from the blackened mirror, that he was wearing the uniform of a naval lieutenant, and his hair was cut short in the new, modern Brutus cut, curling just a little over his collar. He had olive skin, and he was quite handsome.

When it was his turn to ask a question, he leaned almost too close. "To what ship will my next posting be, and what will be her fate?" He had a faint Catalan accent.

I mumbled some nonsense and looked in

the mirror. And then I saw it in my mind's eye, a small ship in a harbor I did not recognize, wreathed in mist. I told him what I saw. "She waits for you in port," I said, "in a broad port beneath a headland with a single lighthouse. The seas are steel gray and the wind blows straight into the harbor. She's a small ship, with only one line of ports down her sides, and six guns on deck."

"Is there a figurehead?" he asked keenly.

Lebrun moved as if to stop me, but I went on. "Yes," I said, trying to see more closely. "It's a woman carrying a shield. There's a head on the shield, a device of some kind."

"Minerve," the young man breathed.

One of his friends spoke. "*Minerve* is under repair at Le Havre."

Lebrun stepped forward. "Enough, Lieutenant. You must not tire our Sibyl. Please let the others have their turn." He didn't like it when people pressed me to be too specific.

After all the guests had left that night, Lebrun came up to me as I was putting my cloak on. "All right?"

I nodded. "Fine."

He put his hands in his pockets. After a moment, he looked at me sideways. "How do you do it?"

"Do what?" I was hunting for one misplaced glove.

"Tell them things that are true. Things you can't guess. And don't tell me you know where half the frigates in the French navy are berthed. Or have some idea what that fellow's posting will be. You don't even know his name."

I shrugged. "I don't know," I said, carefully not looking at him. The glove was on the floor under the chair. "Sometimes I just know. I make things up and I know they're right."

"Have you ever done this kind of thing before?"

I looked at him then. There was no mockery in his face. "No," I said. "I can read tarot cards. And my mother said . . ." I hesitated to tell him.

"What?"

"That women in our family can see things in mirrors. My mother is crazy, mind you. It doesn't mean anything. That we're Doves, whatever that means." I shrugged again to show him I didn't believe any of it, and that of course I wasn't curious. "Do you know what that means?"

Charles Lebrun sighed deeply. He sat down on the chair. "I do," he said. "That's what some traditions call the person who's supposed to scry. In the old days it was a virgin boy or girl, usually a child, who was supposed to be the vessel for whatever invoked entity they had called. More recently, it's a young woman." He grinned. "Not necessarily a virgin."

"I suppose not," I said. I sat down next to him on the other chair.

"I've never done that kind of work," he said, "invoking demons. I know there are some people in Paris who do. It's too dangerous."

"You mean you believe they're real?" I was startled. "But this is a scam!"

Lebrun raised an eyebrow. "Is it? Aren't you telling them the truth?"

"Yes," I said. "At least, as best I can."

"You're the real thing," he said. "I'm surprised, but I've heard of such. A natural Dove. I imagine you could host a demon if you tried."

"I'd rather not!" I said.

"I thought you didn't believe in demons?" he said. "This is a scam?"

"I'm not even pretending to be possessed by a demon," I said. The entire idea filled me with dread.

"How about an angel?" Lebrun asked. "Angelic possession is much easier, I'm told. I've got some clients interested in doing an angelic invocation, and they've done all the regular sessions before. I either have to cut them loose or give them something better. And I'll share the cut with you fifty-fifty if you'll do an angelic possession." He touched my arm. "You can fake it, you know."

"I'll think about it," I said. "How much are we talking about?"

"Seven hundred francs, split two ways," he said. "Thereabouts. After I've paid the Elemental Spirits."

"Who do they want to invoke?" I asked.

"The Archangel Michel, patron of battles," Lebrun said.

RENÉ

A few days later, I was to meet Lisette for lunch in a café just off the Palais-Royal. It was the first day of the year that really felt like spring, and I asked for an outside table even though the air was still a little chilly. Lisette was late, but the café was cheap and I was early for lunch, so the waiter didn't care if I sat for a while.

The crowds in the Palais-Royal had picked up. Lots of people were taking advantage of the sunshine to stroll and to look in shop windows. Several flower vendors were doing a brisk business, and right next to the outdoor tables a pair of street musicians had settled in, a woman singing and a man who played the Breton harp.

I ordered white table wine, which the waiter brought immediately. The sun was warm. The glancing sun struck sparks off the glass, reflections in the wine, winking off cutlery like a mirror, reflections of remembered fire, like Lebrun's mirror. The woman's voice was clear and true, like some other I had known but couldn't remember, could not put a name to.

. . . an old-fashioned tower room and a woman singing, her long red hair caught up in pins at the back of her neck, pale as a swan's in her square-necked dress of black velvet. She smiled, and her smile was for me. Her eyes were warm, and her expression was just like Ney's, open and fair and just a little awkward. She didn't sing before company often, I thought. I knew that about her. And in a moment she'd move, tilt her head another way, and I would remember her name —

"Mademoiselle? Are you well?" A voice beside me interrupted me. I looked up, startled, into the concerned eyes of the young naval lieutenant from the last scrying session.

I jumped. "Yes, quite well," I said. "My mind wandered for a moment, that's all."

He nodded very seriously. His arm was still in a sling, but his uniform was freshly tailored and probably new. "I think we've met. Though under the circumstances, I don't know your name. But you were quite right about me being posted to *Minerve*. My orders arrived yesterday. I'm to report next month. I can't imagine how you did that."

He pulled out the chair opposite me. "Lieutenant René Gantheaume. I don't suppose you know my name either, unless Lebrun told you. He's an old faker, but my friends told me that you were the genuine thing, so I had to come see." He looked at the chair he was holding. "May I?"

"I'm waiting for a friend," I said.

Gantheaume grinned. "He's late and I'm not."

"She," I said, smiling. It was hard not to respond to his infectious charm. I held out my hand. "And it's Madame St. Elme."

He bent over it gracefully. "I should have known. All the pretty ones are married."

"Tragically, I'm a widow," I said.

He glanced at my light-blue spring dress. "I trust your bereavement wasn't recent?"

"Several years ago," I said. "As you can see, I'm prostrate."

He laughed and sat down opposite me. He was dark and graceful, and hardly more than a year or two my senior.

"How is your wound?" I asked. "You don't seem to be suffering greatly."

"It was painful enough to begin with. But now it's quite bearable, thank you. I can still manage quite a lot, even with a broken arm."

"Is that a threat or a promise?" I asked,

cutting my eyes at him. His uniform was indeed new, and the braid was real bullion.

"Whichever you prefer." He signaled to the waiter. "I'll have what the lady is having." The waiter nodded and disappeared.

"Do make yourself at home," I said.

"Thank you, I will." Gantheaume set his hat on one of the empty chairs and grinned again. "I have so few days to have lunch with pretty ladies before the coils of war again ensnare me."

"Alas," I said, smiling. "And you cherish every opportunity to make precious memories to sustain you amid your travail?"

"Couldn't have put it better myself," he said. "Spoken like a cavalry lieutenant. They always say they're better at gallantry than us poor navy boys."

"You look like you're doing well enough," I said.

The waiter returned with his wine. "I have a rich and doting uncle and a pocket full of prize money. And just twenty-nine days to enjoy it before it's back to Le Havre and the sea." He raised his glass. "To liberty. And a pleasant leave."

I touched my glass to his, smiling. "You are the most transparent rogue," I said. "What makes you think I don't have a protector?"

He shrugged. "If you had, you would have said so by now. Or perhaps you'd not mind a charming and transparent rogue on the side? A genuine naval hero who could go to his doom with the image of your fair countenance before his eyes?"

I burst out laughing. "Lieutenant Gantheaume —"

"René. I insist that you call me René."

"René, then. Just what did you have in mind?"

"Dancing at the Exchange tonight? An intimate midnight supper?" His black eyes were bright.

"How intimate?"

He grinned again, showing very white teeth. He hadn't been at sea long enough for them to be otherwise, presumably. "For only two. I don't intend to share you with all my friends."

"That would be extra," I said, still smiling.

He looked at me as though he wasn't sure whether to take me seriously or not.

I raised my glass. "The kind of memorable leave you seem to be proposing isn't cheap. I hope you have plenty of prize money. My last protector was a cabinet minister."

He hesitated a moment, then touched his glass to mine. "Why the hell not? I've got twenty-nine days, and if I go back to sea flat broke it won't matter. Better to have a leave to remember."

"I'll make it unforgettable," I promised. After all, why not? Why not someone my own age who was handsome and charming?

I had expected that he would have a hired room, but instead that evening he took me back to an elegant old house on Île Saint-Louis. A bewigged butler opened the door. "Master René," he said, bowing respectfully.

"Good evening, Louis," he said, handing him his hat and my wrap. "I trust you've got a collation laid out."

"Yes, sir. In the green room, sir."

René escorted me down the hall to a lovely little Louis XIV parlor where a table was drawn up near the fire, two gilt chairs beside it, the cushions worked with golden roses on a celadon background. He held my chair for me with a flourish.

"Very nice," I said. "Surely this isn't yours?"

He sat down opposite me. "I told you I had a rich and doting uncle. Admiral Gantheaume. I thought you would recognize the name. But he's at sea right now, and fortunately told me to make free with his house while I'm in town."

"I don't know the naval commanders," I said. "Mostly the army."

"Aha!" René exclaimed. "I knew you'd gone with some army fellow or other. Probably someone who ranks a measly lieutenant."

"I was with General Moreau for nearly two years," I said.

He whistled. "Ranks a measly lieutenant indeed. I thought for a moment you were going to say Bonaparte."

"Why should you think that? I've never met him," I said. "I don't really have an opinion of him." Moreau, of course, had a great deal to say about him, but I wasn't quoting Moreau anymore.

"He's a genius," Rene said. "I met him in Alexandria last year, when we were supplying the Expeditionary Force. Best general the Republic has, in the opinion of this measly lieutenant. He talks to you like you're really there."

"What does that mean?" I asked, helping myself to the smoked trout.

René took a moment to gather his thoughts. "Most senior officers don't notice lieutenants any more than you notice a waiter or a footman. When you're a lieutenant, you're part of the furnishings. Part of the military trappings. Bonaparte sees you.

He actually talks to you. He remembers people's names and what they do. I think half his staff is in love with him."

I laughed. "That's the kind of thing the army says about the navy and the navy about the army! We all know about sailors, don't we?"

He took it in good humor. "I'll show you all about sailors after a bit! If you've never had one before, you should come over to our side. You'll never go back to great brutes smelling of horse." He shrugged, and his face stilled. There was a good mind behind those laughing eyes, I thought, a young man with more to him than bravado and charm. "Not like that, I mean. He looks at you, and it's like he's not just seeing you. He's seeing what's inside you. Something more. You reminded me a little bit of him, just a shadow. He's more than real, maybe. Like the realest thing in the world."

I shivered involuntarily. "A general who reminds you of a woman who does séances? I'm not sure that's a recommendation."

"A general who reminds me of a companion? I'm not sure that is either." René grinned. "Not really. Not what I meant by love. I shouldn't have expected you to understand."

"Why should I? You know what I am," I

said, shrugging prettily. "I'd much rather you showed me the truth about sailors."

But I knew what he meant. I knew far too well, and a sorrow I could not place pierced me to the heart. I kissed him so that I could forget it.

Perhaps that conversation was what spoiled my mood. I went through the evening feeling slightly off-kilter the entire time. It was nothing René did. He was handsome and considerate, and after Chaptal's heavy-handed intercourse he should have been a fresh wind. He was certainly skilled enough. If his tastes were less extreme than Moreau's, at least he could think of something to do besides the obvious.

And yet I was oddly detached. My mind kept wandering. I was thinking about the rent and the book that I would now be able to afford since I hadn't counted on a month of companionship. I kept falling out of that place where one should be making love, losing the rhythm and pushing myself back into it. And a few minutes later I would drift off again. I pushed myself hard to come, and finally did with his hand on my pearl and his lips against my throat. But it didn't feel quite right, and when I lay beside him afterward I could not sleep.

I rolled over to the edge of the bed, beyond his outflung hand. Would it be different if it were someone else? Or was it that I missed Moreau's games of passion, and now answered only to dominance and humiliation?

Get a grip on yourself, I told myself sternly. *René is a kind young man, a charming lover, as pleasant and accommodating as any woman could want. If it's Moreau you're missing, you'll have to get used to it. And if it's Ney or some other dream lover you're wanting, then you need to grow up. Don't throw away a piece of luck because it's not your beautiful ideal. What's a month with a handsome, generous man? Enjoy it while it lasts and make the most of it, as he will.*

René Gantheaume left for Le Havre and the frigate *Minerve* a week before Walpurgis Night. It had been a perfectly spectacular leave. We had dined out somewhere nice and expensive every night; there had been fireworks displays over the Seine, picnics in the Bois de Boulogne, theater and dance halls. And night after night at the Admiral's house on Île Saint-Louis.

I saw him onto the coach for Le Havre, kissed him goodbye to the cheers of two of his friends. And of course the coach didn't start right away. He got back out and came and stood with me while the coachman and the stable master discussed the foot of the left rear horse. René loosened his stock. It was going to be a warm day. "Will you be all right?" he asked.

"Of course," I said. "It was fun, wasn't it?"

He nodded, and there was something wistful in his face. "Another month and I might have won you."

"I think you've already had me quite thoroughly."

"Not really." René looked over at the equine mysteries transpiring. Now there was a farrier in it, pointing and gesturing. "Your heart . . ."

"My heart is not for sale," I said gently. "Or even for rent."

"Who does it belong to? Moreau?"

I shrugged. "René, would you believe me if I told you that it was a man I've met one time, who probably doesn't even remember my name? And I have no idea why."

"I would believe you," he said. "There are some strange things in this world, like currents that cross beneath the sea. Who is he?"

"A soldier," I said. "I dream about him. I dream that I know him, that we are meeting in some distant place and we are old friends, that he's my lover, my husband, my son, my master, even my prince. Sometimes I hear something and it brings it back to me like a punch in the stomach, like seeing an old lover across a crowded street." I didn't know why I was confiding in René, but how could it hurt? He was off for Le Havre and the sea, and he had been kind.

"Perhaps you've known him before," René said. "In some other life."

I looked around at him sharply. "You believe in that kind of thing?"

René shrugged. "I don't know why not. I'd rather believe in Virgil's underworld than Dante's."

"As simple as that? You can dismiss eighteen centuries of Christianity like that?"

"Why not? If men can worship Reason or the gods of India, pray to Buddha or a Deist clockmaker, why not Mars or Aphrodite? Doesn't it all come down to the same thing in the end?"

"Does it?" I asked. "To dismiss Church and Reason both?"

He put his hands gently on my shoulders. "I'm a sailor, Ida. I don't claim to understand the workings of eternity. But a simple builder who hauls stone to the work site doesn't understand the plan of the great cathedral he builds, how the mathematics of the buttresses work, how the windows should be made, and yet he contributes to the work. I'm a sailor, and you're a courtesan. Neither of us can see the pattern. But that doesn't mean it's not there."

I looked at him, and it was as though I were really seeing him for the first time. There was a tiny squint line beginning between his brows, the shadow of a beard on his face though he had shaved only a few hours before.

"Make up a story for me," he said. "Don't worry about whether it's real. Just tell me a story."

I dropped my eyes to the glitter of braid on his arms, tried to catch a reflection of the sun. "A rower," I said. "A rower with a wounded shoulder. On a galley under sail in a heaving storm." I could imagine the green sea washing up her sides, the movement of the deck beneath me, the cold seawater around my ankles as I struggled to move an unmanned oar, to get it inside so it didn't foul the stroke. The wind tore at me and the rain lashed down. "A wounded rower," I said, "with an arrow in his shoulder —"

"Gantheaume? Are you coming?" They had finished whatever they were doing with the horse, and the driver was swinging up.

"I have to go," René said.

"I know." I held on to him for a moment. The transition was too abrupt.

"Find out," he said. "What do you have to fear from knowledge that's worse than ignorance?" He leaned forward and kissed my cheek. "Good-bye, pretty lady."

"Good-bye," I said. "Until we meet again."

When I got home, there was a note waiting for me from Lebrun.

Dear Madame St. Elme,
Have you decided whether or not you will take on the challenging prospect we discussed? If so, Walpurgis Night is the ideal time. I await your answer.
                    I am your servant,
                    Charles Lebrun

I put the note down on the table and went to open the window to the street. From four stories below the sounds from a greengrocer's stand floated up to me, and the fresh smell of herbs brought in from the country. The old plaster was cool against my hand as I leaned against the window frame. What did I have to fear indeed? I got out paper and quill and wrote to Lebrun.

Dear Monsieur Lebrun,
I will do the thing we spoke of. I should
like to talk to you before Walpurgis Night
so that I may know what to expect. I will
call your angel for you.

Ida St. Elme

WALPURGIS NIGHT

I went to Lebrun's house before sundown on Walpurgis Night. He showed me the room and walked me through the procedure carefully, though I already knew my lines. He seemed nervous.

"There are only four clients," he said. "Just four. You've seen Monsieur Husar before at scrying sessions, so there's nothing to worry about from him. Also Leroy, the jeweler. He's been here too."

I nodded. "I know them both. It will be fine. Who are the other two?"

"Noirtier," he said. "The one who always asks too many questions. And Bonnard, who is new, but he's in banking and has a huge amount of money. I've heard he bought his way into Grand Orient." He paced around the room. "I don't need to tell you to be careful. And stay inside the circle. Don't break the circle."

"You've told me twenty times," I said. "I'd

be more worried about Bonnard wandering off, if I were you."

This time my gown was sheer white muslin, with no trim or ribbons anywhere, and my arms were bare. It was more like a chemise than anything else, but if part of the charm of this little scenario was me in my underclothing, then that was well enough. I had certainly been seen in far less by some of Moreau's guests on at least one memorable occasion.

Then Lebrun's clients arrived, and I lost myself in the ritual.

There is a grace to it that you don't feel until it becomes custom, until the movements and words within the circle of candles become second nature, until they are no longer lines that you have learned but things you know. This night was the first time it was that way for me. Perhaps because this was the first time that I was willing to believe. Or at least to forget that I tried not to believe.

The candlelight, the incense, the darkness of the room outside the circle drew me in, pulling me into that feeling of strangeness, of uncanny concentration.

"Spirit of Air, morning's breath and dawn's light . . . Spirit of Fire, noontide's heat and day's brightness . . . Spirit of

Water, evening's tide and twilight's softness . . . Spirit of Earth, night's peace and
midnight's skies . . ." The words blurred
together, and I was no longer conscious of
them as words, but of their meaning, the
wheel turning and turning, dove-gray dawn
to brightness, afternoon's glare to evening's
purple shades, fading to midnight and the
cool before dawn, turning and turning
again.

Lebrun began chalking the floor around
where I knelt on a black silk cushion. Greek,
Hebrew, a little Latin. Symbols that didn't
match the words. I was glad that it was no
demon he summoned. The circle he chalked
was wrong. Why I thought that, I could not
say. I had never seen one like it, but I knew
it was wrong, that it would hold nothing
that did not wish to be held.

— *It's impolite,* something whispered
amused in my head, *to invite a guest and tie
him up.* —

Unless he likes that sort of thing, I thought.

— The sense of amusement was stronger.
*If you want to speak with an enemy, you send
a challenge, a summons to do battle. But if
you want to speak with a friend, it's much
more polite to just send a note.* —

I smiled.

Lebrun raised his arms and murmured a

series of nonsense syllables. "Enochian," he said aside for the benefit of the guests, "the ancient and secret language of the angels."

Really? I thought.

— *No,* said the voice beside me, still amused. *Angels speak whatever language you do, because they speak the language of the heart.* —

You're talking in my head, I thought. *Are you real?* A moment of panic overtook me. I was like my mother. I was hearing voices, talking to people no one could see. I was going mad and —

— *Calmly,* he said. It was like a steadying hand on my shoulder. *Think calmly. If you are imagining me, good for you, putting a character and a voice to your own common sense. And if you're not imagining me, then you can't be going mad, can you?* —

But I . . .

— *But how do you know I'm not a demon?* The sense of amusement was still there, as though he were smiling. —

Well, yes. I mean, if there are angels, are there demons?

— *Most certainly.* No amusement now, just grim agreement. *People are all too adept at imagining evil.* —

Then how do I know that you aren't one?

— The same way you know if anyone else is evil or not, he said. *See what I do. Judge me by my actions and the results of those actions. Don't believe my words. —*

Lebrun had come to the end of his lengthy speech. He stopped with an imperious gesture, pointing at me. I dropped my head as I had been told to.

He wants you, I said. *He wants to talk to you.*

— A hesitation. *You are frightened. And it is intense. —*

Having you inside me?

— Not quite the way you're thinking. There was the smile again. *Both more and less intimate at once. Perhaps it's better if I talk and you just repeat. —*

I suppose he felt my relief. "Yes," I said aloud.

Lebrun tried not to grin. He looked solemn indeed. "Are you indwelling within this receptacle we have prepared, this Dove of a line of Doves, this perfect vessel?"

"Yes," I said.

"Are you in fact the Archangel Michel, Commander of the Hosts, Bearer of the Flaming Sword?" Lebrun demanded. I saw one of our guests shudder in the background. I thought it was Bonnard.

"Yes," I said.

— *I didn't bring it with me,* he said. *It's rather inconvenient, going everywhere with a flaming sword.* —

You are clowning so I will not be afraid.

— *Yes.* —

And there was a wealth of compassion in that word. I felt behind it the power tightly leashed, controlled and banked to nothing but the faintest touch of warmth, the kindness brought to bear at the very extremity. But for a moment, I knew the power was there.

— *Too much,* he said. —

I know.

"We have summoned you here so that we may know the fate of the armies of France, so that we may know the fate of our nation in war."

— A shrug. *Everyone wants to know what will happen. If that's what they want, they'd be better served by you than by me.* —

I can't say that, I thought.

— *Very well, then. The paths of the future are determined by mortal actions. Why do you trouble the minions of Heaven with these questions?* —

"Very well, then," I said. "The paths of the future are determined by mortal actions. Why do you trouble the minions of Heaven with these questions?"

Lebrun looked at me with a faint frown. Why wasn't I leading him? What did I think I was doing? "O Archangel," he said, "can you not provide us with some wisdom? Tell us how our armies will fare?"

— *Since you ask nicely.* —

I almost laughed.

— *And because I suppose we should keep your stock up, Dove of Doves.* —

Don't call me that, I thought.

— *Which name shall I call you then? Ida? Charles? Elzelina? Or by the name of some other mask that you do not remember but that seems as close to me as the face you now wear? You do not remember me, but I remember you.* —

I only want to know what will happen, I thought.

— *Isn't that always it? A simple answer, then. Your armies are at peace, but peace will not last.*

I covered my confusion and just repeated the last: "Your armies are at peace, but peace will not last."

"That is no more than we know already," Noirtier said from behind Lebrun. "Whose shall the victories be? Which general's star shall rise? Bernadotte? Bonaparte? Moreau?"

I don't want to know what will happen to Victor, I thought. *Don't tell me.*

— A very gentle touch. *I can't tell you what will happen. You understand that I do not know. But you know him very well. Do you think he will win the great victories of the age?* —

No, I thought. *Victor is too cautious. He trusts people too little. He's good, and he's professional. But his desire always exceeds his reach.*

— *Say that, then.* —

"It will not be Moreau," I said. "His desire always exceeds his reach."

— *And Bernadotte?* —

I cast about mentally. *I have never met him. I have never laid eyes on him. How should I know?*

— *He is a better courtier than a general. In the field, he's not quite Moreau's equal, good but not great. But he's much better at making himself liked.* —

"Bernadotte shall rise, but he is not the champion you seek," I said.

— *And Bonaparte?* There was a stillness, as though he were testing me, carefully keeping me from hearing some thought. —

The chariot, I thought unbidden, *the white horse and the black pulling in opposite direc-*

303

tions on the tarot card, held in check by the Emperor's reins.

— His touch, like a hand at my back, like some long-forgotten moment in childhood with my father. *Say it, then, Elzelina.* —

"Bonaparte holds the black horse and the white in check, and guides the chariot," I said.

Noirtier's eyes were greedy. He almost pushed Lebrun aside. "Who else?"

The names came from my lips, but I did not know them. "Masséna. Desaix. Augereau. Lannes."

Noirtier's eyebrows rose. "Lannes?"

— *And you shouldn't be surprised, Noirtier,* he said behind me, or at my ear, not quite inside me but like a whisper, like the not-quite-touch of skin on skin when you feel the ghost heat but not the touch. *Trust you to sensualize angelic presence,* he said, amused again. —

I don't mean to, I protested, *it's just . . .*

— *How you perceive,* he said. *You are who you are, and you sense this way. There is no error in it. Passion and death are sides of the same coin; blood and birth and sex cannot be separated.* —

The gateways of life, I thought, as though I were remembering something, something I had known before. *The gateways of life and death. They are sisters, Death and Love.*

— Just so. Fire is fire. —

And I felt it at my fingertips, my palms growing hot with it, limitless and vague, and knew it was only the smallest part. *Desire,* I thought. *Pothos.*

— He smiled. *And Eros. And Thanatos. And lots of other things besides. —*

"O Dove?" Lebrun's voice cut through, and I realized I'd been silent, wavering. The room blurred in front of me.

"I . . ."

"It is too much for the Vessel. You should dismiss," Noirtier hissed at Lebrun. "You should dismiss now."

End, I thought. *Yes.* I was very tired, and hardly knew why.

— Dismissing is very rude, he said. *It's like pitching your friend out the front door when you're ready for him to leave, rather than asking nicely or saying, "My goodness, it's late." —*

I won't be rude, I thought.

— Nor shall I. —

The room swam, and I fainted.

When my eyes opened, I was lying on the couch. Bonnard was patting my hands rather enthusiastically, and Lebrun was fanning me with a paper.

"Madame?" Bonnard said.

"Yes . . ."

"Are you well?" Lebrun asked.

"Yes," I said. "It was just too much."

Leaning nearer so that the others didn't see, he winked at me. He thought that I had feigned a faint to get out of specific questions, and that it was a good job. I wished the faint had been pretended. I felt terribly light-headed.

In the carriage on the way home, and later lying in my bed, I wasn't sure if it had been real or not. How could one know? How could one prove it? Everything before might have been acting. This wasn't. I wanted it too much, this casual communion with the numinous. It should have been harder. It should have hurt more. It should have been unpleasant and strange, not so oddly comforting, so easy.

Mad. Mad as my mother, preferring her mirror and her ghosts to real life. Of course I would imagine an angel with my father's voice, with Victor's sense of irony, with something in his manner that reminded me of Ney. I would make up a pastiche of men I had loved and admired, a dream of men I had trusted. I imagined that he was near, a concerned expression on his face. I imagined that he spoke. I imagined that someone cared.

I wrapped myself around my pillow and clutched it to me, crying soundlessly. I imagined that someone loved me. That was all. It was pathetic, really.

The next day I sent a note to Lebrun.

Dear Monsieur Lebrun,
While I am sensible of your trust and kindness in offering me a position in your enterprises, I regret that I will be unable to assist you in the future.
Sincerely,
Ida St. Elme

A week later, I signed a contract for three months' repertory work in Marseilles. I would play the nurse in *Violette,* the Sinful Woman in *Heloise,* and Sisygambis in *Alexander in Asia.* Sisygambis in particular was a good part — and, for a change, did not involve a lot of skimpy costumes or comic lines. I left for Marseilles the next day.

NINE OF SWORDS

Of my time in Marseilles, little is to be said. It was summer repertory, with a very small company and all that this entails: the sudden intense friendships and rivalries of people who live and work together day in and day out for a very short time, but would have little to say to one another otherwise. There were many things that seemed important at the time but weren't later.

I remember that I had words with one young man of the company over his appropriation of my cosmetic brushes that seemed likely to burst into deadly enmity, and that I made love with another whose last name I did not know for no other reason than as we sat about drinking on a day we had only a matinee, he offered massages to any who wanted them, proclaiming that he was famous for them. When his hands were on me, I wanted them there. Or at least, I could see no reason not to.

There were some assignations that paid, of course. Gentlemen of the town who wanted to be taken for something, and to whom I had the cachet of novelty. If I did not amass a vast fortune in Marseilles, in three months I was no poorer.

As the summer turned and the days shortened, the days were hotter than ever, and anyone who could desert Marseilles for cooler places did so. The crowds in the theater thinned to nothing. So we ended the run, and some of us began to make our way back to Paris. It was time to cast the shows that would open at the beginning of the winter.

I stopped at a small hotel in Aix. The common room was stiflingly hot. Even so, the custom was brisk, and there were a number of fashionably dressed young people taking a cold supper before the empty fireplace. One of them, a young woman with dark curls fixed in drooping ringlets, looked very familiar. I was trying to place her from one of the many auditions I had done when she looked up.

Her eyes widened and she smiled, getting up and coming over to me. "Ida St. Elme? Is it you?"

"It is," I said. "Isabella Felix?"

"The very same! I remember you from the

auditions for *Iphigenia in Aulis.* You didn't get a part. But then I didn't either."

"What are you doing here?" I asked. "I thought you were in Paris."

Isabella shrugged. "I was. But now I'm stuck here."

"In Aix? Why?"

She rolled her eyes toward the party at the table. "We're in pawn, my company and I. Moiret handles all our business. He's the leading man, and the chariot is his. And we've spent too much, so it's impounded until the theater manager at Digne sends us an advance on our contract. We're supposed to play there next, but who can tell if we'll ever get there? We need seven hundred francs to get out of this mess."

"That's a lot of money," I said. It was about what I had with me from the summer contract, and from a number of liaisons along the way.

"I know," Isabella said. "And we're short-handed, too. Two of the troupe decided not to wait and see if the manager would advance the money, so now when we do get to Digne we'll need a new Third Girl and a new page."

"I'm on my way back from doing Sisygambis in Marseilles," I said. "I'd be your third girl in Digne. What are you doing?"

"Not *Alexander in Asia!*" Isabella said. "Don't tell me you just did it."

"I did," I said. "Everyone's doing it this year, I hear. Is it one of yours?"

She nodded. "We've got *Alexander in Asia* as our history, *Blue Beard* with singing, because you know how they go in the provinces, and we're doing *The Comical Romance* as our comedy. That's the one that will be hard to recast."

"I don't know it," I said.

Isabella nodded. "If you've got Sisygambis, you could learn Sébastienne fast enough. She's the girl who for some complicated reason is dressing up as a boy named Sébastien, and Orlando (he's the hero, of course) falls for her without knowing that she's really a girl, and all sorts of complications ensue, assisted by his old nurse who is in love with Sébastien's valet, a silly sort named Roland who knows that his mistress is really a girl and the heiress of a vast fortune that's coveted by a rogue named Thierry who —"

"I think I get the idea," I said. "So the part open is the girl who dresses as a boy?"

"Yes. And carries off the masquerade in breeches onstage. The men come to watch a girl with nice legs. And, of course, you've got Pompey onstage, which is always an

311

adventure."

"Who's Pompey?" I asked.

"Moiret's pug," Isabella said. "He loves to be onstage, and Moiret swears he's a trouper. He's always good for a laugh." She sighed. "But we're still stuck here until the manager advances the money. Hoping he will."

"I'd lend you the money," I said. "But I'd have to have it back soon. It's all my earnings from the summer. If you'd take me on as third girl. I'm not especially in a hurry to get back to Paris."

The next day I was off for Digne with Isabella's company. The "chariot" turned out to be an open farm wagon that someone had enterprisingly painted bright green. It carried the costumes and baggage of the company, plus the eleven human members, Pompey the pug dog, the soubrette's parrot, and Isabella's Angora cat. We looked something like a circus as we traveled along the road at a snail's pace, practicing the songs from *Blue Beard* while Pompey and the Angora snarled quietly at each other from under the sideboards.

At last I got out and walked, wearing the old pants and coat belonging to Charles. Moiret and the others agreed that I cut a nice figure in pants, and would be just what was needed for Sébastienne.

Isabella laughed. "You carry that off so well that they'll think you're really a young man until unveiled as Sébastienne! They'll be wondering if we have a woman dressed as a man or a man dressed as a woman dressed as a man!"

I shrugged. "That suits me," I said. "I enjoy it."

"I believe you do," Isabella said, looking at me more keenly.

"I do," I said. "Who wouldn't prefer to be a man if they could choose? If I could live my entire life as a man, I should."

I spent three months with the company in Digne. We barely broke even financially, the old problem with provincial troupes. I got back most of my seven hundred francs in the end, but I did not return to Paris until fall was ending and winter coming. In my absence, Lisette seemed to have become nearly entirely nocturnal. She had acquired an opium hookah and supplemented her income by giving parties that went on and on until dawn. Most of the young men who came were students or young soldiers. The money was terrible, and the job worse than Lebrun's had been, but by the middle of the winter I was desperate.

The smell of the opium penetrated every part of the apartment whether I wanted it or not, whether I stayed in my room or not. I might as well go out and join in. A few breaths, and half the time the boys hardly knew if they had me or just sprawled boneless in the cushions that Lisette had gotten to create oriental ambience, and if they suckled a little at my breast in their dreams, it was enough. If it wasn't, I hardly knew it myself.

It was one of those times. I knew it must have been. I had been very careful, otherwise. Victor had insisted upon it, and I had learned all the ways. I had always insisted on the English letters with Chaptal and Gantheaume and the rest.

My courses had always been regular. Two weeks late, and I knew. I had felt that tenderness in my breasts before, the swell of their flesh and the darkening of my nipples. I knew. After all, I had been pregnant twice before.

I sat among the pillows in the late afternoon, wishing that the rooms were warmer, wishing that I could conquer this panic welling up in me. *I will just sit still,* I thought. *I will just sit still. Nothing bad will happen if I don't move.* And so I sat while the light crept in the window and across a purple and red brocade pillow beside me.

Lisette knew someone, of course. She swore the woman had done for her last year, and for half a dozen women she knew. "These things happen," she said practically, flipping back her long red hair. "Madame will put you right in no time."

She nearly killed me instead. I remembered the blood and the cramping and cramping, lying in a pool of my own blood listening to her talking to Lisette, just out of sight of the bed. I knew it wasn't going right. It was so much easier, I thought, to have a child than not to.

I was dying. I hoped Delacroix and Lisette would spring for the pauper's field. Otherwise, I was sure that my fetus and I would make an interesting lecture at the university. "See, gentlemen, the distention of the uterus? Seven or eight weeks of pregnancy, by my estimation." Very educational for the medical students, cutting me open.

I tried to scream, but nothing came out. My voice was already not my own.

"She's delirious," I heard the old woman say.

"There's too much blood," Lisette whispered.

"I am not responsible. Sometimes it goes

315

wrong. . . ." Her voice shook.

I wanted the dreams. I wanted to walk there and never come back. I would not come back to see what happened to my body. Surely I would be somewhere else.

My father had been right: When you die, you simply stop. No heaven. No hell. I would even welcome hell, about this time. I would settle for demons.

Dark. Night. Sticky blood around me. Every limb filled with ice.

I wandered in deep caves, and they were home. *I will stay here,* I said.

— *You can't,* someone whispered behind me, magnified by the caves, whispering around the walls. *I am not done with you.* —

Let me stay, I whispered. *Let me stay. I am done. There is nothing. Let me stay here with this daughter who will never be. Let me forget.*

— *You asked for the gift of memory. Now you will never forget.* —

Light grew, and I stood in the half-lit cave. He wore the dark blue coat of the Army of the Republic, a tricolor sash about his waist, its ends weighted with bullion fringe. His face was plain and beautiful, and behind him wings unfolded in a riot of white feathers, every pinion glittering with imprisoned light.

"Elza," he said, "and Georg and Jauffre

and Lydias and Charmiane and more besides." His voice was like rain on the trees,
like fire whispering in the grate. "You taught
me about faith when I had lost hope. Have
you lost it now?"

"My lord," I said, "let me begin again." I
fought back tears. "I am in too deep. There
is no way out. Let me go, and begin again.
In the name of mercy."

He shook his head like a soldier who sees
danger and must yet go forward. "I can't."

I walked toward him across the cave, and
I did not know if the face he saw was mine
or some other, if the hands I reached toward
him had ever belonged to Elzelina. "Why
not?"

"I need you too badly, scarred as you are.
And there is no time. If you begin again, it
will be too late." His eyes were filled with
terrible compassion. "I must use you, and
use you I will." He took my hand, and his
touch was like liquid fire in my veins. "I'm
sorry."

"I know you are," I said, and looked up at
him. I thought his eyes were blue, and that
they were like some I knew, in some place
far distant from this.

He said something that might have been a
reason, or a word, or a promise. But it
wasn't. It was simply love.

"Is it so odd that I should love you," he said, "when I send you to suffer? And can promise nothing, only that it is the best that I can do?"

"No," I said, and clutched his hand as if I could grasp a brand, or grasp the wind. In this place, it was solid. "I love you too."

His mouth twisted. I closed my eyes, and felt the world move. I was a bird in his hand, white-winged and strong, my heart beating fast. A dove?

He laughed. "No doves for you, dear one. A gull. To face the winds far out to sea, and come at last storm-tossed to shore, if you are lucky." He raised his hand and I took off, spiraling upward toward a circle of light at the apex of the cave, leaving behind the bright angel in the dark.

GRAND-SAINT-BERNARD

To my surprise, I didn't die. It was hard to say that I lived either. Winter wore on, grim and gray. I hardly ever left the apartment, even when I was strong enough to get down three flights of stairs to the street. Sometimes there was food and sometimes there wasn't, depending on whether or not Lisette's friends brought enough money with them for food and opium both, and whether or not anyone bothered to go get some.

One day I was hungry and there was nothing, but there was money lying around. I had no idea who it belonged to, but I took some and went down the stairs. It took a long time. The stairs made me dizzy.

It was cold outside, and the skies were leaden. I went across the street to a café and ordered bread and a hard-boiled egg. I ate the egg very carefully. It was good. There was butter, and the bread was nicely crusty, with just a little ash from the oven clinging to the bottom.

Nobody looked at me. It was the middle of the afternoon, I guessed, too early for dinner and too late for lunch. February? March? Could it be March already? I saw my reflection on the inside of the window overlooking the street, and I looked like an opium eater, wan and listless, with lank, tangled blond hair. I ordered a glass of bad burgundy and drank it watching people walking around on the street.

Two men were moving a cartload of furniture. From the printer's shop a boy emerged with a wrapped bundle, going on an errand. A young girl in a thin cloak carried a magnificent hatbox, probably delivering a purchase. The night-soil cart went along, the old horse patiently waiting while two men swept the streets in a desultory fashion.

And, I thought with a curious sense of detachment, *a young prostitute sits in the window of the café, eating bread and an egg and wondering what happens next. If it's so damned important for me to be here, I'd really appreciate a hint about why. What I'm supposed to be doing that's worth living for.*

Except that, having lived, I could hardly die. Of course, plenty of people killed themselves. My mother had tried often enough. But I had always known that some-how I would never go through with it, never really mean it. It simply wasn't in my nature to go quietly.

And maybe that's it, I thought, sipping the sour wine quietly. *I'm alive because I'm not dead. And I've got to find something to do. Because otherwise it's back to the same old thing, back to Lisette's friends and her boys, until it all happens again. And I'm not doing this again.*

It took me most of the afternoon, stopping whenever I got dizzy, but I found a tobacco shop with paper and sent a message to Isabella Felix.

Dear Isabella,
As you may know from our mutual friends, I have recently been ill, but I am glad to say that I am now fully recovered, and I feel my strength returning every day. I wonder if you have yet engaged a third girl for touring this summer. If not, I would be eager to renew my contract with M. Moiret's company and to join you on the road wherever you happen to be engaged.
With warmest regards,
Ida St. Elme

Isabella did better than answering. She sent

that she should like to meet me for lunch in the Palais-Royal three days later. I agreed, of course.

It was March 26, 1800, by the old calendar, the one people still thought in and nobody used. I had lost track of time so thoroughly that I'd imagined it could be no later than early March.

I had trouble finding anything to wear. Where had most of my clothes gone? And why was everything dirty? I couldn't remember the last time I had sent anything to a laundress. The only clothes that weren't worn or filthy were Charles's.

I dug out a pair of dove-gray pants, a ruffled shirt with half a handspan of lace on the sleeves, a subdued gray waistcoat, and a dark-blue coat, then put my hair back and looked in the mirror. Not bad. Too thin and too peaked, but not bad. I still looked like Charles. And best to be Charles anyway. None of this had ever happened to Charles. Charles was a man, and he was strong.

He raised an eyebrow and gave me a half smile. "Wages of sin, my dear," he said sardonically.

Isabella grinned when she saw Charles come into the café. "My goodness!" she said. "I had no idea I would be lunching with such a handsome gentleman!" Isabella looked like a cat in cream, sleek and well groomed, with perfectly painted fingernails. Her dress was new and, if not the most expensive material, it was well cut and fashionable. Her dark hair was swept up with a pair of tortoiseshell pins that she hadn't had last year.

"Charmed," I said, bending over her hand and smiling. Charles must pay her due attention. I sat down across from her.

"Sébastien, is it?" she asked.

"Something like," I said. "Charles van Aylde. I have decided to be entirely Charles this year. You're looking well. New man?"

Isabella laughed. "Go right to the point, don't you? Yes, a new man. He's an artillery colonel, Auguste Thibault. He's paying my bills now, and staying with me in a nice little third-floor apartment in Grenelle."

My heart sank a little. "That sounds nice," I said. "I take it you're not planning on touring the provinces this summer, then?"

"No," Isabella said. "I've got something better. Auguste is a lodge brother of General Lannes, and he's been assigned to Lannes's corps of the Army of Italy, under Bonaparte. I'm putting together a troupe to follow along with the baggage train. We're going to Italy. Want to come as second girl?"

"Italy?" For a moment I was stunned.

Italy. Where I had grown up, had gotten what Cousin Louisa described as an ideal education for an adventuress. Italy. Where I had been happy. I did not need to consult my cards for this, dug out of the trash that Moreau had thrown out and carefully kept in their bag. I knew a good thing when I heard it.

"Well?" Isabella asked. "Are you interested?"

"Absolutely," I said. "I'm yours whenever you're ready to go."

We left on a gorgeous morning at the beginning of May, a company of six with a wagon and two servants. I didn't ride in the wagon. Instead, I sold everything left of my finery and things in Paris and bought a horse. He was a fifteen-year-old gelding, a bit slow and short of wind, but he was sound enough. I named him Nestor, and we got along fine.

I was Charles on the road. Of course, the company and the servants knew that I was their second girl, but none of the fellow travelers met at inns or on the road did. It seemed safer that way, since the leading man and the second man were both rather timid sorts, and the second man was at least sixty and prone to drunkenness. He was a thoroughgoing professional on the stage, but offstage he was insensible most of the time. I didn't ask what misfortune had put him back on the road at this point in his life. It seemed rude.

Charles didn't have a sword, but I talked the second man into loaning me one of his pair of horse pistols. It was safer to be armed, under the circumstances.

We made slow time across France. The supply columns for the Army of Italy stretched seemingly endlessly, and in the glorious spring weather it seemed that everyone in France must be on the way to Italy. Sutlers, farriers and horse copers, cantinières, and replacement troops all crowded the roads.

While I had been paying no attention, the Directory had given way to the Consulate, in which a triumvirate of worthy men held executive power rather than the band of Directors. Foremost among them was Bonaparte.

What Moreau thought of this, I could only imagine. But perhaps he had his hands full. One of the first acts of the Consulate had been to restore him to his overall command on the Rhine. He now commanded the largest French army, with more than 120,000 men facing the Austrians. The First Consul,

Bonaparte, preferred to take on the supposedly softer wing of the Austrian army in Italy, aided by the men to whom Moreau had referred once to me as a band of undernourished schoolboys and grimy old grumblers.

Presumably the latter had referred to General Masséna, who was presently holding the city of Genoa against a besieging force twice the size of his. Everyone said that eventually he must surrender. The question was how long they would hold, and whether Bonaparte's army would reach Italy before they were lost. Everyone wondered. In each inn all across France, men talked of nothing else. Not once did I hear the name Moreau. *Victor might have the greater command,* I thought, *but once again he is not making himself loved.*

Traveling in what was essentially one giant baggage train, with papers signed by General Lannes, we met little trouble.

As we rumbled along with our wagon, Nestor keeping pace beside it, I felt a stirring. Nestor was strong and solid, and days in the sun and good plain food made me feel myself again. Or at least made me feel Charles. He was less cynical than previously, more willing to be charming, more willing to lean from the saddle and pay elaborate compliments over Isabella's hand while the Angora cat spat at him. I liked being Charles. He could rise to any occasion, get out of any trouble with a twist of a smile and the right word, a golden trickster who feared nothing. He was the master of his own fate.

Unwillingly, I felt my spirits lift. How could I not, with the open road in front of me and the glorious sun of spring in the heavens, with all the trees in bloom and the shadow of the Alps growing closer every day? I had not seen those peaks since I had come this way as a child. Snow-covered, they glittered like a promise, closer each day. Soon we were in the foothills. Cloaks came out of our packs.

We stopped at an inn before we began the ascent. Isabella had us sing for our supper, playing *Blue Beard* before the fire in the main room. I sang the ghost of his wife, and it was eerie and strange, coming in a dusky alto from what appeared to be a slender young man. It was there we heard that Bonaparte had beaten the Austrians at Marengo.

The next day we started up the pass. The weather was good and it was June. The army had crossed a month earlier in a howling storm. In the gullies we could see what was left of the carcasses of their foundered mules and horses. Now the rocks were studded with alpine flowers.

With each step, something lifted. I was young and I was free, like the hawks that soared on the updrafts over the valleys. Once, I thought I saw an eagle.

What did it matter if I was poor again, and if I had no idea what awaited us in Italy? I had a horse and a pistol at my side, my health and friends. If I had no lover, so much the better. Perhaps I would not need one.

Or perhaps even now the dice were rolling, the cards turning. That night, encamped on the mountain beside a small fire, I took out my deck and felt them in my hands, cool and smooth as silk. Wordlessly, I laid them out. The Chariot gleamed gold and white, the Emperor's red cloak billowing soundlessly behind him. The Star gleamed in the heavens. The Sword Queen held her blade before her while the tempest raged about her, grip foremost, like a crusader bending to kiss the cruciform hilt. Six staves entwined, gold and blue.

Isabella came and sat down opposite me wordlessly, her pink shawl bundled tightly around her shoulders.

"What is next?" I asked, and turned the card.

The Emperor sat enthroned, the orb of the world in his hands.

"What do your cards say will happen in Italy?" Isabella asked.

"Battles," I said. "I didn't need the cards to say that. Masséna has surrendered Genoa, but Bonaparte and Lannes are on the move. Battles go without saying."

"Masséna surrendered?"

I nodded. "I heard it from a man going the other way, a horse coper going back to get more remounts. He said they got terms and surrendered the city, but took the wounded out and paroled everyone else."

"I wonder if Auguste is all right," she said.

"I'm sure he is," I said. "He's with Lannes, after all."

"You can win victories and still die," Isabella said.

The next day we saw the carts. We had just begun the descent and they were on the way up, carts drawn by donkeys on the steep path. The little beasts put their heads down, but they kept moving slowly upward.

I rode down on Nestor, moving in reverse along the column, looking for the easiest place to get our wagon down.

Some of the men in the carts were sitting up, joking and calling out. Isabella appeared, walking beside the wagon in case of a runaway, and her beauty seemed to make a great hit. She returned their calls gaily, blowing kisses and promising them tickets someday.

I stopped to wait for her. "Carts," I said.

A donkey cart toiled slowly up beside me and halted. Isabella was standing beside the cart just ahead, letting a gallant with one arm kiss her hand, her shawl stirring in the fresh breeze. I looked down.

A young man was lying in the bottom of the cart, a cloak half thrown around him. His long black hair was matted with sweat and had escaped from its queue to lie across his shoulders. His skin was the faded, sick color of olive skin pinched by the starvation of a siege, then bled white from a wound. I stopped. I dismounted without hardly being aware of it.

Lying in a cart like this, a cloak half across him, long black hair . . .

His head moved a little from side to side in some fever dream, and I let out a breath that I didn't know I was holding.

"The wounded from Genoa," Isabella said, coming up beside me.

He had fine, strong lines to his face, a face

I should have known, so like was it to some other. No doubt his eyes would be dark, if he opened them.

The column started moving again, the patient donkeys plodding forward.

Isabella reached for my hand. "Come on, Charles," she said. "Let's lead Nestor and give him a little rest going down."

I nodded. The cart moved past. What was I to do? Follow it for no reason at all? Because something in the face of a stranger filled me with a sorrow I could not name?

We reached Milan a few days behind our troops, some of whom had returned to the city following the twin victories of Marengo and Montebello. The Austrians had been soundly defeated and were in full retreat.

Isabella had us ready to perform inside of a day. We opened in the camp with *The Comical Romance* and moved on to *Alexander in Asia,* a special double program — three francs for both shows.

The audience was beyond enthusiastic. When I let down my hair and opened my shirt to show Sébastienne's camisole, the men cheered and roared with such enthusiasm one would have thought that I was Venus rising from the waves. And that was the camp show. We were to have the finest theater in Milan the next night to perform for the officers.

Isabella ran about madly, producer and leading lady at the same time. "We need a prologue," she said. "Something appropriate and martial. Something flattering but not sycophantic. If I write it, can you learn it by tonight?"

"If it's not long," I said. "Twenty or thirty lines I can do. Fifty and I'll flub."

It was nearly fifty. And it sounded like it had been written on the fly, which of course it had.

I was to wear a filmy white dress meant to resemble classical drapery, and to represent "the Spirit of Triumph, or Fama Who Rests Her Hands Upon Laurel'd Heads." I was to carry a laurel wreath, which took most of the day to locate. Isabella could not be convinced that such wreaths were not for sale on every street corner in Italy, regardless of ancient Roman triumphs. Fortunately, the Italian I had spoken as a child came back to me, and I managed to find someone to sell me enough leafy branches to make into a circlet. Then I had to learn my lines.

Fama volat, I began. When I stood at last onstage in Milan's Opera House, looking up at the tiered boxes in scarlet and gold, a frisson ran through me. I could not make out any faces. The lights in my face were too bright. But here and there I could see the telltale glitter of braid, of diamonds, of bright decorations. I thought the Consular box must be to the right, so I addressed myself there:

"Fama volat. So slaves spoke to Caesar,
    reminding him
In his glory that Time itself does not stand
    still
That the procession of years renders
    glory itself faded.
But still there is that which remains
Virtue and manhood, courage and destiny
Triumphant over the centuries themselves
That men might know and emulate
    Caesar."

A stillness came over the theater.

"Thus spoke the Sibyl of Cumae
And thus spoke Caesar's slaves
That all glory is fleeting
But virtue and love endure."

The glitter in the dark. Someone had moved, but how I could not see. I looked out into imagined eyes, but all I could see were the lights.

> "Fortune's Darling, know
> that Time himself cannot tarnish
> the wreath that rests upon your brow
> though Fame pass and laurel wither.
> As Achilles or Alexander
> your name shall endure."

I sank to my knees gracefully, my dress puddling around me in soft folds.

> "Take then this wreath
> this tribute of my hands
> Caesar, I lay this at your feet."

I extended the wreath I had made and laid it on the stage, my head bent in submission, sweetly and sensually, as Victor had taught me, holding the pose kneeling in the silence.

One clap began it, then the applause was thunderous. Fame knelt before the First Consul, her blond hair spread across her shoulders and her hands stretched in surrender, and her eyes were full of tears.

I barely had time to get backstage and change for Sébastien. I had no idea what people were saying. So it was a surprise to come off at the interval to find a solemn aide-de-camp in the dressing room.

Isabella had come in too, and he looked

from one of us to the other. "Which of you ladies is Madame St. Elme? The Prologue?"

I exchanged a look with Isabella. I hoped her poetry hadn't been badly received. I stepped forward. "I am Madame St. Elme," I said evenly.

"The First Consul would like to see you after the performance," he said. "He would like you to join him for a private supper."

I heard the hiss of Isabella's indrawn breath.

My voice was entirely steady. "Please tell the First Consul that I would be delighted."

THE FIRST CONSUL

I hardly recalled the second half of the performance. I tried to keep my eyes from straying to where I thought the Consular box must be, despite the fact I could see nothing. Afterward, I ran back to my dressing room to change. Isabella came in hot on my heels. "I'm so sorry," I said. "Isabella, this should be you."

"Don't be stupid," she said, grabbing my best dress and tossing it over my head. "Can you see me explaining to the First Consul that I can't take supper with him because I prefer an artillery colonel?"

I stuck my head out the top of the dress. "Do you really?"

Isabella started doing up my buttons. "I do. Auguste isn't so much to look at, but . . . I'd hate to lose him. And I can't expect him not to yield me to the First Consul, if I had his eye. Or not to feel like I'd set my cap for better and been disappointed if I didn't keep it."

I looked at myself in the mirror. I seemed awfully pale in white satin. I wished I still had the lovely blue dress I'd had when I was with Moreau. "I'm not sure I want the First Consul either," I said. "I haven't had a lover since . . ."

Since I'd ended the child, I thought. No man had touched me. And being Charles had not exactly encouraged male admirers.

Isabella knew what I meant. She began to do up my hair with quick, deft fingers. "It's not as though you'd decided on a life of celibacy."

"No," I said slowly. The way she was putting it up was all classical simplicity, better with no time for curlpapers. "But I hadn't expected to go back to it when . . ."

"The stakes were so high?" Isabella raised an eyebrow at me over my shoulder in the mirror.

I nodded. "Too high."

"Who knows when you might catch his eye again? And if you refuse or say you're ill . . ." She spread her hands.

"I know," I said. "It's not just me. It's the company. We all need this job, and we could all use the patronage. And I need the money. As much as is forthcoming. It's just that . . ."

"What?"

I picked up my lip brush and wetted it with paint. "Moreau detested him. He said Bonaparte was an ambitious, boorish social climber with no graces, that he stormed women as though they were cities under siege. I really don't want that right now. And while I hope I can do it if I need to, I don't know if I can make it look good. Isabella, I really don't!"

There was a knock on the door. Isabella's eyes met mine. "You'll be fine," she said, and squeezed my hand.

The splendidly dressed aide was at the door. "Madame St. Elme? The First Consul has sent a carriage. Would you accompany me?"

Once I would have thrilled at this. I would have played out all my schoolgirl fantasies of being Madame de Pompadour or a daring spy hurrying away to a secret rendezvous with the king. Now I wished I had different shoes. And that the rainstorm that was coming would not break before I got inside, and that it would not reduce my hair to draggles. I wished I could go have dinner with the company and go to bed alone. Looking out the window at the lowering clouds over Milan, I shook myself. I must get into a better frame of mind. I must get in control.

And Charles was no use to me. This was beyond his ken.

The carriage stopped in front of a grand entrance, clearly one of the great houses of Milan. A bewigged footman dressed as though it were still 1780 came forward to open the door and help me out. I stepped down and under the portico as the first drops of rain splashed on the street. The thunder curled high above. It was ten o'clock and not yet full dark.

An officer in dress uniform hurried forward. "Madame St. Elme, I am General Duroc. I am the First Consul's personal assistant."

I held my hand for him and he bent over it correctly.

"If you will come this way, I shall inform you of what is expected."

I raised an eyebrow. Moreau had not kept this state. Barras hadn't either. "You are the First Gentleman of the Palace? Or perhaps the Groom of the Bedchamber?"

He turned and looked at me solemnly. "I would not be rebellious if I were you. Simply be agreeable and charming, as I'm sure you are capable of. And do not fear if he asks you about Moreau."

So that was known. Well, how not?

"If he says anything against Moreau, I am

leaving," I said. "And so much for the First Consul."

Duroc's expression did not change. "There is no need for all that. Some spirit is good, but too much is unattractive. I only tell you that you need not worry that he will hold some grudge against you because of Moreau." He opened the door and led me inside. "The First Consul is properly addressed as sir at all times, not Your Excellency."

"How very Republican," I said dryly. The halls were carpeted deeply, a few candles illuminating alcoves, gilt mirrors reflecting back their light.

He led me into a study or library. It was dimly lit by candelabra on the desk, and the shelves of books stretched up to the ceiling except where there were windows high up. The curtains were open and the windows as well, and the smell of rain blew in, causing the flames to gutter.

"Sir, here is Madame St. Elme as you requested," Duroc said. He stepped back and closed the door behind me.

Bonaparte stood up from behind the desk. He was a slender young man, perhaps thirty years old, with dark brown hair that fell across his brow, too long for a fashionable new haircut and too short for a queue. It brushed his collar, which was dark blue and crusted with gold acanthus leaves. Beneath it he wore a white shirt and waistcoat, the plain white trousers of the dress uniform he had worn to the performance earlier.

He walked around the desk and stood before me, a somewhat quizzical expression on his face. "Do you know that you look several years younger here than on the stage?"

"I am happy to hear it," I said evenly.

"You used to be intimate with Moreau," he said. His eyes were very dark and betrayed nothing.

"Very intimate," I said.

"He did some foolish things for your sake." He clasped his hands behind his back, and I thought for a moment that he would cross behind me while I stood still, the oldest trick in the book for establishing dominance. Instead, he walked over to the desk and leaned on the edge of it.

"I suppose he did," I said.

"And yet you are here," he said. "Why?"

"Passions change," I said, and was surprised at the bitterness I heard in my voice. "And we women are pawns on your chessboard. I have no choice."

Bonaparte did not look away from me. It was my eyes that avoided his. "Do you want to leave?" he asked. "If you do, I will call Duroc and have him return you to your lodgings. If your heart is given to Moreau, I will not try your loyalty."

I looked at him suddenly.

He shrugged. "I don't need to best him that way." Bonaparte smiled, and the smile was like sunshine, like an invitation to a wonderful conspiracy, a joke only the two of us shared.

"I can see that you don't, sir," I said.

"Share my supper," he said. "What is half an hour of your life? And perhaps I can convince you I am not the ogre that Moreau believes me to be."

I stepped forward. There was a cold supper laid on a little table between the library shelves, a chicken and a salad, some cold potatoes dressed with mayonnaise. A bottle of wine stood sweating in the warmth of the room.

"I do not believe you an ogre," I said. "But why should you care what I think? I am no one of importance."

He held one of the chairs out for me. Standing beside me, we were the same height. Not a tall man, but he did not need tricks to impose. "How should I know who is important?" He seemed genuinely surprised by my question. "No one who is of any rank now was important ten years ago, saving Talleyrand perhaps. None of my generals, none of my companions, were born to it. Who's to say what you'll become?" Bonaparte sat down opposite me and began to help himself to the chicken, using his fingers to separate the wing and leg.

"I do not think I am likely to become a general, sir," I said. "You know what I am. An actress."

"Yes, the troupe," he said. He gestured for me to help myself, and I tentatively did so. "I understand you're following Lannes's corps. Then where do you plan to go?"

"Perhaps the Tyrol," I said, thinking of Isabella's vague plans. "Or possibly to Munich."

"Are you German then?" he asked, taking a quick gulp of wine and refilling his glass.

"I was born in Italy, but my heart is French," I said. He did not pour for me, so I waited until he put the bottle down and helped myself. He ate at a furious pace, like a schoolboy who is afraid that the plates will be taken away.

"Do you like acting?"

"I'm not very good," I said. "But I like it. I like the freedom. And I like the road." I took another sip of wine. "I don't like belonging to someone."

"That's what my wife said about you," Bonaparte said, putting the chicken bones by. "She said you were to be trusted."

I nearly choked on my wine. Of course he knew who I was. He was Joséphine's husband. Or rather, she belonged to him as well as to Barras. And given her bargain with Barras, why should not this young general command her loyalty instead? Now Bonaparte eclipsed even Barras.

"It is kind of your wife to recall me," I said.

"She said Moreau cast you aside senselessly, with no eye to your use."

I met his eyes across the table. "It is true that Moreau acted with little regard for my use," I said. "My affections may be for sale, but my loyalty is not."

Bonaparte smiled as though I had passed some hidden test. "I would not put a price on your loyalty, Madame. Or your affections." He shrugged. "And aren't our bodies all for sale? Whether we sell them for sex or for cannon fodder? A recruit is less expensive than a prostitute."

"How much is a general?" I asked.

He lifted his glass to me, still smiling. "About the same as a companion. They used to be the same word, you know.

Hetairos. Hetaira."

"I know," I said. I remembered René Gantheaume suddenly. "I knew a naval officer who said your staff were all in love with you."

To my surprise, he laughed. "I hope so," he said. "It's better to govern men by love than by chains."

"Love itself can be a chain," I replied.

"The strongest chain there is," he said. "We will all do anything for love."

"Even you?" Someone else would have meant it as coquetry, and I wondered if he would take it that way.

Bonaparte put his glass down. "Can you counterfeit desire, Madame, to the point where your patrons are none the wiser?"

"No," I said quietly. "Not if they care to know. Most men don't want to know. It doesn't matter to them if desire is mutual or not. But if they do care, I can't deceive them. I'm not that good."

"Neither am I." He stood up, draping his napkin over the chair arm. "Good night, then."

I was startled, and it took me a moment to rise. "Good night?"

"Good night," he said, and bent over my hand, his lips just brushing my fingers, smiling so that I would know he wasn't angry.

"Duroc will get the carriage to take you home. Perhaps I will see you again."

"I hope so," I said, and was surprised to find that I meant it.

I reached our lodgings long before Isabella, who had gone to dinner with the company. I was curled in a chair before the fire in the room I shared with her, listening to the rain against the glass, when she returned.

"Ida? What in the world are you doing home so early? I thought . . ."

"He didn't want to make love to me," I said. "We ate dinner and he asked me questions about Moreau, and that was that."

Isabella spread her soaking shawl to dry. "So it was politics, then." She came and sat by the fire to get warm. "You must be relieved."

I said nothing.

"Aren't you?" She looked up at my face.

"I suppose," I said. "I should be, shouldn't I?"

Isabella spread her hands. "You didn't want to. He didn't want to. End of story. So what's the matter?"

"I liked him," I said.

Isabella carefully removed one of her slippers and threw it at me. I ducked. "What in the world!" she said. "You didn't want to sleep with him, and you didn't have to. Now what? You wish you had?"

"Almost," I said. "Isabella, I liked him. It was so strange."

"Not an uncouth social climber?"

I shrugged. "Well, his table manners were a little rough. But he was a perfect gentleman. No foul language, no crude demands. None of the little things that one does to establish dominance or to intimidate."

"Maybe that's not what he likes," Isabella said. "Maybe it was all about politics."

"Don't I look good enough? I mean, I didn't have time to dress very much, but —"

Isabella threw the other slipper at me. "You're utterly impossible! You want to attract him but say no?"

"I don't know what I want," I said, catching the slipper before it hit me. "It's mildly humiliating to have liked him. And at the same time —"

"At the same time," Isabella said, "he's a handsome young general who is suddenly incredibly wealthy and happens to be the head of state. I can't imagine why a woman would want to catch his eye." She rolled her eyes at me. "Go to bed, Ida. You are so perverse sometimes."

I heard the door close softly behind her.

The shadows shifted on the walls with the shifting flames.

"Like touching fire," I said.

The next morning we were awakened by a lackey at the front door. The second man answered, and brought me up a package. I opened it sitting up in bed next to Isabella, who looked as though she were only half awake.

There was a purse with fifty gold livres in it, and a letter sealed with cream-colored wax.

"Oh, my God," Isabella said. She didn't seem to care that the second man was seeing her in her chemise. I was sleeping in one of Charles's big shirts, and was as covered as anyone could be. "Did he send that?" The gold spilled out and over the sheets.

"I don't know who else could have," I said, lifting the letter.

"Open it!" she said.

I broke the seal and read it. It was short enough.

My dear Madame St. Elme,
This is by way of thanks for our pleasant conversation. I hope that you will join me again tonight.

Bonaparte

The second man drew in a breath, then let out a whoop. "We're rich! We're all going to be rich! Madame, you will save us all if you can get the Consul by the balls!"

"Shut up!" said Isabella.

I read the letter again. "Fifty livres? For talking?"

The second man plunged forward and kissed my brow. "The kind of talking Madame can do! Oh, those sweet lips!"

Isabella cuffed him lightly. "Behave. Let's all keep our priorities straight."

I tested a coin with my teeth. "And that is?"

"You need a dress," she said.

I took some of the money and went in search of a dressmaker who could put something together for that same night. Thankfully, the classical styles in vogue were not nearly as ornate as the styles of my youth, and could be cut and stitched in a day if the need were great enough. And if the customer was willing to pay. The dress was azure blue silk, necessarily simple in style, caught beneath the breasts with a rope of false pearls. The seamstress swore it would be ready by six o'clock.

I was wishing it were possible to get shoes made in a day, when I heard a shout behind me. "Madame Ringeling!" I turned as if I had been shot at.

Colonel Meynier was jogging across the street, dodging under the heads of a matched pair of bays pulling a green phaeton, his hat under his arm.

I stopped and waited for him. "Colonel Meynier!" I said. "This is an unexpected pleasure! How did you know me?"

He bent over my hand and kissed it. "Madame Ringeling, you are unforgettable!"

"Please," I said, "not that name here. I have left it behind me for reasons you can guess all too well. I am Madame St. Elme now."

He straightened up. "Of course," he said. "I did not mean to be indiscreet." I noticed that his moustache had been joined by a pair of hussar braids dangling on either side of his face. The ends were neatly weighted with little gold beads.

"You look well," I said. "Are you assigned to General Lannes's corps?"

"Bonaparte's," he said. "I'm sure my friend Ney misses me on the Rhine. He told me that he met you in Paris. You made quite an impression."

I found myself blushing. "I'm sure I did," I said. "I babbled like an infant about fish. I can't imagine his impression can have been a positive one."

"Maybe he likes women who talk about fish," Meynier said. "Some do."

I laughed. "I hope so. I . . ." I ran out of what to say.

Meynier looked at me keenly. "Don't tell me you were as taken with him as he was with you!"

"He wasn't," I said. "He couldn't have been."

"He's talked and talked about you. And sent you flowers at the theater, he said."

"What? When?" And then I remembered the white roses. "The roses," I said slowly. "The ones with no card."

"Have dinner with me tonight," Meynier said. "I'll tell you all about my friend Ney."

"I can't," I said. "I have other plans. Another night?"

"Of course," Meynier said. "I am entirely at your disposal. You can find me at the Hotel Battachio."

"I will," I promised, and bade him good-bye. I had the First Consul to think of.

FIRE FROM HEAVEN

The First Consul sent the carriage for me at nine. Isabella had done my hair in ringlets pinned on top of my head and cascading down in artful disarray. My blue dress was ready. It was beautiful, except where the neckline didn't quite fit in the back and it pouched out a little.

"He's not going to be looking at your back," Isabella said. "Don't worry so much."

I gave her a quick hug, carefully, so as not to crush my dress.

"Go!" she said, and handed me up into the carriage.

This time I wasn't led to the library. Duroc came down to greet me and led me this way and that through the house, up a marble staircase to the second floor and down a long corridor decorated with Flemish tapestries of flowers.

"Madame St. Elme, sir," he said, opening a door.

It was a very small study with a single window covered in green velvet drapes. A compact desk took up most of the floor space, laden with maps and papers. There was one armchair, and a fine globe stood at a tilt, its feet half on and half off a pile of papers that seemed to have slid over.

Bonaparte sat in a straight chair behind the desk, a quill in his hand. He looked up and nodded.

Duroc withdrew.

Bonaparte bent his head to his papers again, dipping the quill and writing very quickly on the sheet before him.

I stood.

He laid the sheet aside and picked up another, beginning again. Somewhere, on the mantelpiece, a clock was ticking. It was a fine German clock, all gilded shepherd-esses. Beside it lay a piece of blotting paper, a lead musket ball, and a small pile of books. I walked over, casting a glance behind me.

He did not look up.

Volume four of Gibbon, looking as though coffee had been spilled upon it. A translation of Schiller's *Wallenstein*. A travel book on India.

After a moment I sat down in the armchair beside the fire. I cast glances at him, trying not to watch him openly, but he seemed entirely oblivious to my presence.

He was, I thought, handsome in his way. It was not so much his features as the motion to them, the changes of expression in response to words only on paper, words I could not see, mobile and warm, then grave and still by turns. And it was his hands, long and white as a girl's, and as graceful. It was hard to imagine them handling shells and wadding, but he had begun as an artilleryman. No movement was extraneous. And yet it was beautiful to watch him sand the dispatch he had finished, to blow the sand off, and lay it aside. The light touched one side of his face only, rendering it like a cameo against the dark.

He looked up. "Are you tired of waiting?" he asked, glancing at the clock. Fully fifteen minutes had passed.

"That would be impossible," I said.

"Why?"

"I'm witnessing the work of a great man," I said. "How could that be boring? Surely there are many who would find this of great interest." I stood up.

Bonaparte put his head to the side for a moment, almost quizzically. He walked around the desk toward me. "Is that flattery?"

"No," I said. I did not look away. His dark eyes were exactly on a level with my own. "I imagine you are used to flattery."

"I have become used to it in recent years." He reached out and put his hand on my upper arm, where the cascades of blue silk fell away, but his eyes did not leave my face. "You've changed your mind?"

"Yes," I said, and lifted my chin.

He did not kiss me, though he was close enough that I could feel his warm breath. "It was the money," he said.

"Almost entirely," I said.

"Almost." He nodded. "That will do."

"Will it?" I raised my hand and rested it against his cheek, flesh and smooth skin, the faint stubble of evening. "You do not want me to worship you?"

"On bended knee?" Bonaparte smiled against my fingers. "I prefer sweets to spices. And I think I see enough sycophancy."

"Do you always know exactly what you want?" I asked.

"Yes," he said, and I kissed him, drawing his face to mine.

His arms went around me, not tentative and gentle, but hardly as though storming a fortress either. Solidly.

Our kiss was a ballet of tongues, slow and warm as though we expected an audience, as though dancers reached and touched in sensuality that was ritual. Like gypsies at a fair, I thought, my hands sliding up his back under his coat, like commedia dell'arte, improvised and polished at once. And there was pleasure in the grace of it, each movement matching.

The door opened, and there were heavy footsteps. I sprang away from him.

An enormous man with a long black moustache wearing outrageous Mameluke garb stood just inside the door, a huge scimitar at his side. He scowled.

Bonaparte seemed unconcerned. He dropped his hand from my waist and walked over to the desk. He bundled up the papers in an oilskin pouch. "Here you are," he said cheerfully, handing them over. "That's the lot of them."

Wordlessly, the Mameluke bowed and walked out, the papers clutched close to his massive chest. For some reason, his silence discommoded me more than censorious words would have.

"We could go into the other room," Bonaparte said, stoppering the bottle of ink on the desk. "People feel free to disturb me in here." He looked up at me, eyebrows raising in one last question.

I nodded.

He lifted a tapestry aside that half-covered a door, motioned me through. It was a small enough bedchamber, obviously recently redone, with a draped ceiling styled to resemble a tent, striped scarlet and gold, and a massive bed decorated with gilded laurel wreaths. It looked like a schoolboy's fantasy of a Roman conqueror, lacking nothing but a couple of recumbent Gauls.

Instead, there were windows opening into the branches of an almond tree and the warm Italian night. I heard the distant sound of thunder. Storms had rolled across regularly every night in the heat, light playing over the city.

He came and stood behind me, bent and kissed my neck, lifting the tendrils of curls with careful hands. I leaned back against him.

I remembered this. What it felt like to be worshipped, to be all that was beautiful for a moment, to fill the senses like Venus.

He slipped his arms around me, and I turned in his arms, kissing him again. There was no hurry. "The night is long enough," he said.

I bent my lips to his throat, feeling with a sense of triumph the racing of his pulse just there, where his life lay beneath my lips. I laughed, and undid his neckcloth and the top of his shirt. He shrugged out of his coat, which fell to the floor in a heavy pile, weighted by the gold bullion. His hands slid around me, reaching for the buttons at my back.

"Did you know," he said, "that your dress doesn't fit right in the back?"

I leaned my forehead against his. "I had it made today. There wasn't time to make it perfect."

"Then you should take it off," he said. "Nothing should be imperfect."

I reached back and undid the buttons with one hand. "Nothing is perfect." I lifted the dress up and over my head, let it fall in sus-urrant folds to the floor between us. I wore nothing beneath it.

"You are," he said, watching me. I saw his breathing quicken.

I shook my head, smiling, and walked forward into his arms.

It was long and slow and quiet. There was nothing we needed to say, just the move-ment of bodies in the darkness, darkness in darkness. Only a moment of fumbling over shoes and stockings, but I knew well enough how to get around that. When he laid me back on the bed, my hair spread out in a glory of gold beneath him, escaping from pins he removed one at a time, carefully.

"You wouldn't want to get stuck," he said.

"No," I replied, running my hands along his back, the shape of his lean shoulders. Affection is harder to pretend than passion, but fascination and desire require no pretense. When he thrust into me I was ready, slick and waiting, and the pleasure caught me by surprise. My hips rose, and I grasped at him.

"Did I hurt you?" He held still, joined, both of us held perfectly in check.

"No," I said. "It's been a long time."

That pleased him. I could tell from the smile, and the tremor that ran along his body. He murmured some wordless Italian endearment, and bent his face to mine.

When he finished I was so close that I nearly shrieked in frustration, so close and yet not quite there. He slid off me and to the side, and forgetting everything else, I seized his hand and brought it where I needed it, pressing against the side of his hand, rocking against him.

"There, *cara,* there," he said, and I felt the rolling change, not deep as it had been, but enough.

And then I clung to him as though he were my friend, as though I claimed him, as a wounded man clings to the hand that offers him water, with no thought of who he was, a head of state, an important man, a patron. I held on as though I were drowning. I closed my eyes and turned my face to his neck.

He said nothing. He stroked my long hair spread across the pillows and waited until I lifted my head.

"You know," Bonaparte said, smiling, "I wondered at first if your hair owed more to art than nature, but I see now that it doesn't."

"No," I said, "it's really that color."

He pulled his arm out from under me, and for a moment I wondered if he meant for me to leave so abruptly. Instead, he crossed the room to the little table beside the window and poured a glass of cool water out of an earthen carafe that waited there. He took a long drink, half-turned to the window. The lightning was playing in the sky far away, and the freshening breeze stirred the leaves outside. It felt good.

"Do you want some water?" he asked.

"Yes, please." I sat up and he brought it to me, sitting down on the side of the bed. I took the glass between my hands and drained it.

"Are you always that intense?"

"No. Yes." I stretched to put the glass down. "But I told you it had been a long

360

time. Since things were like that, at any rate." I did not look at him, but stretched out on the red sheets on my stomach, pulling one of the pillows under my chin.

He slipped under the sheet, propping on his elbow. There was nothing but curiosity in his voice. "Did you love Moreau so much, then?"

"No," I said. "But I respected him. And he was very good to me. I can speak no ill of him."

"He never knows what to do with loyalty," Bonaparte said, running one hand down the curve of my back, admiring white skin against the scarlet sheets. "He spends it like coin, and never thinks where more will come from."

"And you?" I asked, turning my head.

"Loyalty is a treasure beyond price," he said, twining one lock of my hair around his finger, all his attention focused upon it. "You can buy sex. You can even buy men who will die at your word. You can buy gratitude or cooperation or peace. But you can't buy loyalty. If I had the loyalty of one such as you" — he paused, and his eyes met mine — "I would not squander it."

"Sir, what would you do with a whore's loyalty?" I asked, pressing my cheek against the pillow.

"The same thing I would do with anyone else's," he said. "See what you are made of, and let you do it." He released my hair, watching the lock uncurl in the dim light.

I closed my eyes, hardly knowing what to say. The words that crowded at my lips were ridiculous, words meant to be said over a blade in a chapel, or on some bloodied field. They were not meant to be said by someone like me. If I were younger, perhaps I would have said them, if I had still believed in heroes and the sons of gods. Instead, I lowered my head against the pillow.

"So tired, then?" he asked.

"A bit," I said. "I hardly slept last night, thinking."

"If you were a better coquette, you would say 'thinking of you,' " he said, and there was amusement in his voice.

"You know that part," I said. "You have the power to throw all into disarray."

He shrugged and moved a little closer, one arm stealing around me. "I do. But order is much harder. It's easy to make a mess of things. Bringing order out of present chaos is much harder."

"Is that what you are doing?" I looked up at him. "Reordering the world?"

"I put it to you that the world has already changed," he said. "In the last century, we have charted the globe, even to the vastest reaches of the South Seas. We have created machines that do the work of men, and now words may flash across the miles faster by semaphore than any dispatch rider ever rode. Our governments must change along with it. If we do not accept the realities that already are, and change our way of doing things accordingly, we will all be swept away by the tide and engulfed."

"Like the Terror," I said. "If change is blocked, when it breaks the dam it runs wild. I had not thought of it."

"Most people don't," he said. "Most people don't think far enough — or if they do, they see only vast tides and can't see the waves right before them."

"You see both," I said.

"The flood is here," he said. "We will never return to the *ancien régime,* to the way things were. We can either learn to master the flood and to make deliberate choices about what we do, or just be swept along." He snorted. "In Austria, they pretend there is no flood. In England, they say that it can be resisted, that their houses will stand against it. It has already washed over our rooftops. It would be purest folly to pretend. We must instead be the masters of our fate."

I rolled over on my back and stared up at the draped ceiling. "I wish I were the master of my fate. Instead I am a bark that has been thrust here and there by the tide."

"Give up, Madame," he said, but not angrily. "You make choices, some for good and some for ill, and you reap the consequences. No storm has tossed you here."

"No," I said slowly, looking up at the carved wreaths holding the curtains. "I suppose not." I knew well enough that if I had refused or pleaded illness, he would not have forced me to come. For that matter, I was in Italy of my own choosing. I had asked Isabella for a place, taken an opportunity that came. I was not a child bride, given to a man who owned me body and soul, or even a virtuous wife bound by law. If law did not protect me, it did not bind me either. No one owned me.

And for the first time I felt a curious lightness, as though I understood the word for the first time. "Liberty," I said.

"Liberty is hard, Madame," Bonaparte said, one hand tracing a pattern down my arm. "As we are all learning."

"Yes," I said. I was still filled with this idea, so vast and uncontrollable that it seemed I held it only by the corner. These politics that Jan had played, that Moreau

had played, were more than just a dangerous game for money or position, more than
the snapping of dogs over spoils. It was a
game for life itself, for who we are to be, a
game stretching centuries behind and dizzying centuries ahead, a game of deciding
what we would believe and how we would
live, whether I should be regarded or de-
spised, freed or imprisoned.

"How much the common good may demand of us . . ." I said, trying to get my
head around it.

"And how much our individual inclina-
tions, how much our natures, may be given
free rein," he said.

"Whether I am an abomination —"

"Or a treasure," Bonaparte said. "Just so."

I looked at him. "And you think?"

He put his head to the side. "Everyone
has their uses. And I see nothing in you to
despise."

"Not my loose virtue?"

He laughed. "*Cara,* if every woman of
loose virtue were an abomination, I should
be Augustine, not Napoleon!"

"And why should there be a different
standard for men than for women?" I said,
thinking of Charles and the liberty I felt in
his clothes, in his skin.

"There is," he said.

"But why should it be so?" I asked. "You have put it to me that we may change civilization as a whole. Why should I not wear trousers and ride into battle, or choose my lovers as a man does? Why should I not face the same dangers and dare the same risks? Why should I not be your Paladin, as surely as Lannes or Masséna?"

He ran his hand over my golden hair, a strange and rueful expression on his face. "You are running far ahead of me. I think there are not any Amazons. But if there were, I am sure you would be one."

He did not know the half of it, I thought. He did not know Charles. He did not know how thoroughly I could be him.

Instead of a hot retort, I put my arms around him, feeling the solidity, as though he were the realest thing in the world. "Love me again," I said.

His eyebrows rose. "Politics is an aphrodisiac?"

"Yes," I said, and drew him down to me.

FAMA VOLAT

In the morning he was awake a few minutes after five, something I was less than enthusiastic about, since we had not slept until after two. I was generally an early riser, but this was ridiculous. I moaned and pulled the sheet back over my head, not stopping to consider that he was the head of state, and that it was probably a severe breach of etiquette.

He laughed at me and hurried into the adjoining dressing room. The sounds of very noisy bathing drifted out to me. It was impossible to sleep through all the splashing and talking with his valet and the singing of random Italian comedy songs. By the time he returned, I was sitting on the edge of the bed, wrapped in the sheet. He wore a cream-colored dressing gown and was toweling his hair dry.

"Do you never sleep?" I asked.

"As little as possible," Bonaparte said,

shaking out his hair like a dog. "Whatever is taken from sleep is added to real life. And there are never enough hours for everything."

His valet followed him in, and I pulled the sheet more tightly around me. Bonaparte ignored it, and continued talking while being handed smallclothes and breeches, shirt and waistcoat and stockings. "And now especially there is no time. I have written the Austrian Emperor to begin negotiations, and we must gain as much as we can before a treaty is proposed."

"Why?" I asked.

"To keep what we have won." He looked at me sharply, in the midst of shrugging into his coat. "Politics, Madame. It may interest you to follow it."

I flushed, still wrapped in the sheet. My dress was on the floor some little distance away.

The valet picked up the wet towels and carried them out.

Bonaparte walked over to me, lifted my chin, and smiled. "I'm leaving for Paris tomorrow, so I won't see you again now. I will be interested in seeing what you do with money and liberty both."

"I am sorry to hear that, sir," I said, rather stiffly. I had not expected more. I had not expected anything of longer standing. But I felt a real reluctance to say good-bye that had less to do with money than I had thought. I wanted to know more. My fascination was not quenched.

He picked up my dress and brought it to me, smoothing out the folds and tucking a bulging purse into it. *"Fama volat,"* he said.

I took it from him. "Do you always spend so much money on women?"

He lifted the dress and held it for me to duck into it. My head emerged. He gave me a half smile. "It stimulates the economy of France."

"Ah," I said, slipping my arms into the sleeves, "I'm glad to know that's what it stimulates."

Bonaparte laughed. "Good-bye, Madame. I will see you again." He did up the buttons on my dress with deft fingers, planted a kiss at the base of my neck, and went off about his work whistling, all before six in the morning. I watched from the hall as his trim form went down the wide marble staircase, his cocked hat in his hand.

I went back to my lodgings and fell sound asleep almost before my head hit the pillow.

It was late afternoon when I awoke, almost time to be at the theater. I got up, splashed my face with tepid water, changed clothes, and ran. I made the curtain, but it was a rather breathless Sébastien in the first scene.

Isabella passed me in the wings during the first comic interlude with the servants. "Are you all right?" she whispered, her long purple wrapper drifting around her trailing feathers. She was about to go on as the beauty who sought the hero's hand and would be sadly disappointed.

I nodded. "He was fine. But he leaves for France tomorrow."

Isabella rolled her eyes. "Well, a small windfall is better than none."

"Yes," I said. And of course it was. While the money wasn't enough to set me up in style, it was more than enough to live on for a few months. Enough to rent an apartment of my own when I got back to Paris, without having to worry how I should pay for it for a while. By the time the money ran out, I would have had time to find a new patron. Or succeed as a great lady of the theater. Or something.

The next morning I went in search of Colonel Meynier at the Hotel Battachio, where he had said he was staying. I arrived not a moment too soon. Meynier was in the courtyard saddling a lean ebony gelding, its tail clubbed with green ribbons.

"Madame St. Elme!" He took both my hands in his and kissed each, his pleasure in seeing me evident on his face. "I hoped you would come before I left."

"Where are you going?" I asked. "I thought you would be in Milan for a while."

"The First Consul is going to Paris," he said. "And I am with Bonaparte's staff, as I told you."

"You leave today?"

"Almost this moment," he said. "I had hoped for the pleasure of your company at dinner, but I fear that we will have to postpone that reunion."

"We will," I said. "And I am terribly sorry. I had no idea you would be leaving so soon."

"Nor did I," Meynier said. "But Bonaparte moves fast. If you have an hour to prepare, you're lucky." He grinned at me, and took hold of the reins. "Do you mind if I tell my friend Ney where you are? He thought you'd disappeared off the face of the earth."

I felt my heart quicken. "Surely he would not wonder so much."

"He might," Meynier said. With one smooth motion he mounted. "May I ask a personal question? Are you presently . . . engaged?"

"No," I said, and hoped he didn't see the

flush rising in my cheeks. "No, I am alone at present."

Meynier bowed from the saddle. "Then until we meet again, Madame."

I did not really expect anything to come of it. I did not expect him to write to his friend and tell him of a chance meeting, and still less for Ney to write to me. It was nearly a month later when the letter came.

We were still in Milan. *The Comical Romance* was still a great hit, but we had been obliged to learn a new history, *Antony and Cleopatra,* so that we could leaven our standard fare with something new for officers who had now seen *Alexander in Asia* half a dozen times.

Of course, we were the only play in town in French, so they might have seen it twenty times yet, but it helped the box office to expand a bit. Isabella was a lovely Cleopatra, all melting warmth. I was her handmaiden. I had all the sharp lines, which I thought was interesting, if not quite as I imagined the character.

The letter came right before the opening curtain on a sweltering night in July. I considered waiting to open it, but I didn't. I couldn't go on not knowing.

His handwriting was slanted and legible,

like a schoolboy with a ledger that he would be graded on.

17 Messidor, Year VIII

Dear Madame St. Elme,
I have had the Pleasure of Mail from Colonel Meynier, who is known to us both. He said that he had greeted you in Milan. I am happy to hear that you are well. He said that you were the very picture of Health. I am glad the climate of Italy agrees with you. He said that it did. I am pleased that you suffer no ill effects and that you are comfortable.

He suggests that I should write to you and renew our Acquaintance, distant as it may be. And that moreover I should tell you some Interesting Military Anecdotes that are Revealing of my Character. I am uncertain of the wisdom of this, but I bow to his Superior Understanding of Women.

We are currently in Munich, having won at the Field of Oberhausen on 9 Messidor, and marched into the City without further Resistance. The Bavarians, for their part, are not eager to support the Austrians, and do not seem Dismayed at the Change in their Fortune.

The enemy flies whenever we are near.

We have taken more than 20,000 prisoners in these Late Months, and widespread desertion makes the Fearful Plight of the Austrians worse. Ulm, which had only a weak garrison, surrendered Without A Shot, to my satisfaction. I hope that Victory, which is with our arms everywhere, will soon end this Struggle and give us Peace. Then I shall hasten home to Enjoy Her Blessings.

Your Obedient Servant,
Michel Ney

I read and reread the letter in my dressing room. I just had time to tuck it in my bosom as I heard my cue. I hurried onstage.

"My dear lady," I said to Isabella-as-Cleopatra, "must you give this Roman such credit?" I knelt beside her throne and spread my hands. "Antony is not Caesar, and the gods did not sire him."

Isabella looked down at me, her voice scathing. "How can you know whom the gods begot, you who were gotten on a slave? Antony is the noblest man who ever walked the Earth, and into his hands I place my safety."

"Dear lady," I said, "he is a hero, of this I have no doubt. But the fire of genius is not his, to command where others fail, to win love and renown together. He is not Fortune's darling, as Caesar was."

She rose, gathering her robes about her, one hand opening to the audience. "Antony is true and brave, and none gainsay it." She swept from the stage.

I looked round, still kneeling, into the footlights. "He is not Caesar," I said, dropping my voice. "Lady, I fear for you. I fear for us all."

I answered the letter that night.

My dear General Ney,
I can hardly express my pleasure upon receiving a letter from you! I did not think that you would remember me based upon our brief acquaintance. I am glad to know that you do.
The climate of Italy is very agreeable, and we are having considerable success with our plays. We are doing The Comical Romance, which is very light and pleasant, and also Antony and Cleopatra, which is tragic but is much appreciated by our troops. Every performance is packed. I don't imagine most of the men have ever been to a play like this before, but everyone seems to enjoy it. Is that not the truest form of Republicanism, to make avail-

able to everyone entertainment formerly reserved for the wealthy? I cannot think but that we are all better for it. And certainly the troupe is better for packed houses. I am playing Sébastienne in The Comical Romance, who is one of the young ladies courted and won in the last scene. Also the Handmaiden, in Cleopatra.

I hope that this letter finds you still at Munich and still safe. While I know little enough of military endeavors, I can still read between lines and tell that your peril has been grave. Pray be safe, and write to me again!

Ida St. Elme

Ney must have replied almost by return post. His letter came in the mailbag of a courier, who dropped it off at my lodging with a grin.

"Special mail and special delivery. The general was sending dispatches and other things to General Lannes, and asked me to drop this for him." The courier was a weedy-looking boy with a Gascon accent.

I tipped him generously. "Are you returning to Munich anytime soon?"

"General Ney's not at Munich anymore," he said. "We're at Parsdorf now. Or we were when I left. I'm going back directly tomorrow, and I'll have to hunt the General up and down Bavaria as usual." He swung back on his horse. "If you've got a return letter, I can stop by tomorrow and pick it up."

"I will," I said. "I will look for you in the morning."

11 Thermidor, Year VIII

Dear Madame St. Elme,
I am glad to know that your plays are doing well. I did not see any until I was in the army, but now I like them very much. I should like to see you as the Handmaiden in Cleopatra, though the idea disturbs me somewhat. It is such a sad play, I expect. I mean that the ending cannot be good. She must die by poison, if I remember. I should not think that I would enjoy watching you do that, even the counterfeit of it. But I suppose it would not be the same play were someone to provide an eleventh-hour rescue.

I hear that Peace has been proposed. In the meantime, we are Making Certain of our position. Which involves a great deal of running at Alarms and snapping back and forth like a dog on a chain, not venturing too far from Munich and yet charging at any Rumor of an Austrian advance.

My Peril, as you put it, is not so very great. There is that Austrian army of 100,000 warriors that was not only going to invade the Alsace, Brabant, and so on, but was going to change our political status entirely and end the Republic. There is that Army, I say, reduced to 40,000 runaways not daring to face Republican Phalanxes, which are in rags but are full of courage and sauce. They will make peace, of that I am sure.

Your servant,
Michel Ney

We did not play that night, for there was a musical performance instead, and I sat up composing my reply.

Isabella came in and found me at it, writing by the light of one candle. "Can you be writing to that man again?"

I nodded absently, dipping my quill again, trying to recapture what I had been saying.

"You've met him once?" Isabella came and looked over my shoulder at Ney's letter. "It's not exactly the picture of romance."

"No," I said.

She shook her head and walked off. "You're hopeless."

I was.

My dear General Ney,

I do not think the Handmaiden would thank you for an eleventh-hour rescue from her fate. Surely the only thing more tragical that she could endure would be to outlive her mistress, knowing that she has been untrue and failed in her charge. How should you live, an outcast man, who had the misfortune to live when your world is gone? Pity the poor Handmaiden her death if you will, but do not wish it otherwise, I pray. She would rather your tears upon her faithful grave.

I have never yet been to Bavaria, so I do not well imagine your endeavors, your running back and forth. But I am pleased to hear that it is going well, and I thrill to imagine your feats of arms!

You have saved the Republic, you and men like you. We do not even reckon the worth as yet, for most of us are still sleeping and do not understand the liberties we should lose if you should fail. I know what I should lose. I have my own money in the bank. I could not keep it if the Republic fell, for before I could not have a bank account separate from my husband. I have my own lodgings. How should I live if I could no longer be party to contracts and I could not rent? I may travel freely and live as I like, with liberty unknown to females of other states.

I am no longer sleeping, but awake, and the cause of liberty is dear to me. Know then, that you are a hero in my eyes for preserving that which is as necessary as breath to me.

Ida

I sent the letter in the morning, and it was seven weeks, as they still called them in Italy, before his reply came. I wondered if I had offended him. I wondered if my letter had gone astray and had not reached Ney.

Isabella was beginning to talk about wintering in Italy. Some of the company wanted to stay and some didn't. I thought that Isabella was reluctant to leave Auguste Thibault, who seemed to eat out of her hand.

He was a nice enough man of medium height, with sandy hair and a pair of wire-rimmed spectacles that he wore for reading or anything else at close range. Otherwise he squinted, which gave him a somewhat comic look. It was obvious that he thought the sun rose and set around Isabella, while she, for her part, treated him with a comfortable familiarity that seemed more warm than passionate.

I wasn't sure whether I would winter in Italy or not. An armistice had been signed, and most of our troops were going home. I had not decided what to do when Ney's letter reached me.

7 Vendémiaire, Year VIII

Dear Ida,
I should rather live, for life is hope, and that which is lost may always be regained. If we fail in our charges, what can we do except strive for better, and by our atonement remedy our flaws?

I cannot imagine that you have ever been sleeping.

I have taken some trifling wound to the leg weeks ago, before the armistice. It was a close skirmish, and while there was not much they could do, and indeed some had begun to surrender, this bastard got me with the bayonet along the back of the knee just above the top of my boot. I was on horseback and he on foot, so perhaps it was all he could reach. But it is nothing but a Nuisance. I limp about a bit and shall until the muscle heals.

I am on my way back to Paris, the peace

having been signed. Perhaps you will be there?

Your servant,
Michel

THE ROAD HOME

In the end, Isabella decided to return to Paris after all. Auguste Thibault was being reassigned, and he and his artillery unit were to go north in a few weeks. This decided most of the company. We should all return to Paris together.

I wrote to Ney to tell him this.

My dear General,
Our company has decided to return to Paris, and I expect to arrive there at the end of the summer or early in the fall. We are accompanying an artillery brigade, so our speed will not be great.

I hope that the wound you have taken is not dangerous. You make light of it in your letter, but I do not know if it is such a little thing, or if this is just your way.

I would like to see you. When you are in Paris.

Ida

■ ■ ■ ■

Traveling with an artillery train was very different from following after an army, as we had done on the way to Italy. For one thing, the cannon tore up the roads to such an extent that it was sometimes difficult to get our wagon through, especially on hills and slopes when the ground was wet and the road was mud. For another thing, they had their own extensive baggage. Each cannon had its caisson, with shot, chain, swabs, and other supplies. Then there were the powder caissons, packed close and carefully, drawn by horses with their hooves muffled lest their iron shoes throw off sparks from stones in the road.

After this came the baggage train proper — the feed wagons for the officers' horses and for the horses who drew the cannon and the carts and caissons, the baggage wagons with tents and cooking pots, rope and lentils, beans and grain and great barrels of wine, vinegar and oil. There was the harness master's wagon with leather and supplies, driven by the harness master's apprentice. There were the noncommissioned officers' wagons, carrying their clothes and private provisions, and the cook's wagon with chickens and ducks in cages, three nanny goats tied on behind, chewing philosophically as the wagons rolled along the road.

Then came the sutlers and the unofficial baggage — the wagons hired by officers who clubbed together, carrying folding cots and camp tables, wine and bed linens and shuttered lamps. The sutlers, of which we had two, had fancy foodstuffs for sale, as well as soap, playing cards, novels, eau de cologne, English letters, cognac, and a litter of purebred dachshund puppies. Behind came the laundresses in two wagons. The five of them were all wives or women of various enlisted men among the gun crews, and they took in washing to defray the costs of the road.

We came after, our gaily painted wagon the court jester at the end of the baggage train. The second man drove the wagon, as the first man was one of the few who'd stayed in Milan. Isabella rode on the box with him while the dresser/understudy and the soubrette sat in the back with the costumes and trunks.

I rode alongside on Nestor. In my man's clothes, no doubt I looked like the first man, the handsome one who always plays the hero. I probably could in a pinch. By now I knew all Antony's lines by heart.

In the morning we would all start out together, but by nightfall the cannon and their crews would have drawn ahead, the first wagons well out of sight along the bends of the road. It took us some half an hour to come up to them at the halts.

Three days out of Milan, I was nervous. Or perhaps it was Nestor who was nervous. He had been a cavalry horse, and keeping to the decorous pace of an artillery column bored him. It was one of those glorious end-of-summer days of Northern Italy, when the setting sun gilds the snow still remaining on the distant peaks as though they were dipped in gold, while plunging the valleys into shadow. A slow purple haze spread over the world, and the sounds of the insects were loud. The sky was very blue and very far away. Though the day was warm and I had removed my coat in favor of shirt and waistcoat, the evening chill already spoke of the mountains. Autumn was coming, especially on the heights.

Most of the wagons were out of sight. Only the laundresses were visible ahead, and when the road curved we could sometimes see the sutlers. It was almost time to make camp. I hoped the head of the column had stopped.

I was about to ride ahead on Nestor to see if it had when it happened.

I didn't see the men come out of the underbrush in the gulley. The first thing I knew was when the soubrette screamed, more startled than afraid. There were six of them, unkempt and bearded, all dressed differently. Not an Austrian patrol or even deserters. They were bandits. No doubt they had been waiting as the column passed, hoping for an easy target at the end.

One of them grabbed the bridle of the cart horse, a long knife in his hand. Two more closed in on the wagon, while the other three blocked the road ahead and behind. The two ahead looked at me. One of them took a step forward. Nestor was a prize worth having.

Our second man shouted something, and the cart horse backed, whinnying, not liking the unfamiliar hand on his bridle. Nestor's ears went back.

The one before me held a long knife. I could see with sudden startling clarity his bristled chin, the small scar at the corner of his eye, the red laces on his shirt. "Drop the gun, boy," he said in peasant Italian, "and get off the horse."

The second bandit moved closer. He made a grab for Nestor's rein just as Isabella screamed. I saw, from the corner of my eye, that she was struggling with one of them on the box, heard the ripping of fabric as her dress gave way.

Nestor shied, and the bandit missed his rein by a finger's length.

Absolute, cold clarity. Somewhere Elza might be frightened, but the part of me that was Charles was not. He had done it all before. The bandit was on my right side, but I wore the second man's pistol on my left.

Swearing. The sounds of a scuffle. Our second man was lying on the ground in front of the wagon, the cart horse restive at the smell of blood.

"Get down now, boy," the other man said.

I heard the smack as a blow caught Isabella on the side of the head, tumbling her backward onto the chests and the understudy.

I raised the pistol in my left hand and brought it across me as Nestor backed a step. "No," I said, and fired it point-blank in the bandit's face.

Blood and brains exploded across me, part of his jawbone catching on the lace of my cuffs, teeth still in it. I shook my wrist and it flew. Nestor backed away from the falling body, the acrid powder smoke.

The other bandit snarled and made a lunge for me, but Nestor backed again. I felt the sudden rush of warmth between my legs as irrelevantly my bladder gave way. Not important right now. I had one shot and no sword, and now they were after me, except for the two still struggling with Isabella, the understudy, and the soubrette in the wagon.

Two of them, crowding in close ahead.

The horse. I had the weight of the horse. Like movement underwater, every moment seemed to take forever, like movements of a dance I knew, a dance Charles had known forever. And Nestor had been a cavalry mount. They rushed in, and I pulled back sharply on the reins. Nestor rose on his hind legs, flailing at them with his sharp, heavy hooves. A squeeze and he plunged forward, striking one of them sharply. I brought the pistol butt down hard on the back of the man's head as we lunged past, saw him fall insensible.

I pulled Nestor around, and he had the bit in his teeth now. We charged back in as though I had a saber in my hand, Nestor's weight bowling another over into the mud, though I don't think he was hurt. "Back!" I said, hauling him around.

And now they were converging, all four of

them. I backed away. I could escape into the woods or down the road toward the column. But that would mean leaving Isabella and the others. I could not reload — the second man had the powder. And I had no sword.

"Come and get me then!" I yelled. "Pissant sons of bitches!" They would have to try to corner me without getting close to Nestor's forelegs. Nestor stamped for emphasis.

And then there was a thunder of hooves. Auguste Thibault and two of his officers charged into it like daylight into snow, a flurry of swords and Thibault's white warhorse. Auguste's hat was off and his glasses clung to the tip of his nose, an expression of grim fury on his face, his epée in his hand.

It was over very quickly. Two of the bandits went down in the first rush. One ran, and in the confusion escaped into the gulley. The last one, his right arm clenched bleeding at his side, sank to his knees in surrender. A lieutenant I knew by sight alone dismounted and tied him up.

The other lieutenant rode up to me. He must have been no more than seventeen or eighteen, with wide hazel eyes. "Are you all right?" he asked. My clothes were a mess of blood and powder and bone.

"Yes," I said. "I'm fine. I don't know about anyone else."

The understudy was moving. She had a bruise along the side of her face and her nose was bleeding, but she was climbing out of the wagon and kneeling down beside the second man. I saw her checking him, talking softly. His unfired pistol lay on the road beside him, the mate of mine.

Auguste swung from the saddle to the wagon box, reaching down for Isabella.

She got up gingerly. Her dress gaped open to the hips, her breast streaked with blood where someone had clawed at her, and she clutched at Auguste's hands as though he were her savior.

"I heard the shot," he said. "God, Isabella, I'll never forgive myself. You could have been killed. Without you, I'd have no reason for living." His glasses had been lost in the fight, and in the expression on his round face I suddenly saw what Isabella had seen in him. "You are everything to me. Every-thing, my dearest love. . . ." His last words were muffled as Isabella stepped into his arms, holding on to him and bursting into wild tears. Auguste rained kisses on her hair, murmuring incoherently.

I slid off Nestor. My knees shook a little, but I could control them. The brains on my hands were sticky. For a moment my stomach turned over.

No, I thought savagely. *No.*

I put my hand against Nestor's warm side. He turned his head to me and butted me softly. "You were perfect," I said to him. "You're the best horse."

He nickered and put his head against my shoulder. I rested there, leaning on him. Then I carefully put the pistol back in its holster on the saddle, and reached for my saddlebags, suddenly acutely aware of the dampness of my trousers. I had a spare pair in my bags. I would change before anyone noticed. And no one would remark on my changing clothes, given the blood everywhere.

I changed behind Nestor. When I came out again, the second man was sitting up in the wagon with the soubrette and the understudy holding cloths to his head. He had a large purple lump rising and it had bled a little, but he seemed to be talking coherently to them.

Auguste swung back onto his horse, Isabella before him, her draggled skirts spreading over his stirrups. It was getting dark.

"Lenotre, will you bring the wagon along and escort the ladies? Paul, can you take the rear? Let's get everyone into camp. I am taking Mademoiselle Felix ahead with me."

The one he had called Lenotre looked up. "What about the bandits, sir?"

"Leave them where they fell," he said. Auguste glanced at me for the first time. "Madame St. Elme seems to have accounted for two of them. Perhaps you will ride with the boys there and bring the wagon in?"

I nodded as smartly as I could.

Auguste held out his epée. "I think you've earned this." He put it into my hand. "I've another."

"Thank you," I said.

He touched his heels to his horse's sides and trotted away into the gathering darkness, Isabella clasped tightly before him, the white horse shining in the last light.

I rode behind with the two young officers, bringing the wagon in, the epée naked in my hand. Auguste had forgotten to give me the scabbard.

The rest of the trip to Paris passed without incident. I got the scabbard from Auguste the next day, and wore the epée with Charles's clothes for the rest of the journey. It was not too heavy for me. With a straight blade and a narrow blood channel, it was unadorned and none too fancy, but it was light and cold and very, very sharp. I made sure it was very, very sharp from then on.

Nestor seemed inordinately pleased with himself, as well he might. He practically frisked his way up and down the passes. I spoiled him a bit. He deserved it.

We reached Paris as autumn began. I used the First Consul's gold to rent an apartment on the third floor of a respectable house — one large salon with a Franklin stove at one end so that I could cook, and a bedroom. I would have no roommate this time.

Isabella would hardly be available. She and Auguste set up housekeeping together in Rue de Turin immediately. Which of course meant that they needed furniture. Isabella and I spent a happy day in the flea markets getting a few things that would make it possible to live in some comfort. She spent Auguste's money. I spent Bonaparte's.

A pair of Louis XV armchairs, the pale-blue upholstery softened by time, would grace the salon, along with a modern table with sphinx claw feet à la Égyptienne. I bought some pots and china, a nice tea set that had three cups and a saucer broken and could consequently only serve five, and scarlet velvet curtains in a vast lot, which turned out to be enough curtains for the salon and the bedchamber, plus an extra pair that I hung over the door from the salon to the bedroom, looped back with the gold tasseled ties. I bought a somewhat battered four-poster, but then sprang for a new feather bed, white linen sheets, and a set of gold satin curtains and a gold brocade cover for a feather duvet. I stopped then. The money needed to last. And I had spent more than half.

There was also the expense of Nestor's stabling. Isabella suggested that I should sell him.

"I don't think so," I said, balancing packages one on another. Isabella wanted to go look at crystal.

She looked back at me over the top of a huge box, her bonnet feathers nodding from a fashionable brim. "It seems contradictory to me to build a nest and keep your horse for the open road."

"It may be," I said. Isabella had had quite a bit to say about staying in Paris from now on. "But I don't know what I'll do next. There's Ida and Charles both, both my lives."

"I think you take Charles too seriously," she said. "Sometimes it scares me. You know, you're not really him." Her dark eyes were worried.

"I am," I said. "Charles is every bit as real as Ida. It's not as simple as a masquerade."

"I wish it were," Isabella said. "I wonder about you sometimes."

"So do I," I said. Surely if anything was a symptom of madness, it was Charles. And yet I had spent some of my happiest days as Charles, freed from everything a woman should be and should do, invulnerable in a waistcoat. Men did not feel as women did, did not suffer. But truly, what did it matter if I was mad? Who in all the world truly cared, if I did not?

And we bought crystal. She bought a great deal. I bought a pair of wineglasses, long and graceful, with knobbed stems, the rims touched with gold.

When I got home, a boy was waiting with a message for me. I gave him a coin and read it, waiting for my purchases to be brought up from the wagon Isabella had hired.

17 Vendémiaire, Year VIII

Dear Ida,
I am returned to Paris after a fortnight in the Saar with my family. I know that you are also traveling, and perhaps this is the reason I have had no letter from you. I

hope that you are well and that the weather has held fine.

I have just this day arrived in Paris, and I asked about until I heard that you were here from a friend of mine who heard from an artillery colonel with whom you had traveled from Italy. In short, we're both here now.

I should like to call on you, if I may.

Michel

It took some time to find ink and a quill and paper, my heart beating fast all the while. I hadn't bought any when I was shopping with Isabella.

Dear Michel,
I would be pleased if you could come for dinner tomorrow night. It would give me the greatest pleasure if you would present yourself at eight o'clock.

I hope that you are well, and that your leg is much better.

Ida

Since I had just moved in, I spent the next day running around madly preparing for dinner. I bought table linens, and then spent most of the afternoon buying food. I decided not to get overcomplicated. A good mushroom soup was not beyond my skills as a first course, and could be made on the Franklin stove without difficulty. A roasted chicken could be purchased ahead of time and served cold, dressed up a little bit. A salad was easy, and there was nothing in it that needed cooking. Bread, naturally. A Spanish Manchego to go with Madeira and fresh plums as a last course would round it out nicely. Not a formal meal, but then formality would be hard to manage with no cook and no servants.

Trying to impress the peasant general with your housewifely skills? my Inner Moreau asked sarcastically. I wasn't much interested in my Inner Moreau's opinions anymore. I knew exactly what Moreau thought of Ney, and exactly what he would think of my dinner efforts.

Ney was punctual, knocking on the door exactly at eight. Patting my hair into place, I went to open it.

He was taller than I remembered, and fairer. A summer in the sun had bleached his hair more red than bronze; it was caught behind him in a long, old-fashioned tail that went halfway down his back. The same sun that had bleached his hair had left his face sunburned and freckled, and his eyes looked very blue against his skin. His hat was under his arm.

"Madame St. Elme?" he said, as though for a moment he wasn't sure. Perhaps I had changed too.

I stepped back from the door. "Please come in, General Ney. I'm glad you were right on time."

He pulled out his watch from an inner pocket. "Actually, I was early. I've been waiting down in the stairwell until it was time."

I couldn't help smiling. "You could have come up."

He looked around for a place to put his hat that wasn't either on the table set for dinner or on one of the chairs. "I couldn't have. My mother always hated it when guests were early and threw all her plans off."

I took the hat from him and cast around. No place to put it. "I've just moved in," I said. "I'm afraid I'll have to put it on the bed in here." I scurried into my room and dropped it on the bed, then popped back out from behind the curtains.

He was standing in the middle of the salon. The windows were open, letting in the last warm air, though the sun was setting. It was really fall now, and over Paris the stars were high and far away, the evening star glittering through the smoke and cloud, Sirius rising cool in the sky.

He seemed to fill up my room, though he could not be that tall. Still, it was strange to look up a good six inches. I was a tall woman, and unused to it.

I went over and closed the windows to give myself something to do. "It will be cold later," I said.

"Probably," he said. "It was last night."

"The weather is often variable at this time of year."

"Yes," he said. "The weather can be different from day to day."

I looked at him. Blue coat, gold braid, the tricolor sash wrapped around his waist. I had imagined him often, tried to remember what he looked like from that one brief meeting. I had imagined him before that, the King of Chalices in my tarot deck, the red-haired king, swift in every feeling. And yet the reality was strange. He had a square jaw like a street fighter, but he stood like cavalry.

"Are we going to talk about the weather?" Michel asked.

"We don't have to," I said. "We could talk about something else." He had a small scar across his jawline on the left side, white against his sunburn. A practice foil? A childhood accident?

He looked down, almost as if he had read my thought in my eyes. Down meant straight down my cleavage. I was wearing my new pink gown, a rose so dark it was almost red, with gold trim at the sleeves and waist. Then he took a step back and pulled something out of his pocket. It was a grubby piece of paper, folded many times over. "I brought your letter back."

For a moment I didn't know what he meant.

"The one you meant for someone else. 'I am sending your boots as you requested, along with several pairs of new stockings. I have taken care of the table linens. . . .' "

He held the paper out to me.

I felt myself flushing wildly. "You must think me a complete idiot."

"The letter was for General Moreau?"

"You know that I was with him," I said, taking it from him.

"I didn't, but I certainly found that out," he said. "When Moreau called me into his office last spring and upbraided me for being no gentleman, the kind of cad who cuts in on his senior's territory, and warned me that if I intended to keep my command in the Army of the Rhine, I had best learn how things are done."

I drew a deep breath and half-turned away. "I am so sorry," I said. "I never meant that he should hold it against you. I told him that nothing had ever happened between us." I put the paper down very carefully on the table, next to the pewter forks that served me for plate. For a moment I felt my eyes swimming.

"You got worse," he said. He stepped closer, and I could almost feel him behind me, as solid and trapping as a wall. "I heard he threw you out."

"He did." I shrugged. I didn't look at him. "That's how it goes sometimes." I turned and gave him a brilliant, brittle smile.

"I didn't know," Michel said. "I'm sorry. I

thought you were an actress. I saw you on the stage later."

"You seem to have turned up for all my most humiliating moments," I said.

He smiled, and it was grave and kind, not mocking. "You were very bad. But I liked it anyway."

"I've gotten better," I said. "I only got that part by sleeping with the right person."

"The fat man I saw you with after?"

I nodded.

"I thought so," he said. "So I didn't come up to you."

"But you were watching me," I said. "You sent the roses. There was no card."

"There was when I left them," he said. "It must have gotten lost."

Along with my shoes, I thought. Oh yes, I could see too easily how that had happened. "He gave me money and a part," I said.

Michel put his head to the side. "Are you trying to make me think worse of you?"

"I want you to know what I am," I said. "I want you to have no illusions about me."

"I know what you are," he said. "At least, I think I do."

I looked away. I could not stand the expression on his face. If I looked at him another moment, I would do something I would regret. Like burst into tears. Or kiss him.

"Dinner is nearly ready," I said. "Would you open the wine?"

I put the length of the room between us, ladling soup and getting out the bread. He handed me into my chair as soon as I had put the plates on the table, and poured the wine deftly.

"I'm sorry," I said. "I've just moved in. I have no servants yet."

Michel shrugged, breaking off a piece of bread. "I never had servants at all, growing up. We all just did for ourselves. My father was a cooper for the vineyards at Saar-Louis, and there were five of us children, so we all had to do our part. Mother couldn't have kept up otherwise."

"Are you the oldest?" I asked.

He shook his head, his mouth full of soup. It took a moment before he swallowed it. "I'm the middle one. My sister Sophie is the oldest. She's six years older than I am. She was married long before I left home. Margarethe is my other sister, and she's five years younger, and still lives with my father. Joseph was my older brother, and he was two years older. He was killed at Trebbia last year."

"I'm sorry," I said. "That must be hard."

He nodded. "And then Charles was my younger brother, two years younger. He died when we were children."

I caught a sudden breath, as though something had punched me.

"What's the matter?" Michel said, laying his spoon aside.

"I had a brother named Charles, too," I said. "Two years younger. He died when I was eight."

"I was nine," Michel said. His hand reached for mine across the table. "I didn't mean — what's wrong?"

"I can't even begin to tell you," I said. "About Charles. About my family. It's so complicated." I shook my head. "It's too strange. You wouldn't believe it."

Michel shrugged. "I believe some pretty strange things."

"You?" He seemed the picture of a big, honest Saarländer.

"I'm not as wholesome as I look," he said, smiling.

I couldn't help but smile back. "You can't be as bad as you think."

"Try me," he said. "Maybe I just need some lessons."

I laughed and looked away. The desire on his face was so plain. Every emotion was written all over him. I could read him like a

book. "Like a soldier from the country looking for sophisticated vices?"

He shrugged again. "In Saar-Louis, vice is
having a baby six months after the wedding.
We're wholesome people. Salt of the earth.
Hardworking and early-rising and all that.
We love our vineyards and our farms and
orchards and wells, and our big families and
our excellent ham."

"And you?"

His smile faded. He leaned forward, his
elbows on the table. "I never belonged
there. I've always been in love with blood."

A chill ran down me.

"As a child, I always wanted the darkest
stories. When the old men would sit around
in the tavern talking about the Seven Years'
War, I wanted to see the stumps of their
arms, to touch them. And wondered how I
would feel, knowing my arm wasn't there,
how it would feel to lose it, half frightened
and half fascinated." He picked up his glass,
the light playing on the stem, on his clear,
passionate eyes. "I ran away to the army
when I was sixteen. I'd never wanted anything else. This was in '85, when if I served
all my life, I might end a sergeant. A half-
lettered thug with a really big sword."
Michel raised an eyebrow at me. "I was a
sergeant at twenty. Then the Revolution

came. And suddenly it was a good time to be a thug with a really big sword."

"I think you're more than that," I said. "You couldn't look at yourself with irony if you weren't. Man of blood you may be, but you're a good deal more than a thug."

"If so, it's because I chose to be," he said, lifting the glass again. "If there's one thing that the Revolution taught me, it's that we're all inches from savages. It's just that I know it more than most. I can't dress it up in pretty explanations when the bloodlust is on me, pretend that I'm fighting for anything else than the joy in it. That's why I have to be so careful. And trust in God to help me moderate these passions."

"You believe in God?" I got up to fetch the chicken and its accompaniments and bring them to the table. "That's very dated."

Michel didn't seem offended. "I do. I believe in God and the teachings of Christ, in the brotherhood of mankind and the inexpressible love of the Holy Spirit."

I looked at him, as shocked as if he had muttered obscenities. I couldn't remember hearing anything of the kind before, except as a pious platitude or a clever mockery. It simply wasn't said in society by intelligent people. But he sat there perfectly composed, getting ready to carve the chicken.

I sat down across from him. "I am only wondering how you can be anything but a rationalist after what you have seen," I said.

"Like Moreau?" he asked, looking at me, one eyebrow cocked.

I didn't rise to that bait. Instead I sat back in my chair, my fragile muslin dress looking the color of old blood in the light.

"How can you be anything but a cynic after the things you have seen? How can you really believe that, other than some vague humanistic aim of good government and freedom from foreign oppression, that there is any greater good in all of this?"

He looked at me, startled. "How can I not?"

Two years ago, I had fancied him my eternal love. Instead he was a stranger, a man I didn't know. Not really. I wanted to reach out and touch him, for him to tell me something, to know it all and understand. But he was a stranger.

"Don't you believe in anything?" he asked quietly. "Not gods or destiny? Not justice or beauty or Heaven?"

I took a quick gulp of the wine. It stung my throat and my eyes. "Heaven is no comfort for me," I said lightly. "I hope it does not exist, as I plan never to reside there. Which is just as well, I suppose. It would be awfully boring, sitting around with Augustine and the Church Fathers, playing the harp and wearing a little white chiton. I'm all fumbles with stringed instruments anyway. Can't you just see me taking up foot washing in the St. Mary Magdalene room, having seen the error of my ways? Forgiven, but only so much?" I spread my finger and thumb apart.

He raised his chin. "How many men have you killed?"

"What?" There was, unbidden, falling past me, the bandit on the road with no face, the other whose face I had never seen.

"How many men have you killed?" he demanded again, leaning forward, nothing nonchalant in his pose now, just intensity of line and feature.

"One or two, perhaps," I stammered. "Does it matter?"

"451 dead at Heinsberg, 72 at Maastricht, 967 at Altenkirchen, 244 at Winterthur, close to 1,200 in other actions. These are my casualties, my troops killed by my orders. Close to seven thousand of the enemy. Hundreds who have lost legs or arms or their sight." His voice was perfectly steady and terribly precise. "So you have shared men's beds. You have not dismembered them, or seen your own wounded hacked to pieces by surgeons in a futile attempt to save their lives. You have not written the letters. 'Dear Madame: I send you your son Jean-Paul in three pieces. I am dreadfully sorry. I made a stupid mistake in the disposition of my left flank!' "

Michel reached for the wine again. "So when I am here, safe and sound, where there is only the guillotine and a crowd of mad ex-Jacobins to fear, please forgive me if I do not die of guilt at the thought of spending the night with a woman I am not married to, or in some other sophisticated vice. It pales next to more than nine thousand counts of murder."

I sat there in stunned silence while he poured carefully and drained his glass. "And you believe in God?" I asked.

He looked up at me over the gilded rim of the glass. "Of course I believe in God. I have come within inches of death more times than I can count. Men have fallen at my back stricken with the bullets aimed for me. A saber once turned in the air above my head as though it had been stopped by a blade I couldn't see. I believe in God. I must. In all these slaughters, I am spared. God has something else in mind for me. And given the slaughters to which I aspire, I can only say" — he paused and took a sip of the golden wine. "He delights in it."

"Delights? You don't believe, then?"

"In a good and just God?" Michel met my eyes. "Oh, yes, I do. Because, hackneyed as it is, I believe in the Republic. I do believe that this is necessary. It's better. Not perfect, because nothing made by the hand of man ever is, but better. Better than starvation under a corrupt king. Better than hundreds of thousands of lives stifled and dying for lack of air, living and dying in ignorance, spirits broken by the sameness. By doing as their fathers and grandfathers and great-grandfathers before them, with no hope and no choice. It is better that the responsibility of sin be taken on by those who agree to do it."

His eyes were shaded in the flickering light. "Make no mistake. Our enemies mean to destroy us. If they should win, it will be French citizens who bleed under a Terror like we have never known before, and French children who grow up in ignorance and poverty, condemned to accept it with the fatality of the inevitable. If we go back, we will go all the way back. It will be 1648 again. Who knows how many hundred years it will be again, before we once again have the idea of revolution?" He gave me a sideways smile, rueful and sharp. "But that doesn't mean I don't know that my hands are covered with blood."

I looked down at the chicken on my plate, half touched, then looked up. "How can you do it? Wide-awake, knowing what you do?"

"It's what I was born to do," he said, almost gently. "We are both who we were born to be."

"You can't know who I am," I said. I stood up a little unsteadily, knocking against the edge of the table. The plate and china rang. "And you wouldn't like it if you did."

"Ida —"

"Don't call me that," I snapped.

"Why not? You can call me Michel."

"Because it's not my name," I said, turning away. The cheese. The Madeira. The plums. That would be a distraction.

"Not your name?" He tried to make a joke of it. "Then who are you? I thought that I was having dinner with the famous Madame St. Elme."

"It is a stage name," I said with some annoyance. "Do you think I would use my own name as I have used this one?"

"What is your name, then?" he asked gently. I heard the chair move as he stood up.

I took a deep breath. "Elzelina van Aylde Versfelt Ringeling." I didn't look at him.

"Elzelina," he said quietly. He stood behind me. "Elza."

"Yes."

Reaching around me, he took my hand in his and pressed it slowly to his lips, leaving a trail of fire that made me shiver, his eyes warming me to the bone. "Hello, Elza," he said.

I gathered my wits about me, looking anywhere but at his face. "Do not tell me that you will not hurt me," I said harshly. "That is a promise you can't keep, and I would as soon that you never made it. And do not ask if I will be faithful. I am not the kind of woman who can be faithful, even to someone she feels sincere friendship for."

"That is as well," he said evenly. "I am not the kind of man who can be faithful either. Certainly not when I am away in the field."

"That would be unreasonable to expect," I agreed. "I could not be faithful if I were left behind."

"No fidelity, then." He shook his head. "And the money? I am not a rich man, and I live on my pay."

"No fidelity. But I must live."

Michel sighed. "So must I. And I actually live on half my pay. My father's arthritis is so bad that he can't work anymore, so I send half my pay to him and Margarethe, who takes care of him. I'm still paying off the farm I bought them. It has a little orchard that I thought could be Margarethe's dowry if something happened to me."

I blinked at him. "You do know that you're too good to be true," I said flatly.

He shrugged, looking for a moment like an embarrassed schoolboy. "Anyone would do as much."

"No, they wouldn't," I said.

"I'm not in a position to make any offer you could accept. I can't afford two establishments. I have rooms like this." He looked around. "I'm renting from an old woman on Île Saint-Louis."

"We'll manage," I said. "You should try selling some favors in the corps."

"I would never —" he began hotly. Then he saw my face. "Elza."

I looked at him then, and he was smiling, his face half-turned from me. "Michel," I whispered, "it is better if we never begin this."

"You were not frightened two years ago," he said, reaching for my hands and drawing me toward him.

"I was a different person two years ago."

"Two years ago, you were my commanding officer's mistress," he said. My eyes came just to the level of his shoulders. Moreau had called him an Alsatian bull. He might have been right. I wanted to press against those tight pants, see if all that bulge was real.

"It would be better if we were only friends," I said. "I do have a sincere regard for you."

"And I have a sincere regard for you," he said. My face must have been disbelieving, for he smiled at me and said, "Elza, surely you don't want me to say that I love you." His long fingers brushed at my cheekbone, at the curve of my face. "You wouldn't believe me if I did. You are so young and so much a woman of the world."

"I am twenty-four," I said, trying not to sound breathless. I wanted him as I had never wanted anyone in my life.

"And I'm thirty-one," he replied.

"I know." He was an innocent anyway, much more than I had ever been. I had never been wholesome.

His mouth was drawn, fine and strained, his eyes searching my face. "Is it ordinary, do you think, to remember a woman you met once, two years ago, who sent you an inexplicable letter, so vividly that you must go and find her two years later?"

"Of course it's not ordinary," I said, trying to ignore the touch of his hand on my face. "You aren't an ordinary man."

"Elza, why are you fighting me?" he asked, one thumb tracing my jaw lightly. "What do you have to lose?"

I shook my head, smiling at him. He was so beautiful, this stranger, but familiar all the same, as though I had known him in distant infancy and only forgotten. "You are arrogant, and you are shamelessly manipulating me."

He cupped my face, brushed back a stray tendril of hair. "I thought I was being pretty transparent." I could feel the sword calluses on his palm, the rough places where reins would lie.

"Let me think," I said, and he released me. I sat down in my chair and leaned back, telling myself that my head was only spinning from the wine. I closed my eyes.

How could he be different from any of the others who lay with me for a night or a week or a month, and whom I was forgetting? *If I have him, he will be no different,* I thought, *one more lonely soldier, one more Gantheaume, whose face I barely recall. If I do not, I can continue to love the idea of him, my modern cavalier, flawed and dangerous, the imperfect ideal of everything a man should be. If I do not have him, do not know him, he cannot disappoint me, or tear away the last thing I have to believe in.*

I heard him get up and cross behind me, his booted footsteps hesitant. "Elza?" He was behind my chair, but he didn't touch me. "Would you like to go to a concert tomorrow night? It's a drinking kind of party, and I don't know if you . . ." Oh yes, I knew what he was really asking. Will you or not? he wanted to know.

"I don't know either," I said. "Shall I let you know in the morning?"

"Yes, of course," he said. "It's after midnight now."

"Goodness, is it that late?" I said, getting up and trying to look businesslike. "I didn't realize." I tried not to look at his face.

His voice was not cool and sophisticated, even though he said the right things. I could hear the hurt. "Perhaps I should be going," he said, looking behind the table for his gloves. "Thank you for an excellent dinner."

"I enjoyed it very much, too," I said, going to get his hat and handing it to him. "Let me show you down. I'll have to lock the street door behind you this late."

I unlocked the door to the hall, still not meeting his eyes. My body was aching for him, yearning toward him, aroused by the mildest of touches, by one almost-kiss.

The stairs were narrow, and there were four flights and four turnings to the bottom. I held one of the candles high so that we could see our way, lifting my skirts and holding the banister with the other hand. He was behind me on the stairs, his boot heels heavy on the polished wood, walking with the heavy scuff that always means cavalry, a man used to walking in spurs.

When we reached the bottom, I already felt the draft of cold air under the door. I put the candle on the stand while I unbolted the heavy door, my back to him. "Good night, Michel," I said.

"Good night," he said, sliding his arms around me. I turned, and somehow we were locked together, all the warmth of him flooding into me like a tide submerging all the rocks. My arms went around him, pressing him to me, feeling the scratchy wool of his coat on my bare arms. He pushed me back against the door, its solidity holding me up. My mouth opened under his, and I felt the warmth and hardness of his body against me, slipping my tongue into his mouth, pulling at him.

I came up gasping, but there was no respite. His lips were on my neck, the smoothness of his shaven cheek against my throat, one of my hands tangling in his hair. I moaned and pressed against him, his knee in the cleft between my legs, his hardness against my thigh.

He bent his head, his mouth opening and closing on my nipple through the thin muslin. With a ragged breath, I started tearing at the cravat at his throat, dropping it and ripping the buttons open so I could get at his flesh. Our mouths met with some sort of primal sound. His hands were on my breast, and I could taste the wine on his breath. Upstairs, I heard a door open and close.

"Michel." I tried to surface, pushing against his shoulder. I didn't dream of this, to be taken like an army whore drunken in a stairwell and forgotten tomorrow. Better the ten-course banquet we had both imagined.

He raised his face to mine, flushed and intent. "Elza?"

"Let's go back upstairs," I said. "It's more comfortable there."

He put his arm around me, his hat suddenly in the way. "Elza, I promise you —"

I put my hand to his lips. "Don't promise me anything, Michel. Then it will be easier when you don't do it."

I couldn't see his face in the shadows. "If

you trust me so little, why do you want to make love with me?"

"Do you think I have to trust you for that?" I asked with a smile that didn't reach my eyes.

We went upstairs together. I locked the door, then took one of the candles from the table and carried it into the bedroom. He followed me.

Light made everything spring into place at once, the crimson curtains at the window and door, the bed with its gold covers and curtains, the gilt mirror over the dresser reflecting and refracting bottles of oil and perfume, the curved handle of a hairbrush, the china box that held my tarot cards. The light left shadows in the corners. One candle does not show too much.

Michel stood just inside the door, something oddly uncertain in the way he stood, like a man who has gone into a secret place and doesn't know what to make of it. The flickering candle turned his red hair bronze again.

His shirt was open, and I could see the pulse at the hollow of his throat. Below the sunburn his skin was redhead fair and freckled. He took his coat off and looked for somewhere to put it, settling for hanging it on the end of the screen that separated the necessary pot from the rest of the room. I walked over to him and undid every button on his waistcoat.

He reached for me, but I pushed his hand back. "Wait," I said. "Let me do this. Let me see you."

He stood still while I hung the waistcoat. I walked behind him and undid the black ribbon that held his hair, spreading it in a copper river down his back. From behind him, I lifted his shirt over his head.

Redhead fair, indeed. Long red hair and skin as creamy as a girl's. But no girl was ever muscled that way. I ran my hand along the line of his shoulder, traced one long white scar around his ribs. His stomach was flat, and he shivered at my touch.

"Beautiful," I said, looking up at his face, at the longing there, his lips slightly parted. "Do you know that you're beautiful?"

Michel blushed. He glanced away.

I put my hand to his face. "Look at me," I whispered. "I want you to see me looking at you."

He turned his face against my hand, kissing my palm. His eyes met mine, scared and hungry at the same time, half wanting and half dreading what I seemed to promise.

"And be still," I said, smiling.

I put my hands on his shoulders and ran them lightly down his chest, so lightly that I felt the goose bumps rise. Pale skin and bronze curls, running in a straight line down to his waistband. I stopped and played with one nipple, feeling it slack between my fingers. Then I bent and suckled it, drawing and licking as though he were a woman.

He certainly wasn't, from the size of the erection pushing at me through his breeches. He made some incoherent noise. His hand moved, then stopped as I closed my fingers around his wrist, pressing it back to his side.

"Be still," I said. "Wait."

I unbuttoned his breeches and pushed them down around his hips; sharp bones and another scar, this one across the top of his hip, angling toward the groin. His phallus was hard and thick, jutting straight forward out of a nest of red hair, almost purple with blood. Very deliberately, holding his eyes with mine, I went down on my knees and took it in my mouth. He moaned and swayed, catching on to the edge of the dresser for balance. The flame dipped, shadows moving around the room.

Large and thick. I couldn't take all of it at once, so I played with it, drawing and licking, almost letting go and just pressing my lips to the tip. I looked up at him. His face was almost white.

"This can't be taken," I said. "It can only be given."

I worked his breeches off, boots and stockings. More scars. The half-healed one on his right leg crossed over an older one, while his left foot a mass of seams like a starburst. I ran my fingers along it.

"Bayonet through the foot," he said, somewhat breathlessly. "Now . . ."

I shook my head, smiling. "Go and lie down. I don't want you to fall over."

I led him to the bed and sat down beside him, pressing him back against the pillows. Moreau had had this power over me, but until now I had never understood what he felt, the power of someone lovely and trembling in your hands, ready for you to make them into another person.

It was almost too much for him, keeping still. Almost, but not quite.

"Open your legs," I said, and knelt between them, my rose dress falling around me in puddles of soft fabric, half concealing and half disclosing. And then I bent over him again. As I took him in my mouth, his hands clenched on the bedcovers, his back arching. Not quite. Not quite to the edge.

My hair had fallen down, honey gold brushing against the insides of his thighs. I lifted my head. "Put that pillow under your head," I said. "I want you to see what I'm doing. I want you to see exactly what you look like."

He did it, biting his lip.

I ran my hands along the insides of his thighs, muscled from a lifetime on horseback, a lifetime of fencing, feeling the shape of him under his skin like cream.

I gathered my hair in my hands and slapped the inside of his thigh with it, stinging like a horsehair whip. His entire body arched. Again. I took the flat of my hand and slapped harder, the crack of my hand against him loud in the quiet room. Then I bent and kissed the red mark I had left.

"You like pain, don't you?"

He made some insensible noise.

I slid my body up his, lifted his chin in my hand. "What did you say?"

"Under the right circumstances." He was trying to get at me through my dress, hips moving against me.

"No." I sat up, straddling him. "Not yet. You have to watch." Very deliberately, I lifted my dress. I had nothing under it. I moved on him, closing my hand around him and putting it where he wanted it to go, making him watch every movement. And then I sank down on him, feeling him filling me, wide and stretching. One slow movement.

"Like that," I said. "These are the right circumstances."

He came with a noise that was almost a scream, and I rode him. Not quite enough for me. As he softened in me, I put my hand down and touched, soft flesh parted by him, my pearl tight and needy. And I used him for my pleasure, touching until the ripples built into a flood, one, two, three tight convulsions.

"God," he said. "I can feel you."

"Feel me," I said, and closed my eyes and gave in to it.

Afterward, I unbuttoned the dress and dropped it over the side of the bed, then slid in beside him, skin against skin, pulling the linen sheets loose and the duvet over us. I lay on my side, wrapped against his left shoulder, while he lay on his back. Our hair mingled on the pillow, red and gold alike. I bent my lips softly to his shoulder. He was shaking like a racehorse, the contest over.

"God, Elza," he said, and bent his lips to

my hair.

"Too much?"

"No." He wrapped his arms tightly around me. "Just enough."

I kissed him, sweet as a girl with her first lover, warm and tender with the lethargy of release. It was as though something had broken between us, something brittle that had held back the tide, and now there was nothing between us, no barrier, as though we flowed together like fire and fire.

I felt him close his eyes.

And I just held him while his breathing stilled, quiet in the candlelight.

"You've never done anything like that before," I said.

"No. It's intense."

I nodded. "If it's too much, you can tell me. It's —"

"It's not too much." He shifted a little, pulling me tighter. For a moment I thought he wouldn't say any more, but then he did. "Usually I'm afraid I'll hurt someone."

"I'm more likely to hurt you this way," I said. My leg was against his, the inside of my thigh against his hip. "I suppose you're not used to that idea."

"You won't hurt me."

"I won't mean to," I said.

He turned his head and looked at me. "If

I wanted a woman who wasn't dangerous, I wouldn't have come looking for you."

"I suppose you wouldn't have."

He was quiet for a long moment. Then he said softly, "Elza?"

"Yes?"

"Was there supposed to be dessert?"

He sounded so plaintive that I started laughing. "Didn't you have enough dinner?"

"I've worked up an appetite since then."

"There's cheese and plums and Madeira," I said, sitting up. "I could go get them."

"I could help."

He got up, and we brought everything back to the bedroom. We sat up in bed eating plums and Manchego, sprawling naked in the candlelight, drinking tawny Madeira out of my only two glasses. It was the best food I had ever eaten. The plums were sweeter than any fruit had ever been, and I held one for him to eat and tasted it on his tongue. Watching him eat it out of my hand was oddly sensual.

"I thought grapes were traditional for a conqueror?" he said, leaning back against the pillow.

I laughed. "I don't have any grapes. I didn't see any in the market this morning."

"We could look for them tomorrow," he said. "I've always wanted someone to feed me grapes."

"Maybe you should feed me grapes," I said. "Turn and turn about."

He smiled at me and dipped his forefinger in the glass of Madeira, carefully gilding my breast with one golden drop. Then he bent to lick it off, smoky and sweet at the same time. Which led to a tangle of sheets and limbs, to making love in candlelight, warm and laughing.

It was the hour before dawn when we pulled the sheets back on the bed. The candle had burned out. I lay down on his shoulder again.

I was nearly asleep when he suddenly said, "Letters?"

"It's not the right time to worry," I said sleepily. "My courses are due. I thought of that hours ago."

"I'm glad you have more sense than I do."

"I have more risk," I said, closing my eyes. I really didn't want to think about it at the moment.

His arm tightened around me. "I would never desert you if it came to that."

"No, you probably wouldn't." I put one hand against his hip, feeling the softness of skin over sharp bones. "You think you're a white knight, a Paladin of Charlemagne."

"I am a Paladin of Charlemagne," he said

quietly. "Where do you think they go? Do they really sleep for centuries in the hollow hills, waiting for Roland's horn to sound?"

I smiled and curled tighter. "Next you'll tell me that you threw Excalibur in a lake."

"Not in a lake," he said. "But there was a sword."

"You are the most impossible romantic," I said, and fell asleep in his arms.

IN THE CITY OF LIGHT

I was awakened in the morning by the sounds of Michel behind the screen, going about necessary morning functions. I heard him pouring water in the washbasin, then a loud splashing, as though he had suddenly ducked his head. He came out from behind the screen, shaking his wet head, naked and completely unselfconscious.

I sat up, the sheet around my waist. For a moment we just looked at each other. I wasn't sure what to say that wasn't either too much or too little.

He came and sat down on the side of the bed. "What am I supposed to say?" he asked.

"How about good morning?" I said. He was as awkward as I was. It had been too intimate, too real, and now it seemed odd to find him almost a stranger.

"Good morning," he said. He gathered up my hair in his hands, playing with the long strands, a tentative smile on his face. "And how about breakfast?"

"I don't have anything," I said. "I wasn't really planning —"

"We could go out."

And we did. We had breakfast in a tavern that he knew, a place by the river that was full of soldiers having a late breakfast and teamsters who had hauled in produce for the markets having an early lunch before they started home to the country. We ate fried potatoes and sausages while sitting at a long trestle table. Birds flew in and out the open doors, perching on the rafters high above and flitting down to eat the crumbs that fell beneath the tables. One bold bird landed on our table and begged. Michel threw him a bit of bread, and he took off to the beams above with his prize, followed by four or five other birds.

"Jealous fellows," Michel said. "He'll have to fight to keep it. But at least he's got it to start with."

Afterward, we wandered through the markets at Les Halles. Apples, wine, fish, it was all the same to me. We walked arm in arm in the autumn sunshine, laughing and talking about everything — plays I had been in, places he had traveled, books we had both read. We bought grapes and cheese and bread and beer and ate again sitting on the quay, watching the river traffic. My feet hung down over the water, clad in worn half boots. He put his arm around my waist and I leaned back on him, laughing. I had always heard that Paris was the city of lovers, but this was the first day I'd believed it.

He kissed me, and a couple of sailors cheered, drifting downriver on a powder barge toward the Champs de Mars. Across the river the mellow fronts of townhouses glowed. The Pont Neuf angled toward the Boulevard Saint-Michel. He tasted of beer and warm skin, sunlight and autumn.

When a different kind of hunger threatened, we went back to my apartment. I felt stiff and a bit sore, and wasn't terribly surprised when I went behind the screen and checked that my courses had come on hard. Since I had ended the pregnancy last winter, they had been erratic, sometimes showing up every seven or eight weeks and barely there, other times coming on heavy and uncomfortable. This looked heavy. I wished it could have been any other day. Any day other than the perfect day.

I rearranged myself and came out from behind the screen. Michel was in the salon, building a fire in the stove. The night would be chilly.

The fire flared. His face was solemn and intent, illuminated briefly, then dropped into darkness. Michel stood up, dusting his hands on his coat and closing the stove door. "Are you cold?" he asked.

"A little," I said. Mostly I just felt disappointed. I would need to tell him to go soon.

"I could warm you up," he said disingenuously. A day before I would have wondered if he meant it innocently, but now I knew better. He could manage that perfectly innocent expression, but not hide the amusement in his eyes.

"Lechery," I said. "You aren't as wholesome as you look."

He put his arms around me, but I didn't kiss him. "What's the matter?"

I shrugged. "It's the wrong time. I told you my courses were due. I just hate for this day to end." I didn't want him to leave, but I could hardly ask him to stay and do nothing. And he would hardly want more, under the circumstances.

Michel took a step back. "Don't you want to go to bed?"

"Well, yes," I said. This was not the sort of thing one talked about, and it felt distinctly awkward, too intimate. "I mean, I want it, but men find it kind of disgusting."

His brow wrinkled. "You think I'm afraid

of a little blood?"

"When you put it that way . . ."

He put his hands on my shoulders. "Show me what you like. It doesn't bother me if it doesn't bother you."

And so I showed him. Lying together in the dark, he put his hand over mine and I showed him exactly what I liked, exactly the pressure, exactly where, hearing his breathing quicken with mine, knowing that it excited him to excite me, to hear my moans and to feel the wetness. If he was not as practiced a lover as Moreau, he was no green boy either, and he knew enough to know that every woman is different. I said so afterward, when we lay together half asleep.

"So is every sword," he said. "Or every flute."

I looked up at him, a vague shadow in the darkness. The curtains were drawn. "You play the flute?"

He nodded. "Not very well. But I enjoy it."

"You are so strange sometimes," I said, leaning back against him.

"What's strange about playing the flute?"

I searched for the words. "It just doesn't fit with the image."

"I should play a more manly instrument,

like the bassoon?" Michel laughed. "Consider where I'd carry a bassoon on campaign. And how much it would bother the camp to have me practicing the bassoon late at night."

I giggled, imagining the general's tent with the sounds of bassoon practice emerging. "I suppose the flute is practical. But it seems so contradictory."

"And everything about you fits together neatly?"

"No," I said. It was easier to talk in the dark when I couldn't see his face, just feel the warmth of his arm around me, his scarred shoulder against my cheek. "There's Charles."

He was quiet a moment. "Is Charles your son?"

I took a breath, but couldn't quite answer.

"I saw the stretch marks last night. I thought that you must have a child, and I wondered . . ." He stopped, then went on. "I'm trying to say, if you have a child farmed out somewhere because you . . . Well, if you wanted to have him here with us — I mean, with you — it would be better, wouldn't it? I like children. I grew up with a big family, remember? And if you wanted him here with you . . . . Is he Moreau's son? Because if so, that makes him an even bigger ass —"

I put my hand to his lips. "Michel, no." Tears stung my eyes, and I pressed my face against his shoulder for a moment. One of his hands moved against my hair. Something hurt, and I wasn't quite sure what it was.

I lifted my head. "I have two sons," I said. "Klaas and Francis. They're with their father. I haven't seen them in four and a half years. They think I'm dead." It had hurt for so long. Who could I talk to about it? Moreau would not even have begun to understand. He would have been jealous of anything that claimed my attention from him, even a child of his.

"Who's their father?"

"My husband," I said. "Jan Ringeling." I hadn't said his name in years. It seemed like another person who had been his wife.

"Oh." He took a breath. "I thought you weren't married."

"He's Dutch," I said. "He won't divorce me. I left him years ago for Moreau. And then you know how that went."

"I do," he said. "Barras's lady told me."

"Joséphine?" I was surprised he knew her. This was safer ground.

Michel seemed to understand that. "Yes. Madame Bonaparte. I've talked with her several times. The first time I was in Paris was when I went to that party of yours, and I met her then. Director Barras asked me to stay at his house. Which was sort of . . . unexpected. She's very nice. And I mean that truthfully, not in the false way people mean when they say that and mean that someone is boring."

I couldn't help but smile. "Politics," I said. "I can see exactly why he invited you to stay. Moreau was out of favor, so Barras was entertaining other generals from the Rhine. I imagine he found you weren't enough of a political animal and didn't invite you again."

Michel shifted uncomfortably. "Either that, or it was because I assaulted his valet."

"You what?"

His voice was a little defensive, his provincial accent a little broader. "I didn't grow up with servants, remember? I don't know what they do, creeping around the house when everyone is sleeping. His valet came into my room early in the morning to brush my coat or some other damn-fool thing, and I thought he was a thief."

"Oh no," I said.

"I pinned him up against the wardrobe doors and threatened to rip his head off. It was a little awkward."

I burst out laughing. "Oh, Michel! I imagine it was!"

I heard him smile despite himself. "Half the household came rushing in when he started shrieking, and I wasn't wearing a nightshirt, and Madame Bonaparte was there, and . . ."

Still laughing, I asked, "And what did she say?"

"She didn't say much, but she seemed to be enjoying the view." He was laughing now. "I grabbed a towel off the washstand, but that didn't really cover very much. I begged the poor fellow's pardon and tipped him, but Barras never asked me back again. It wasn't the best first impression I've ever made."

"I imagine it made a good impression on Joséphine," I said. There was something ironic about Joséphine appreciating Michel in the nude, considering how I knew her husband.

"It seemed to have done," he said.

I propped up on one elbow, snuggling closer. "You are beautiful, you know."

"I know," he said. "That's why I wear those tight white breeches." His hand strayed across my stomach caressingly. His fingers were damp. "A good soldier should always make the most of his assets. If ladies of fashion like to look . . ."

"Just a provincial lad, knowing nothing of

439

the ways of the big city," I said airily. "Perhaps someone should show him around. I'm surprised you haven't been shown around thoroughly." It pleased me obscurely, to think of him showing off that way, made him a bit like Charles.

"I've been around the gardens a time or two," he said. "But I never —"

I pressed my hand against his lips firmly. "Don't say it."

"Say what?"

"Say you love me." How many times had he said it, and to whom? I had never felt jealous before. It had not really mattered to me whom Moreau slept with, and it had never occurred to me at the time that Jan might even be capable of infidelity.

He took my hand from his lips and kissed it, even the tips of my fingers. "Why not?"

I closed my eyes. "Because I'll believe you." He could hurt me. He could hurt me more than anyone ever had.

"Oh."

I couldn't look at him. "Don't do that to me. Don't make me believe in you. Just let this be what it is."

"And what is it?" he asked quietly.

"An interlude," I said. "A wonderful, glorious, passionate interlude. We both know it can't last. It's as fragile as this peace treaty.

In a few months you'll be gone back to war, and I'll be working again, being with whomever. And the time will come when you marry someone else and send back all my letters." I gulped. "I want this to be good while it lasts. I don't want any lies."

"You don't believe I could really love you?" His hands never stopped moving, caressing and slow, gentle almost.

"No," I said. "You have no idea who I am. You have no idea the things I've done. What I'm capable of doing." And yet some traitorous part of me wanted him to know, wanted him to know everything, to have every power.

"You don't know what I am either," he said. "I might be a rapist or a torturer. I might beat you or cut you for fun."

"I don't believe that."

"Isn't it likely? Knowing what you know of me?"

"No," I said, "it isn't. Tell me the worst thing you've ever done. I can hear whatever it is."

Michel was silent for a long moment. His hands finally stilled. "No," he said quietly, "I can't. Not yet."

"Then don't tell me you love me." I put my face against his shoulder. It was too good. I must not believe too much, be drawn too deeply into this spell of passion, this illusion of friendship and mutual desire. "Live for half an hour in the world as it is."

"A world without magic and love? With nothing more than flesh and bones and old blood?" There was a sadness in his voice I hadn't heard before. "I don't think I could survive half an hour in that world. If this is madness, then so be it." His hands started again, slow and gentle. "If we compromise with sanity to create the worlds we love, the places where we thrive, then we do."

"I want to be sane," I said. "I don't want to believe in visions and portents, in angels and demons and ancient gods and old oaths dragging me into stories I don't understand. I just want to survive."

"Maybe you'd survive better if you stopped fighting the current," he said. "Like a swimmer pulled out to sea. Stop trying so hard and let go."

I held him tight. *Tomorrow,* I thought. *It will be different tomorrow. We will wake and these illusions will fade. But it's not tomorrow yet.*

And he said nothing, just rocked me against him until we both fell asleep.

In the morning, Michel woke me with a kiss. "I have to go back to my rooms," he said. "I need to get a clean shirt, and I need to check on Eleazar. Livery stables sometimes don't bother to exercise a horse if the owner isn't checking in. I should take the poor boy out myself."

I unfurled from the covers, stretching. "I could come with you," I said. "Nestor could use a run too."

"And clean up a bit," he said. "Do you want me to tell the landlady to fetch you up a bath?"

I shook my head. "She'll charge two sous to have her boys bring the tub up and fill it."

"I don't care," he said. "If you want it, I'll dress and pay her. They can put the tub in the other room, so you don't even have to come out until it's ready."

I did want it. And I wanted to think about this, now, not some other things. My eyes went back to him, wondering if I had managed to completely disgust him with the female process.

Instead, he was getting hard. The expression on his face warred between arousal and embarrassment.

I slid over to the side of the bed and ran one stained hand up his thigh, watching the muscles twitch at my touch. His bloody phallus was half-erect beside my fingers. I understood something about him suddenly. "You like that, don't you?" He moved his head, but didn't answer me. "The idea that you've used that kind of force."

"Elza, no. I would never — I have never —" He looked away. "I'm not like that. It's not that I've never had the opportunity. God knows I have, more than I would like. But I swear to you, I've never done it. I've never forced anyone unwilling. I've never done it." His voice shook.

"But you wanted to." He had. I knew that. He wanted to rape.

He closed his eyes, and his voice was ragged. "God help me, yes."

A weight lifted from me that I hadn't known was there. Michel sat down next to me, and I put my arm around his shoulders. "If you wanted to and didn't, it doesn't count. A sin you only think about isn't the same as something you've done. Something you've wanted isn't the same as something you've really done to another person." That was the fear I had never named — what would a man do to me if he could get away with it, if there were no servants, no people who would talk? With him, I knew. And I knew he wouldn't really do it. "What is it you want?"

He shrugged, and his shoulders moved

under my arm. His face was turned away. "I don't know. To tear into someone. To listen to them scream and beg. To throw her down and take her like an animal." He put his head in his hands. "I wouldn't do it, Elza. I really wouldn't. I haven't, when I had the chance and other people were."

"What did you do?" I asked, my mouth dry, wanting to know and not at the same time. "When other people were."

"Started shouting and laid into them with the flat of my sword," he said. "Kicked some noncoms in the ass who really deserved it. They knew better. You can't have that kind of thing. I wound up killing one of them. I didn't mean to, because I just struck him in the arm to get him off her — but the wound putrefied. I swear to God, if I were the corps commander, rape would be a hanging offense."

"And then?" My voice was very quiet and calm, like a priest in a confessional. But a priest would not understand this. A whore would.

"I got the town doctor out. He was hiding in the cellar of his house, and I scared him half to death. I put the girls in his care. He knew who they were, who their families were. He could get them home. I put everyone on report, and brought the ones who were the leaders, the ones who'd actually done it, not the ones who were watching, up on charges. Six months' pay and two weeks in chains. Not enough, but it was the maximum in the corps."

"Moreau's corps," I said, remembering the cantinière in camp with a rush of shame. I had not done half what he had. I had gone to bed, telling myself I needed a thicker skin. "Yes, I know about that."

He nodded. "It's not what I did that bothers me. It's what I felt." He took a racking breath. "I was helping one of the girls to the doctor's house. The street was rutted and she was shaking, and I . . ." Michel turned his head away, his face drawn. "This Franconian girl my sister's age, with long brown hair, and what had just happened . . . What kind of monster am I to think that?"

"What did you do?"

"I took her arm and helped her to the doctor's house, and said some things about how I would arrest the men and that I hoped she would be all right and that the doctor would get her home." His shoulders shook. "Surely God will judge me by what I did, not by what I thought."

"I will," I said. I put my arms around him and held him close, his head against my shoulder, searching for the words. "And if you believe in a forgiving God, then surely that grace is easier to reach than a whore's absolution." I stroked his brow. "Michel, you can't help your nature."

He made some sound against me that wasn't a word.

I ran my hands down his back. Last night had not even been the pretense of violence. It had been love and tenderness. "Michel," I said, "you didn't hurt me. Remember? It's just the thought. Just the idea. There's nothing wrong with that."

He lifted his face to mine, looking for something there. If it was fear, he didn't see it, because I felt none. Perhaps I should have been afraid of him, but I knew in that moment that I never would be.

I kissed his cheek softly. "Really, my dear. I promise I would tell you if you hurt me. But it doesn't bother me at all for the idea of hurting me to excite you. If you want to take me right now, I'll even scream and struggle a bit."

He laid his cheek against mine, two days' beard prickling. He hadn't bothered to shave yesterday. "Don't tempt me that way."

I took his hand and closed it around my wrist, letting him feel the shape of the bones, letting him see what it did to me to test myself just a little against his strength.

"Why not?" I said. "If it's a game between lovers, and no one is hurt? It's just a quirk."

He felt me shiver as he tightened his fingers, solid but not quite bruising, just on the very edge of pain. "And what are yours?" He smiled against my face, and his voice was almost normal, leading him back out of the dark places.

"I like dominating men twice my size," I said almost playfully, leaving it so he could take it as a joke if he wanted, leaving me a way out, "and I like being made to come in public, and the pretense of seduction. And I like dressing in men's clothes and sleeping with women."

"That's quite a list," he said.

"Do you think you're up to it?" A glance showed he clearly was. I didn't frighten him or disgust him any more than he did me.

"I love a challenge." He smiled again, and this time it touched his eyes. "But I don't think I can manage the being a woman part. This is the body I have right now."

"We can work around it," I said, and kissed him.

Autumn

The weeks that followed were the happiest I had ever known. Michel moved his things over and let go the rooms he had taken to save on rent. There was no sense in his paying for rooms he was never in. We were together every moment, as lovers are when no sense of fatigue has set in, and when neither has any more pressing responsibility than to be together night and day.

On clear days we rode in the Bois de Boulogne, cantering through the parks and scattering the squawking ducks and geese, taking the bridle trails at breakneck speed. Nestor didn't have Eleazar's wind or his stride, but he did his best to keep up.

Michel leaned out of the saddle, laughing, waiting for me to come thundering up beside him. Nestor and I were both sweated. My hair had escaped from its binding, and Charles's shirt stuck to my body beneath a waistcoat. We walked the horses under the trees. Michel's boots were scuffed, and the fallen leaves crunched under his feet.

"I look terrible," I said, taking my hair down and trying to tie it back more neatly.

"You worry too much," he said. "You look beautiful no matter what you wear. It's disturbing." He looked at me sideways.

I paused, hands raised to tie my hair back. My coat was stuffed in my saddlebag, and I wore dove-gray breeches and a black waistcoat, cut a shade higher than the current fashion so that it came just above the line of my breasts. With the fullness of the shirt and cravat above, there was no curve at all, just long slim legs and golden hair in a tail. I looked like a young man of seventeen or so. "Disturbing?"

"You carry it off well," Michel said. Nestor stepped between us, so I couldn't see his face.

"What, being a young man?" I almost said *being Charles,* but stopped myself in time.

"It's the way you walk. The way you move. When you dress like that, you don't move like a woman at all."

I took Nestor's reins and held him by the head, so I could see around him to Michel. One golden leaf had fallen and caught in his red hair. "It's safer on the road to travel as a man. And my father taught me to fence, which I suppose accounts for the way I move."

"Really?" He looked at me around Nestor's head.

I nodded. "And I've taken lessons this way. People see what they want to see."

"Are you any good?" That gleam he'd had in his eye galloping across the park was back.

"I'm not bad," I said. "But I'm not about to cross swords with you. You've got a head of height on me, and six inches of reach. Not to mention a much heavier sword."

He wore it even in Paris, and glanced down at the belt now, a worn general-issue saber weighing a good ten pounds. "No," Michel said. "You'd need something lighter. But it's not all weight and reach. I wish it were."

"I'm left-handed," I said. Perhaps a gentle introduction to Charles was best.

"I have to see this," Michel said, grinning with delight.

Nothing would do then but that we had to go to the fencing *salle* he favored right away. It wasn't one of the fashionable ones, but I was coming to expect that. The owner was a wicked Sicilian with muscular thighs and an old-fashioned curled wig. His rooms were popular with young army officers who wanted to fight dirty, and with green boys who needed a quick turn or two before an affair of honor.

He greeted Michel like a brother. Michel hung about his neck, pounding him on the back, while they cheerfully insulted one another, Michel in bad Italian and M. Vincenzio in worse German.

"My young friend," Michel said, "is in need of a few lessons. Perhaps you could take him through a pass or two and tell us what is needed?"

M. Vincenzio looked me up and down with a somewhat skeptical expression on his face. His ornate brocade coat looked as though it were ten years old, and smelled like it too. "The boy has to fight a duel?"

"He often travels," Michel said smoothly. "And it would be well if he could defend himself."

Vincenzio raised one eyebrow and addressed me. "How fortunate you are to have such a friend who has concern for your well-being. Have you ever crossed swords in earnest?"

"No," I said. "But I killed two men with a pistol on the road from Milan this summer." I was not about to be cowed. And Charles would never be, arrogant as he was. I put one foot forward, standing negligently, as the young bucks did. I flicked my cuff back as though to take snuff.

The other eyebrow went up. "You are a fair shot?"

"I am a fine shot," I said. Which was true. Not that it took much of a marksman to hit someone with a horse pistol at point-blank range.

"And where have you learned to fence?"

"My father taught me, having been a swordsman in the service of the Czar. And then I had lessons in Italy when I was a youth."

"With your pretty face, you'll need all the lessoning you can get," he said. "We'll try a pass or two as a favor to the general here. It seems it would disturb him if you were to be scarred." He walked over to a group of foils hung on the wall and selected one for each of us.

Michel gave me an encouraging smile, apparently entirely oblivious to the implications flying over his head. *Sometimes,* I thought, *it's like he just crawled out of a cabbage patch.*

I took the foil Vincenzio offered and tried the balance. A bit battered, but a serviceable practice weapon, tipped with a nub of India rubber. It would bruise if it connected, but not really do much damage unless wielded with exceptional force. I stepped back, saluted, and sank into guard.

He pressed me almost at once. My footwork consisted mostly of retreat and endless riposte. He touched on my off shoulder in seconds. I went back to work, circling grimly. I knew I was outmatched, but I wouldn't make this easy.

The next touch was a glancing one on the sword wrist, a disarm that didn't quite work. Vincenzio nodded approvingly. "Better, my boy! That would be a pinking, but it wouldn't stop you, not in a real fight. This would."

He lunged. The third touch was an absolutely stinging blow to the back of my left hand. Even tipped, it broke the skin a little, a star-shaped red mark spreading.

Vincenzio lifted his blade and saluted formally, handing off his foil to an assistant.

I shook out my hand, trying to feel my fingers.

Michel grinned like a proud papa. "My friend's not so bad, eh?"

"I've seen worse," Vincenzio said. "I see the eastern influence. A guardsman's style, not a nobleman's. I bet that father of yours was in some keen fights, not affairs of honor. None of the extraneous flourishes the Austrians are teaching these days. Was he foot or horse?"

"I don't know," I said quietly. "He died many years ago." And I didn't. I had assumed he was an officer and a gentleman, but an illegitimate son left to make his way in the world might just as easily have been a street fighter. For the first time in years, I felt suddenly close to him. Perhaps he would have been proud of what I had become, little Elza who could deal with the world being a dangerous place. An adventurer, like her father.

My chin rose. "Will you teach me, Monsieur Vincenzio? I see that I have a lot to learn."

"If you'll work at it," he said. "And if your friend will pay." He looked at Michel.

Michel shrugged. "Once a week?"

"Three times a week," I said. "If I'm to learn it, I want to learn it well." I glanced at Michel. "If you're paying."

He laughed. "I'm paying. And three times a week, if you want it. You'll be so stiff and sore you won't be able to move, but I suppose I can deal with that."

I found myself blushing with as much embarrassment as if I had been Charles. I nodded and wandered off by the door to put on my coat while Michel dickered about the cost of lessons with Vincenzio, who swore he had a special stop thrust that he would show Michel himself for just a little extra, the perfect lethal move only for a man of his skill, shown only to very special pupils for a very special price. He came over to join me shaking his head. I handed him his hat.

"Did you pay for the very special stop thrust?" I asked as we went down the outside stairs to the street.

"I will," he said. "Sometimes Vincenzio has some good things. And he's practical. He'll teach you how to handle people a lot bigger than you are."

"You could show me that too."

"I could," Michel said cheerfully. "But I'm not a good teacher. I'd probably lop your ear off in the process." He threw an arm about my shoulders enthusiastically. "I've never seen a woman who was as good as you."

"You know," I said, stepping around a market stand of apples that spilled onto the sidewalk, "he thinks I'm your lover."

"You are my lover," Michel said, jostling me as he avoided the mud splashed by a bottle-green phaeton passing at too quick a pace for the city.

I looked at him sideways. There was mud on his boots anyway. "He thinks I'm your lover and he thinks I'm a man."

Michel stopped. I walked a couple of paces farther before I realized it, then went back. He shrugged, but the smile didn't reach his eyes. "You're not."

"No," I said, linking my arm through his and drawing him to walk down the street, "I'm not. Not physically."

"But you think people will think so, when you dress like this?" He kept pace with me now, his voice dropped.

"They usually do," I said. "You said yourself how well I passed." I didn't want him to decide whatever it was. It was too much to expect that he should love Charles as well. A tentative truce between the parts of my life was the most I could hope for.

He stopped walking again, stood facing me, one small line furrowing between his brows. "You're the only woman I've ever met who wanted to ride and shoot and fence and talk about interesting things, never mind all the rest of it. That I know what to say to out of bed."

"And in bed's not bad either," I said, reaching for his hand. I held it. "But if I hold your hand in the street dressed like this, you know what people will think of you and of me."

"It's a masquerade," he said, but he didn't

sound sure.

I shook my head. "No, Michel. It isn't." I could not pretend, not with him. "This is who I really am."

"More than a quirk?" His blue eyes were very serious, and I couldn't tell what he was thinking.

"Yes," I said, and my heart sank. "More than a quirk. More than a costume."

He looked down. His hand in mine, big and callused, long fingers scarred from too many things; my hand small and tense, a swollen red mark from Vincenzio's touch blossoming. It didn't look like a woman's hand, not emerging from a man's coat sleeve, the lace cuff falling short of the first joint. Michel looked at it. Then, very deliberately, he lifted it to his lips.

He kissed my hand in the open street, reverentially, like a lover who has achieved a great prize. His eyes met mine over it as people walked around us, curious or knowing or censorious.

I looked back at him, and something broke inside me. "I love you," I said.

Michel fell into pace beside me, walking down the street, still holding my hand. His steps were light. "I had to know if I could," he said. "If I'm brave enough."

"For what?"

He shrugged. "For whatever. And I love you, too."

I stopped suddenly, pulling him around, and kissed him passionately in the middle of the sidewalk, my arms twining around his neck.

People jostled past us. I couldn't have cared less what they said, what they thought, whether they laughed or disapproved or just wished we'd go somewhere private; I kissed him in men's clothes in the middle of Paris, and he kissed me back. He could live with Charles, and it was more than enough.

Autumn came in earnest. A cold rain blew in from the north, and the leaves were scoured off the trees and lay in sodden heaps on rooftops and in streets. The nights were cold, and we went to bed early, curling into bed to do soft things under the covers and whisper when it was done. There was magic in our flesh. I felt the binding grow tighter and tighter with each touch, with each secret told in the dark.

The news told a different story. Britain had paid the Austrians, it said. Sixty thousand pounds had been the price if the Austrians would break the armistice. The peace was ending.

We knew. We knew the next courier might

be for him. Michel bought some small supplies, shaving soap and a few books, new quills and a compass in a leather case to replace one he'd lost.

We drank burgundy at the table in the apartment out of my two wineglasses, finishing a stewed rabbit we'd brought back from a tavern. Outside, the rising wind made the windows shake.

"I'll pay the rent for next month in advance," Michel said suddenly. "And I'll have my agent pay it each month while I'm gone. You won't have to worry."

I looked down at my plate, then back up at him. I didn't want to talk about it, but we had to sooner or later. "I suppose you'll leave your things here."

"If that's all right with you." Staking a claim. It would deter other lovers, his things all over the house. How he had got so many things here in only six weeks was something of a mystery.

"I could come with you," I said.

Michel put his glass down. The wine looked like blood in the dim light, an old comparison but an apt one. His eyes met mine across the table. "I'm given a divisional command, nine thousand men. The largest command I've ever had."

"That's good, isn't it?" I said.

"I'm under Moreau's direct command."

I took a breath and let it out. "Damn."

"Yes." Michel poured more wine for both of us and took a big drink of his. "If it were anyone else. Or if I wasn't going to be directly under him, with Moreau in and out of my headquarters all the time . . ."

"If he sees me, your career will go up in flames," I said. "You have no idea how vindictive he can be."

"I'm getting a pretty good idea," Michel said. "He already thought I was having a secret affair with you behind his back. If you come with me —"

"— he'll decide that he was right," I said. "And believe me, Michel, he will make your life miserable. If you're lucky."

"If not, I'm Uriah the Hittite."

I looked at him blankly. "You're who?"

"Uriah the Hittite. David saw Uriah's wife, Bathsheba, bathing and sent him off to the front lines to take a spear through the middle." Michel took another big gulp of wine. It was rougher stuff than I usually bought, but it had been on sale.

"Oh, the Bible," I said.

"How you managed to grow up a perfect heathen is something I can't understand," Michel said, one eyebrow raised. "I can't bring you, Elza. If Moreau found out, it would be the end of my command. He could do that."

"And he would," I said. "I know he would." I looked away.

"I can't risk it," Michel said.

"I know." I wasn't going to cry. I wasn't going to plead to go. I knew all the very good reasons. And it would be selfish to ask him to sacrifice his command for me, just so I wouldn't have to stay bored and safe in Paris, living on his money. That was not, I thought, how a lover should act, how a lover should be. I should love his honor as my own, and be as zealous for his glory as he was. That was what Plato counseled lovers, a counsel far more real to me than Uriah the Hittite.

"I don't want to go," he said. "This . . ." He gestured around the apartment.

"You do want to go," I said. "Michel, this is an interlude. It's not your real life. Your real life is out there, in the field, doing the things you do best. You may wish you had a longer holiday, but you do want to go."

He smiled ruefully. "I do. But not yet."

I nodded. "And I wish I could go with you. I would go with you on a moment's notice, except —"

"— for Moreau," Michel finished. "And it's not a very safe place for you. It will be

462

the dead of winter soon, with an army on the march. I don't know how I can even think about taking you into that anyway."

"Women go," I said.

"It's a rough life," he said. "Always the first to go without food and shelter, the last out in a retreat. The prey of unscrupulous men and scoundrels on both sides. I wouldn't want it for you."

"I would," I said, raising my chin, "if I could be near you always and see you every day. And it's not as though I haven't been in a baggage train before. I can take care of myself."

"I know," he said. He reached across the table and took my hand, just looking at it. The touch from my first lesson had faded to a yellow bruise, but there were fresh ones, and a long scab along my thumb from the flat of the blade on a bad disarm. But I was getting better. "I'll be back in the spring."

"I hope you will," I said. "Michel, I hope so." My voice broke.

And then we both started crying. Which led to kisses and comfort and going in the other room to forget, kissing the tears from his eyes and at last curling sleepily together. I listened to his beating heart. "When?" I whispered.

"At the end of the week," he said. "Four more nights."

FAREWELLS

The next day was gray and colorless. It was hard to recapture our carefree mood now that our days together were numbered. I went with Michel to his tailor's shop to pick up half a dozen new shirts, several pairs of flannel underdrawers, a pair of dress pants, and two pairs of wool uniform pants reinforced with leather for riding. I liked the pants with the leather between the legs and in the seat, and said so. Michel said I should order a pair for myself for riding and put it on the bill, even though I said I didn't really need them.

We shopped a bit more. It wasn't raining, though it looked like it would at any moment. I was officious about what he would need, trying to send him off as I had sent Moreau, with a full kit and a few comforts. Michel took being fussed over fairly well, though he protested that he didn't need jam or mustard, since he didn't have a cook, and his orderly wouldn't remember to put them out with meals anyway.

Instead of going out to dinner, we went back to the apartment and made love while the rain came down in sheets against the windows and the room was filled with gray light. We went to sleep fitfully in the afternoon while the rain still fell.

We woke to a knock on the door. Michel swore. I felt the bed give as he rolled out. "Probably a courier. Damn." He raised his voice. "Just a moment."

I curled up in the warm place he had been while he found his trousers and thumped out into the salon. It was morning, but the light was still gray. And it was cold, since no one had lit the stove.

Michel's voice and another man's. Not a stranger — Delacroix. I pulled myself out of bed and was finding my dress when Michel stuck his head in. "Elza? There's a friend of yours here."

I pulled my dress over my head and he quickly fastened up the buttons in the back for me. His face was solemn.

"Is something wrong?" I asked.

"Let him tell you," Michel said gently. I felt terror grip me, and I hurried out.

"What's the matter?" I asked. "Why —"

Delacroix looked drawn, and he was wearing his best black coat. With a pang of regret, I thought that I had barely paid attention to him or any of my other old friends since my return to town, so focused had I been on Michel and this wonderful new romance. I hadn't spoken to him in weeks. "Ida, I . . ."

Michel's head rose at the name. He had forgotten about Ida.

"What's happened?" I said.

Delacroix took my hands. "It's Lisette. She's dead."

"Oh," I said. "Oh." It had only been six months since I'd moved out, since I took the road to Italy with Isabella. It seemed half a lifetime ago. But it had not been long. "What happened?"

He glanced at Michel, but shrugged when I didn't seem to mind if he told me in front of my new man. "She was upset. I don't know about what. She drank half a bottle of laudanum, and then decided that she didn't want to die. I think that's what happened. She tried to make herself throw up, but she was drifting in and out. She choked on her own vomit."

I closed my eyes. I couldn't feel anything. Nothing but Michel standing behind me, his hands on my shoulders. There was nothing but this chill horror spreading through me.

Delacroix went on, his voice roughened. "Clemence and I and some others are arranging for the grave in the pauper's field. I thought you'd like to know and come in with us, or at least come this afternoon. It's not much, but it's what we can do, and —"

"I will," I said. "I'll be there. I can give you some money toward it too." My voice sounded perfectly steady. I was surprised by that. "Michel, where did I put my reticule?"

"It's over here," he said. "On the chair." He handed it to me, a blue brocade purse swinging on satin strings.

There was money. We had been shopping, but I hadn't bought much. I gave Delacroix all that was left. He looked at it.

"Are you sure? It's more than your share," he said.

I shoved it into his hand. "It's fine."

"I'll see you this afternoon at two, then," he said. "I'm going to run by the theater and see if I can catch Dorée before her rehearsal and tell her."

Michel went to the funeral with me. He wore his best dress uniform, which I had not seen before, the coat stiff with gold braid, and a tall bicorne with a black plume.

468

It made him look roughly ten feet tall. He wore his saber instead of a dress sword, which I was concluding he didn't own, and the long tricolor sash of the Army of the Republic with its fringe of bullion. It was quite a show for a prostitute he'd never met.

It was respect for me and for my friends. I knew it, and it made tears start in my eyes.

I wore my one black dress and a long cloak, and a black velvet chip bonnet that wasn't really appropriate but was the only black hat I owned. My wardrobe did not run to somber.

Delacroix was there, and Clemence and Dorée, the tall African girl who was now at the Théâtre-Français. There were several young men, bleary-eyed and unkempt, who stayed far away from Michel with his glitter and his sword. I couldn't remember their names, or if I had slept with them last winter. I might have.

They had sewn her body into a cheap linen shroud. I didn't see it. I didn't really want to remember her face that way. There was no priest. Delacroix said a few words about how she'd been a good friend, and Dorée gave Cleopatra's lament over Antony while the gravediggers stood about in the cold, sharing a flask and telling each other jokes, leaning on their shovels. Their laughter was somewhat discouraged by Michel's gimlet gaze.

They dropped her down in the hole. Beneath her there was a thin layer of dirt over the shrouds of the others already in the pit. Dorée started to walk away as they threw in a few shovelfuls of quicklime. Michel took my arm.

"See you around town?" Delacroix asked me.

"Absolutely," I said. "Thank you for coming and getting me. I mean it."

He looked up at Michel, who was towering. "See you soon."

I nodded. Behind, there was a *thunk* as the gravediggers started throwing earth. They would just barely cover Lisette over. The quicklime would prevent the stench from being unbearable when they put the next one in on top, today or tomorrow or next week.

We walked home. It wasn't raining, though it looked like it would. Michel had my arm and was mercifully silent.

It was ten blocks before I spoke, the words running round and round in my mind, before I could find the thing that I truly feared. "That's where I'm going, you know," I said. "Where I'll end up. One of these days." It would be me in the pit with a few shovels of quicklime to keep the smell down.

He tucked my hand in the crook of his arm. "I'm for a mass grave on a field somewhere," he said evenly. "With or without all my limbs attached. I don't particularly mind the idea of dying, but I do mind being carved up first."

Not for us, the ancient sleep in quiet tombs. It would be decay or fire. I looked up at him. His profile was hard and still as a bronze somewhere, distant.

Michel turned to me, his eyes blazing, and took me by the shoulders. "Hang Moreau! You're coming with me. We're not for the grave yet," he said, and kissed me hard.

"I will go anywhere you go," I said. "Let me live every moment that I am living." My heart lifted, a curious kind of ecstasy, as though we were twinned birds of prey lifting onto the wind. This was what I yearned for. This was where I belonged.

"Amen," he said, as though it had been a prayer. And maybe it was. His God might answer these things, if all we asked was to face whatever it was together. Michel believed in that sort of mercy.

"I'll just stay out of Moreau's way," I said. "If he doesn't see me, he won't know I'm there. And he's never seen Charles."

"Charles?"

"Me in men's clothes. He has a name," I said, a little flustered. "I mean, I have a name. I use my brother's name. Charles van Aylde."

"Oh." Michel's brow furrowed again. "Do you have papers for him, or do I need to arrange them?"

"I don't actually have papers," I said, swallowing my surprise. "You're taking this all in stride."

He shrugged. "You don't want to be riding all over Germany as Charles with papers that say you're Ida St. Elme, do you? That's going to involve a lot of confusion."

"No," I said. "I can see that it would." Michel had gone straight to the practical. Whatever he thought about Charles was now buried under a pile of logistics.

He took my arm again, and we kept walking home. I thought it was getting colder. "And it's better if Moreau never hears the name Ida St. Elme anywhere," Michel said. "Not on papers, not on any list, not from anybody. Just Charles van Aylde and Elza."

"He knows my real name," I said, "but he never called me Elza. How are you going to arrange legitimate papers?"

"I can have a servant," Michel said. "Most officers above a certain rank do. I've got a military orderly, but there's no reason I

472

can't have a civilian servant too."

"And who pays attention to servants?" I asked cynically. "Certainly not Victor Moreau. He might not notice even if he were looking straight at me."

"Let's not try that," Michel said fervently. "God, we're crazy to do this!" He saw me open my mouth and ran straight on. "Don't say we can't. I'm not leaving you in Paris, and we're going to get by with it. You want to, don't you?"

"Absolutely," I said. "I can't think of anything better than being Charles all the time on a winter campaign with you." And it was true. I couldn't.

We spent the next two days madly putting together a kit for me. Fortunately, I had practical clothes for Charles as well as drawing room finery, so I needed to add some things, not start over entirely.

Michel approved of Nestor as a mount, solid and not flashy, the kind of horse that a young man who wanted to get some military experience would ride. I was allowed to take only what would fit in my saddlebags: two pairs of pants besides the ones I stood up in, three shirts, a waistcoat and coat besides the ones I wore, a baggy flannel tunic to go under my shirts, a couple of plain stocks, a scarf, two pairs of gloves, and a new hat. Also a new cloak, as Michel pronounced my dark wool one to be of too thin a material for the campaign. The new one was black wool lined in silk, with a double layer of wool batting between. It was quite warm, and as nice as his.

The rest of my things consisted of a rolled bag with a few toiletries, a couple of books, my cards wrapped in oilcloth and silk, and a new leather flask of brandy. I should have no more than any young man would, no forbidden dresses or fripperies. Michel would have nothing held up on my account, and neither for my part would I.

His luggage was a bit more extensive, though nothing to what Moreau had traveled with — two cases and a long wooden map case moroccoed and sealed with leather. I smiled when I saw, in the last stages of the packing, that he had slipped one of my dresses in with his things, a sapphire-blue wool that was practical and not too fine, but was also the color of my eyes. I didn't tell him that I knew it was there.

The other thing I did was cut my hair. While Michel was out arranging his last business with his agent, I went as Charles to a fashionable barber. When Michel came back, he stopped dead in the doorway.

"Do you like it?" I asked. "I thought it would be better. Moreau is used to my long hair, and this is more stylish now."

It was the Brutus cut, trimmed in layers a finger long from my crown to the nape of my neck, falling to my collar in the back with a certain fullness, like a Roman captain's. Everyone was wearing it now, abandoning the ubiquitous queue. It felt very strange to have such short hair. Looking in the mirror, it suited Charles.

Michel came over and looked at me, a somewhat bemused expression on his face. "It's very . . ."

"Short?" I supplied.

"Disturbing," he said. "You look more like a boy than ever."

"That's the idea," I said, brushing back a piece or two in the mirror. The way it was cut on the sides implied sideburns without actually requiring me to grow any facial hair.

"I can see your neck now," Michel said, standing behind me and looking down.

"Yes," I said. "It's always back there."

He bent and kissed it, just a brush of lips. "There's something . . ."

"There is, isn't there?" I said, turning into his arms. And so we spent our last night in Paris.

■ ■ ■ ■

Moreau had always traveled by carriage, his work desk on his lap. Ney rode, with his baggage following behind, and he set a grueling pace. The first night, I could hardly sleep despite the comfortable inn, because of the aches and pains. I was a good rider, but I wasn't used to ten or twelve hours a day in the saddle. In the morning I had locked up so stiffly that Michel had to pull me out of bed, laughing.

I was less amused. "Don't you hurt?" I said. "You've been resting for a few months. Surely you're out of form too."

"Of course I am," he said, relenting and sharing his coffee with me by way of amends. "But what's a little pain?"

"Right." I sipped at the scalding coffee. It was terrible. "You like pain. My legs hurt like hell."

"And it's a good thing that I do," Michel said, dressing quickly because of the chill in the room. "If we weren't short of time, I'd stop and massage your thighs." He raised an eyebrow at me as he pulled his shirt over his head.

"And that would take all day," I said, grinning. "You can come massage my thighs anytime you want."

"Not and get to Munich in six days," he said, tucking his shirt in with one hand. "Come on, lag-abed!"

He hurried downstairs shouting for the stableboy, leaving me to ruminate on why military men always wanted to get up at five in the morning.

ON CAMPAIGN

It finally stopped raining, and frost clung to the trees in the mornings, my breath coming in white clouds as we rode into Bavarian winter. Michel took command of his division, and I soon found that traveling with him was very different from the time I had spent in camp with Moreau. For one thing, I had actual work to do. Michel needed a competent orderly more than he needed a mistress, and the orderly he had was hopeless. Private Barend was barely twenty, and his eyesight was so poor that he posed a clear and present danger to any man in range who wasn't sitting atop an elephant and waving French colors. His supposed saving grace was that he had been a footman before patriotism had brought him stepping to the drum. This, in the eyes of the sergeant, qualified him as body servant to a general. Michel had no idea what a body servant was supposed to do anyway, so he overlooked the fact that his shirts were always dirty and that meals were irregular at best.

"Michel," I said, on the fourth or fifth day of this, "you are not supposed to have to think about supper. You are supposed to think about the enemy, and your orderly is supposed to think about supper. That's why you're a general and he's a private."

Michel muttered something or other over his map. It was spread out on a trestle table, the edges held down by an ink pot, a filthy glass from the day before yesterday, half a loaf of stale bread, and the compass he was getting ready to lose again. Dispatches were stacked haphazardly, the candle on top of them at an angle that ensured that one good puff of wind would set the entire mass alight.

So I set about pushing Barend about and trying to turn him into a proper body servant. This involved details such as laundry that had been above his station as a footman. When I made it clear that these considerations reflected his improved status, he was pathetically grateful and began to follow me about, asking about table settings and bed making.

I was concerned solely that there should be food on the table, thinking that the setting was probably beyond Michel's interest, and that as long as there was a bed, Michel would sleep in it. If there wasn't, he would roll up in a blanket in the corner and be asleep in five minutes anyway.

Which he was, every night. For that matter, so was I. Even after we joined his division and our mad dash across Europe slowed to the pace of the caissons and the cannon, every day was exhausting, beginning before dawn and ending long after sunset. That the days were short this time of year didn't help.

We would strike camp just after sunrise, which meant that I had been up an hour and a half before, preparing breakfast in the darkness. We had a store of coffee, which I ground with a hand grinder that one of the aides had brought, then heated the water over the fire that we built up, poured it over the grounds, and pressed it out, adding a full spoon of sugar for Michel's cup so that it was almost an espresso syrup, very hot and very sweet. Sometimes there was day-old bread for toast. There was no jam, because Michel had said we wouldn't need it. Occasionally there was butter, if we had been able to buy some from a farmer the previous day. It was the wrong season for eggs, and nothing else would cook fast enough in the morning, if the camp was to be entirely struck in an hour. Often Michel still had his coffee in his hand when he swung up on Eleazar.

After two hours on the march, we would halt for a few minutes so that everyone could smoke and trot out into the woods to do the necessary. That was the hardest part for me. Every tree had a squatting soldier behind it, and finding any place private enough to do my business alone required stomping off into the woods a considerable distance.

I traveled in the rear, in the baggage train, while Michel was at the head of the column as usual. Because each division followed another on the road, the back of one division was the front of the next. Other troops of the Army of the Rhine followed us.

One fine, clear day as we swung along after the morning halt, I heard a cavalry column coming up behind us. All of us with the baggage moved to the side of the road to let them pass through, as was customary. As they drew nearer, I saw that it was simply an escort of light cavalry, chasseurs from a brigade I didn't recognize, escorting staff. Right in front was Moreau.

I hadn't seen him in nearly three years. Not since the morning he had slammed the door on my clawing fingers, throwing me out of the house he had given me. I couldn't look at him and feel nothing.

Compact and precise, he rode a coal-black horse, looking straight ahead, his insignia glittering in the sun and his gaze alert and dark as a hawk's.

I had dismounted when we heard the column coming, so I ducked behind Nestor's head. Moreau could see my feet and legs, but there was nothing remarkable about them. The column clattered past.

I was surprised to find myself shaking. Whether it was the ghost of the desire I had once felt for him, or the urge to hit him, or sheer terror that he would see me here and punish Michel, I wasn't sure. Perhaps it was all three.

I looked out as the escort passed, three chasseurs bringing up the rear, the last a lieutenant on a dapple-gray mare who was frisking at the tight rein he held her on. I held on to Nestor's head. My knees were water.

The lieutenant on the gray mare twisted in the saddle and looked back at me, giving me a sudden, charming grin. I gulped like a fish, and he gave me a knowing, flirtatious look as he turned back to the road.

Was it so obvious? I thought. If the lieutenant had seen straight through me, perhaps my disguise wasn't as good as I had hoped. Something gave me away. But perhaps it was only my shock at seeing Moreau. Certainly I had never seen the lieutenant before.

That night we stayed near Mühldorf, in a small town in forested country where the farms were few. Moreau and his staff took over the mayor's house, while Michel and the Hussar general, Richepanse, took the inn. Moreau had the generals and their staffs to dinner and to a long planning meeting, so I was left somewhat at loose ends. After gathering up all Michel's dirty shirts and explaining to the innkeeper's wife in my extremely halting German that I needed laundry done for the general and I would pay, my chores were more or less done.

Michel had the best room, since he ranked Richepanse, with a fireplace and a big box bed with cornices that looked like they'd been there since the Thirty Years' War. The linens were impeccably clean, the floor swept and tidy, the sconces filled with fresh tapers. I hung his coats for a change to let them shake out. Then I went downstairs to find dinner for myself.

The taproom of the inn was full, and I was pleased to see that it was a fairly orderly crowd. The only women sitting on laps were the ones we had brought with us. The innkeeper and his teenage son were circulating with huge steins of beer. This was a good sign — plentiful beer never hurt anyone, but anything fortified in large quantities was bound to result in fights before the evening was over.

I squeezed into a corner far from the fireplace and managed to get the attention of the teenage son, who understood my gestures and *bittes* enough to bring me a bowl of stew with potatoes and rabbit and some warm bread to go with my beer.

I ate, a sense of contentment stealing over me despite Moreau's proximity. After all, I'd been in the same town as Moreau for years when he knew what I looked like. The last place he'd be looking for me was a Bavarian inn in the company of Richepanse's hussars.

A group by the fire had started a song, something about a girl from Aix and a sergeant. Several of our girls who were clearly working had sized up the biggest spenders in the room. And the beer was very good.

"May I sit here?"

I looked up. It took me a moment to recognize the lieutenant from the road. He was of medium height, with an ordinary face framed by elaborate hussar's braids, each one worked with a gold thread. He was holding a bowl of stew and a stein.

I shrugged and moved over into the corner so he could have a bit of table.

He put his food down and took a bite. "Quite a crowd, isn't it?"

I nodded, bending over my bowl. If he had already noticed my secret on the road, I didn't want him to blurt it out in a busy inn. There was too much chance of idle talk getting back to Moreau.

"I'm with the Twentieth Chasseurs à Cheval," he said with a friendly smile. It reminded me suddenly of René Gantheaume. He had the same cocky air, the same open charm. "Are you with the General?"

"Yes," I said, looking away from his face. It took nerve for a lieutenant to come on to a general's woman.

The lieutenant shrugged elaborately. "My friend, don't you think he's a bit old and serious? Wouldn't you rather have a bit of fun with someone your own age?" His hand stole onto my thigh under the table.

I turned and fixed him with a steely stare, though my voice was still low, glad I wore the epée openly now. "My friend," I said, "I may be a woman, but if you don't get your hand off my thigh, I will use this and you won't like it."

He moved his hand as if I had burned him. For a moment he gaped, and then he laughed, bowing slightly from the waist, his eyes bright with laughter. "A thousand pardons, Madame! Had I known you were a woman, I should never have taken such liberties!" He gave a self-deprecating shrug. "I thought you were a pretty lad to be a servant to General Ney. They said your name was van Aylde, and that you were a volunteer."

"I am a volunteer," I said, "and I am with General Ney. And my name is van Aylde, and I am also a woman."

He lifted his stein and took a drink. "Good luck to you, then, Madame. You carry off the masquerade as well as any I've seen. I hope you will forgive my impudence?"

I found it impossible not to. "You are forgiven," I said. "And may I have the name of the man I forgive?"

"Lieutenant Jean-Baptiste Corbineau," he said. "And you are?"

"Charles," I said. I steepled my fingers around my stein. "Let's leave it at Charles."

"What a coincidence!" he said. "I'm

sometimes called Charles too. It's my favorite alias for losing at cards."

I burst out laughing. "Do you lose often?"

"Continually," he said. "If it's a foolish gamble and angels fear to tread, there goes the cavalry."

"I'll toast the cavalry," I said, lifting my stein.

Instead of touching his stein to mine, Corbineau got to his feet, raising his in the air instead. "Gentlemen!" he said loudly. "My friend here proposes a toast to the cavalry!"

Since the inn was full of Richepanse's men, the roar was thunderous. "The cavalry!" It was a full shout, every glass raised, as I looked at them in bemusement.

Corbineau sank back into his seat beside me as a group by the fire started toasting everyone they had ever met in Auvergne.

"You're drunk," I said.

"Not as drunk as I will be, fair lady," he said, motioning for more beer. "If I'm out of luck tonight, I may as well enjoy the beer."

I raised an eyebrow. "And what would you have done if I had said yes? Assuming you were correct in your assumptions, that is?"

He laughed. "You can't think of anything? Perhaps Red Ney is wooden after all!"

487

"I'd know and you wouldn't," I said rather tartly.

Corbineau grinned at me again. "No offense intended. I think the world of him, in truth. I'd follow him straight into the mouth of hell on horseback — he's that good, and I ought to know, the son of a horse trader that I am. And there's not a braver man or a better one to serve, even if he's hard as hell on malingerers. But sometimes his dignity is just a priceless backdrop for a *bon mot.*"

"And you always have one of those, don't you?" I said. A joker, so that no one would know if his advances were intended or not. Unless they were taken up. Another stranger in this land.

"I do," Corbineau said. "But the battle will be joined within the next week or two, and you know who will be riding screen tomorrow. Damned if I'll do that stone sober."

"Riding screen?"

Corbineau spread his hands. "Light cavalry fans out in front of the line of march, staying just in sight of each other. We scout the terrain and, most importantly, we look for the enemy. Usually we find them. And when we do, we put our spurs to it and get back as fast as we can. If we can. Because *they* send out cavalry skirmishers to do the same thing." He interlaced his fingers. "And sometimes we cross like that, our screen and theirs."

"I see," I said, imagining the cold woods and the tension, waiting for a movement that would mean something.

"It's been raining on and off for weeks," Corbineau said. "The mud is almost knee-deep in places. And it hasn't been cold enough for everything to freeze solid. It's pleasant, let me tell you."

"I see," I said again. There was some part of me that wanted to try it, rather than ride with the baggage train.

"A keen lad?" His eyes twinkled.

"Something like that," I said. "It's hardly fair you should get all the fun."

"If you get bored being a servant, you could be a chasseur," Corbineau said. "You'd pass as long as no one looked under your tunic. But I suppose your general wouldn't like that."

"I suppose he wouldn't," I said. But I wondered if I could do it anyway.

Michel was late coming in that night, carrying his map case with him and opening it on the table upstairs in the bedchamber. I sat up in bed, wearing one of Charles's shirts, watching him. As he leaned over the map, light from the single candle gleamed on his hair, on the braid at his shoulders.

"What are you doing?" I asked.

"Fixing the positions in my mind." He looked around at me. "Do you want to see?"

"Isn't it secret?" I asked, getting out of bed.

"There's no reason you can't see what half the army will see before tomorrow." I looked over his shoulder as Michel smoothed the map out. "There are two roads," he said, "the one from here to Munich, and the one from Munich to Wasserburg. They both pass through the forest of Hohenlinden, here and here. The Austrians must use the roads to move as many men as they have, with all their guns and equipment. There are footpaths through the forest as well, but none of them are suitable for a wagon or a gun."

"How many men do they have?" I asked.

Michel looked at me sideways. "Our best estimate is around sixty thousand men. To our total of fifty thousand or so, nine thousand of which are mine. Not such great odds. And they have many more cannon."

I looked at the map, and it seemed for a moment I had seen it before, stretched out in candlelight like this, an iron candlestick weighting it instead of pewter, forest and roads engraved fine. "But if they must keep the guns on the roads," I said slowly, "then they can't use them easily, and not at all except there."

"Exactly," Michel said. "And so we must get around behind them while they are in column, advancing, and at the same time hold them here, at the village of Hohenlinden, where the road leaves the woods and crosses the river here." He pointed. "General Moreau's plan is for us to move the main body down here to wait, and send Richepanse's men around to flank."

"A waiting game?" I asked. "That's like Moreau."

"He's good," Michel said. "Whatever I think of him privately, he's as good as they say he is." He let go of the edge of the map and it rolled up. He carefully rolled it the rest of the way and put it in the case. "The problem is," he said, as he sat down on the edge of the bed to take his boots off, "we don't know exactly where the Austrians are."

I thought of the lieutenant, going off at dawn to screen in front of the army. "I imagine we'll find them, won't we?"

Rather, they found us.

The next day was cloudy and cold, with

the whisper of snow in the air. It smelled like snow, though not a flake fell.

We were between the first halt and the midday halt when a furor erupted toward the head of the column, a sudden rolling echo of shots loud enough to startle all the roosting birds, which took off out of the fir trees into the sky. It was the first time I had heard firing in volley.

Nestor didn't even prance when I hauled him up sharply in my surprise.

In the wake of the shots came the yells, one shrill shriek and a great many shouts. Then came sporadic shots in reply.

In the back of the baggage train, there was a great deal of swearing as horses shied and teams fouled their reins. Some people started rushing forward and some started rushing back. The only thing I could think was that Michel had been at the head of the column as usual, glittering with braid, an obvious target.

Something ran through me, the same elongation of time, and an utter lack of fear. I had Auguste Thibault's epée, and I drew it left-handed, the reins in my right hand.

"Come on, Nestor," I said, and touched my heels to his sides.

It wasn't very far. The Twenty-Third Infantry Demibrigade had been thrown back in disarray at the first volley, which had been straight into their flank as they came over the crest of a hill in the forest. The Austrians were in the woods. Now they charged out en masse, bayonets fixed, into the carnage and confusion.

"Shit," I said, as I saw the one who had marked me. He had very light gray eyes, running over the muddy ground.

And then I was lunging forward, pulling to the right so that at the last moment I passed him on the wrong side, the off side where a cavalryman doesn't want you — unless he's left-handed. It threw him for a split second. That was the second that mattered. A squeeze, and Nestor went halfway up, his weight on the descent adding momentum to the thrust of the epée, hitting the Austrian full in the breastbone with the point. The impact tore the sword out of my hand.

I pulled Nestor round in a hard circle. The man stood there almost stupefied, the epée protruding from his chest. His hand opened, and his musket and bayonet dropped to the ground. I made a grab for the sword and got the hilt, the blood spurting as I pulled it free.

Nestor went up again. To my right, an Austrian was trying to get at us with fixed bayonet without getting close enough to Nestor's hooves. I swung him around, keeping his belly clear. My sword rang against the bayonet's blade, parrying just as I had been taught. Strike, strike, a double beat with the forte, a disengage to the left faster than anyone could do with something as ungainly as a musket. A thrust that opened a wound down the side of his face and neck, the epée sliding almost cleanly through flesh.

And then we were past him, plunging among our infantry. They were rallying into line.

Michel's voice cut through the din. "Don't unlimber that gun, you sons of bitches! Get the hell back! We're covering your retreat. That gun is worth more than your sorry lives!"

Relief flooded through me. His hat was gone, and Eleazar's white stockings were splashed with gore. His face was as red as his hair, and his aide and two cavalrymen were trying to keep up. The four of them charged into a knot of Austrians who were reloading, and I charged after.

One of them brought his musket up, half-finished, and fired. The ramrod went straight through the cavalryman to the right, standing out from his back a handsbreadth. He swayed and pitched from the saddle.

I took the infantryman, who was looking at his gun in astonishment. He never saw me cut him down.

And then Michel was stirrup to stirrup with me. He grabbed my reins. "What the hell do you think you're doing?"

"What does it look like?" I shouted back, my bloodied epée in my hand, my glove soaked through with someone else's blood. "You do your job and trust me!"

Something passed over his face, and he gave me a brisk nod. "I do," he said, letting go of my reins. He raised his voice. "The One Hundred Third to the fore! Everybody else, get your butts back out of the way. I want the Twenty-Third in line behind. You there! Get on over there! Any stray cavalry, come with me!" He looked at me. "It's the main body of the Austrian army to our nine thousand men."

Michel turned away. "Form up! We've got to get those skirmishers out of the wood line. Ruffin, who are those chasseurs? If they're here, they're with me."

There were six of them, one of them the lieutenant with the dapple-gray mare, Corbineau.

At the edge of the wood there was a sudden flash of light and smoke, an instant before the crashing sound of the volley. It was fifteen or twenty men, but it sounded like the vast army that was rolling up the road at a marching pace, bayonets fixed. The main body. Sixty thousand men on nine thousand.

A bugler sounded charge, and Nestor leapt forward with the rest, straight into their guns.

But they had already fired. Only one shot sang past me, someone reloading too slowly for the volley. I didn't think it hit anything.

And then we were among them. The dapple mare plunged in front of me, taking down a man with her hooves and teeth, almost dancing. Corbineau's face was set, his own teeth bared.

I got one of them in the arm, the point straight into the fleshy part of the upper arm, and saw the blood bloom on his coat. He dropped his musket, and then I was past him, ducking under heavy fir branches that tore at my sleeves and hair.

"Turn! Recall!" Michel was shouting, presumably in absence of the bugle signal. I swung about, finding myself once again beside Corbineau as we emerged again from the woods.

Off to our left, the entire Austrian army came on in perfect ranks, regiment upon regiment along the road, bayonets fixed and muskets loaded, every step in drill-perfect precision, lined up from here to heaven knew where. To our left, our artillery was towing the last of the field guns away as fast as possible, and four ranks of infantry waited, the first rank kneeling, holding their fire for range.

Michel galloped toward our ranks, calling out something to an officer standing at the end, and the rest of us followed.

Corbineau glanced at me and his eyes widened. "Charles?"

"It's me," I said, taking off my bloody glove to wipe the sweat from my face.

"I love a lady who likes it hot," Corbineau said with a grin.

"I'm no lady," I said. I felt exalted. No opium, no hashish had ever had the power to make me feel this way, light as a cloud and made of fire. It was like sex and joy and the primal urge of childbirth, like being wind off the mountain, like being chained lightning. Only the barest bit of sense kept me from charging straight into the Austrian army.

"Cavalry, get back!" Michel shouted. We were between our men and the approaching Austrians. The range was still too great, but it was closing.

We spurred forward, passing through a gap in the ranks between companies. The infantry gave us a cheer. We had given them time to form up. Now they would fight a rearguard action to give our column time to escape.

Michel sat on Eleazar just behind the fourth rank, his aide Ruffin beside him. Eleazar's breath came in great clouds of steam in the frosty air.

Closer and closer, their feet marking time.

Michel raised his sword. The infantry officers watched him. It would be death to fire too early, and would waste the shot.

Something blurred my vision. I put my hand to my face and felt it melt, the first snowflake. I looked at Corbineau. A white flake clung to the shoulder of his blue tunic. Another drifted down between us.

"Snow," he said.

"Yes." I didn't quite understand why he was grinning.

With a crash like thunder, our first line opened up. The powder smoke rolled back toward us with the wind in a great stinking cloud. They knelt to reload, the second rank stepping forward.

A shouted order, and a hundred muskets blazed in the smoke. I could see nothing of whether or not the shots told.

Then there was the crash of the reply. I heard screams, but they could have come from anyone. The Austrians couldn't pick out targets in the smoke, only fire in the general direction of our men.

Again our guns crashed. The third rank, I supposed.

The heavens opened and the snow came down thick and fast, as though the sound of our guns had cracked the clouds. It swirled on the wind, powder-scented.

There was movement. Our ranks were retreating slowly, each rank as it fired backing off and waiting for the others to pass through in their turn, a fighting retreat. Again the guns blared.

I couldn't see the Austrians, had no idea what was happening.

"We should back off," Corbineau said, "stay behind the last rank in case we need a countercharge against cavalry."

"Is that likely?" I said. I could imagine what he meant, almost feel what it would be to do it.

"Not so much in this," Corbineau said. "They can't see anything either."

I couldn't imagine that anyone could. Between the rolling smoke and the flying snow, I could hardly see a length beyond Nestor's head.

Three times more our guns sounded. We were taking fire as well, farther forward. Three more times the ranks passed through to reload, and we backed up again, almost into the thick trees along the road.

And then our guns went silent. For a moment, I could almost hear the swishing of the snow, starting to stick to the thick branches, sticking to my hair.

A couple of infantrymen came past, half-dragging a friend between them. One of the caissons sat along the road, its team held tightly by a pair of privates. The infantrymen hoisted their friend up on the caisson.

"Get the wounded back!" Michel shouted from somewhere ahead in the fog. "Everyone else, stay in line. Ruffin, what do you see?"

Ruffin must have ridden out in front of the smoke, but I could not hear his reply. The guns remained silent. As the smoke thinned, I could see them standing like ghosts in the falling snow.

"Pull back!" Michel shouted. "The One Hundred Third back behind the line of the Twenty-Third!"

I could see the Twenty-Third up the road from us a bit, the brigade disordered on the first attack, now formed up waiting. Line by line, we backed up to them.

Corbineau and I stood still and waited. Two of the officers of the Twenty-Third came forward to where we were.

Michel and Ruffin rode back, following the second line of infantry. "They're holding position," Michel said. "I don't think they've got pursuit orders. Which suggests they didn't know where we were either, and we ran up on one another. If they're waiting for pursuit orders from the Austrian command, they'll wait a year and a day for them. Archduke Johann is uncertain and untried."

He looked from one face to another. "We'll retire in order to Hohenlinden. Moreau can't be far behind us." He glanced at me, and I saw that he felt it too, this passion half-leashed by intellect. He would not go charging into the middle of the Austrians. But it was there. He looked like an angel of battles should look, bloody and bareheaded in the swirling snow, strange and familiar at the same time, obscene and beloved.

Echoes of a Beating Drum

We bivouacked that night half a mile from the village of Hohenlinden on the edge of the forest. Moreau's men occupied the town, which was our headquarters, and Ney's men moved into position to hold the left. Other generals would have kicked a junior officer out of quarters in the town, but Michel did not want to be so much as half a mile away from his men, so his tent was set up in the camp.

Settling in took a considerable amount of time. The snow was ankle-deep when it ended at nightfall, and by moonrise the night was clear and cold. Twenty-seven men had fallen in the skirmish, mostly men of the Twenty-Third who had been shot in the first few volleys. For the first time I saw the grave-digging details, heard the bugler play the final calls over a burial in the moonlight.

I had not known any of them personally, and I stood back from the fires that had been kindled to keep the diggers warm and to light their work. Michel stood near one of the fires, and when it came his time as general to speak, he stepped out solemnly, the smoke unerringly flowing away from him, as though he had done this a thousand times before. Perhaps he had.

The firelight played across his face, glittered on his gold braid and his hair, washing his face with light. It seemed to me for a moment it was some other face I saw there, in the light of a pyre for men I had not known, under these same wheeling stars. I could almost see him clearly, the prince of a people who were no more, brown hair pulled back from his face just so, a young face, a decade younger than Michel. How many times had I watched him thus? I wondered. It felt like a million, like a moment of touching eternity.

I shook myself. I had closed those doors, I thought. I had said no more omens and half-remembered faces. But this was not frightening. This did not verge on madness. Instead, it seemed safe and familiar. Michel spoke different words, but the sense was the same — *these are our comrades, we bid them farewell, farewell to the lost, until we meet again.*

Michel stepped back from the fire, and

the gravediggers went to work filling in the graves. Twenty-seven more for his lists.

I fell in beside him as we walked back to the camp, laid out in precise rows in the moonlight. There was none of the disorder I remembered from Moreau's camp. This was the night after a small battle, with a greater looming on the horizon, a camp at watch, the men catching what sleep they could.

Private Barend had redeemed himself by managing dinner, potatoes fried with a bit of ham with mustard on the side, Maille's finest seasoned with tarragon. It was the kind Moreau liked best, that I used to order for him on campaign. I didn't need to ask to know that Barend had traded for it with someone at Moreau's headquarters.

We ate in silence, and then Michel went back out to go round the sentries. It had gotten very cold. I heard the snow crunching under his boots as he left, the ice on top forming a fine crust. I got out all the blankets, which between us were four, and spread them on the slung camp bed. It was technically wide enough for only one person, but we could both squeeze in if we were close. I left the lamp alight, because it did give off some warmth that the tent trapped, took off only my boots, and rolled up in the blankets.

I must have dozed. The sounds of the camp softened. Michel came back, and I woke when the light changed as he blew out the lamp. He lay down beside me in the dark, curling gratefully into the warm place beside me. His hands were like ice. His face was cold.

His arms went around me and he sighed. "All right?"

"Yes," I said. And we slept.

We expected the Austrians to attack the next day. Before dawn a fresh cavalry screen went out, careful on the snow, spreading out through the woods. All day riders came and went.

And still there was no attack. The temperature rose enough for the snow to begin to melt where the sun touched it, leaving patches of bare ground here and there. Riders came and went. Soon everyone knew what the scouts had said. The Austrians hadn't moved at all.

When Michel came back to his tent before dinner, I asked him what was happening.

He shrugged, gathering up his map case. "Archduke Johann is young. A more experienced commander would have attacked today. Instead, he's given us time to prepare for him, and time for General Moreau to think of a thing or two. I'm off to a staff meeting." He leaned over and kissed my brow. "Don't wait for me. I don't know how long I'll be."

"I won't," I said. It was the first time in days that he had looked at me as though I weren't Charles. We hadn't spoken of the skirmish. There was nothing we needed to say that we had the words for.

Michel ruffled my cropped hair, a half smile on his face. "You know, it's still disturbing."

"I imagine so," I said, smiling back. "More a squire than a maiden fair."

"You do a fine job of arming me," he said. "Don't think I haven't noticed that I'm not hungry and frozen."

"More useful than bedroom arts right now."

"More to your taste?" He rested his hands lightly on my arms, looking at me.

I shook my head. "Both, Michel. I'm both." I didn't know how to say it, so I leaned forward and rested my head against his shoulder. "Squire and courtesan both. They used to be the same word, you know. *Hetaira* and *hetairos,* courtesan and knight companion."

"Did they?" he said bemusedly. His arms went around me, holding me tight.

"Someone told me that once," I said, trying to remember who.

I didn't remember until after he'd left for the staff meeting, his map case in his hand and his cloak pulled close against the wind. It had been Bonaparte.

All the next day we waited. Still the Austrians didn't move. The day was a bit warmer, and the snow melted in the sun, leaving patches under the trees and on shaded slopes, turning the road to mud. Our provisions didn't arrive. We hoped it was the mud that had delayed them. Otherwise, the Austrians had cut our supply line.

We made do on boiled potatoes that night.

Moreau ordered that watch fires should be built in advance of our actual lines, outside the camp to the north, all along the perimeter toward the edge of the woods. It gave us light, since the sky had clouded over again and the temperature had dropped. I thought it would snow again.

Michel had added to the plan. He had posted sentries out in the woods in a sweeping circle, well ahead of the fires where the light would not affect their night vision, with the river at our backs beyond the camp.

I curled up in the blankets and slept, only to awaken in the middle of the night. There was a movement in the tent, and even in the darkness I knew it was Michel putting his boots on. "Michel?" I whispered.

He leaned toward me. "No need for you to get up. It's four in the morning. I'm just going round the sentries again."

"Can't sleep?" Now that I sat up, I felt completely clearheaded.

"No," he said. "Something's happening." He looked out to the north, like a hunting dog scenting after quarry. "Can't you feel it?"

"Yes," I whispered. "The temperature's dropped again. And it's getting ready to snow. It's darker in here than it was. The clouds have come in."

Michel nodded. "They'll come with the snow. Elza, I don't want you on the front line. You don't know a damned thing about infantry tactics, and you can't fake them." He touched my face with one forefinger. "And I would say exactly the same thing if you were Charles. Promise me you'll stay back."

"I promise," I said. And I meant it. Life was too sweet to have a death wish.

He kissed me lightly. "Good." And then he pulled his cloak around him and went out.

I sat up in bed, fully dressed. It was too

cold to undress. I didn't think I had for about five days. I had not actually made love to him in three weeks, since we joined his division. I missed it, and I didn't.

I wondered if Bonaparte was the same in the field.

A strange and fey mood was on me, and I couldn't sleep. I put my boots and cloak on and went out.

The sky had completely clouded over. The lights of our watch fires were the only bright things in sight. It was dead silent. The river did not even whisper, frozen over between its banks. Not a bough stirred among the massive fir trees. The first flakes of snow began to fall, beautiful and ethereal in the darkness.

Michel stood a short distance away, far enough from the fires to see into the dark. He was alone. I walked up beside him.

"It's strange," he began, but we heard the sound of hooves coming up. Three men on horseback were coming along the length of our lines, cloaked figures dark against the falling snow. I knew the first, even shrouded. Moreau.

I had no time to leave. I stepped back into a shadow, hoping that my hooded cloak hid my features.

"Citizen General?" he called, his voice low

and calm.

Michel stepped forward. "Here, General Moreau. Everything is quiet. It lacks two hours to first dawn."

Moreau nodded, still in the saddle. He did not glance in my direction. His eyes were bright, even in the dim light. "Too quiet."

"I agree," Michel said. "We'll stand to colors at dawn."

What Moreau would have said, I did not know. His horse took a step toward me, and I saw his head began to turn. He had seen my movement, but not my face.

A shot rang out in the woods.

Moreau and Michel both jerked about. There was a shout, and then another shot.

"Bugler!" Michel shouted, his voice carrying about the camp.

A man was running out of the woods, his cloak cast away in his haste. He pounded up at the same moment as the bugler began. "General! The Austrians are moving through the woods en masse. They're wearing white, but we saw them anyway. Probably about three or four thousand men, my best guess."

Behind me, the camp was mustering, shouts and swears intermingling as the units formed up.

"They can't mount an effective charge," Michel said to Moreau. "The ground is too broken. Underbrush, little streams, banks."

"They'll be crack infantry," Moreau said, "on a night attack like this." His horse shied at a shot close by, one of the sentries firing down into the woods. He held on effortlessly, his light body molded to the horse. "Shall I move in Richepanse to help hold them?"

"Why?" Eleazar had been led out, and Michel swung into the saddle. "I'm just about to launch a counterattack."

"Your call," Moreau said. A full volley fired, the first of our units firing into the woods together. I hoped the sentries posted in the woods had gotten out of there or gotten down. "Let me know what you need. I've got to get back to my troops."

The tent was at my back, and I slipped inside, out of his sight. I could still hear his voice, but couldn't make out what he said, with all the running and confusion. And then there was another crashing volley. Right behind it was a louder explosion, one of the field guns coming into action.

I stood in the tent, holding the flap shut. I had promised Michel I would stay back. And in truth, there was nothing useful I could do. I didn't have a musket, and as

Michel had pointed out, I knew nothing about infantry drill. The only thing I could do in those dark woods was make myself a target for our own men.

I listened. After a few moments, I parted the flap and looked out again. Moreau was gone. I could see his silhouette on horseback moving down the lines, toward his own troops. On that end, the muzzle flashes were sporadic. I thought that the main attack was this way, but in the darkness it could simply be that the right side of the line had not yet engaged.

Before me, our lines spouted fire in perfect unison, volley after volley crashing into the darkness.

The return fire was dense off on the far left. Our guns silenced suddenly there, and a cheer went up. With a shriek, our men charged forward on foot, engaging bayonet on bayonet as the Austrians reached close quarters. I could hear, but not see. The snow was coming down densely now.

More crashes. The fire to the right was less. Shouts.

To the left the fight had moved into the woods, and I could see nothing. I went back inside and rearranged things, put on my sword just in case. Then I couldn't stand it and went back out.

The firing off to the right had fallen silent. I could see people moving in the woods, dark uniforms against the snow, our men who were not camouflaged. To the left, I could tell nothing of what happened.

Dawn came. We had captured more than four hundred prisoners. Another hundred or so lay dead in the woods. We had lost a handful, mostly the original sentries.

In the pale light I made coffee and found Michel. He was talking to two infantry noncoms, his hat crusted with an inch of snow. It was coming down so thickly that already it covered my boots in some places. The sky was dead white.

Wordlessly, I put the cup in his hand. He glanced at me and drank, never pausing, but I saw the gratitude in his eyes. When they had finished talking, he turned to me. "The coffee's good," he said.

"Thank you."

"I want you to go to the village," Michel said. "I'm sending all the nonessentials over there."

"Moreau. . . ." I began.

"Will be with his men," Michel said. "We're striking the camp. The scouts have told us that the Austrians are still advancing. We threw back the night attack, but there are more coming. That wasn't really

513

so many. The village is safer, and that's where our supplies need to be."

I nodded. "I'll do whatever you need me to."

At noon they rolled in, striking again most heavily on the left end of the line, on Michel's troops and the left section of Moreau's. I watched from the village, from a second-floor room of a house that was now division headquarters.

The real division headquarters was with Michel, wherever he and his aide Ruffin were on the field between the river and the wood, but this was where I had the maps laid out on the table and found some food for when they would need it. There's never such a thing as an unwelcome potato soup. With some onions and dried herbs in it, it was pretty good and would keep as long as it needed to over the fire. They would be hungry, wounded and unwounded alike.

By late afternoon the snow was more than knee-deep, and it showed no signs of stopping. It was too much. The Austrians withdrew.

Michel came in at nightfall, Ruffin and his senior officers with him, stamping the snow off his boots, his coat steaming before the fire. There was blood all over his cloak, and no way to clean it just now. His buff pants were almost brown.

He ate some soup, and I got him to change clothes and lie down for a few hours. He had been going since before four in the morning in the cold. He lay down on a bed upstairs, where I had a fire going, and slept until midnight.

I didn't sleep. I stayed downstairs, getting soup for the others who came in, serving it out with Barend and a couple of others. When I ran out, I went into the cellars to see what I could find. More potatoes, more onions, the householder's winter stores. Enough to make another big pot of soup, because the hungry men just kept coming. I wanted bread, and there was flour, but I had never learned to make bread. Fortunately, there was a private from the Somme whose father was a baker, and I set him to making bread in as large a quantity as possible. With cheese and apples from the cellars, it would manage a substantial dinner and breakfast. I left the sausages. We would get to them later.

I wasn't sure how many of the men had figured out that I was a woman, and how many thought that I was simply the general's body servant. It didn't seem to matter. Barend did what I told him, and the rest seemed to assume that I had the authority to arrange the provisions and quartering, whether as the general's woman or as an orderly duly deputized. Or perhaps nobody cared, as long as there was food.

At midnight Michel came down and ate some bread and an apple and some soup with a cup of very hot coffee. He had a clean shirt and pants, though I had been able to do nothing about his coat or cloak. He went straight back out to the lines.

The room quieted. There was no sound but the snores of sleeping men and the crackling of the fire. I sat on a stool beside the fireplace, nodding.

Something brushed against my ankles, a big gray cat with green eyes that reflected the flames. She purred, and brushed past me again. The household's cat, I thought, hiding somewhere all day and now come out when the house was quiet. I petted her and gave her some scraps of cheese. She ate them delicately, as though she wasn't very hungry, stopping to watch me with her enormous eyes. I ran my hands along her back, sweeping over her soft fur. She purred.

The Egyptians thought cats were magic, I thought. Perhaps they were right. This one looked as though she had something to tell me. She leapt into my lap, kneading and purring. I pressed my face against her soft fur. "I'm sorry, dear," I whispered into her pointed ears, "your people will be back soon, when the battle's over. They're probably safer somewhere else right now, you know." The cat in my lap, I watched through the small hours of the night.

In the morning, the great battle began.

HOHENLINDEN

In the night, Moreau had sent off about half his force, nearly twenty-five thousand men under Richepanse. They pulled back quietly and marched away to the east, cavalry to the fore and guns last, the cavalry taking one of the footpaths through the forest. Ney, Moreau, and General Grouchy formed a bastion about the town of Hohenlinden, with General Legrand, whom I did not know, in reserve. Given the talk of flanking maneuvers, I assumed that this was the plan — to somehow get around behind the Austrians using the poor trails through the forest. By morning the snow was fourteen inches deep, and still coming down in occasional flurries. I didn't think this would make it easy.

Michel came in right after dawn and ate some soup. The potatoes had cooked to bits by now, but it tasted wonderful. "Thank you," he said quietly.

I nodded. "It's a good thing I learned to cook," I said. I wondered if he would say any of the things I hoped he wouldn't, things about if something happens or just in case.

He didn't. "Very useful," he said. He didn't touch me, and there was nothing affectionate in his manner, nothing inappropriate for a servant, except his expression, the warmth in his eyes when he looked at me. If any man in the room didn't guess, they certainly thought it was an interesting relationship with Charles. If they cared, which at the moment I doubted anyone did.

And so I did not say good luck, good-bye, or any of those other things that women in stories say on the cusp of a battle. What could I say that I hadn't said in soup?

He went out as though it were a bit of business he meant to attend to, a battle of a hundred thousand men on which might rest the Republic. In an hour they were all gone, all the men who had crowded in overnight and through breakfast. There was no one left except nearsighted Barend, whom I set to washing up. I sat by the fire and had a bowl of soup myself.

Three years ago, I would not have cared if the Republic fell or flourished. Governments come and go, kings and princes, committees and consuls, up and down on Fortune's Wheel, with no real difference between. But there was. Here I had liberty, the freedom to be who I truly was with no censure, no fear. I could have my own money in the bank. I could rent rooms without fear that a man could take them away. I did not belong to Jan. I was more than a vessel for wealth, more than an ornament whose education was to the glory of her husband and sons.

Should Michel have been a cooper? Should he have been a sergeant all his life, doomed to the lot of his forefathers because he was born a peasant with no hope of advancement? I knew now that the stiltedness of his letters was because he had ended school when he was twelve. What use would the son of a peasant have of more knowledge? Everything he knew, everything he was, he had won himself out of pure desire.

The same was true of every man here. Their dreams were different — glory or money or the esteem of a girl — but everyone wanted something that would have been denied, and now saw it within their grasp. Dreams are a thing worth fighting for. Worth dying for. A good many of them would die today, their dreams still unfulfilled.

Not Michel.

I bent my head over my soup.

I had never really prayed, never really understood the form and the need to recite elaborate passages or to spend hours on one's knees; but now I felt my whole self yearning, concentrating in two words: *Not Michel.* Anyone else. Just not Michel. *Let him be right. Let it be true that he leads a charmed life, that he is protected by angels.*

I closed my eyes, reaching for that presence I had felt in Lebrun's rituals. I knew the words, I had been taught them. *Archangel Michel, Guardian of Battles, of the South and of Fire, Patron of warriors and all those who fight for others, watch over your namesake! Guard him with your sword. Keep him safe.*

And then I felt better. Not wild with the ecstasy of battle as I had before, but just better. Not buoyed up by divinity, but calmer, as though my heart was now the mirror of my face. I got up to wash my soup bowl.

With a roll like distant thunder, the guns opened up.

The front of the Austrian advance had come out of the woods straight into the field of fire of Moreau's guns. Caught between their advancing column and the French guns and infantry ahead and the dark forest, the Austrians did the only sensible thing. They charged.

I ran outside and looked, but I could see nothing. There was too much smoke from the batteries, too many men rushing about, and the buildings of the town blocked my view. I glanced up. Even from the second-story windows of the house, I should see nothing. The church stood between it and the road, as well as other houses on the other side. The tower was filled with our men, no doubt, spotters who could send messages to Moreau. The church itself had been made ready as a hospital, the priest and several nuns who normally tended the town's sick waiting for the wounded of both sides. As yet, the town was safe. We were not in range of the Austrian guns.

From the sound of the batteries crashing, I doubted that many of the Austrian guns were in play yet. They would have to be dragged clear of the woods and unlimbered, and I had seen what a laborious process that could be. To do it under fire in fourteen inches of snow would take quite some time, if they did it at all.

I wanted to go nearer, but I didn't. If it was an artillery duel, or the rush on guns by infantry against our infantry, there was nothing useful I could do. Here, at least, there was. I went back in the house and started making a sausage soup.

The sun flirted with the clouds, now coming out for a few minutes, then disappearing again.

For a few moments near noon it seemed the battle was over. The Austrians had backed off to the edge of the woods, unable to make any headway, and the field was covered with the dead and dying. They could not advance and get their wounded, while ours fell near our lines and could be pulled to relative safety. It was only a respite. The young Archduke rallied his men again and charged. From the street I could see little, save that the left was fully engaged.

I would have heard if Michel had fallen. Someone would have said. Messengers were coming and going, and the wounded were being brought back to the church. If something had happened, I would know it.

I chopped up onions and fried them in butter, making a base for the soup. I fried the sausages and found plenty of sage, some barley to go in the pot that would plump up and give it all some body as it cooked.

The snow began again.

I went back out in the street. Now there was something new. Men in the uniforms of the 103rd were escorting prisoners, dozens of them, back away from the town and across the river. Tired and bloody, there were scores of them. No, I thought as I got a better look, hundreds. Hundreds of prisoners were sheltering in the byres across the river, guarded by our men, their paroles given. Hundreds.

It couldn't be long. And it wasn't.

The snow changed into sleet. There was a new sound. Far away, just on the edge of hearing, the answering booming of guns. Richepanse was somewhere in their rear, and his guns marked his position.

The Austrian front collapsed. Pullback became retreat became rout. By the end of the afternoon, Ney's nine thousand men had taken ten thousand prisoners and eighty-seven guns, and the Austrian army had completely disintegrated. Units fled into the forest, while a small number retreated in order. All in all, we had more than twenty thousand prisoners.

Our losses were comparatively small, by military standards — a few thousand, a few hundred of whom were Ney's. He would count every one.

He did not come in until midnight. The sausage soup was gone. I thought that I had seen every hungry man in the division. I'd made onion soup with some bacon in it. When that ran out, we were back to potato soup again.

Michel came in from the dark, ice glittering on his hat from the sleet that still came down. The kitchen was full of men, most of them grabbing something to eat before going back out.

He looked at me and I looked at him. I could see the shadow of that exaltation on his face, the last bit of that passion that transported me beyond myself, that had lifted me on the wings of eagles.

I ladled out a bowl of soup and brought it to him with a wooden spoon.

He took it as though I had handed him the Host. "Isn't this the same soup?" he asked, his eyes meeting mine over the steaming bowl.

"No," I said. "It's different soup. The other soup ran out and I made more soup. Twice."

His face was red and raw from the cold, two days' beard on his jaw, his hair damp with ice and blood. A powder burn streaked one cheek. He had been firing a musket at some point.

"Oh," he said, and lifted one hand from the soup bowl, cupping my jaw and pulling my face to his in a kiss, savage and tender with the remains of that passion. Someone hooted and someone else laughed, making a jest I didn't hear. It made my head swim.

He released me. His expression was slightly sheepish above the soup bowl.

"Michel," I said a little breathlessly, "eat your soup."

And he did, sitting down at the trestle table and putting his hat beside him.

"How about bringing me some soup?" a wag across the room called.

"I didn't get any of that with my soup," a corporal remarked. "How about some more for me, pretty one?"

I ladled out a dish for the wag and gave it to him with a smile and a flourish. "I'll give you soup but nothing more. Go get some oak leaves on your shoulders, and I'll bring you soup to remember!"

A stocky sergeant with his arm in a sling reached for the second bowl I brought. I leaned down and kissed his brow. There was a hooting cheer. "And that's for you, with your honorable blood. The rest of you, go to work like Jean here and see what you get!" I winked and went and sat by Michel.

His eyes were amused. "When did you get to be the wife of the brigade?"

"Sometime in the last two days I've spent

feeding them," I said. "It's what I can do. There's not one of them who would hurt me."

Michel looked around the room, taking its temper in a glance. "No, there's not. Good fellows all, and you belong to them. They'd kill any man who took liberties with you, whether they think you're a boy or a girl."

I followed his glance around the room. "This is where I belong," I said simply.

He looked up, the spoon halfway to his mouth. "Yes," he said. "You understand."

He meant more than this room. He meant the madness that possessed him, the glory that filled and receded like an unconquerable hunger. And he meant the life of the camp, the life of the road, of seeing morning breaking over strange fields.

"I do," I said, and leaned on his shoulder for a moment.

Then I went back to ladling out soup.

Richepanse was sent in pursuit of the Austrians because his men had taken the least damage in the battles. Moreau followed after toward Munich. Michel was left to parole the prisoners and have a day or three of rest, his men having borne the brunt of three days' battle. We were four more nights in Hohenlinden before we moved out for Munich. Michel spent most of the nights on his feet, what with one thing and another, catching a few hours' sleep in the early mornings. I cooked, and slept on what seemed to be an entirely different schedule.

On the last night, I woke to find the bed empty except for the big gray cat. She lounged, purring, on my feet. I sat up and petted her. "Don't worry," I said to her, "we're leaving. And your people will be home soon, I expect. They'll miss their potatoes and sausages, but they'll be glad to see you."

We left for Munich on a cold, clear day. The snow had stopped, but it hadn't been warm enough to melt anything. I rode Nestor at the front of the baggage train, ahead of the hospital wagons and the supplies and caissons, just ahead of the wagon with Michel's tent and cases. Nestor was in fine spirits, prancing and blowing a bit just to show that he could. We camped that night along the road, and the next day came into Munich.

The city had already surrendered to Moreau long since, with deputations from the city fathers and the Church, Moreau giving his guarantees of safety and nonmolestation. In return, certain public buildings were opened for our troops, and officers and others who would not fit should be quartered in private homes. Moreau, of course, was at the Residence with the sovereign duke, Max Joseph.

Michel and his immediate staff were assigned to the mansion of a wealthy doctor, an eminent man whose anticlerical sympathies were something of a scandal. Perhaps, his peers thought, if he was so fond of the Republic, he should have them in his house, stomping around his polished floors and leering at his daughters. Michel's response was to behave as an honored guest, greeting his host in perfect German with a grave and thoughtful manner.

I wondered precisely what role I was expected to play here — Charles would in all propriety be quartered with the footmen. Not only would that make it impossible for me to stay with Michel without scandal, but I doubted that I could carry off Charles in a garret with three or four other men.

Uncertain, I went to Michel's room to unpack his things. There would be dinner with our host and his wife and some distinguished friends, Michel's best coat needed airing and brushing, since he didn't have a dress coat with him.

The room was beautifully appointed —

clearly the best guest chamber of a wealthy family, with a copper bathtub behind a screen in the dressing room and the walls hung in celadon-green silk. The bed was also curtained in celadon, high and fluffy with goose down. It looked heavenly. My desire for the footmen's beds in the attic waned still further.

Michel had been one step ahead of me. Laid out on the bed was my sapphire-blue wool dress, the one that had been in his case. I picked it up. It seemed like a very long time since I had worn it in Paris. Had it really been only a month and a half ago? The fabric seemed so soft against my fingers. I held it to my face, smelling the faint scent of leather that clung to it from Michel's bags.

He opened the door and came in. I knew his step and didn't turn.

"What's the dress for?" I asked.

"For dinner," he said, putting his hands on my shoulders. "For Madame St. Elme, my dear companion."

"You will make the Munichers accept me and greet me in polite society? I'm not sure that's wise," I said. Moreau had been careful not to have me in company where my status might give offense. It didn't in Paris, of course, but France was not like the rest of the world, and Michel was trying to put a good foot forward here. "And what about Moreau?"

Michel swore long and hard. Eventually he paused to take a breath. "You can say you're Madame Versfelt or Madame St. Elme or Cleopatra for all I care! I'm sick of sneaking around Moreau! He's the one who threw you out almost three years ago. If he can't accept that you have a new lover, he's deranged."

"He's still your commander," I said, turning in his arms. "And he can still do you great harm."

"I can think of one name that won't give offense," he said, his teeth clenched. "Madame Ney."

"Michel, you are out of your mind! Don't you think Moreau will wonder who that is? Don't you think he'll expect to meet her? Unless I have some name that isn't anything he's ever heard."

"Maria," he said. "You look like a Maria. Every third woman is named Maria."

"Maria Kuller," I said, thinking back. Berthe had been my nurse in those horrible years after my father died. And she would never begrudge me her name. She had taught me to cook. Maybe I was thinking of her because of all the soup. "Madame Kuller."

"Good," Michel said. "Get dressed, Madame Kuller. Dinner is in less than an hour."

I looked at him. He was smiling at pulling this off right under Moreau's nose, a silly risk and a dear one. "You're mad, you know," I said fondly.

CEASE-FIRE

Dinner was not terribly formal. This was fortunate, since neither of us had any dress clothes. The gown Michel had brought for me was a day dress, not an evening gown, and he didn't have a dress uniform coat or waistcoat. Also, neither of us had bathed in nearly seven weeks. There's only so much you can do out of a basin of water. Michel's long hair was high on the list of things that weren't fixable before dinner, though he did shave. My hair was decidedly sticky. Also, it was growing out from its Brutus cut, and looked more like a deranged pixie than anything else. It certainly didn't make me look like a respectable woman.

I went down to dinner on Michel's arm with some trepidation, clunking on the stairs. Michel had packed a dress for me, but no slippers, so I had to wear Charles's boots under it or go barefooted. I nearly ran back upstairs in embarrassment.

Michel's hand tightened on my arm as though he anticipated flight. "Steady, Elza," he whispered. "Remember, we're the conquerors, and we can wear boots to dinner if we like." He didn't have any shoes either.

My morale was lifted by the sight of the first person at the bottom of the stairs, looking up from a knot of strangers. He wore an elegant red pelisse trimmed in fur thrown over one shoulder. The other arm was supported by a black sling. He grinned at me in unmitigated delight and came forward to kiss my hand with a flourish as though we were in Paris. "My dear Madame! How ravishing you are! You put the very stars to shame!"

I couldn't help but smile. "Lieutenant Corbineau! I'm surprised to see you here rather than with General Richepanse."

Corbineau shrugged. "As you can see, I had some small difficulty at Hohenlinden. I broke my right wrist, and since it is now impossible for me to wield the sword for some weeks, I have been assigned as maid of all work to General Ney. I have some facility in speaking German, and I have had the misfortune before of being put in charge of stabling and feed arrangements. It is no small matter to quarter nine thousand men in Munich without giving offense!"

Michel was greeting our host and his wife in German, and now turned to present me. "May I present to you my dear companion, Madame Maria Kuller? She has traveled in arms with us, and borne every danger and privation."

Our host, the Doctor, bent over my hand very properly. His wife hesitated, and did not offer the kiss of greeting. "I am delighted," I murmured, but I felt myself coloring. I looked terrible and I knew it. In the field it didn't matter, but here in the drawing rooms of Munich it did. I was not a respectable woman, and we were not in the Directory salons of Paris.

I was then introduced to the Doctor's oldest son, a serious young man in his late twenties, and his plain, thin wife. She didn't actually speak to the likes of me. There were three other men whose names I didn't catch, as well as Michel's aide Captain Ruffin, Colonel Joba of our Fourth Hussars, and young Colonel St. Jean of the Twenty-Third Infantry. All of the latter were quartered in the same house, the rest of the brigade officers being quartered elsewhere.

Dinner was fairly interminable. I was seated between the Doctor's son and Colonel Joba. Joba ate as though he hadn't seen food in a month, and made no attempt at keeping up the conversation. I spoke almost no German, though fortunately the Doctor's son spoke good French. To his other side, Corbineau carried his assault with the greatest ease, flattering our host's wife and daughter-in-law in two languages, his dark eyes sparkling and his repartee this side of outrageous, witty and wicked enough to make them feel that they sinned just a little, but not too much. After all, there was no harm in flirting with a handsome wounded cavalry officer. I could see why Michel had brought him, though he was the most junior officer present.

Michel, meanwhile, was engaged in serious discussion with the Doctor and his friends. I could hear a bit of it over the thunderous silence from Joba. Politics. The Doctor and the dark-haired man to his right favored liberal ideas and were staunch supporters of the Duke, Max Joseph, who wanted friendship with France rather than enmity. The other two gentlemen seemed of the other party.

"Is it not true," the elder of them said, "that the ultimate outcome of unbridled liberty is chaos? Why should any man feel safe in his property or person when the mob may break free, as it did during the Terror? It behooves me to ask, General, how many innocents you led to the guillotine."

Silence fell over that end of the table.

Michel shrugged almost negligently. "For my part, sir, none at all. I had never so much as set foot in Paris at the time. I was a lieutenant with the Army of the Rhine, and my whole occupation was fighting Austria. Surely you have no love for Austria?"

"Indeed we do not," the Doctor said. "I think any true Bavarian will say as much." He glared at his guests, daring them to disagree.

"I do not deny," Michel said evenly, "that some tragic events occurred. I think we all can admit the truth of that. But the men who did those deeds are for the most part dead, or fallen from power. The First Consul had no part in those events, nor any man here who now defends France."

I thought of Moreau and his profiteering off the homes of the condemned, and wondered if Michel might be stretching the point a little. Or perhaps he simply knew nothing of how Moreau's wealth was founded. We were neither as bad as they feared, nor as good as Michel believed.

"But what is the line," the gentleman said, "between liberty and libertinage? Men follow their worst instincts, given the freedom to do so."

"It all depends," I said, "on what we believe of the nature of man."

Michel blinked, looking at me as the other gentlemen looked round.

I toyed with the stem of my wineglass. "If men are by nature little better than beasts, and the common man an unruly mob trammeled only by the firm hand of Church and state, then his liberty is indeed to be feared, for such men can only spread chaos and destruction in their wake, bringing an end to fragile civilization. But if men are by nature the beloved children of God, made in His divine likeness, then surely the liberty that allows all men to seek the greatest good and happiness will eventually transform civilization for the better."

The Doctor smiled broadly. The other gentleman frowned. "Such a fragile hope, Madame, on which to place our safety. Naïve, I believe."

"And yet I have placed my safety upon it these last months, and my trust in the good of man is fulfilled," I said.

"All men are not saints, Madame," he replied.

"No, of course not. There are always scoundrels and villains and venal men who look for nothing but their own treasure. But

I will not fear them while there are such good angels as these men here to preserve liberty with both strength and compassion." I smiled brilliantly at Michel and Ruffin, and at our host.

The Doctor's eyes crinkled in an answering smile. "Well said, Madame! Let us toast Liberty, then."

"And Friendship," Michel said, raising his glass. "Liberty and Friendship, gentlemen."

Dinner ended early. Our host said that he understood that we must all be greatly fatigued from the road, and so it was barely nine-thirty when we went upstairs. I went ahead of Michel, who had stopped to speak to a servant in the hall. He came in behind me, tossing his coat onto a gilt chair.

"You can thank me," he said.

"For what?" I sat down to take off my boots. Tomorrow I was going to look for a cobbler and a dressmaker. If we were to be in Munich for more than a few days, I should have to have clothes. This was embarrassing.

Michel looked pleased with himself. "The servants are bringing up water for a bath for you. I thought you'd like it."

"I adore you," I said, laughing. "Adore. Will worship you with slavish abandon. Will do anything in the world for a bath!"

"I thought you might," he said, grinning. "But I'd rather have you clean for that part!"

"And I'd rather have you clean, too. You get the second bath. Michel, you . . ."

"Stink?" He raised one eyebrow. "Yes, probably."

And then we were both laughing. He picked me up and tossed me backward onto the feather bed, where I sank like a stone. He jumped on me, tickling, and we rolled around giggling and poking each other. He had a terribly ticklish spot just under each arm that almost paralyzed him with laughter.

A soft knock heralded a procession of servants with buckets of hot water. They filed in and out of the dressing room through a hall door, one after the other. It took three trips to fill the tub. When they were done, I went into the dressing room and stripped off every stitch gratefully, hanging up my only dress to let the steam get the wrinkles out.

There were a couple of bottles of oil on the shelf in the dressing room and a cake of milled soap. I opened one of the bottles. Rose. That would be lovely. I poured some in and sank in the tub up to my chin, then dunked my head and washed my hair twice.

Michel came in and sat on the delicate

boudoir chair, one booted foot against the edge of the tub. He watched me as I scrubbed every limb. It was deliciously sensual to bathe under his gaze, though he didn't touch me or even speak.

The water was gray when I finished. Michel held a towel for me as I stepped out, wrapping me in it so my arms were held at my sides and bending to kiss me.

I took a step back. "Not yet," I said, dodging his kiss. "You still stink."

He laughed. "Give me a few minutes, then." He opened the door from the dressing room to the hall and called for the servants again.

I went back in the bedroom and tried to get the tangles out of my hair with a comb. As short as it was, it dried quickly, and in the candlelight shone golden and glossy like a cherub. I put on an old soft shirt of Charles's that was the cleanest one I had. Its hem came halfway down my thighs, and the lace on the cuffs dangled over my hands. A dandy shirt, not one of the ones I'd bought for the campaign. I turned back the celadon silk coverlet and thick linen sheets and sat on the bed.

Michel came in from the bath and stopped dead in the doorway, a towel wrapped around his middle. "Oh, God."

"Yes?"

"You look like a demon," he said. "Like some Renaissance angel up to no good. Corrupting mankind." He took a few steps toward me.

"Up to no good," I said, tilting my head to the side with all Charles's arch manner. "A succubus?"

"Nothing that feminine," Michel said, and his voice was a little strained. Above the towel, the breadth of his shoulders gleamed in the candlelight, slick with rose oil, each red hair burnished and bright. The towel barely went around him, and it seemed a little strained, too.

"No?" I purred, crawling forward on hands and knees to the side of the bed. I pulled the towel away.

His phallus strained forward from a nest of red curls, lengthening at the touch of air. He made some muffled noise.

I knelt up on the edge of the bed, Charles's shirt open at the throat, and took him in my hand. The lace ruffles cascaded down over my hands, roughened by weeks in the field, a young man's hands, not a courtesan's. The lace whispered against his flesh. He closed his eyes.

"Look," I said in a low voice, tracing one long vein a little roughly. "I want you to see what it looks like. I want you to see me."

Michel looked at me. "You look like . . ."

"Charles," I said. I felt him firm in my hand, and I knew this was affecting him as strongly as it did me, wanting him this way.

He swallowed and said nothing, that hunted and hungry look in his eyes.

I smiled, a predator's smile, the smile Charles had used haunting the ballrooms of the spas, had used on Thérèse. "Watch me," I said, and took him in my mouth.

He groaned. And he obeyed. His hips shook and he pressed forward.

I let go. "Not yet," I said. I had expected this, had known what we would both need.

"The damn letters," he said, swaying a little against the side of the bed.

"Right here." I produced one from my sleeve like a conjuror. I smoothed it onto him, weighing him with my hand, looking up with a Charles expression that was pure evil, tugging at his hair just enough to make him wince, winding it around one finger. "You've always wanted this," I said, sliding up him, the lace at the front of my shirt against his chest. "Always." I kissed him deeply, mouthing at his chin.

He reached for me, but I leaned back out of reach. "Michel," I whispered, "I know what you want. Do it." I knelt on the bed, looking back at him over my shoulder, my hands against the soft linen. Charles's shirt didn't quite cover my buttocks.

He closed his eyes for a moment. Then he slid down behind me, his hands running up under the shirt, along the planes of my back, up to my shoulders and back down.

I nudged back against him, feeling him there, warm and hard.

With a breath he thrust into me, tight and slick. I rocked forward on my elbows, then shoved back against him, pushing in counterpoint.

On and on without a word, our bodies moving together, time narrowing to this moment, this yielding cloth beneath me, a rhythm stronger and stronger, like our beating hearts. I put my weight on one elbow, slid my hand down to feel each movement. My pearl was hot and swollen. My hand moved against it in time with each thrust.

When the change came, it started as the tremors deep inside, rolling outward, my breath catching and my eyes going dark. He made some noise as each spasm curled around him, over and over, deep as night, until I cried out and put my face against the cool sheets, wrung out as he finished.

It was a long time before the world stopped moving. He lay down beside me, his face buried in one of the pillows.

The candles flickered slightly. The celadon silk bed curtains swayed a little, whispering softly.

I put my hand against his back. "Michel?" His face was turned away from me, his long red hair in tangles across the sheets. I stroked it. "Beloved? Was that too much?"

"I don't know. No." He turned his head, and his face looked almost blind with desire, with the separation from self. He put his hand against the side of my face. "Charles."

"And Elza," I said. "It's me, you know."

"God help me, I know," he said, rolling over and putting his arms around me, drawing me against his shoulder.

I reached down and pulled up the sheet and coverlet. It closed us in within a cave of warmth. I stroked his cheek. "It bothers you to want Charles. But you do."

"You drive me mad," Michel said, and kissed me. "I have no idea what to do with you."

"Love me," I said, holding him tight. "Love me as I love you. All of me, forever and ever."

"I do," he said, and kissed me again.

CHRISTMAS IN THE FIELD

Michel was up at dawn. There were nine thousand men all over town who had to be drilled and reviewed and disciplined, not to mention fed. He kissed the top of my head before I was really awake and thumped down the hall.

I couldn't get back to sleep. After tossing and turning for a little while, I got up, put on my only dress, and went downstairs. The house was very quiet. From one direction came the faint clink of silver and a low voice. I tiptoed across the carpets to investigate.

Breakfast had been laid out on the sideboard in the dining room, and two bewigged footmen stood ready to assist with the serving. As yet, they had little to do. Michel had presumably been and gone, and only Corbineau was sitting at the table, eating a huge plate of sausage en croute and reading a book.

I came in and joined him. Coffee was truly a wonderful thing.

"Up so early, Madame?" Corbineau asked, looking up over the edge of his book. He had it propped in his bad hand, while he tried to eat left-handed.

"Yes," I said. "And today I'm going shopping. You may have noticed that the General has no clothes. Where did you get the uniform you had last night?"

"I brought it with me," he said. "But if you have a mission, I am happy to assist. I may not be much use at carrying packages, but I do speak German. And the plan seems to be that we shall be quartered in Munich indefinitely."

"Then I need clothes," I said, "and would be happy for your translation assistance, Lieutenant."

"Jean-Baptiste," he said, his eyes sparkling. "You must think of me as your brother, Madame."

"My rakehell brother, perhaps," I said, smiling.

"Perhaps I should consider you my rakehell sister," he said. "I'm a mere boy of twenty-two, so I suppose you are my senior."

"You might," I said. With a pang, I realized he was the same age as Charles, as the real Charles would be, had he lived. I missed him still.

A few days later the news came that Riche-panse had defeated the Austrians again, at Herdorf on 24 Frimaire, which people out here in the rest of the world called the 15th of December. The Austrians withdrew again toward Vienna, with Richepanse still in pursuit.

Ostensibly, it was to celebrate the season, not our victory, that the Duke decided to hold a ball at the Residence in Moreau's honor. Michel, of course, was to go. I, of course, was not.

Madame Kuller could have gone and indeed was included verbally in the invitation, but it would be tempting fate for me to go. Moreau would expect to meet General Ney's lady. Instead, Madame Kuller pled a heavy cold, and I had to spend several days stuck in the house.

Michel went to the ball. I saw him off with good grace, though admittedly it was with seething resentment that Moreau once again prevented me from doing what I liked. It would have been something to attend a duke's ball at Michel's side, in a palace all aglitter for Christmas.

It snowed in Munich on Christmas Eve.

Michel did not want to impose on the Doctor and his family, who had a family dinner planned and would have felt that they must make room for half a dozen semi-welcome guests. Also, there were other officers quartered around town who were at loose ends, so Michel had Corbineau and Ruffin arrange a dinner for his officers at a guildhall rented out for the occasion. I was there, as were nearly all of the women who had traveled in the baggage train.

The guildhall was gorgeous, decorated with holly and evergreen, not that it needed any decoration over the lovely carvings and bright paint that adorned every inch of wood. There were candles everywhere. The scent of roast pork filled the hall, with apples and plenty besides. There were also several casks of brandy. I had no idea where Michel had found them.

"Moreau's contribution to the feast," Michel said quietly. "He's at the Residence with the Duke, keeping Christmas." Hardly a more secular man than Moreau had ever lived, but I'm sure he found it good politics.

Michel, on the other hand, was in his element, toasting everyone, clapping shoulders, and generally behaving like a feudal lord in his hall. I lurked in a corner with a glass of brandy while Michel led a straggling version of a Christmas song in French and German at the same time. A bunch of Bavarian officers had joined us, and Michel seemed to be making them feel very welcome indeed. Corbineau kept pressing brandy on them.

Yes, there was something of the brigand chief in him, I thought. He was standing on a chair, waving a glass of brandy and singing, his hair escaping from its tail. It had been nearly ten years since the Church was expelled from France, but almost everyone knew the song except me and a few diehard Republicans who also lurked in the corners drinking. Even they looked reasonably convivial. As for the rest, perhaps they were happy to have Christmas back.

The party broke up just short of midnight. Wrapped in my cloak, I followed Michel out into the street. Snow was falling, sticking to roofs and trees, big, puffy white flakes so thick you could almost hear them whispering as they landed. The cobbles were wet but not snowy yet. I felt warm and cheerful from the brandy. Michel was a little flushed. It took a lot of drink to make him unsteady, but his redhead's complexion showed every glass.

Michel took my arm. "Let's go to midnight Mass," he said.

I looked at him doubtfully. "Mass?"

"At the Frauenkirche," he said. The snow was sticking on his hat, lying across the shoulders of his cloak.

"I . . ." I began uncertainly. I hadn't set foot in a church since the day my son was christened. I wasn't sure I wanted to, or what would happen if I did. "I'm not sure I'm Catholic."

Michel blinked. "Dutch Reformed? I should have thought that since you're Dutch, you're probably Protestant. I don't know why it never occurred to me."

"Maybe?" I said doubtfully. "My mother was Dutch Reformed. My father was an atheist, and I was baptized Catholic in Italy when I was a baby because they were afraid I'd die, and my mother wanted me christened by somebody. I don't really believe in anything. Unless it's the Olympians," I said, trying to make a joke of it.

Michel smiled at me through the snow. "It's Christmas Eve. No one will care. It's special." He held out his arm to me again. "Come on, Elza. I promise no one will check your catechism at the door."

"If you put it that way . . ." I took his arm. I wasn't sure it was right to go, but Michel was the one who actually believed, and if he didn't mind, then perhaps it really didn't matter.

Lots of people were making their way to the Frauenkirche. It was the largest church in the city, old and severe compared to many, with their Baroque ornamentation and organs. It was big and plain, and at first seemed almost austere.

Michel stopped just inside the doorway and crossed himself, looking toward the altar.

One of the several priests waiting about made his way toward us, drawn no doubt by the excess of gold braid Michel wore, and the fact he towered over nearly everyone. He spoke to Michel in good French. "You are welcome in the Church of Our Lady, my son. Would you like to confess before the Mass?"

Michel glanced at me sideways, then gave the priest a thin, rueful smile. "I'm afraid not, Father," he said. "You see, I'm not sorry."

The priest's mouth twitched, and for a moment I thought he would laugh. "Very well," he said. "But you know that if you have sins on your conscience, you may not approach the altar."

"I understand," Michel said gravely.

We went and waited toward the back for

the Mass to begin. Above us the plain walls soared into blackness. The light of the candles did not reach the dim ceiling.

"Michel, I shouldn't have come with you," I said. I didn't belong here. I was not part of this, part of his life this way. I could only embarrass him. It frightened me.

"It's not your fault," he said, squeezing my hand. "I'm not hypocrite enough to repent conveniently."

And then the music began.

I could almost forget myself in it. Perhaps I had heard the Mass sung before, as a child. Perhaps my nurse had taken me in Italy. It was familiar and lovely at the same time, warm and quiet and sad at once. Michel bent his head and closed his eyes. I wasn't sure if I should too, so I didn't, but just waited, listening, letting the music soar around me.

I stopped being frightened. Somewhere in the words I didn't understand, in the counterpoint of Kyrie Eleison sung by a boys' choir, a warm thread ran through me, quiet and still. *This, too, is magic. These too, these white walls, belong to the world. The Frauenkirche does not sit in heaven, but in Munich, the work of men's hands, the labor of their lives. Not separate, but love made manifest. It surrounds Her people like a mother's arms, sheltering them from the cold, singing to them on a snowy night, the church of Mary, Queen of Heaven, Lady of the Stars, a young mother who had borne a son long ago, strangers sheltering in a barn.*

I had borne my sons in fear and resignation, in anything but love. I had never sheltered them, never even given them the vague unformed memory of perfect safety. And the last child, the one I had not even borne . . . I blinked, then closed my eyes on my tears.

I was everything they thought I was, an abomination, all my dreams of freedom no more than a convict's desire for escape. I squeezed my eyes shut on my guilt and pain. What was I thinking, to imagine that I had any right to love and liberty?

The music wrapped around me, voice to all I felt. *Kyrie Eleison, Christe Eleison.*

Rage and pain and grief, tangled and entwined. And then, like a child's gale of tears, it passed, soaring with the music into tentative peace. Presence. Love. Understanding. Love that knew me as I was, needed me as I was, changing pain into purpose, some faint sense of deep-held contentment I barely remembered.

A little later, walking out, Michel took my

arm again, a look of concern on his face. "Was this a bad idea?" he asked. "I'm sorry if it was. I —"

"No," I said. "Not a bad idea." I tucked my hand into the crook of his arm. I had no words, nothing I could say that would share it with him. The snow was sticking on the street now.

We walked in the falling snow blowing pale in the lights from people's windows, the sounds of laughter coming out into the street, Munich on Christmas Eve. Every gable, every stone, sang of love, of joy, of the beauty of the world. Under their Gothic arcades, some of the shops around the Marienplatz were still open for the last late-night revelers, the scent of chocolate and ginger coming out into the streets.

Michel was beside me, earnest and complicated and beautiful, angel of death, ardent as a schoolboy, cruel as a captain must be, devout as a child. Surely if anything were proof of love made manifest, it was he. Blasphemy, perhaps, or simply my nature.

"Look!" Michel said, dragging me toward one of the still open shops. The sweet smell of baking poured out, cloves and cinnamon and nutmeg, the round cookies only made in Bavaria. "Lebkuchen!" Michel pulled me over to a shelf of cunningly made containers, tin and cartonnage, formed in the shapes of animals and buildings, eggs and angels. One gorgeous painted one was in the form of a castle. Each battlement sported a tiny tin flag snapping in an imagined breeze.

"It's lovely," I said, and it truly was, intricate and delightful.

Nothing would do but he had to buy it immediately for me, though I protested. "It's Christmas Eve," he said, looking at me sideways, as though he were embarrassed. "I haven't gotten anything for you yet. I meant to, but I haven't had much time."

"You wanted to get me a Christmas present?" I looked at him blankly. It had been five years since I had imagined anything of the kind.

"My family always did presents on Christmas Eve," he said, "when we were growing up. After Mass. I suppose . . . I mean, if you mind —"

"No," I said, smiling at him in the falling snow, clutching my painted castle. "No, I don't mind. It's beautiful. It's wonderful. It's just that I haven't anything for you. I haven't done this in years, you see, and I . . . I never gave Moreau anything."

"You're all the present I need," he said with a grin. "Unless you'd like to share some of those lebkuchen with me."

Quietly, my hand in his, we walked back to the doctor's house. We did not speak. There was nothing more we needed to say. The snow whispered down, catching in my eyelashes.

A tall carving of an angel looked down from a Baroque building, stern and cold and nothing like the angel I imagined. *Thank you,* I thought. *If you are here, thank you.*

I almost heard a laugh behind me. — *Anytime,* he said. *Anytime, my dear ones.* —

I looked up at the sky, watching the snow falling. Michel laughed and held me up when the falling flakes' swirls made me dizzy. I almost fell over when the bells began, first the high notes from a church near the Residence, then the lighter bells in the valley, then the rich dark notes from the Frauenkirche, followed by all the bells of Munich.

"What is it?" I said. "Is it midnight?"

"Long after," Michel said, grabbing the sleeve of a man hurrying by and speaking to him quickly in German. I didn't understand a word, but the man seemed pleased and in a hurry. He answered rapidly, then dashed off through the snow toward the Marien-platz.

"What?" I said, reaching for Michel.

He turned back, a broad grin on his face. "The Austrians have signed an armistice with Moreau. It's peace!" He picked me up and swung me around. "The Austrians surrendered! Victory!"

I swirled around, caught in his arms, caught in happiness, as around us all the bells of Munich rang out for peace. "I don't want this to ever end," I said. Snowflakes were sticking to his hair, and for a moment I felt as though I might lift into the sky, borne on wings of joy.

"It never will," Michel said. "I promised that I would love you until the end of the world."

"So you did," I said, and kissed him amid the falling snow.

AUTHOR'S NOTE

The General's Mistress is a work of fiction, but it is based on the memoirs of Ida St. Elme, courtesan, soldier, and ultimately author of a dozen books. Chatty, scandalous, entertaining, and heart-wrenching by turns, her memoirs provide a unique view of the people and places she knew and loved. Many of the incidents described in *The General's Mistress* really happened, and often I have been able to use original dialogue, as in her first meeting with Napoleon. Hers was a fascinating and turbulent life. *The General's Mistress* only scratches the surface, the first twenty-four years of an amazing adventure that a mere writer of fiction could never hope to invent.

No less a literary figure than Chateaubriand, who hated her, named her "the widow of the Grand Army," and so she was, eulogizing not only the famous men she had slept with but the entire way of life of the baggage train.

Mariska Pool, of the Royal Netherlands Arms and Army Museum, who recently curated an exhibit about the women who followed the armies of Napoleon, said, "These women barely escaped oblivion, yet they deserve far more prominence than all those well-known noble and elegant ladies who found a place in the history books purely by reason of their family connections or because they were known by such euphemisms as *grande horizontale* or *scandaleuse.*' But Ida gave all the women a monument, the brave ones, the unfortunate ones, the ones with no choice, the ones who really loved, the opportunists, the mistresses, the wives, and all those others who had their own private reasons to sign up."

I hope that Ida would be pleased with the way that I have retold her story.

ACKNOWLEDGMENTS

I owe thanks to many, many people for their help and encouragement with *The General's Mistress* over the twenty years from the time I wrote the first scenes to its publication in 2012. Foremost is my father, who read the earliest parts before his death, and who was always my first and biggest fan.

Yet there is one person without whom this book could not have been written, my partner, Amy, who first encountered Elza's adventures as the project of a distant acquaintance when she was a college student and was fascinated by my obsession. She was the one who went with me to hunt down memoirs in rare book collections, who made the pilgrimage to Davidson with me, who prowled around the Met comparing sets of horse pistols, and who has always provided both perspective and love. She jokes sometimes that she married Elza, and in a sense that's true! She's lived with this

561

story day in and day out for twenty years, and I expect she's in for it for a good many more. I could not tell this story without her.

I would also like to thank the many friends who have helped me with research over the years, especially those friends in Europe who have gone places I could not or who read languages I don't. My thanks go to Anne-Elisabeth Moutet, who sent me scans of rare books from Paris and deciphered El-za's illegible nineteenth-century script, as well as being my constant culture-checker on whether the coffee should have cream and how long it takes to walk from one place to another. I'd also like to thank Tanja Kinkel for the Christmas Market in Munich, the lebkuchen, and calling her father and asking him about the species of trees at Hohenlinden, as one can't tell on Google Earth! I also have many thanks for Anna Sitniakowsky, who translated recent articles for me from Dutch to English; Anna Ki-wiel, who has proved of invaluable assistance with all things Polish; Jasna Stark, who gave me a copy of Eric Perrin's biography of Michel Ney long before it was available in the United States; Nathan Jensen, who always straightens out everyone's service record, and many others who have rendered assistance over the years. I also must thank my aunt, Polly Hartman, who had no idea what a monster she was creating when she let me crash with her in Paris for two weeks back in 1991!

I also would like to offer heartfelt gratitude to the many pre-readers who have given me their thoughts on draft after draft, including but certainly not limited to Lesley Arnold, Gretchen Brinckerhoff, Mary Day, Imogen Hardy, Mary Kate Johnson, Wanda Lybarger, Gabrielle Lyons, Kathryn McCulley, Anjali Salvador, Melissa Scott, Lena Sheng, and Casimira Walker-Smith.

READER'S GROUP GUIDE
THE GENERAL'S MISTRESS

JO GRAHAM

Introduction

The General's Mistress invites readers into the world of Elzelina, a young woman living through the turmoil and excitement that followed the French Revolution. Based on the historical figure, Elza — sometimes known as Ida St. Elme, sometimes as Charles Van Aylde — follows her passions, her heart, and her own independent spirit as she flees her coldhearted husband in Holland for a series of fiery romances in Paris, Italy, and Germany. Her adventures take her into the arms of General Victor Moreau, a tryst with a coy and ambitious socialite, a turn as an acting troupe's "second girl" and casual prostitute, a foray into fortune telling, and even a taste of war when she disguises herself as a man and joins the French military campaign in Germany. Throughout it all, she is haunted by two mysterious obsessions: General Michel Ney, a man she loves before ever meeting him, and the seductive, protective, and dangerous presence she senses in her dreams and in psychic trances: the Archangel Michael, the Warrior's Saint — and the Angel of Death.

Topics and Questions for Discussion

1. Early in the novel, Elza leaves her cruel husband and their two sons in Holland. What did you think of her decision to leave her sons behind? Do you think it was the right decision? Did this choice make her less sympathetic? Or more?

2. Elza first discovers her psychic abilities when playing with a deck of tarot cards. Her cousin tells her that they answer a question in three parts: "The first one is the what, the second is how, and the third is why." Elza asks if she will find a man she truly loves. She sees a red-haired man bearing a chalice, an illustration of Fortune's Wheel, and an emperor in a chariot. How did these predictions play out over the course of the novel?

3. Elza travels in disguise as a man — specifically, as her late brother Charles. At first this seems to be little more than a game to placate her grief-addled mother, and a convenient way to avoid the dangers

facing women who travel alone. But over the course of the novel Charles becomes an increasingly crucial part of Elza's identity. Why do you think this is? In your opinion, is her "dual identity" a solution to a problem, or another problem in itself?

4. Throughout the novel Elza is visited by an otherworldly being, who gradually reveals himself to be the Archangel Michael. In Roman Catholic teachings, Michael is the Angel of Death and the fierce defender of the faithful against evil — including one's own nature. How do you interpret his role in Elza's life?

5. In your opinion, what does the Archangel Michael want from Elza, and why has he chosen her to see him?

6. Elza seems disinterested in politics and the recent French Revolution when she is first introduced. How did her awareness of and interest in the events unfolding around her change over the course of the novel?

7. Elza's sexual adventures often seem to give her more than just physical pleasure: with each new lover she plays a different role and explores a different aspect of herself. Which of these "versions" of Elza did you find most appealing, and which the least?

8. There is a theme of duality running through this novel: double identities, conflicting forces of light and dark, matched pairs. Was there any instance of duality that struck you as particularly surprising, or insightful? Do you agree with Elza's description of herself as "courtesan and knight companion both," both roles being equally valuable?

9. Michel Ney also exhibits contradicting traits. He is gentle in person and violent on the battlefield, a kind and romantic soul who secretly fantasizes about rape and murder. Did these dark aspects of his nature make it difficult for you to see him as a romantic figure? Would you have preferred Elza's true love to be more heroic, in the traditional sense?

10. Discuss the role of sex in the novel. Were the steamy segments a diversion from the plot or did Elza's sexual encounters add something to her story and development as a character — intertwined with her life outside the bedroom?

11. Elzelina is representative of many women in the Napoleonic Era: women who lived on the margins of society, travelling with soldiers and drama troupes, often working as prostitutes. Do you think the author succeeds in giving a voice to

these women and some insight into their lives? How has the novel changed your perception of the women of this era?

Enhance Your Book Club

1. Jo Graham drew inspiration for *The General's Mistress* from the memoirs of the real Elzelina, published under the name Ida Saint-Elme as *Memoirs of a Contemporary.* Find a copy at your local library or bookstore and read passages aloud at your book club discussion. How does it compare to *The General's Mistress?*

2. To learn more about the real Ney, Moreau, and Napoleon, visit: www.napoleonseries.org. Be sure to read the article "Four Men and a Woman," which Jo Graham quotes in her author's note.

3. "The Campaigns of Napoleon" is a multi-part documentary on the Napoleonic Wars. Watch the first installment with your book club members to learn more about the battles described in *The General's Mistress.*

A Conversation with Jo Graham
How did you first learn about Elzelina and what drew you to her story?
Actually, it was Michel I found first, when I was fifteen. I applied myself to learning

everything I could about him, and that was why four years later I found Elza's memoirs in the original French in my university library rare books collection. I knew I would write her story then, and I began it in 1992. Elza is unique, sensual, brilliant, clever, brave, and ultimately strong as mountains. Her story was irresistible.

What resources did you use in researching her life and this era in European history?

I've been researching this story for twenty-nine years now, so it's hard to pick out a few references, as I've probably literally used nine hundred or a thousand sources. The ultimate, invaluable one is Elza's own *Memoirs of a Contemporary,* particularly the unabridged French edition, as the English one is a Victorian translation and cuts a great deal and cleans up a great deal more!

The real Michel Ney does in fact sound like a romantic hero: warrior, patriot, and called "the bravest of the brave" by no less than Napoleon Bonaparte. It must have been a pleasure to flesh him out on the page. Do you think the real Elza felt as passionately for the real Ney as "your Elza" does?

Oh yes! I'm certain she did. She makes it very clear in her memoirs that he was the love of her life. At one point she says of going to join him in the field, "I went from Florence to Perpignan as one goes from Paris to Versailles. In love, one is like the gods of Homer — in two jumps one could go to the ends of the earth," and "Oh the happiness given to me by this great man, full of unspeakable delights! Our hearts, separated for a long time by great distances, had ceased at nothing, tasting pleasure with like convictions, one with our equal communing of emotions. New fears could not suspend our enchantment, and we seized it as sort of a prize for victory."

What inspired the inclusion of the Archangel Michael in Elza's story?
Michael has been a character in my books before, in *Black Ships* and *Hand of Isis,* and it seemed natural for him to return in this one.

Were you already familiar with the mythology of St. Michael, or did you do some biblical research as well?
I was pretty much already familiar, because as I said I'd written him twice before. I was fairly certain of where I was going.

It can be risky for a novelist to turn historical figures into characters in her story, particularly when they are as well known as Napoleon. Were you hesitant to include him in the novel, or did you always know he'd play a role?

I always knew he'd be in the book. His scenes in Elza's memoirs are so memorable and distinctive that I was certain those scenes needed to be included. I kind of have a soapbox about this — Napoleon is portrayed horribly inaccurately in popular media, either as a strange, short, ranting man who is a figure of fun, or as some early version of Hitler. Neither of these things is remotely true! He was charming, charismatic, and had a talent for inspiring devotion in those who knew him. It's very strange that in the U.S. we've forgotten that the United States was Napoleon's ally, not his enemy, and that at the time we were one of the few other nations who embraced ideas like the separation of church and state and free public education. Napoleon is absolutely not a villain in my books.

There are some pretty steamy sex scenes in this book! Is it difficult to write effectively about sex? Do you ever make yourself blush? Are there family

members or friends whom you hope won't read those sections?

I never blush! Actually, those are some of my favorite parts to write, both because I enjoy writing steam and because it gives insights into the characters that you wouldn't get any other way. You literally get them naked, without the things they pretend to most of the time.

How closely connected do you think Elza's development as a character is to her sexual exploits?

Very closely. As Michael says to her at one point, this is how she understands the world. This is the lens through which she perceives, and there's nothing wrong with that. Each experience, good and bad, makes her more the person she is able to be. *The General's Mistress* is about becoming, about how Elza begins her journey. It's not the end of the journey. In this book she learns about power, but she's not yet grown into her own. It's coming, and Michel, like Victor, is a catalyst for that. Only unlike Victor, he is someone who can walk along the path with her, travel on a parallel course and understand her completely.

The historical Michel Ney came to a sad

end: condemned to death in 1815 by the new French government. The novel is dark enough that readers might expect it to encompass that event, adding yet more pathos to Elza's life. Why did you decide to end it on a cheerier note, with the two lovers kissing in the snow?

We'll get there! There is much more of Elza's story to come in later books. This is the first pause, two lovers kissing in the snow, having found each other for the first time. This is new love, love not yet tested by the years and by pain. They have a long way to go before 1815!

You are unsparing in your depiction of Elza's darker side: her pragmatic approach to prostitution, her lack of attachment to her children, and even her proclivity toward violence. Did you have to resist a temptation to soften her up a bit and make her a more traditional, morally upright romantic heroine?

I had to resist the lure of cash! *The General's Mistress* was turned down by four editors before it was bought by the wonderful Abby Zidle of Gallery Books — all four times because the editors hated Elza. The temptation was to make her into a more traditional heroine in order to sell the book. But I couldn't do that. Elza is who she is, and she's a real person. I have to write her as I see her, to tell her story with the same lack of apology and with the same boldness and lack of shame as she tells it herself. This is who she is, and turning her into a blushing ingénue would be awful.

Yes, absolutely Elza has a darker side. If she didn't, she wouldn't also be a suitable vessel for Michael. Sex and death are opposite sides of the same coin. Birth is blood and danger, beginnings encompass the potential of endings, and endings hold the seeds of beginnings. Elza belongs to that great Mystery, just as Gull did in my book *Black Ships.* It's expressed differently in the eighteenth century than in the Bronze Age, but it's the same Mystery. She always serves the same Mystery.

Elza's friend Lisette commits suicide, but we're not told why or what had happened to her. Did you intentionally leave that backstory vague — and what *did* happen?
No, actually that was cut for length! I needed to remove 14,000 words in order to bring the length down to something reason-

able for a trade paperback. The backstory with Lisette was less necessary than a lot of other things, so it went. In the original version there was more of her drug habit and her violent relationship with her boyfriend. I don't think she actually intended to kill herself this time — I think her overdose was a bid for attention, a cry for help as the cliché goes today, but no one saved her.

You've set other novels in historic epochs as well: the reign of Alexander the Great, Cleopatra's Egypt, and ancient Troy. Where (and when) do you think you'll go next?

Next up is the second book about Elza, covering 1800–1805, in which Elza takes on a new task and a new adventure. Tentatively titled *The Emperor's Companion,* needless to say Napoleon is back! When Victor Moreau is arrested for treason (and he is guilty!) Elza is blackmailed by the Minister of Police into working as his agent to spy on her former friends and associates, including Therese Tallien. But when this blackmail requires her to betray Josephine, Elza has a choice to make — her life, or to be true to the deepest part of herself!

ABOUT THE AUTHOR

Jo Graham is the author of the critically acclaimed historical fantasies *Black Ships, Hand of Isis,* and *Stealing Fire.*

The employees of Thorndike Press hope you have enjoyed this Large Print book. All our Thorndike, Wheeler, and Kennebec Large Print titles are designed for easy reading, and all our books are made to last. Other Thorndike Press Large Print books are available at your library, through selected bookstores, or directly from us.

For information about titles, please call:
   (800) 223-1244

or visit our Web site at:
   http://gale.cengage.com/thorndike

To share your comments, please write:
   Publisher
   Thorndike Press
   10 Water St., Suite 310
   Waterville, ME 04901